PRAISE FOR SHANNON K. BUTCHER AND THE SENTINEL WARS

Falling Blind

"Amazing and dramatic . . . heart pounding [and] heart-breaking."
—The Reading Cafe

"A taut mixture of action and suspense."
—Smexy Books

"I like this author's voice and have enjoyed journeying with her into this paranormal world filled with monsters, aliens, talented women, and powerful men."
—Fiction Vixen

Dying Wish

"You'll be thrilled, entertained, enamored, and when it's all done, you'll be begging . . . for more."—Fresh Fiction

"[A] fascinating, gritty read."
—Night Owl Reviews

"Unexpected twists and turns."
—Romance Junkies

"I loved *Dying Wish*. . . . If you have not started this series, please do not miss it."
—The Reading Cafe

Living Nightmare

"There's only one way to describe this book to me: fabulous!"
—Night Owl Reviews

"[An] action-packed story of the brooding and angry warrior Madoc and his journey to the future. This series rocks!"
—Fresh Fiction

continued . . .

THE EDGE NOVELS

Edge of Sanity
Razor's Edge
Living on the Edge

NOVELS OF THE SENTINEL WARS

Willing Sacrifice
Falling Blind
Bound by Vengeance
(A Penguin Special)
Dying Wish
Blood Hunt
Living Nightmare
Running Scared
Finding the Lost
Burning Alive

EDGE OF
BETRAYAL

AN EDGE NOVEL

SHANNON K. BUTCHER

A SIGNET ECLIPSE BOOK

SIGNET ECLIPSE
Published by the Penguin Group
Penguin Group (USA) LLC, 375 Hudson Street,
New York, New York 10014

USA | Canada | UK | Ireland | Australia | New Zealand | India | South Africa | China
penguin.com
A Penguin Random House Company

First published by Signet Eclipse, an imprint of New American Library,
a division of Penguin Group (USA) LLC

First Printing, November 2014

ISBN 978-0-451-46551-1

Printed in the United States of America
10 9 8 7 6 5 4 3 2 1

*For Gretchen Jones, who always has the best ideas and
is constantly ready for an adventure,
and whose sense of direction is so good,
it must be some form of dark sorcery.*

Chapter One

There were only two men in the world Mira Sage had ever hated enough to consider killing with her bare hands, and only one of them was still breathing.

She watched the man on her tablet, ignoring the fact that she was breaking about seven laws by doing so.

Adam Brink was up to something, and no matter how many bugs she had to plant, no matter how many traffic cameras or surveillance systems she had to hack into, she wasn't letting the man out of her sight.

His tall, lean body glided swiftly over the cracked pavement in the alley behind a vacant distribution facility. His arms were filled with more boxes of who knew what—just like the boxes he'd been carrying in for the last hour. He glanced over his shoulder occasionally, checking to make sure he wasn't being followed.

Even from this extreme distance, with the poor camera angle and night descending on the area, Mira swore she could see guilt riding his angular features.

Whatever he was doing, she was going to catch him in the act. Maybe then her coworkers at the Edge would believe her when she said Adam Brink was still the enemy.

Mira started her car's engine and moved in on his location. Still out of sight, she slipped from her car and did her best to slink closer to the building where he was up to his nefarious deeds.

Without any windows in the building to peer through, she had no choice but to slip inside and follow him. There was no way to know what greeted her in there—dead bodies, illegal human experimentation, a meeting of twisted scientific minds—but she was ready for anything.

The gun holstered under her arm still felt awkward. She was a much better shot now, thanks to her boss's insistent training, but skill and resolve were two different things. As much as she wanted to believe she could shoot someone if she had to, she wasn't sure she had it in her.

She knew intimately just how much being shot sucked.

Bella had promised that the will to survive would shine through if Mira got into trouble, and that she'd be able to pull the trigger. She wished she had even half of her boss's confidence.

The employee entrance, at the back of the brick building, was unlocked. There was no light spilling out from under the door. No sign that anyone was inside.

With a deep breath for courage, she drew her gun, turned the doorknob, and slipped inside.

There was little light to see by—just the glow from another room ahead beckoning her forward, and even with that, all she could see was dust and open spaces. She heard nothing but the frantic drum of her own heartbeat. Beneath her clinging black layers, sweat collected along her spine. The revolver in her hand trembled.

You can do this, she told herself. *Bella has trained you well.*

A deep, melodic sound rose from the glowing opening ahead.

Singing? The sound seemed so out of place here, she was sure she had to be imagining things.

As the sound continued, she realized that she knew that voice. It was filled with quiet strength and, like everything about Adam, skill.

Hearing him do something so normal gave her pause. There was no evil in the simple act of singing. It was all too human, shaking her resolve.

And that pissed her off.

Adam Brink had tricked her, lied to her, drugged her, abducted her, and delivered her to her father, who had been more than willing to kill her to get what he wanted. A sweet, crooning tune didn't change any of that.

Mira steadied her weapon and moved forward, being careful to follow in the footprints left behind in the dust. For all she knew, this place had been filled with explosive traps to keep out unwanted visitors.

As she moved forward, the singing grew louder. There were no other voices, but she could hear low strains of music filling the lighted space that was blocked from sight by the wall on her left. She vaguely recognized the tune as one from the 1940s. Dramatic, romantic, and filled with the hope of new love.

The way Adam sang it almost made her forget he was a monster.

She steadied her weapon and eased around the corner just enough to get an idea of what faced her on the other side of the wall.

Adam sat at a table covered with a pristine white cloth. Atop it was a glass bowl filled with water topped with floating candles. She could smell something savory, sinfully rich, and loaded with garlic coming from the room. Two dome-covered plates were laid out, along with sparkling stemware filled with deep red wine. Candlelight glinted off the flatware and made Adam's pale gray eyes sparkle with warmth as they met her gaze.

"I was hoping you'd come," he said.

Mira jerked her head back around the corner and stood on the other side of the wall in shock. He was

alone. There were no instruments of torture, no screaming human subjects, no evil scientists. Just Adam and a
candlelit dinner for two.

She was so confused by the sight, she looked again.
Sure enough, nothing had changed. He hadn't even
shifted in his seat.

"Will you join me, Mira?" he asked.

He'd seen her. There was no sense in pretending he
hadn't.

She stepped around the corner, revolver raised and
aimed at his chest.

"Your hand is shaking. I'd really prefer not to be the
victim of an accidental shooting."

"Wouldn't be an accident. Bella told me never to
point a gun at anything I didn't want to kill."

A sad flicker of disappointment wrinkled his brow. "I
see."

"Who else is here?" she demanded.

"No one. You've doubtlessly been watching me all day."

How had he known? She'd been so careful in her surveillance.

Adam continued. "Have you seen anyone else enter
the building?"

Mira hadn't, but she wasn't about to say so. "I'm the
one asking questions here."

He leaned back in his chair and crossed his arms over
his chest. His shirt pulled tight across his shoulders, and
for a second, the memory of him covered in blood sprung
back into her mind. She wanted to feel some kind of
satisfaction in his pain, but all she felt was a queasy swell
of nausea.

"Ask away, then," he said.

She swallowed hard, shoving the bloody image from
her mind. "Why are you here?"

"Isn't it obvious?"

She steadied the weapon, forcing her shaking to even
out. "I don't assume anything you do is what it seems."

"In this case it is. All that's going on here is dinner."

"Who's coming?"

"You."

That news rattled her, but she tried to hide her surprise. "You didn't know I was coming."

"Of course I did. You've been watching me for weeks. All I had to do was give you an enticing enough reason to investigate."

"All this trouble so I'd come to dinner with you? Even you aren't that desperate."

"I've tried to talk to you at work. Repeatedly. You walk away and lock me out of your office every time. I went by your house. Twice. You refused to answer the door even though I knew you were home. You've left me no choice but to resort to extreme measures to gain your attention."

"I don't have anything to say to you."

He glanced pointedly at the barrel of her revolver. "I beg to differ. You're speaking eloquently right now."

"Are you mocking me?"

"Never. All I want is a few minutes of your time. After that, I'll leave you alone."

Mira didn't see how that was possible, considering they worked at the same office. She had made it clear to her boss that she couldn't stand the man, but Bella had made sure that Mira knew that hiring decisions were none of her business. She would work with Adam, or she'd find a new job.

No way was Mira going to let Adam scare her away from the job and friends she loved.

"The weapon isn't necessary," he said. "I'm not going to hurt you."

"Again, you mean."

Adam winced but didn't break eye contact with her. Nor did he try to pretend that he hadn't done to her what he'd done. "Yes, Mira. Never again."

"I don't believe you."

"I understand why you wouldn't, but I'm trying to do the right thing by you. Please, just have a seat."

"If you think I'm going to let you drug me again by eating your food, you're insane."

"Fine. Don't eat. Just listen."

"Why would I listen to you? I know how well you lie."

Adam stared at her for a moment, regret plain in the lines on his angular face. Somehow, the emotion made him even more handsome than he was naturally. She knew it was an act—everything he did was a carefully planned series of lies meant to fool her into trusting him—but that didn't mean she didn't notice his appeal. Being honest about her feelings was the only way to combat them.

There had been a moment not too long ago that she'd actually believed she could fall for this man.

How wrong she'd been.

Mira had always been gullible like that—willing to trust any kindness offered her, no matter how fake, no matter the ulterior motives.

His posture shifted, moving from relaxed to alert. She could almost feel him coiling to strike. Even so, his voice remained quiet and gentle. "You've been ignoring me since I started working at the Edge. I gave you time to heal from your wounds. I gave you weeks to accept that we are now coworkers, but it seems that you're as immovable as your father."

A violent surge of fury consumed her, clenching her jaw around her words. "Don't *ever* compare me to him. Do you understand?"

"Finally, a reaction. You've been so cold I wasn't sure there was any fire left in you."

Her fingers tightened around the butt of her revolver and she lifted her aim. She wasn't sure if she was brave enough to pull the trigger, but after what Adam had done to her, scaring him was the least he deserved.

Not that anything she did could scare a man like Adam Brink.

He ignored the weapon aimed at his head and stood. As he glided closer, she swore she could feel the heat of his body shimmering out of him. There had been a time—a few insane moments last December—when she would have done anything to get closer to him. He'd fooled her into thinking he was a decent man. Right before he'd drugged and abducted her for reasons she still didn't fully understand.

"Be as angry with me as you like," he said. "It's no less than I deserve. But it's a wasted effort. All it's going to do is wear you out. There are other things that demand our attention."

"Like you care. You don't get to pretend like you give a shit about me now. I know better."

His mouth shifted slightly, his lips pressing together. A flicker of pain wrinkled the skin between his pale gray eyes. Regret hung around his shoulders, making them droop more than she remembered.

It had been a mistake to come here. He was too handsome, too intriguing. Once her gaze was on him, she started to forget that inside that lean, masculine package was a monster. A cold, calculating beast willing to use whoever crossed his path.

"I'm not pretending," said Adam. "Not anymore."

"And you just expect me to believe it? How the hell did you get Bella to agree to hire you, anyway? Is she so blown away by your good looks that she lost every bit of good judgment she ever had?"

"Bella doesn't find me attractive."

"How do you know?"

"She doesn't look at me like that."

"Like what? With drool running down her chin?"

"No, like you look at me."

Mira hated it that he could see through her so easily. She wanted to deny it, but what was the point? It was better to send him away than to be lured into conversation with him. That's what he wanted.

"I'm leaving." She lowered her revolver and started to turn.

Before she could, he reached out, offering her an envelope. Only then did she realize exactly how long his arms were and that she had been within his grasp the whole time. He could have touched her if he liked, just as he had the night they'd gone on their one and only date.

A shiver of something raced through her, gone before she could tell if it was nervousness or excitement.

"What is that?" she asked, diverting her gaze to the envelope.

"Open it. It's important."

"If I do, will you leave me alone?"

"Yes, as much as our work will allow." He seemed sincere.

It was probably another of his lies, but that was a chance she was willing to take. She holstered her weapon and did as he asked. Inside the envelope was a lab report listing test results for a series of diseases. HIV, hepatitis B and C, and a whole list of things she'd never heard of. All test results were negative.

"I'm sorry it took so long to get the results. I didn't think clearly enough to have myself tested until I'd recovered from my injuries. And then, of course, there was the issue of your unwillingness to speak to me."

He'd been in the hospital for three weeks after that horrible night last December. Her father, Dr. Richard Sage, had shot him. Shot her, too. But her father was dead now, unable to hurt anyone else.

For that Mira rejoiced. Most of the time.

Confused, she looked up at Adam. Way up. She'd almost forgotten how tall he was, towering over even most men. "What's this for?"

"The bullet that struck you went through me first. I thought it might bring you some peace of mind to know that I'm healthy, that you couldn't contract any diseases from my blood."

That whole horrible night flooded back to her in a heartbeat. The horror of seeing that gun aimed at her. The panic of watching Adam move to block her body just as the shot was fired.

She absently rubbed her chest where the scar puckered the skin along her ribs. The surgeon had told her that if Adam's body hadn't slowed the bullet, it would have killed her. He'd saved her life and he'd never mentioned it until now.

"You didn't need to do this," she said. "My doctors knew I'd been exposed to another person's blood. They took precautions."

"And how many more tests must you endure before they're sure you're safe?"

"It's none of your concern."

"I've done you enough harm for one lifetime. All I want is for you to find some peace."

"Who says I haven't?"

"I've seen you around the office. In the gym. At the range." His pale gray eyes caught her gaze and his voice quieted further. "You're afraid."

Mira stepped forward. At well over six feet, Adam was easily a foot taller than her. She didn't care. She got right up in his face as close as she could and growled, "I'm not afraid of you."

"I would say that's good—I don't want you to be afraid of me—but I don't believe you."

"I don't care what you believe. Just keep your distance and no one has to get shot. Again."

He winced, pain flashing in his eyes for a split second. "I never wanted you to get hurt."

"Yeah? Well you should have thought of that before you agreed to trade my life for whatever was in that precious envelope my father gave you."

"I never agreed to trade your life. That exchange wasn't about you."

"No, it was about my best friend and using me as bait

to lure him in." She smacked his chest with the lab report, wishing she had the nerve to hit him with her fists instead. "Did you ever stop to think what my father was going to do with me once he had what he wanted? Did you ever think about what he'd do to Clay once he had him?"

"He was your father. I believed him when he said he wasn't going to hurt you."

"Shows how much you know. I meant no more to him than a lab rat. He would have used me and dissected me with as much concern, too. If Leigh hadn't come in to save me, I'd probably be dead by now and no more than a brief note in the margins of his lab reports."

"I never would have let him hurt you. It's why I stayed. Why I refused to let you out of my sight after I realized the true nature of the situation."

"Which would have been all heroic if not for the fact that I was only there *because of you*."

His eyes closed briefly with regret. "I'm sorry for the pain I caused you, Mira. I always will be."

"Be sorry all you want. It doesn't change anything."

He took the report and tucked it into her jacket pocket. "I'm sure you'll want to verify that the information is true. If you have any questions, I gave Dr. Vaughn permission to speak to you about my medical records. Anything you want to know."

"All I want is for you to leave. Preferably out of state. Thanks to my father, there are all kinds of people in those files we found who are in need of help. Go find one of them, do your job, and leave me the hell alone."

He stared at her for a long moment. The heat of his body flooded over her skin, bringing with it his scent—one that brought back memories of another candlelit dinner when there had been no fear between them, only a shivering kind of excitement she could barely believe was real. "I'll respect your wishes and stay away. Whatever you need, Mira. It's yours."

Chapter Two

Adam was waiting for Bella Bayne when she unlocked her office door the next morning. "What's up?" she asked, juggling a full mug of coffee and her keys.

Bella was tall, with the kind of self-confidence that commanded respect. She didn't wear the typical tailored suit one would expect of a CEO, but rather preferred jeans, combat boots, several weapons, and an air of capability that warned others not to cross her. With her glossy black hair pulled back in a no-nonsense ponytail, she almost seemed like a normal woman. Adam knew that in her case, looks were definitely deceiving.

"I need to speak to you."

"Sounds serious. Come on in."

Adam followed his new boss into her office and shut the door behind him.

Light filled the space, highlighting a massive glass desk and minimalistic, modern chairs gleaming with chrome. There was no clutter here, only a laptop, phone, notepad, pair of pens, and neat stack of folders.

"Hit me," said Bella as she settled in her chair.

Adam was uncertain how to start—a feeling so unusual he wasn't sure quite how to handle it.

Walking away from Mira last night had been harder

than he would have thought possible. All he'd wanted to do was beg her for forgiveness, but that would have been its own kind of selfishness, and he'd already caused her enough pain for one lifetime.

He shouldn't have cared—not that his presence upset her or that he'd once felt *something* for her. Still felt something. It lay hot and vibrant in his chest, urging him to act. But feelings didn't matter in his world. Only results.

Which was why he was following through on his promise to give Mira the space she needed.

Bella glanced up at him, her eyebrows raised in impatience and expectation.

Adam cleared his throat. "I think my usefulness here has come to an end."

"Mira's idea?" asked Bella.

"You've talked to her, I see."

Bella shrugged. "She talked to me. Loudly. Told me what you did. All of it. If not for the part where you saved her life, I would have shot you myself."

"One more reason among many for me to leave."

"I thought you wanted this job. I was told I didn't even have a choice in the matter of hiring you if I wanted the new contract. My ability to help all those people that Mira's father and the other scientists fucked up was tied to you."

"I can imagine how well that ultimatum must have gone over with you."

She set her coffee down on her glass desk with a precise, controlled movement. "I seriously doubt you can. But there are bigger things in this world than what I want. And you know more than most people what we're up against. I may think you're a disgusting waste of human skin, but what Gage has reported after partnering with you is that you kick ass and you seem to be on our side. These days, that's a pretty short list." She opened her laptop and started typing.

"So I can count on a glowing recommendation from you, can I?" asked Adam, sarcasm scalding his tongue.

"Nope. Not letting you go. I want you where I can keep an eye on you. Besides, we got a lead on one of the folks on the List to track down, and I'm shorthanded as it is. Whether or not I like you, you proved that you can get the job done. The people out there hurting deserve the best we can give, and sadly, that includes you."

He wasn't sure if she lumped him in the category of people who were hurting or as part of the best she had to give. Either way it made him uncomfortable. He didn't like that anyone knew he'd been part of the Threshold Project experiments. Then again, he didn't like people knowing anything about him. And yet he'd just handed Mira unrestricted access to his most personal medical information.

Being with the people here at the Edge—working side by side with them—had changed him. He wasn't yet sure whether or not he liked it.

"I'm making Mira miserable. I should go." He gave Bella a hard stare—one that would make most men cower. Instead, she just grinned.

Bella stared pointedly at her laptop. "She'll get over it. Besides, she needs to toughen up a little."

"You've had her in the sparring ring and at the range nearly every night since she recovered from her wounds. I think she's tough enough."

"Hardly. Which is why I'm sending her into the field."

The thought of Mira in danger made some dark, violent force lunge from somewhere deep inside him. He tamped it down, but only barely. Even his best effort to control himself couldn't keep the heat from his tone. "You can't. She's not ready for that."

"She's as ready as she's going to get until she has some experience under her belt."

"A woman with her intellect must be of more use to you here, behind a desk, where she'll be safe."

Bella didn't even glance his way. Her focus was on her laptop. "Her tech is mobile enough. She can still do her job from the road."

"Have you even talked to her about this?"

Bella turned her laptop around, showing Mira's enraged expression. She was saying something, but the sound had been muted. With the click of a button, Bella turned up the volume.

"What's he doing there?" raged Mira. A second later she disappeared from the screen, leaving her desk chair empty.

"She knows," said Bella. "We've been discussing it for a while. Like you, she's been . . . hesitant."

"Surely she's smart enough to stay here."

"It's not her call," said Bella. "It's mine. The decision is made."

Accusation filled his voice, making it boom out into the space. "You're going to get her killed."

"Like you almost did?" asked Mira from the doorway. She must have run all the way here from her office.

He couldn't tell if the pretty pink flush covering her cheeks was due to exertion or anger. Either way, her pull on him was too strong for his peace of mind. Every time he got near her, all he wanted to do was get closer. That wasn't fair to her or to him. He'd destroyed his one and only chance with Mira when he'd abducted her and taken her to her father. It didn't matter that he'd done so only to find his baby brother, who'd been lost to him for more than twenty years—a brother who was suffering and in need of help for all Adam knew at the time.

The irony was that while his brother had no clue who Adam really was, he worked at the Edge and knew what Adam had done to Mira. Whatever connection he'd hoped to have with Eli was now lost to him because of what he'd done to find Eli. Lost, just like that instant attachment Adam had formed to Mira during a few shared moments. He'd traded Mira to reach Eli, and because he'd done so, Eli would never trust him.

"That's enough," said Bella. "Adam is an asshole, but he's a skilled asshole. And he's proven he's willing to take a bullet for you, which is why I'm partnering the two of you."

"No way, Bella," said Mira, her tone final.

Adam agreed. "I don't think that's a good idea."

"I don't care what you think. Either of you. I'm headed out of town to track down one of the victims of the Threshold Project who's just been located. Riley will be back in the office in a day or two, but until then, there's no one else around to take on this assignment."

"I'm not working with Adam," said Mira.

"You're not ready to work alone yet, sugar," said Bella, "and I still don't trust Adam enough to send him out on his own."

Adam spoke up, hoping to defuse the situation. "I thought Gage was my keeper. You've had me paired up with him for weeks now. I'd rather work with him."

"He has more important things to do."

"He didn't mention anything to me," said Adam.

"Because I ordered him not to. I might be forced to have you on my team, but no one can force me to trust you, and what Gage is doing is way too sensitive for you to know about."

"I see," said Adam, trying not to let her mistrust of him chafe enough to show.

"I don't," said Mira. "Either this assignment is too important to let Adam touch, or it's unimportant enough that it can wait until I have someone else to go with me."

"Not your call, sweetie. This is happening. Your only choice is whether or not you enjoy it."

"I could quit."

"You could. But then you wouldn't get a chance to help all those people your father fucked up. I know you better than that, so please don't waste my time bluffing." Bella pulled a file from the stack and tossed it on the corner of her desk nearest Mira. "This is information on one of the men on the List. All I have is a name and address. Research him today. Make contact only after you're sure of what you'll face. If he shows any signs of cracking, bring him in."

"Whatever," said Mira.

Bella rose, making full use of her impressive height. She gave Mira a stare cold enough to freeze her in place, warning clear in her tone. "If you leave this office to make contact or do surveillance, Adam goes with you. Clear?"

Mira scowled.

Adam nodded. "I'll make sure of it."

Mira scowled harder, aiming it in his direction. "I know the drill."

"Perhaps, but you haven't executed it yet," said Adam.

"I have. Several times now."

Bella pulled a pistol from her shoulder holster and checked the weapon with fluid, practiced movements. "And so far, it's gone well. See that the trend continues. And if Mira comes back to me with so much as a hang-nail, we're going to have words."

"Your warning is overdramatic but clear. I won't let her get hurt," promised Adam.

Mira's nostrils flared and the file folder crumpled in her fist. "*I* won't let me get hurt. I don't need him."

"Your opinion is noted and ignored," said Bella as she holstered her weapon. "Play nice, kids. I've got lots to do before I hit the road." She swept out of her office with her coffee, leaving a fuming Mira in her wake.

"I can't believe she would do that to me," said Mira. "She knows how I feel about you."

"Everyone who works here knows how you feel about me. The question is, are you adult enough to put your feelings for me aside and do your job?"

"Easy for you to say."

"Of course it is. Compartmentalization was merely one small part of my training. Was it part of yours, Mira?"

She flinched and tucked her brown hair behind her ear with shaking fingers. "What my father did to me is none of your business. You gave up the right to care when you sold me out."

"I am responsible for everything stemming from my actions last year. There's plenty of blame to go around, certainly, and I willingly accept my fair share for what was done to you. The question now is do you really think that your hatred of me is going to help anyone in need now?"

She closed her eyes and let out a weary sigh. "Probably not. My father left one hell of a mess, and there aren't nearly enough of us left to clean it up."

"We're making progress. Today, you and I will make more."

Her green eyes lifted, meeting his. That connection rocketed through him, startling him down to his bones. He didn't know what it was about her that pulled him in and held on, but whatever it was, its grip was tight enough to drive the breath from his chest.

"I won't trust you," she promised.

"I know. I won't waste time asking you to. But we do have to find a way to work together."

Her gaze slipped away and her voice rose slightly, giving away her tension. "Give me some time to accept the situation and do the research. Tomorrow I'll find a way to get past my feelings for you and do what's right."

She was lying. Hiding something. The list of reasons why she would do that was short.

Adam nodded, struggling to keep his disappointment hidden. "Tomorrow, then."

Before he could destroy her willingness to put herself within his reach, he turned and left. Mistrust was a two-way street, and while she didn't trust him not to betray her, he didn't trust her not to do something foolish and go out on this assignment alone, just to prove she could.

Adam had promised Bella he'd keep Mira safe. If that meant checking on her every hour to make sure she didn't do anything foolish, then so be it. It wouldn't be the first sleepless night she'd caused him. And likely not the last, either.

Chapter Three

Mira glanced up as Bella poked her head in the doorway of the computer room that doubled as Mira's office. She quickly closed the program she'd had open on her desktop, hiding the evidence of her spying efforts.

Bella's dark hair was pulled into a tight ponytail that dangled down her back. Dressed in clinging workout clothes that showed off muscles Mira could only dream about having, Bella was either on her way to the gym or had just finished there. There was no sign of sweat or fatigue to give away which one, but then again, Bella always looked fabulous, even when she was sweating.

"Ready for some sparring, sugar?" asked Bella. "As mad at me as you are, I thought you might enjoy it."

Mira was mad, but not at Bella. Adam was the real villain here—something Mira refused to forget even if others here did. "I thought you were leaving town."

"I am. Plane leaves in a couple of hours. Thought I'd kill some time in the ring. Wanna join me?"

"Not today. I have something I need to go do."

Bella propped a hip on Mira's desk, showing off an envy-inducing body of Amazonian proportions. "You're not planning anything stupid, are you?"

"Just a personal errand."

"Liar. You're up to something."

"You're imagining things. I have a very secretive pile of laundry that needs to be dry-cleaned."

"It's not even six yet. Since when do you leave work before ten?"

"Since I was shot. I'm still not one hundred percent. I get tired easy."

"Bullshit, doll. Since we've started sparring, you've got more stamina than ever."

"Maybe I'm just tired of spending my life on work. Ever think of that? I am capable of having a personal life."

Bella snorted. "Yeah, right. You've spent more time here since leaving the hospital than you ever did before. So. Why all the lies? You know you can trust me."

"As much as you trust me?"

"What's that supposed to mean?"

"I told you Adam Brink was bad news. I told you what he did to me. And you *still* hired him."

Bella's amusement dried up. "I had no choice. His employment here was part of the contract."

"You could have negotiated harder."

"You think I didn't try? Of course I didn't want the man who'd drugged you and sold you out anywhere near here. Hell, I would have put a much-needed bullet through his dick if it had been left up to me. But it wasn't. Would you have rather I'd turned down the contract?"

"We could have found another way to help those people without it."

"Sorry to burst your bubble, sugar, but that's not true. As much as I couldn't care less about the money, it goes to buying things like shiny new weapons. Not to mention the access to intelligence we've gained in the deal. You can't say government resources haven't helped."

"I do like having access to the toys, but that means Adam has access, too. You know we can't trust him."

"I *don't* trust him. But I do have to find a way to work

with him. So do you. This is bigger than either of us or our feelings. People out there are suffering. They need all the help they can get, even from Adam. You should hear Gage talk about how badass Adam is. I swear he uttered three whole sentences. In a row."

Mira didn't bother hiding her shock. "That was a lot for a man of few words. But what if Adam is only helping for some nefarious purpose?"

"Then we stop him. However we have to. At least we know where he is if he's working with us every day. Dr. Stynger is in the wind, and we haven't had so much as a hint of where she may have gone."

Mira nodded, trying to keep the sick feeling in her gut from showing on her face. "I've been searching for her. Scouring the data we recovered last year for any clue as to where she might be." She hadn't been spending as much time on it as she should have, though. Too many hours had been spent watching Adam, tracking his movements, monitoring the cameras she'd planted in his house and car. No one else could do the work for her because no one else could know what she was up to.

Even now, Mira itched to open the program she'd closed so she could follow his every move.

Bella sighed. "Stynger's a ghost. It's why she's been able to do so much harm. But we *will* find her." That was Bella's scary voice—the one she reserved for the people she planned to kill.

"I have programs running even as we speak," Mira assured her. "If anything pops up, we'll be alerted so we can pounce."

"Guess that's all we can do for now." Bella pushed away from the desk. "Are you sure you don't want to go a few rounds with me?"

"Not when you're pissed off like this. I still have bruises from the last time."

A slight smile tickled the corners of Bella's lush

mouth. "I still have a few you gave me, too, honey. You're getting better all the time."

"You haven't given me much choice."

"Now you know how I feel about employing Adam. I don't like him. I don't trust him. But he does a hell of a job. He's found and helped more victims of your father's experiments than the next two men combined. Think what you want about him, but he is one efficient bastard."

Apparently, Adam had worked his charm on Bella, too. If there was one way to worm his way into her good graces, it was by doing his job well. A few weeks from now and Bella would forget all about how her new star employee had come to them.

"I'll agree with the bastard part, at least," said Mira. "Just hope he minds his manners while you're away. I'd hate to use what you've taught me in the ring and break your new favorite toy."

Bella grinned in amusement at that. "If you do decide to break him, promise you'll let me watch. I'd pay good money to see that fight."

Mira rolled her eyes. "Sure. That'll happen."

"Don't underestimate yourself. You may look all sweet and gentle, but there's a fierce streak in you half a mile wide. My guess? Adam's going to bring that right out. I'm counting on it."

With that, Bella left Mira to the hum of her computers.

Mira spent the next hour completing her research on the man in the file Bella had given her. It didn't take long for her to lay out a picture of his life. Like so many other victims of the Threshold Project, Corey Lambert led a life that was bleak and filled with pain. All thanks to her father's work.

It made her wonder if there was hope for any of his subjects to find happiness.

Including her.

Those thoughts were too dark for her to face now, so she distracted herself with what had become an all-consuming hobby of hers: tracking Adam.

She pulled up her surveillance video and audio recordings, sending them through several filtering programs designed to call her attention to key words and actions. Every conversation Adam had, she recorded. Every place he ever went, she tracked him. Every room in his home had hidden cameras and microphones. His car was bugged with surveillance devices as well as redundant tracking systems. She could find him through his phone, his company-issued dog tags, his keys, his car; even the soles of his shoes had been implanted with tracking devices while he'd been in the shower at the company gym.

Wherever he went, whatever he said, whomever he met, Mira would know. And when Adam finally showed his true colors and revealed his real boss, she'd know that, too. So would Bella and everyone else.

Maybe then, after he was thrown in some dank prison cell, she'd be able to stop thinking about him.

By the time she'd gone through all the recordings and reports her programs had generated, it was well after dark. The office was empty. She was exhausted and probably should have gone home to sleep, but her mind was still reeling, trying to assimilate the news that Adam was now her partner.

The lab report he'd given her sat on her desk, taunting her. The results were easy enough to alter—at least they would have been for her—but why would he go to so much trouble? What possible goal could he have for putting her at ease?

Maybe he was trying to get her to lower her guard.

Not in this lifetime.

Mira brought up a screen showing Adam's current location. Several different transmitters confirmed that he was at home, so she activated the cameras she'd hidden there until she found him.

He sat alone at his kitchen table, eating a microwaveable dinner. He stared straight ahead, eating methodically, almost robotically. There was no TV on in the background. No radio. He had no book or cell phone to distract him. Just dinner and the rhythmic pattern of the fork moving between the plastic tray and his mouth.

Oddly, the sight reminded her of the one meal they'd shared a few months ago. He'd been so animated then, so warm. He'd paid attention to her every word, touching her hand now and then with a gentle caress of his fingertips.

That night she'd anticipated each touch with nervous, girlish excitement. She'd barely tasted her meal for all the butterflies fluttering in her stomach.

His attention on her had been rapt. Absolute. He hadn't even glanced at anyone else, including the pretty waitress who'd served them or the busty hostess who'd seated them.

She'd felt beautiful that night—something she had never felt quite so keenly before or since. No other man had ever put her under his spell so completely.

Mira could have fallen for the man who'd sat across from her that night. Which made her a total idiot.

The real Adam was the one she watched now. Cold. Methodical. Robotic.

And now he was her partner.

Bella was insane for forcing the two of them together. Mira could have worked with anyone but Adam.

Then again, Bella was known for testing her employees. Their work was high-pressure, high stakes. If Mira was going to crack by being paired up with a man she hated, then how could she ever expect to be allowed in the field?

And she had to be allowed in the field. It was the only way to undo some of the damage her father had caused to countless innocent lives.

If working with Adam was the only way to make that
happen, then she would be the best partner the man had
ever known. He'd hardly have to lift a finger. Bella could
have no excuse to keep Mira behind a desk the way
Adam wanted.

As far as Mira was concerned, pissing off Adam was
just icing on the cake.

Once again she opened the file Bella had given her.
The subject's information stared up at her, black-and-
white proof of her father's evil.

The secret files that had been recovered last year had
all been decoded. There was a massive amount of data,
and Mira had spent the past several weeks working to
organize it into some helpful format. Test subjects were
referred to by codes, and small bits of information about
them were scattered through dozens of different files.
She had done her best to construct a database to merge
all the information together, but there were so many
missing pieces. Some victims had been assigned multiple
IDs for different experiments. She could spend the rest
of her life trying to piece it all together and the picture
would still be incomplete.

But there were some pieces that were visible. A few
names. People like Corey Lambert, whose file she held
in her hands.

His life was a wreck, thanks to Mira's father. Police
records showed he'd been jailed a handful of times,
mostly for disorderly conduct and assault. He'd filed for
bankruptcy a couple of years ago. He was chronically
unemployed. Two marriages, two divorces—both within
the last three years. No children, which was a small blessing.

Mira still had no way of knowing if what her father or
the other scientists had done could be passed on to future generations. There were mentions of genetic ma-
nipulation, but she was no doctor, and the notes she'd
decrypted made little sense. From what Dr. Vaughn had

said, most of the notations seemed to refer to ideas rather than actual research.

But they'd discovered only a small number of files—a tiny fraction of the whole puzzle. There was no way to know if those ideas had turned into something more as time went on.

Movement on her monitor brought her attention back to Adam as he rose from his kitchen table. Cameras followed him to a spare bedroom filled with exercise equipment. He stripped off his T-shirt, leaving him wearing only a pair of knit running shorts.

Lean muscles followed the contours of his body, easily covered by the suit he usually wore. The scar where he'd been shot was a faint, pinkish pucker of skin in the midst of his naturally tan complexion.

She absently rubbed her matching scar where the bullet had gone through him into her. She hated that they had even that small connection.

He got on a treadmill and started to run.

Mira knew from experience that he'd be there for at least a couple of hours. She had no idea how he could sprint like that for so long, but she'd seen it often enough to know how much stamina he had.

So far, he hadn't found any of her surveillance devices.

Unless he had, and this recording of a marathon running session was his way of distracting her while he slipped out to do something horrible.

That had to be it. No real person could run like he did for hours, breathing evenly, barely sweating. It had to be a trick—a way to bypass her surveillance measures with a repetitive, monotonous activity that was easily reproduced.

A welcome wave of anger swelled in Mira's chest, distracting her from thoughts of her soulless father and all the damage he'd caused.

Adam wasn't going to trick her so easily. She was going to collect proof that he wasn't the man he pretended to be, and once she had that, Bella would have no choice but to send him away and find Mira a partner who didn't remind her of just how gullible she could be.

She gathered her coat and purse and headed for the door. Only when she was halfway there did she stop. After several long seconds, she turned back to her desk and pulled out her revolver. There was no way to know how Adam would react to her discovering his lies, and she needed to be ready for anything.

A few minutes later, she drove by his house. Through the plain, functional blinds covering his windows, she could see his shadow moving as he ran.

All that anger trickled out of her.

She'd been wrong. He really was still here, not slinking around out in the night, torturing kittens or whatever it was he liked to do in his spare time.

Her head fell back on the headrest with a thump.

At this rate, she was never going to find proof that Adam was evil all the way through.

Which made her wonder . . . what if he wasn't? What if she was the unreasonable one, hoping to see what she wanted? If that evil streak wasn't there, she was wasting a hell of a lot of time looking for it.

She had to remember her real goal. Adam was simply a distraction from finding and helping the people her father had hurt. Even now, while she sat in her car outside of Adam's house, Corey Lambert was in pain. Suffering.

She had the power to help him, or at the very least tell him why he felt the things he did, why he couldn't seem to get his life under control. Maybe the simple relief of knowing that he wasn't alone would be enough for him to get himself back on track.

It had worked for others. The lucky few who hadn't fallen too far to be saved.

What if tonight was the night Corey cracked? What if

tonight was the night he gave in to the urge to do that one unspeakable act for which he'd never forgive himself?

Mira wasn't going to sit around and simply hope it didn't happen. She was going to *do* something.

Bella would have told her to go knock on Adam's door and drag him along with her. She would have lectured her that it wasn't safe to go alone.

But what Bella didn't yet realize was that it was far safer to walk into a bad situation alone than it was to go into one with a devil by her side. For all she knew, Adam would turn on her the first chance he got.

He'd done it before.

Mira had spent her life trying to prove herself to others. First to her father, then to Bella. It was time to start proving things to herself.

She was smart. Strong. Determined. And armed. She could handle a conversation with one broken man who couldn't even manage to keep a job.

And if she couldn't, she had no business being in the field at all. Better to know now before she got someone she cared about killed.

She pulled away from Adam's house and headed across town. At the first stoplight, she made sure her phone's tracking system was on and the panic code that would dial her best friend, Clay, was partially keyed in. All she had to do was hit one button, and Clay would come running.

Now, *he* was a man she could trust. Too bad she'd never felt more for him than she would have for a brother. He was happily involved with Dr. Vaughn, and Mira could not have been more pleased with his choice.

She doubted it would be long before the wedding invitation arrived.

With that happy thought in mind, Mira pulled into the run-down neighborhood where Corey Lambert lived.

A lot of trailer parks were really nice, filled with shiny,

well-kept homes inhabited by people who took pride in where they lived.

This was not one of those places.

The mobile homes here had seen better days. Patches of long, winter-brown weeds grew everywhere. The most prevalent colors were rust and the sad, dingy yellow of decaying paint. A few large trees had grown up here, indicating the age of the trailer park.

Mira inched along the cracked road, searching for the right address. A lot of the lots held vacant, collapsing mobile homes abandoned by their tenants long ago. Even the boards over the windows looked rotten and on the verge of collapse.

The whole place had a sad vibe that made her wish her father was alive to see the price of his precious experiments—right before she forced him to live in one of these run-down deathtraps.

She didn't need to check the house number to know she'd found the right one. Standing outside a rusting trailer was Corey, furiously pointing his finger at a small woman. She cowered back from him, wrapping her arms around her middle and hunching her shoulders as if to make herself a smaller target.

The woman backed up another step, until she ran into the chipped metal railing along the stairs leading into the house.

Corey looked just like his photo: worn-down, angry, desperate. His shaggy blond hair and beard needed a good wash, as did the pit-stained wifebeater he wore. His gut stretched the fabric enough to show her that visits to the gym weren't high on his list of priorities.

That gave her the confidence Mira needed to get out of the car. She kept her headlights splashed over the scene and the car's engine running, just in case. Her cell phone was in her jacket pocket, and under her left arm was a shoulder holster filled with enough firepower to remind her to be careful.

"Corey Lambert?" she asked as she approached.

He turned and squinted, lifting his hand to shield himself from the glare of her headlights. Even from here, Mira could see how bloodshot his eyes were, how much his hands shook.

He was not a well man.

"Did you call someone?" he asked the woman, his tone sharp with accusation.

She flinched and hugged herself tighter. "No. I'd never do that to you."

Corey took another step toward the woman.

A little ripple of fear slid up Mira's throat. She slipped her hand into her pocket and gripped her phone. "No one called me."

"You a cop?"

"No. I'd like to talk to you."

"I'm busy."

"Busy making what might be the biggest mistake of your life," said Mira. "Now, please, all I need is a couple of minutes."

"Whatever you're selling, I'm not buying."

"I'm not selling anything. I swear. I'm here to help you."

He whirled on her, his face warped with anger. "Do I look like I need your help?"

That ripple of fear turned into a full-blown wave. She had to fight the need to take a step back, away from his anger.

Calm. That's what she had to be now. Firm but calm. Nonthreatening. Reasonable.

Honest.

"Yes," she finally said. "You do need help. I know what was done to you. I know how you suffer."

"Pfft," he hissed. "Get the hell out of here, lady. You don't know shit."

"I do. You have headaches. Maybe even black out sometimes. And the nightmares . . . they seem so real. You're angry all the time. Cry for no reason."

He looked at the woman and issued a harsh "Get in the house."

The woman scrambled away fast, as if glad for any excuse she could find to leave.

Corey turned back to Mira. "You're seriously starting to piss me off, lady. If you know what's good for you, you'll get the fuck out of here."

Mira didn't budge. This was too important. Corey had been damaged by her father, perhaps irrevocably. It was her duty to see to it that he got whatever help she could offer.

She squared her shoulders. "You hear things, maybe smell them, and it sets you off just like that." She snapped her fingers. "You can't control what you see or how you feel. The terror is so real, you swear you're still in that room with the doctor and all those needles. He's hurting you, and he won't stop, no matter how much you beg."

Some of the anger fell from his face and his skin went pale behind his beard. "Who the fuck are you?"

"A friend. I want to help."

"Just leave me alone. That's all I need."

"No, it's not. What was done to you can be fixed." She hoped. "I know people who can take away the headaches, end the nightmares. All you have to do is come with me."

Skepticism quavered in his voice. "Where?"

"I can't tell you. You have to trust me."

"I don't even know you. For all I know *they* sent you here."

"They?"

He moved closer. She wasn't even sure how he got that far that fast until he grabbed her arms.

Corey lifted her up until only her tiptoes reached the ground. His grip was crushing, making pain shoot down to her fingertips. Fear exploded in her gut, and her fingers scrambled to hit the right button on her phone to call in reinforcements.

He snarled, his face only inches from hers. She could see each vein in his bloodshot eyes, each groove that fear and pain had carved around his mouth. "You go back to wherever it is you came from and tell them to back the fuck off and leave me alone. I know they're watching me. I know they have some way of getting in my head. You tell them to stop." He punctuated his words with another hard shake that dislodged the phone from her hand.

"No one's watching you. I can prove it. Just come with me."

His hand flashed across her face so fast she didn't see it move. It was the jerk of her head to the right and slightly delayed pain that told her she'd been hit.

Shock numbed her for a second as she struggled to digest the fact that she'd been hit—that she was in far more danger here than she'd thought.

The tang of blood hit her tongue.

Corey tightened his grip on her arms and shook her hard enough to rattle her skull. "If they get in my head again, I'll come find you," he promised. "I'll make you pay. Understand?"

Honesty was quickly becoming difficult, but she wasn't sure what else to do. "I swear no one is in your head. That's just a side effect of what was done to you when you were a kid. Please let me help you."

"They got to you, too, didn't they? Filled your head with lies, made you do things you didn't want to do?" There was a crazy light in his eyes—one that was starting to glow a bit too bright for her peace of mind.

She shook her head. "This isn't about me. I—"

He hit her again, and this time the blow was hard enough to send her flying back onto the concrete. She landed hard. The back of her head hit something even harder.

The edges of her vision went swampy for a second before she managed to fight it off. By the time she did, Corey was standing over her.

He reached down and pulled her revolver from inside her open jacket. "You came here to kill me, didn't you?"

She tried to deny it, but her tongue was stuck to the roof of her mouth. Her whole body felt slow and heavy, and her normally swift mind was drawing a total blank as to what to do now.

"Maybe this will send them the message to stay the fuck away from me." Corey aimed the gun at her chest.

Chapter Four

Adam continued with his usual routine so that Mira wouldn't suspect his mistrust of her. He'd gone home while she was still safe at the office to eat and get in a quick run before executing his plan to spend the night parked in front of her house.

Then she'd surprised him by coming to his house instead. He'd seen the headlights bob across his front windows. His proximity alarms had sounded, activating the cameras aimed out from his house. But a moment before his phone had vibrated to draw his attention to her, he swore he'd *felt* her presence.

There was no other way to describe the odd connection he'd made with her last year. And there was no rational reason why he'd feel any connection to her at all.

But he did, and Adam was not a man to deny instincts. His had screamed at him to follow her, and he was glad now that he'd listened.

Mira was sitting on the ground, slumped against the front bumper of her car. Fear bleached her skin, and there was a dazed, sluggish quality to her movements.

An unkempt, beer-bellied man stood over her, seething with rage. In his hand was a revolver, and it was aimed right at Mira.

Fury swept through Adam, too swift and hot to control.

He lifted his suppressed weapon and fired it into the thigh of the man who'd dared to point a gun at her.

It wasn't until after he'd pulled the trigger that he realized he'd let his emotions rule his actions for a single, split second. Dangerous for a man like him, and completely uncharacteristic.

Corey Lambert collapsed, screaming in pain and clutching his leg.

Adam kept his weapon along his thigh but in his hand as he approached. In a controlled voice, he said to the man, "Put pressure on the wound or you'll bleed out."

A woman came running from a nearby trailer, her screams adding to Corey's.

Adam kept them both in sight while he knelt beside Mira. "How badly are you hurt?"

"I'm fine. How did you get here?" Her voice trembled, which added to the rage he now kept carefully banked.

"I drove."

"I know that, but why did you come?"

He spared her a quick glance then and wished he hadn't. Blood trickled from the corner of her mouth. One side of her face was bright red, and he was almost certain he could see the outline of a man's handprint burning in her skin.

Fury shoved upward, threatening to break free. He pulled in a deep breath and let it out slowly before responding. "I'm your partner. I will always have your back."

The woman ran back into the house, presumably to call for help.

They were running out of time before police and ambulances trapped them here in this dismal excuse for a neighborhood.

Adam left Mira's side just long enough to pick up the

weapon Corey had dropped. He pinned the man with a cold stare and warned him in a whisper Mira could not hear, "Mention her in any way, and I will find you in the hospital and kill you in your sleep."

The man's widened stare of fear was enough to tell Adam that his warning had been received.

He lifted Mira to her feet and tucked her in the passenger seat of her car. As he walked around the vehicle to get in behind the wheel, he saw there was a dent in the bumper where her head had hit.

Another swell of anger threatened to burst free, but he held himself in check and shoved that anger into a tidy box. He slid the seat back to make room for his body and calmly drove out of the trailer park.

A few blocks later, a police cruiser flashing its lights zoomed past them.

"What about your car?" asked Mira.

"I'll go back for it later." Or not. There was nothing tying the vehicle to him. Let the police find it. His tracks were always carefully covered.

A professional requirement for a man like him.

He drove toward the nearest hospital. "How is your head?" he asked.

"Thick enough to handle a blow like that, apparently."

"Any blurred vision? Nausea? Dizziness?"

"No, but my pride is plenty bruised."

"Good. Maybe that will remind you not to go into dangerous situations without your partner."

"I was careful."

"Apparently not careful enough."

"No, just not quick enough. I should have dialed Clay before the jerk grabbed me."

"Clay?" Now Adam was *really* getting mad. "His place is all the way across town, easily twenty minutes farther away than I was. I should have been your first call."

"Well, you weren't."

"Just what, exactly, did you think he would be able to do for you that I couldn't?"

"I trust him."

Of course. It always came back to that with her.

And why shouldn't it? He was a creature of logic. He understood how putting one's hand into the fire twice would be a stupid thing to do.

Then why did it piss him off so much that she refused to give him a second chance?

"We're almost to the hospital. Would you rather go there or to see Dr. Vaughn?"

"Neither," said Mira. "I'm fine. Really."

"Then you won't mind proving that's the case to the good doctor."

"It's after ten. I'm sure she's asleep."

"And I'm sure I don't care. She's paid well for her time—paid to be on call when we need her. The dent in your front bumper makes it clear that you need her."

"Just take me home, Adam."

Rain began spitting against the windshield. It was too warm for snow, but only by a little.

At the next stoplight, Adam texted Dr. Leigh Vaughn. By the time he pulled into Mira's driveway, Leigh was waiting for them.

"You called her?" asked Mira, accusation in her tone.

"I did." He parked the car. "Do you need help inside?"

"From you? No, thanks. I'm fine."

Mira made her way into the house without his aid, though he held an umbrella over her head, using that as an excuse to hover close enough to catch her if she'd overestimated how well she felt.

"Thank you for coming," Adam said to Leigh.

She pulled a leather bag from her car and followed them in. "Sure. Glad to help."

Mira flopped onto the couch. "I'm fine, Leigh. Adam is just rubbing my nose in the failure of my first job."

That's what she thought he was doing?

Her thought patterns were so bizarre, he could hardly keep up. Maybe that was why she intrigued him so much.

"I'm only making sure you're not permanently damaged. Bella would kill me if I did anything less."

Leigh glanced between them, obviously trying to figure out what was going on. "Adam, will you please go make Mira some hot tea?"

He was being sent away, but he accepted the dismissal and did as he was asked.

Mira's kitchen was like the rest of her house: tidy and small, with quirky decorations he couldn't quite understand. There was a clay pot in the center of her kitchen table, and in it was a spray of antique glass doorknobs planted in the dirt. Her curtains were covered with cartoon images of flying squirrels. In the far corner was a one-armed mannequin wearing only a hot pink apron and what looked like a beret made of bacon. The remaining arm seemed to serve as some kind of white board for her grocery list.

Like the woman herself, none of it made any sense at all to him.

Adam made the tea and brought it out. By the time he did, Leigh was already packing her medical bag.

"You're leaving?" asked Adam.

"She's fine. No sign of concussion. Just keep watch over her tonight to be sure."

"What?" screeched Mira. "He's not staying here."

"Someone has to, and it's not going to be me," said Leigh with a womanly grin. "Clay is waiting on me to get home."

"I'm surprised he didn't come with you," said Mira, sounding a little hurt.

Leigh opened her mouth, but Adam spoke before she could. "I asked her not to tell him. I know how worried you are about his stress levels, and hearing you were injured would definitely be stressful for him."

"Oh," said Mira, frowning. "That was nice of you."

Adam set the tea on the table beside her. "Don't sound so shocked. I am capable of basic human decency."

"And this is my cue to leave," said Leigh. "Call if you need me. If she shows any signs of concussion, take her to the hospital and I'll meet you there."

Mira sighed. "I'm fine."

Leigh pulled out her keys. "Tell that to the bruise you're sporting. And if you don't want Clay moving you into our place for the foreseeable future, I suggest you use some good concealer before you see him next."

"I will. He has enough to worry about."

"He's tough," said Leigh. "Getting stronger every day. I'm honestly not even sure how that's possible, but he keeps surprising me."

"Well, go home and let him surprise you some more. I'm good."

Adam walked Dr. Vaughn out and locked the door behind her.

"You can go, too," said Mira.

He ignored her comment as absurd. "Did she give you something for pain? I bet your head is throbbing."

"It's not that bad. And yes, she gave me some ibuprofen."

"When did you eat last?"

She paused as if trying to remember.

He went back into the kitchen and got the box of crackers he'd found. "Here. Eat some of these so the pills won't upset your stomach."

"I'm really not that much of a wuss."

He set them beside her. "Fine. Just know that if you throw up, I'll assume you have a concussion and move in here for at least a week, just to make sure you're safe."

She opened the crackers and stuffed one in her mouth. "Happy?"

"Deliriously."

He settled in a chair as far from her as possible. There was no getting rid of him tonight, and the last thing he wanted was to make his life difficult by putting her more on edge than she already was.

Adam watched her eat, enjoying the shape of her mouth. Of course, he liked the way the rest of her was shaped, too. She was curvier than the other women at the Edge, and with the way she sat with her legs curled under her, her entire body was one intriguingly sinuous line.

The lamp beside her made her dark hair shimmer with glossy highlights. She wore no makeup, or so little he couldn't detect any trace of it. Even so, she always had a lovely pink tint to her cheeks and mouth that was more alluring than any blush or gloss could ever be.

"Are you tired?" he asked.

"No. But if you are, feel free to go home. If you want, I can text you every hour so you know I'm not dead."

Not good enough. Not even close. "I don't sleep much."

She froze in the act of eating another cracker. "Neither do I. Is it the dreams, or what was done to you?"

"I don't dream, or if I do, I don't remember them."

"Count yourself lucky." She tried to stifle a shiver, but he saw it anyway.

He crossed the room and reached past her for the throw on the back of the couch. It was printed with large blocks of Swiss cheese and made absolutely no sense to him as a decorative item.

Mira flinched as his hand passed her shoulder.

Another inconvenient burst of anger flew through his veins, forcing him to freeze with his fist around the fabric while the emotion faded. He didn't dare move when he felt like that—not when she was so close. The last thing he wanted was for her to see his fury, rush out into the rain to escape him, slip, and hit her head again.

When he was once again calm enough to control himself, he lifted the ridiculous blanket from the back of the couch and wrapped it around her shoulders.

"You look cold," he said, to ease her apparent worry over what he might do.

He was close enough to her to smell the shampoo she used—something sweet and tart that made his mouth water. Beneath that was a hint of warm skin and a single note of fear.

The need to bury his nose against her neck and breathe her in was nearly uncontrollable. He had no idea what it was about Mira that distracted him so deeply, but he needed to find a way to make it stop.

She was the key to his future. Without her trust, no one at the Edge would every truly welcome him as one of their own. And he needed his brother to accept him. Desperately.

After all the years he'd spent searching, for Eli to reject him now would be a mortal wound.

Mira clutched the edges of the fleece blanket, gripping it tightly enough that her knuckles bleached. The urge to unclench her fingers and rub the tension away hit him hard.

Instead, he arranged the fabric around her body, covering as much of her as possible. Maybe if he couldn't see her curves, they wouldn't distract him so completely.

When he was done, he picked up the mug of tea and handed it to her. "This will help you warm up."

She blinked up at him. Her green eyes were lovely, even narrowed in skepticism the way they were now.

"Why are you doing this?" she asked.

"Doing what?"

"Being nice to me."

"You're my partner. It's my job to make sure you're safe."

"I'd be safer if you left."

Adam wasn't entirely sure she was wrong. The things he felt for her were strange. Potent. She was a constant distraction in a job where such things could get a man killed. Or a woman.

Still, Bella had entrusted Mira's care to him, and he refused to let his new boss down, even if that meant coping with distraction.

He lifted the mug of tea closer and waited to see if she'd take it.

After what felt like far too long, she let go of the blanket and wrapped her fingers around the warm ceramic.

The tip of her thumb grazed across his finger. Her skin was cold. Her hand trembled slightly. Even so, that simple, innocent touch streaked up his arm and all along his spine, tingling as it went.

Before he could think twice about it, his hands covered hers, caging them against the hot mug.

She froze like a startled rabbit. Her green eyes widened. Her pupils shrank. "What are you doing?"

"Your hands are cold," he said, hoping that would end any further questions.

Her breathing sped, making her blanket slide from her shoulders to pool around her waist. From where he stood above her, he could easily see a shadow of cleavage that made his mouth go dry.

Her voice was weak. "I didn't say you could touch me."

"This is hardly touching, Mira." Though it felt very much like the real thing.

"It's more than enough. You should let go."

He tried to. He issued the order to his hands to move, but they stayed curled around hers, enjoying the smooth feel of her skin inside his grasp.

To cover his lack of discipline, he said, "Am I hurting you?"

She swallowed hard enough that he could see her throat move. He swore her pupils flared, and if he didn't know better, he'd think she was looking at him the same way she had the night of their one and only date—like a woman who was very much interested in the fact that he was a man.

"That's not the point."

"No. The point is you're not the kind of woman who likes to ask for help, which forces your partner to be the kind of man who gives it to you, whether or not you ask for it."

Anger forced a snarl on her lips a second before she shot to her feet. The mug tilted wildly, sending the hot tea all over his front.

She'd doused him like this once before, only that time, he'd arranged for it to happen. She'd been extremely apologetic, too—something the look on her face told him was not going to happen this time.

"Just stop it with the partner bullshit. Whatever game you're playing, you won't win. I won't fall for you or your lies again."

Which meant she had fallen for him before.

Strangely, the idea that he'd had her romantic attention and lost it was what upset him most. Not the drenched shirt or the burning skin. Not her current anger or her refusal to trust him. It was the idea that she could have loved him that he found most compelling.

No one had ever loved him before—at least not that he could remember. His parents had birthed him and his brother as an experiment, just to see if their theories were correct. Even his baby brother had clung to him more out of fear than love.

What would it be like for a woman as fierce and intelligent as Mira to love him?

A tiny part of him grieved that he would never know.

Mira stormed off, slamming her bedroom door behind her.

Adam found a towel in the kitchen and dried off as much as possible. The damp fabric felt cool against the slight burn of his skin. He was sure it was all the comfort he would find tonight.

Not that he needed comfort. That was for other men. Real men—not the product of human experimentation. Adam was designed to need very little to survive, and things like love and comfort were merely foreign concepts that gave him something to ponder as he made a slow security sweep of the house.

Tonight, Mira would be safe, and that was really all he needed.

Chapter Five

Riley Conlan barely heard the knock on his door over the sound of rain pounding on his roof.

It was nearly midnight, and he'd been lying awake in bed, hoping for sleep to find him. His body was exhausted from the job he'd finished earlier tonight, but his mind was slow to process and had not yet let go of the details.

The sheer magnitude of devastation the Threshold Project had caused was utterly staggering. So many lives ruined, all in the pursuit of power.

He rolled out of bed and slid on the pair of sweats he'd shed earlier. His Glock was holstered on his nightstand, and he grabbed it more out of habit than worry.

A glance through the peephole in his front door showed only the top of a drenched hoodie and a slender body hunched against the wind.

With one hand on the weapon he'd tucked at the small of his back, he unlocked his door and pulled it open.

The woman standing there looked up. He knew her instantly. Would have known her anywhere. She'd spent the worst night of her life with him and then disappeared, leaving him reeling.

Riley's heart stopped beating for a long moment as he struggled with his disbelief. "Sophie?"

Sophie Devane stood there, shivering and drenched. She glanced behind her as if expecting Satan himself to be on her heels. Fear quavered in her voice. "Can I come in?"

He nearly smacked himself for making her stand out there this long. Poor thing was freezing to death, and here he was, gawking like an idiot.

He stepped back, giving her room to pass, then closed and locked the door behind him.

There was no car in his driveway or parked on the street. No cab pulling away.

Had she walked in this weather? And what the hell was she doing here?

Riley turned to see her standing at the edge of his tile entryway. She was clearly trying not to drip on the carpet, even though every inch of her was soaked to the skin.

She pulled the hood from her head, revealing a thick, strawberry blond braid. It was dark from the rain, dripping down one shoulder. Her skin was visibly pale, making every one of her freckles stand out in contrast. There was a faint bluish tint to her lips, and her fingers were an angry red color.

She wasn't wearing rain gear or a winter coat—just a lightweight hoodie that was clearly not meant for this time of year. Even in Texas.

"Are you okay?" he asked, trying to wrap his head around her unexpected presence.

She gave a shaky nod. "I didn't know where else to go."

"How did you get here?"

"I walked." The way she said it, he was certain there was more to it than that, but he didn't press for details. Yet.

"You're freezing."

"Yeah. I kinda am. I'm glad you were here, or I'd have been screwed."

She carried no bag. Not even a purse.

A million questions bulged in his mind, but he kept them in check. First things first. "Come with me." He led her to the bathroom and started a warm shower. "Take your time. I'll set clothes outside the door. Then we'll talk."

She nodded again. "Thanks, Riley. For letting me in. I don't exactly deserve a warm welcome after the way I left things."

"We'll talk about it later. Just get warm."

He found some sweats with a drawstring, the smallest, warmest shirt he could find, and some wool socks he never wore because they were too hot. He piled everything outside the door while he went into the kitchen and heated up some canned soup. By the time she was out of the shower, he had a stack of blankets on the couch waiting for her, and a steaming bowl of chicken noodle.

His clothes swallowed her up, hiding all but her hands, feet, and head. Her hair was wrapped up in a towel, and a bit of color had returned to her cheeks.

He waited until she was comfortably settled and had a few bites of soup before he let his curiosity free. "What the hell are you doing here? In the middle of the night? In the rain? With no coat or purse?"

The spoon stalled out halfway to her mouth. "I had a chance to run. I took it."

"Run from what?"

She set the bowl aside. "Not what. Who."

"Okay, then. Who?"

Her gaze strayed from his, and he could practically see her shrink. "My dad was a shitty man. Into a lot of bad stuff. He died a few months ago, and the inheritance he left wasn't a good one."

"I don't understand."

She pulled his sweatshirt sleeves over her hands and curled deeper into the pile of blankets. "He owed a lot of people a lot of money. Word got out that I was worth more than he owed if I was delivered to the right people."

"What?" It was more a bellow than a question.

"I know. I thought I left all of that behind me when Soma was killed."

"Who are *the right people*?"

"I have no clue. The men who found me wouldn't say."

"Did you know the men?"

She still hadn't looked him in the eye yet, and he was starting to wish she would. He couldn't tell if she was hiding something or ashamed. Maybe neither, but there was definitely something going on that made her avoid his gaze.

Sophie nodded. "I'd seen them before. Years ago. Same guys who always came around to collect when Dad lost a big bet."

Bookies? Loan sharks? Enforcers? It hardly mattered. They were all bad news.

"Start at the beginning," he said, trying to keep his voice calm. "Tell me what happened, starting with the day you left the hospital without saying good-bye."

Her eyes lifted, and her pale green gaze met his.

He felt like he'd been hit in the gut with a battering ram. There was so much beauty there. So much pain.

He wanted to wash it all away, which made him the biggest sucker to ever walk the planet.

Sophie had left him. After he'd rescued her. After he'd helped her through her miscarriage. After he'd brought her home and made sure she was safe. She'd just . . . left.

She hadn't even said good-bye.

"I didn't mean to hurt you," she said.

"Who says you did?" he asked, his tone chilly.

She looked away again, and he suddenly missed the

connection. Her voice became distant, as if reciting a history lesson. "I went back to Louisiana. Got a waitressing job. I wanted to make a fresh start."

"But?"

"As soon as I called Dad to check on him, I found out that he'd died while I was held captive in Colombia. Guess Benny and his goons had been keeping his phone line paid up, hoping I would make contact. They used the number of the diner where I worked to find me."

"And they drove you all the way here?"

"No. I saw them coming and ran. I didn't know where else to go, so I headed here."

Toward him.

Riley didn't know if he should be more furious or flattered. He was the first person she'd thought of when she'd gotten in trouble, but she hadn't bothered to pick up the phone and call him to tell him she was alive and well?

After what they'd been through, that hurt.

"They tracked you all the way to Dallas?" he asked.

She nodded. "My car died about twenty miles south of here. I abandoned it and set out on foot. It was dark. I thought I'd lost them, but I was wrong."

"What happened?"

The pile of blankets seemed to shrink as she curled up tighter beneath them. "I stopped for water at a gas station this afternoon. They grabbed me. Threw me in their car."

"How'd you get away?"

"One of them made a call. There was a woman on the other line. I could hear her through the plastic. She was angry that they'd taken so long to find me."

Riley couldn't stay on the other side of the room any longer. The fear radiating from her was too much for him to ignore. He had to comfort her—if not for her, then for himself.

He got up from his chair, took a seat on the cushion next to hers and put his hand on her shoulder. "Did you recognize the woman's voice?"

"No. But I could tell she wasn't going to ask me to go for a pedicure with her. I swear she said something about an autopsy. That's when I bolted."

"What do you mean?"

"The guy sitting in back to keep me in line had a pen in his pocket. I stabbed him in the thigh with it and dove out the car door."

She stabbed him? Guess little Sophie was more vicious than he thought. "Please tell me they were parked."

She shook her head. "They were only going about twenty. I landed well. Rolled. It hurt, but I'm fine. Wish I'd taken my purse with me, though. Or at least some cash."

He didn't believe that she was fine. He followed her arm until he found her hand and pushed back the sleeve. Just as he'd thought, her palms were covered in a rash of scrapes and bruises. "Any other injuries?"

"No. Like I said, I landed well."

"Tell that to your hands."

"They'll heal. I'm more worried about staying alive."

"After you jumped, did they come after you?"

"Oh yeah. It took me several hours to lose them before I came here. I didn't want them to find you, so I was careful."

"How did you know where I lived?"

A faint blush crept up her cheeks. "I checked you out as soon as I got home. I even called your mom once. She's really sweet."

He was stunned silent for a second. Sophie had checked on him? Why hadn't she just called him? "My mom told you where I lived?" If so, he was going to have to have a serious talk with her.

"She thought I was selling life insurance and that you

should have some. She thought I was going to mail you an information packet. Don't be too hard on her. She really had no clue who I was."

Riley tabled his anger—at both women—to focus on the problem at hand. "Are these men the kind who give up easily?" He hoped.

"Not a chance. This doctor chick wants me and is willing to pay good money to get her hands on me."

Doctor?

All kinds of warning bells and sirens were blaring in his skull. "Did you get a name?"

"No, but it looks like you might know her."

"I hope not." If he did, Sophie had bigger troubles than a couple of thugs. Not that he was going to tell her that and scare her more. Not when she so clearly needed rest. "You should get some sleep."

"I'd argue, but I'm too tired. It's been a few days since I did more than close my eyes for a minute. I can't even think straight right now."

That made two of them. "The couch is yours if you want it, but my bed is more comfortable. I'd feel better if you took it."

"And what about you?"

"I'll be fine. I have some work to do still tonight, and it won't be the first night I've fallen asleep on the couch this week. Go on. Get some rest." He had some research to do on Sophie.

Namely, why Dr. Stynger might want to get her hands on Sophie and what he could do to make sure it never happened.

It wasn't until Sophie was safely behind a closed, locked door that she let herself cry.

She'd hurt Riley. It had been the last thing she'd meant to do when she'd left. He'd been so sweet to her. So kind.

That was why she'd run away. He was better off without her. He hadn't known it at the time, but *she* had.

And here she was, in his home, asking him to help her again.

But what choice did she have? There was no one else she could turn to.

The fact that she was here now proved just how right she'd been to leave him in the first place. A good woman would have never brought trouble to his doorstep. A good woman would have never been in trouble like hers to begin with.

Lies, bad luck, and bad blood. That was what she had to offer.

He deserved a hell of a lot more than that.

Still, she couldn't bring herself to leave. She needed to feel safe—just for a few hours. Sleep, recharge. Plan her next step.

The only time she'd ever truly felt safe was with Riley. Even with bullets flying and her in the midst of losing her baby, she'd known without a doubt that he would get her out alive.

Her baby.

The tears fell faster now. She had to shove her fist against her mouth to keep from making a sound.

She hadn't planned to get pregnant, but she would have given anything to save her child.

Just one more thing stolen from her, like her childhood, her freedom, and the life she should have had.

Sophie let herself grieve for a full minute before she pulled herself back in control. She needed to sleep. There was no way to know when she might get another chance to rest. She'd learned long ago to take what she could when she could and not ever believe there would always be more where that came from.

There were no guarantees in this life. No certainties.

Except Riley.

She was certain he'd help her or die trying. He was

one of the good ones. One of the few real heroes in the world.

Sophie had preyed on enough of them to know one when she saw him.

And now she was preying on Riley, too.

More tears burned her eyes, but she held them back. She would sleep now because that's what she needed. Tomorrow she'd wake up and regroup, eat and plan, because that's what she would need to do tomorrow.

Everything else, including her feelings for a man too good to be real, was irrelevant.

Chapter Six

Adam was still in Mira's house when she woke up the next morning.

She ignored him as she made coffee. Ignored him as she read e-mail. Ignored him as he moved around her kitchen like he owned the place, making a breakfast that put her usual bowl of cereal to shame.

He slid a plate in front of her, and her ability to ignore him couldn't stand the strain of crispy bacon and fluffy eggs. "Thank you."

He sat down across the tiny table from her. His legs were so long that his knee brushed hers. She shifted in her seat, but there was no escaping him. The only thing between them was her collection of antique doorknobs and a thick slab of awkward silence.

"Did you finally get some sleep?" he finally asked.

"I slept all night."

His fork stabbed a bite of eggs. "You were awake well past two."

"How do you know?"

"I checked on you every hour, just like Dr. Vaughn said."

She remembered. He hadn't even knocked, though she had to admit that doing so would have meant he was willing to wake her when she really needed her rest. It was one of those situations in which he could not win—a fact she grudgingly accepted before judging him too harshly.

Still, every time he'd come in, her eyes had been closed and she'd been pretending to sleep so that he wouldn't talk to her. "How do you know I wasn't sleeping?"

"I know the way your breathing changes when you're asleep."

She tore off a piece of bacon and revved up the sarcasm engines. "Oh, that's right. You drugged me unconscious. How could I forget?"

"You didn't forget. Nor are you likely to do so in this lifetime." There was something else he'd been about to say but didn't. She could tell it by the way he paused before resuming his breakfast.

The idea that she would know him that well was both irritating and intriguing.

She lowered her gaze so she wouldn't have to look at him and be distracted by the way his long fingers made the fork look tiny in his grip. "I need to go check on Corey Lambert today. Do you think they kept him in the hospital overnight?"

"It's likely," he said. "But you can't go."

"I have to. He's our assignment."

"I shot our assignment. I don't think either of us needs the legal problems that kind of thing will bring." He sipped his coffee, the move so casual he could have been talking about the weather. "The police will be looking for us."

"It was self-defense. We did nothing wrong."

"I doubt Mr. Lambert would agree with that assessment."

Adam was right. She hated it that he was, but that didn't change reality. "So what do we do now?"

"I'll arrange a meeting with him. If it goes well, I'll escort him to the facility where he'll get the help he needs."

"And if it doesn't go well?"

His pale gray eyes lifted and caught her gaze. There was no emotion in his face, only acceptance. "Then I'll drag him there."

"Where do I fit in this plan of yours?"

"Behind your desk, in that refrigerator you call a computer room."

"That wasn't the deal. Bella said we were supposed to work together."

He lifted an inky black brow. "Oh, you remember that now, do you?"

"What's that supposed to mean?"

"It means I haven't forgotten that you went out on your own, without backup. It's going to reflect poorly on both of us."

"Worried about your performance review?" she asked sweetly.

"Yes. I am. And if you ever want to be let out of your cage again, so should you be."

He had a point. Again. What was it with him and being right? "Geez. Fine. I'll play nice. No more meeting people alone. But you have to do the same."

Instead of giving her an answer, he checked his watch. "Are you ready to go?"

She looked down. Her plate was clean; her coffee cup was empty. A pile of e-mail requests from the team awaited her attention. "Sure."

"If you don't mind, I'll ride with you until I can get a new car."

"And if I do mind?"

"Then I'll walk."

"It's sixteen miles."

"And?"

She let out a frustrated breath. "Just get in the car."

He followed her out, waiting as she locked the door behind her.

Mira had to move the seat up about a mile before she

could once again reach the pedals. He sat beside her, silently patient. In fact, he didn't say a word the whole drive in to work. By the time she pulled into the garage, she was ready to beg him to say something—anything— if it meant she didn't have to sit in silence, wondering what was going through his head.

She put her car in park. Turned off the engine. Adam didn't make a move to get out.

"Are you coming in?" she asked.

He turned in his seat so he faced her more fully. "Do you ever wonder how things might have been between us if I hadn't decided to use you as leverage?"

Mira blinked in stunned silence. "What?"

He tilted his head to the side, as if truly pondering the question. "I've never second-guessed myself like this before. I mean, I know what I did to you was wrong and that it hurt you—I knew at the time that all of that was true."

"You're really not scoring any points here, Adam."

He frowned and shook his head slightly. "What I'm trying to say is that most of the decisions I've made in my life were necessary. Just as I felt it was necessary to do what I did to you. But it's different this time."

"How?"

"I wouldn't do the same thing again, given the choice. I would have found another way."

He still hadn't told her what was in that envelope he'd earned for abducting her, and she was dying to know what had been so important to him that he'd willingly betrayed her. "Another way to do what?"

"Find the information I needed. Looking back, I think that torturing your father would have been a smarter move."

"Wow. Okay. Nothing sociopathic about that or anything."

He took a deep breath that made his shoulders expand to fill the small space. "I'm saying this all wrong. I only meant for you to know that I'm sorry about what I did to you. If I'd known the kind of person you were—if I'd known what your father intended to do to you—I would have found another way."

"So I guess the envelope wasn't that important after all, huh?"

"It was the single most important piece of information I've ever wanted to know. I'm only sorry it came at such a high cost to you. You deserved better."

As apologies went, that was the most awkward one she'd ever received. Still, Adam was clearly trying to make an effort. A frightening, clumsy effort, but it had to count for something.

"What's in the past is in the past," she said. "I'll be happier if we don't dwell on that horrible time more than absolutely necessary. It gives me nightmares."

"Like last night?" he asked.

"I didn't have any nightmares last night." At least not that she remembered.

He gave her a look that told her he didn't believe a word, but he kept his opinion to himself. "I'll come see you when I find out Mr. Lambert's status. We'll plan our next move then. Together."

His switch from personal to business took her off guard. She took a couple of seconds to catch up. "Oh. Right. Sure. I'll take care of some work and see you then."

By the time Mira unlocked the computer room and settled in her chair, she still wasn't sure what had just happened.

Adam made no sense to her at all. First he terrified her; then he apologized; then he said he wished he'd tortured her father. Before she'd had time to process that, he was back on the topic of work, leaving her feeling like a kid in an overcrowded bouncy castle.

She'd made it through only half of her e-mail from overnight, including an odd request from Riley about information on a woman named Sophie Devane, when Payton Bainbridge settled in the spare chair near her desk.

She jumped, stifled a yelp, and put her hand over her heart to keep it from lurching from her chest.

"You scared me, Payton. Don't any of you guys ever knock?"

"I'm sorry about that. I didn't realize it bothered you." He smoothed the lapels of his perfectly tailored suit. Each strand of gray hair on his head was trimmed and in place. Even though he was well into his fifties, he was still a handsome enough man that women flocked to him. Of course, it could have been his vast wealth they found so attractive.

"Probably because everyone walks in. I really should start locking the door when I'm in here."

He grabbed her chin so fast, she didn't even see his hand move. With gentle care, he tilted her head to the side and scowled. "Care to tell me about the origin of this bruise?"

"It stems from a single bad decision."

"As most tragedies do. Was it Adam? If so, I will kill him." Not a threat. A calm statement of fact.

Strangely, the urge to protect Adam rose, giving her denial a crispness. "No. I went to see one of the victims last night. Things . . . got out of hand."

"How far?" His tone was as cold and smooth as polished steel.

"Far enough. The man is in the hospital with a gunshot wound."

"I'm not sure if I should be more impressed or dismayed. Bella said you were field material, but I honestly wasn't sure I agreed."

"It wasn't me who shot him. Adam did."

Payton eased back in his chair. "I see."

"You say that like you're not surprised."

"I'm not. Adam is as he was created to be."

"A sociopath?"

"Hardly. I assure you his emotions are completely normal. He feels; he simply doesn't allow those feelings to sway his actions."

"Like when he abducted me."

"I don't condone what he did, but I understand it. You were a means to an end."

"One that almost got you, me, and a whole bunch of other people killed. One that did kill my father."

Payton flinched. The move was slight, but she still saw it. "You still grieve for him, don't you?"

"No. I grieved for him years before he died—as soon as I found out the kind of man he really was, rather than the man I needed him to be. He was cold. Evil. Just like Adam."

"Adam isn't evil any more than a knife is. He's a tool. A weapon. I would have thought you of all people would have understood that."

"Me? I was the one he abducted. Why the hell would I understand him?"

"Because of Clay."

"He almost got Clay killed, too."

"That's not what I mean. You saw what was done to Clay—your best friend. You saw him hurt people without remorse. You saw him lift that gun to kill."

"That wasn't Clay. They fucked with his head—made him do things. They used him."

"Exactly. You forgave Clay because you knew he wasn't in control, that he had no choice in his actions."

"So?"

"So maybe Adam and Clay have more in common than you care to admit."

"Bullshit. You're just messing with my head so I won't cause trouble. I know you were one of the people who wanted Adam working with us. Weren't you?"

"What I want is unimportant. All that matters is helping those who need us—helping the people your father damaged."

That was all Mira wanted, too—to make up for some

small amount of pain her father had caused. Maybe if she'd been smarter and less trusting of him, she could have stopped him years ago. Sure, she'd been just a kid, but she was a smart kid.

Her father had seen to that.

"What do you want me to do, Payton? Forgive Adam?"

"I don't care whether or not you forgive him. All that concerns me is how well the two of you work together. That means there has to be some level of trust."

"I won't trust him. Ever."

Payton picked up her notepad and wrote something down before tossing it onto her desk.

She picked it up and looked at the note. The letters *AE* were written, followed by a string of numbers. "What's that?"

"Knowledge. Yours to seek or ignore as you please. Just know that once you see it, it can't be unseen."

"If this is more of my father's depraved human experiments, I think I'll pass. I already know enough about what he did to fuel my nightmares for eternity."

"This has nothing to do with your father. It's all about Adam."

She didn't want to be curious, but she was. She didn't want to ask, but she did. "What about him?"

Payton shrugged. "That's up to you to find out or not. Look at the files or don't. That's all I'm going to say."

"Why do I feel like this is some kind of trap?"

He glided to his feet, smiling in a way that was both devastatingly handsome and chilling, all at the same time. "Because, my dear Mira, knowledge like this always is."

Chapter Seven

Riley pounced on Mira's e-mail the second it hit his in-box.

Sure enough, Sophie's name was on the List—one of the victims of the Threshold Project who'd been experimented on when she was a kid. Mira's father had been the one to alter her.

That's why those goons had been after her. The vicious Dr. Norma Stynger was more than willing to pay to recover any of the children who'd been touched by Dr. Sage's research. Despite the best efforts of the government and everyone at the Edge, no one had been able to locate Stynger and shut her down.

She was a ghost—one smart enough not to show her face when so many people wanted her dead.

Riley scanned the file, then read it again.

Sophie had been volunteered to enter the project when she was four. The name of the person who signed the release was hard to read, but Riley made out enough to see that the person shared her last name. A parent? Probably. If her father had gambling debts, who knew how far he'd go to pay them, up to and including selling his own daughter.

Dr. Sage had paid good money to those willing to

loan him their children. From the inheritance Sophie's dad had left her—armed men hunting her down—Riley doubted that the man would have lost a lot of sleep over the idea of letting some bastard hurt his baby girl.

From what Riley could tell, Sophie had been subjected to the same protocols that Mira had. It didn't mean that Sophie wasn't in trouble, but at least the doctor hadn't done anything to her he hadn't been willing to do to his own daughter.

Enhanced memory, improved intelligence, reduced need for sleep, ability to multitask well and recognize intricate patterns—they were all goals of the brain-altering protocols and chemicals that had been pumped into both Mira and Sophie.

Riley read all the notes, few of which made any sense to a man who was better with his hands than he was with his head. If he could have killed her ugly past with a well-placed bullet or the sharp edge of his favorite knife, he would have done so. But her problems were far beyond that. She'd been hurt. Altered. She needed the kind of professional help only the team Payton had set up could give.

Riley leaned back in his kitchen chair and stared at his bedroom door. Sophie hadn't come out all night. He'd heard her get up once to use the bathroom, but that was all.

He was so worried that he'd wake up and find that she'd taken off again, he hadn't dared to sleep.

As if his thoughts of her summoned her, she opened the bedroom door and shambled out. Her strawberry blond hair had dried overnight, leaving it a curly mess around her head. One side of her face was pinker than the other, showing which side she liked to lie on. She'd taken off the sweat pants—likely because he'd cranked up the heat in his house last night to a balmy eighty degrees to warm her up—and now wore only his sweatshirt. It fell above her freckled knees, skimming the pale skin along her thighs.

A brief flash of the night in the jungle in Colombia flooded his brain. Blood covered her thighs, trickling down her legs into the fallen leaves. He'd felt so helpless that night—unable to stop her miscarriage. He'd been forced to push her onward through her pain, all the time wondering if a woman could lose that much blood and still survive.

Only the sight of her standing in front of him now, whole and safe, made the muscles in the back of his neck loosen.

He cleared his throat so he could speak without squeaking like a teenage boy. "Coffee? Breakfast?"

"Just water. I'm dehydrated. Didn't want to have to stop and use the bathroom when I was on the run, so I quit drinking much a couple of days ago."

He filled a glass and set it in front of the seat across from him.

She took the hint that he wanted her company, and sat down. It took all his willpower not to glance down and see just how far up his sweatshirt had slid, and whether or not she wore anything underneath.

"I washed your clothes," he told her. "Hope you don't mind."

Her slender fingers curled around the glass. "Not at all. Thanks. That'll make it quicker for me to hit the road."

"You're not leaving." It wasn't a question. Riley wasn't the kind of guy who generally bossed women around, but this was important. "You have no car, no money, no phone."

"How do you know?"

"I checked your pockets so I wouldn't wash anything. All that you had on you was lint and an elastic hair tie. That's not exactly going to get you far, especially not with men on your trail."

"I lost them. And money isn't hard to come by."

"What are you going to do? Steal someone's wallet?"

She looked down at her lap. "If that's what I have to do to survive."

"You came here so I could help you. Let me."

"I shouldn't have come at all. If I hadn't been so sleep deprived and scared, I wouldn't have."

That hurt. He didn't know why it should, but the barb still stung. "I've seen you safely through worse situations than this. That has to count for something."

She lifted her gaze to meet his, and it hit him so hard he forgot to breathe. "This is different. This is real danger."

"And flying bullets and a miscarriage weren't?"

"You don't know what you're dealing with, Riley. These men are bad news. They won't just kill you. They'll make you beg them to first."

"How do you know that?"

She looked away again and stared out the kitchen window. "Just consider my leaving as payback for you saving my life in Colombia."

"I'm not letting you go."

She pushed to her feet. "You don't have a say in the matter. The fact that you think you do proves just how stupid it was for me to come here."

As she started to leave, Riley grabbed her wrist. He was careful with his hold, but he knew instantly that touching her had been the wrong thing to do.

He was overwhelmed by the feel of her skin under his palm. She was too soft and smooth for his peace of mind, her bones too delicate for him to even consider letting her face off against armed goons.

For some reason, this woman rocked him all the way down to his foundation, and he had no idea why. He'd barely had a conversation with her. He didn't know how she thought or what she believed. He didn't even know if she was straight. Even so, all he could think about was keeping her close, where he could make sure she was safe. She'd already been through too much.

And Riley desperately needed a distraction from the pain and monotony of his own life.

"I can help," he said, doing everything he could to sound reasonable. Flexible. He wasn't, but that didn't mean he couldn't try to make this easier on her.

She lifted her chin. Even without makeup, she was a natural beauty. Messy hair, freckles—it didn't matter. Sunlight loved her and clung to her like a second skin.

"How?" she finally asked. "Exactly what do you think you can do that I can't do for myself?"

"I know why Soma abducted you. I know who he was trying to sell you to. And I know why."

Her skin paled beneath her freckles. "I don't believe you."

"We've learned a lot since the day you took off. I work for a company that's helping people like you— people who were used when they were children. Hurt."

She took a step back, but his grip on her wrist kept her from going far. "How do you know about that?"

"It's in your file."

Her green eyes flared, and there was no mistaking the fear he saw in her pinpoint pupils. "What file?"

"You were on something called the List. That's why Soma took you, why he was selling you, why these men who are after you now will try to do the same thing."

"What is this list?"

"It contains the names of all the kids who were part of a series of experiments. The doctors and scientists who did the research have all been found or killed. Except one woman. Dr. Norma Stynger."

"I don't know her."

"You might never have met her, but she wants to meet you. She's searching for all of those kids, now grown, so she can continue her work. She knows you exist now, and my guess is she won't stop sending people to find you until they succeed—or you're dead."

She flinched, and he immediately wished he'd sugar-coated the truth a little.

"I'll change my name. Hide. She'll never find me."

"That's not good enough."

"What's that supposed to mean? You have no idea how good I am at hiding."

"Actually, I do. I've looked for you almost every day since you ran off."

"So you know I'm good," she said.

"It doesn't matter. Being found isn't the only thing you have to worry about."

"If they don't find me, what can they possibly do to me?"

"They may have already done it."

"What?"

Riley paused, searching for the gentlest way to tell her what she needed to hear. "Most of the kids grew up fine. But some of them . . . didn't."

"Didn't how?"

"Some of them cracked. Hallucinated. Became violent."

She started to sag like she was going to faint. Riley grabbed her arms and eased her into the nearest chair.

"You're saying I'm going to go homicidal?"

"No. I'm not saying that at all. You're probably fine."

"But if I'm not . . . ?"

"That's why you need to let me help you. We are connected to people who can look at you. Fix you before anything happens."

"Doctors?" she asked, shaking her head. "Hell no. No one is touching me ever again."

"It's the only way to keep you safe. We'll set you up with a new identity, send you somewhere you've never been before, keep you healthy, make sure you're cared for."

"Like some kind of pet? No, thanks. I'll take my chances on my own."

He took her hands in his. Her skin was cold and clammy, but it still felt good against him. "Listen, Sophie.

Please. If you don't let me help, then you'll be out there all alone. Afraid."

"I've been afraid before. It's not fatal."

"Yes, but my guess is you've always been afraid of what others might do to you. Now you also have to worry about what you might do to others. Someone you love could get hurt."

She closed her eyes. He could see the sheen of tears wet her lashes, but not a single one fell.

When she looked at him again, he could see the steel running through her. Her eyes were bloodshot and her nose had turned pink, but there was a fierce look in her that gave him the craziest urge to kiss her.

"No one I love is ever going to die again," she said.

"Then you'll come with me? Let me help you?"

"I'll listen. That's all I can promise right now."

"But what about what you just said about no one you love dying?"

She shrugged, and her sad expression broke his heart. "That's easy. All I have to do is never love again."

Chapter Eight

Mira lasted for all of twenty minutes after Payton left before she gave in to the uncontrollable urge to look at the file he'd mentioned. It was password protected, but that wasn't an issue for her. Less than thirty seconds later, she started reading.

She was still reading an hour later, despite her shaking hands and queasy gut.

Adam wasn't just part of the Threshold Project. He was its pinnacle.

The notes she'd read were well beyond her medical knowledge, but she was smart enough to understand what they meant: Adam's parents had altered him before birth. What they'd done to him was written in his genes—inescapable.

At least with some of the other victims, their programming could be overwritten. The drugs they'd been given had worn off, and with enough counseling, they were able to live normal lives.

Adam would never have that. No matter what he did, what drugs he took, what therapy he received, he would never be able to undo his genes.

Childhood tests showed he was faster than other children. Stronger. His mind worked more quickly, and he was able to compartmentalize better than any of the other subjects.

No wonder he was able to do the things he'd done and not show guilt. It wasn't that he didn't feel it so much as he'd locked it away where it couldn't alter his effectiveness—as he'd been designed to do.

Mira's eyes burned as she sat back in her chair. She'd hardly blinked as she'd read the file. It was all too much to take in.

Adam had never been a child. He'd been a construction. A project.

Even Mira, daughter to a man who cared nothing for her safety or comfort, had a home and a loving mother to care for her between experiments. Adam had had none of that. Both his parents were scientists, committed to the Threshold Project.

So committed that they'd given up their son to the cause.

It was a wonder Adam had even survived. There were no notes in the file about whether he'd been rescued or if he'd escaped. The last entry she read was dated shortly after his first birthday.

She picked up the phone and dialed Payton. "I want to know more."

"You read the file."

"You knew I would. Tell me the rest."

"There is no more to tell. That's the only file I recovered on the subject."

"Why didn't I see it before? Why wasn't it with the others?"

"Even you don't get to see everything. Believe me. That's more a blessing than a punishment." Pain and regret coursed through the words.

Mira shivered. "You're right. The less I know, the better. Except about Adam."

"You know what you need to."

"To do what? You read the file. We can't help him."

"We already are helping him. We've given him a job, a group of people who accept him."

"Except me."

Payton sighed. "No one can make you forgive him for what he did. All I'm asking is that you work with him until Gage is free again. You're both safer working with each other. It's what Bella wanted, and we all need to do what we can to make her happy for a little while."

"You mean you need all of us to make her happy so she won't take out her anger on you."

"Bella's anger toward me is none of your concern."

"The hell it isn't. You two have barely spoken in weeks. If you think that doesn't affect the way this company runs, you're insane."

"Leave Bella to me. You worry about Adam. Despite how you feel about him, he's proven he's willing to go to extreme measures to keep you safe. He deserves a chance."

Mira wasn't sure how safe she'd be with Adam, but at least she understood why he was such a jerk. She even felt sorry for him, but only a little. She'd been used, too, and it hadn't made her abduct anyone. "How long will Gage be?"

"I'm not sure. Bella won't tell me what he's doing."

"She's keeping secrets from you? That's not good news. I'll talk to her when she—"

"Leave it alone, Mira. I mean it. Bella has every right to be angry with me. I can handle it."

"She's pissed that you knew about the Threshold Project, isn't she? You knew that she had people working here that had been victims, and you didn't tell her."

Payton's voice hardened. "I said leave it alone."

"Geez. Chill. No need to bring out Scary Payton."

"Just do your job, Mira. There's way too much work to go around, and every minute you sit around playing peacemaker is another one in which all those people are suffering."

He was right. They all had bigger problems to deal

with than interoffice bickering. "If you see any more of those AE files, you'll send them my way, right?"

"No promises, but I won't hide things from you if I think you need to know them. Which is why I'm going to tell you this: Adam is dangerous, Mira, but he's a logical creature. You're better at seeing patterns than any of the other kids in the project. You're more likely to see changes in him than anyone else."

"Adam fooled me once before. I believed he was a nice guy. Hell, I almost fell for him. What's to keep him from fooling me again?"

"Simple. Now you know it's possible. Your eyes are open. Make sure you keep them that way. And, Mira?"

"Yes?"

"If you see any changes in him—anything you don't like—run. Fast. And don't look back."

The line went dead as Payton hung up. A greasy ball of fear sat knotted in her stomach.

It didn't matter if she ran or not. Adam was likely a hell of a lot faster than she was.

She set down the phone and turned slightly to get back to the familiar feel of her keyboard under her fingers. Sitting right beside her in her guest chair was Adam. He'd come in and she hadn't even heard him.

That greasy ball of fear exploded, snaking through her veins until her whole body was trembling. "How much did you hear?" she asked.

His expression was as cold and blank as a sheet of ice. "Everything."

Chapter Nine

Adam watched the color drain from Mira's face and wished he'd chosen his words differently. "Don't worry," he hurried to say to ease her fear. "I know you all talk about me when I'm not around. I'd expect no less. I'm the fox in your henhouse."

It took her a minute to regain the ability to speak. He watched her delicate throat move, waiting patiently until her nervous system had settled down from the scare he'd inadvertently given her.

"Why do I suddenly feel like a little yellow chick?" she asked.

"I can't convince you I hold no ill intentions, so I'm not going to waste my breath."

She scooted her rolling chair back as far as the confines of her desk would allow. "Payton says you're dangerous."

"You didn't need Payton to tell you that. You've seen what I'm capable of doing."

"He thinks I'll be able to see it if you start to crack."

Adam nodded to the computer screen, where his file still glowed as a reminder of what he really was. "You've read my file. What do you think?"

"I think I'm glad I have a concealed-carry permit."

Adam leaned forward, resting his elbows on his knees. The move put him closer to Mira, more on eye level with her.

She had such pretty eyes. Bright green with little strands of gold weaving through them, nestled right up against her pupils. They weren't always visible, but right now, in the bright light of her office, with fear so recently her companion, he could see every one of the fiery threads.

He waited until her gaze was fixed to his before telling her, "If you feel the need to use your weapon on me, I won't hold it against you."

"What?" she asked in disbelief. "You're giving me permission to shoot you?"

"If you feel as though you're in danger from me, yes."

"Why in the world would you tell me this?"

"Because you have a soft heart. Because you might hesitate if I don't give you my blessing. Because I'm stronger and faster than you, and while I have no intention of hurting you in any way, I've seen the things that the other subjects of the Threshold Project were capable of doing—what Clay would have done to you, a woman he loved. I would be a fool to think that what happened to him couldn't happen to me."

She shook her head, making her dark hair sway slowly about her shoulders. "You're nuts. Completely certifiable. I'm not going to think about shooting you just for fun."

Before she could so much as flinch, Adam pulled her weapon from the holster under her arm. While she was gasping in surprise, he wrapped her fingers around the butt and held the barrel against his chest, pinning her hand in place with his own. She tried to pull away, but he didn't loosen his grip. Her finger wasn't on the trigger, but for this demonstration it didn't need to be.

In a calm voice he said, "I'm faster than you, Mira. Stronger than you. If things go badly, and I come after you the way Clay did, this is where you aim. Don't think. Don't hesitate. Just pull the trigger."

She squeezed her eyes shut. "I'm not playing your game."

"It's not a game. If it helps, just remember what I did to you. Remember how I shot your best friend."

The tension vibrating through her arms went still. She opened her eyes and looked at him. "If you hadn't done that, Clay would have killed all of us. He told me you didn't hit anything vital—that it was the shot he would have picked to take given the choice."

"I also have good aim, which is one more reason for you to listen to me now."

She lifted her chin. "I've dreamed about hurting you. Besides my father, you're the only other man I've ever considered killing."

"Use that, then—whatever it takes to get the job done. You won't get a second chance."

He let go of her hand and watched as she holstered the weapon. She was shaking so hard it took two tries to seat the gun in place.

Adam hated it that he'd done that to her, but it was for her own good. Now that she knew how easily he could disarm her, she had a marginally better chance of surviving if he snapped.

She lifted her chin and gave him a warning stare. "Don't make me shoot you, Adam. I really hate the sight of blood."

"I'll try to remember that." He stood and took a long step back so he wouldn't be towering over her, adding to her tension. "Corey Lambert is being released from the hospital in a few hours. I intend to intercept him on his way home and have him escorted to one of our facilities where they can help him. Care to join me?"

"Escort him? You mean force him to go along with what we want him to do."

"I feel I'm being generous, given the bruises on your

face. The next time he snaps, that frail little woman he was with might be his next victim. It's our job to ensure that doesn't happen."

She pushed to her feet with a sigh. "You're right. We can't let the wild animal roam around free to hurt someone else. Let's go cage him."

Chapter Ten

The operation to get Corey Lambert some help went off without a hitch. They'd waited until a taxi dropped him off at home and left again before moving in. Within seconds, he was subdued and tucked in the back of a van with two armed guards serving as escort.

Mira watched the van drive away, hoping Corey would get the help he needed. He wasn't as far gone as some of those she'd seen. With help and a few months of therapy, he could be one of the lucky ones.

Adam was in the mobile home's kitchen, speaking with Victor Temple — one of the men assigned to oversee the use of government assets at the Edge. Like Adam, Victor's employment by Bella was part of the contract that gave the company the funding and support it needed to locate and help victims of the Threshold Project. Also like Adam, his forced employment was a thorn in Bella's side.

By the time all the paperwork was done and Mira had left evidence on Corey's PC that he'd bought a one-way bus ticket to Florida for a little R and R, it was already dark outside.

The door to the mobile home closed behind Victor as he left.

"How much more time do you need?" asked Adam.

"Just about done. I'm going to have the post office hold his mail so none of the neighbors see it building up. After that, we're good to go."

"I'm starving. Would you like to get dinner?"

"Why? So you can drug me again?" The words fell out of her mouth before she could stop them. "I'm sorry. That was way bitchy."

"But not undeserved." If she hadn't known for a fact that Adam was more robot than man, she would have thought he sounded hurt.

"We're making nice now. I should have more control over my tongue than that."

"Forget it. I should have considered how an invitation to dinner might have made you feel. It won't happen again."

She wasn't sure if she should be more relieved or disappointed, which confused the hell out of her.

After taking care of Corey's mail delivery online, she wiped her prints from his keyboard and turned off the PC.

Adam held the door open for her to leave. Gloves clung to his long fingers as he locked the door behind them and pulled it shut.

They drove back to the Edge in silence. When he pulled up beside her parked car to let her out, she was still wishing she'd thought of some way to make up for being so bitchy to him.

Social graces weren't her strong suit. She was just a nerdy girl who was more hips and thighs than hip and cool. So when he stopped the car, she just got out. "Good night."

"I'll request a new assignment for us to start tomorrow," he said.

"I can do that."

"No. Go home and rest. You didn't sleep very well last night."

She doubted tonight would be any different, but she didn't say it out loud. "Okay. Tomorrow, then."

She felt crappy as she got behind the wheel. Felt even crappier as she ran her snide remark through her mind.

Adam was trying. Maybe he was doing it only to fool her, but she couldn't stand the idea of being *that* girl—the one who held a grudge and spent all her energy looking for ways to get back at a guy who'd wronged her. She was more adult than that. A better person.

At least she wanted to be. Maybe if she pretended she wasn't so pissed, some of her anger would trickle away when she wasn't looking.

She thought about him sitting at his little kitchen table, eating alone in silence, his fork moving robotically to his mouth.

Maybe he got lonely, too. Maybe he hated eating alone as much as she did.

Mira knew that if she went home now, she'd sit in front of her computer screen with her pitiful bowl of cold cereal, watching him eat. Then she'd watch him run. Then she'd watch him lie down and turn out the lights, making it impossible to see him without adding some night-vision capability to the hardware she'd hidden in his house. Then, finally, she'd lie down in her own bed and replay what she'd seen.

How sad and pathetic was that?

No more. He was her partner, and like it or not, she was going to give him the benefit of the doubt one time. Just to see how it felt.

She phoned in an order for carryout and swung by to pick it up on the way to Adam's house. He'd told her today that she could freakin' shoot him and that if she did, he'd forgive her. The least she could do was try to make up for taking his head off after a simple invitation to dinner.

The smell of garlic wafted from the plastic bags she carried to his door. His sleek black sedan sat in the driveway, pointing toward the street as if he was expecting to have the need to tear out of there at any second.

What kind of world must he live in that he thought of little things like that?

What kind of idiot was she that she *didn't* think to do the same thing?

The light on his doorbell winked out for a second as she pressed the button. She could hear the chime through the door, followed by the heavy tread of footsteps.

Adam pulled the door open just enough that she could see his face. He was already shirtless, apparently changing up the order of his routine tonight to run before dinner. "Mira. What are you doing here?"

She lifted the bags. "Dinner. I figured if I bought the food myself, I'd know it was drug-free." Before the words had even finished landing, she winced. "Sorry. Again. I clearly need a little help with this kung fu grip I have on my grudge against you."

"It's fine. But I'm not hungry. You should just go."

"What? You were starving a few minutes ago."

"I already ate."

"When? There was no time."

"Seriously, Mira. You need to leave now." There was something in his tone that tipped her off that things were not as they seemed.

He was hiding something.

She hadn't checked in on him as usual. She had no idea what he might be doing in there. For all she knew, he had a hostage or was building a bomb to take out the entire office.

No way was she letting him get away with this kind of secretive bullshit. "Open the door, Adam."

"I'm not dressed."

Her voice hardened. "I don't care. I've seen you shirtless before. I'll find some way to survive the strain."

"It's a bad time."

Now he was just pissing her off. "Really? A bad time?

Do you have some innocent girl tied up in there or something?"

He looked past her, scanning the street. "It isn't safe for you to be here. Please go."

Now she really needed to get in there and make sure he wasn't doing something horrible. If she didn't, not only would she never forgive herself, but Bella wouldn't forgive her for letting him get away with trouble, either. "Let. Me. In."

Her insistence paid off. He grabbed her arm and practically yanked her inside his house. The door shut behind her. He took the bag of Chinese takeout from her fingers and tossed it aside.

"Hey," she said as she moved to pick up the toppled containers of food.

"Leave it," said Adam. He took her by the shoulders and pressed her flat against the door.

"What do you th—"

He covered her mouth, cutting off her words. Her tongue swept across his palm, tasting salt and man. His scent filled her nostrils, and for a second, she forgot she was supposed to be pissed.

"Quiet," he ordered in a calm voice. "Stay here."

Not going to happen.

She started to push away from the door. He pushed right back, pinning her in place with the hard length of his body. She felt his heat sink into her from her knees to her breasts, and it was all she could do to stifle a shiver.

A hint of anger flickered across his features, hardening them. "We're not alone. The door is armored. Stay here."

Armored? Against what?

As soon as the thought slid into her mind, she felt the door buck behind her. There was a loud pop—the kind a suppressed weapon made when it fired a round.

That's when she realized: someone was firing at them.

The glass in the sidelight to her left shattered. She shrieked behind Adam's hand.

He grabbed her body and flipped her around so that he was between her and the door. "Are you armed?"

She offered a shaky nod.

"Good. Go into the kitchen. I'll cover you. Hide in the pantry until I come for you. Its walls are reinforced and it locks from the inside. On three."

Mira was still reeling from what was happening. He was talking like nothing out of the ordinary was going on, like it was just another Tuesday evening.

The door shook again under the force of another trio of bullets.

"One, two."

Adam pulled a silenced weapon from the back of his waistband.

She wasn't ready.

"Three."

He fired through the broken sidelight as he pushed her into motion. She stumbled into the kitchen, going as fast as her numb body would allow. The pantry was in the corner—on her surveillance devices, she'd seen Adam walk into it more times than she could count.

As soon as she got in, she closed the door behind her. It was heavier than it should have been—proof it was also reinforced. Sure enough, there was a lock on the inside.

She turned the dead bolt and held her breath.

The shelves were lined with food, but now that she was up close, she could see that behind the box of cereal were several magazines stocked full of ammo. Behind the gallon jug of apple juice was a 9 mm semiautomatic handgun. The canned goods hid an array of grenades and boxed ammunition, and the butt of a long combat knife was barely visible inside the stainless steel bowl of a stand mixer on a high shelf.

The seconds stretched on, each one dragging its feet as it went. Nervous sweat formed along her hairline. The gun in her grip shook, and it took every bit of her training to steady it.

Her whole body trembled. She couldn't hear much from outside the little safe room. There was an occasional muffled pop of a silenced round. Once, she heard something hit a wall nearby—whether it was a bullet, person or something else, she couldn't tell. All she knew was that she was still safe and sound.

But was Adam?

Adam paced his shots, giving Mira enough time to make it to safety.

Whoever it was on the other side of his door, he was a professional. Adam hadn't even caught sight of the man hiding behind his neighbor's house until Adam had backed into the driveway.

The plan had been to go about his business, pretend he was settling in for a little time on the treadmill, then wait for his opponent to make his skills known. Could he break in, defeating Adam's security system? Was he silent in his approach, or more the kind of man to use hard, brutal force? Would he be patient and wait for an opportunity to strike, or would he move in fast? Was he alone?

Every bit of information Adam could gather was to his benefit.

And then Mira had shown up, complicating his plans to wait out his opponent.

Once again, the urge to protect her rose to the fore, drowning out all else. It had been like that last year, when he'd made the disastrous mistake of using Mira as leverage to lure in her best friend. Once he'd known what Dr. Sage had in store for her—that the man had no emotional attachment to his own daughter—Adam knew he couldn't leave her side.

Another silenced round slammed through the broken window, taking more glass with it as it passed. It ripped a hole in the wall adjacent to his kitchen. Adam went back through every one of the precautions he'd taken to ensure that his pantry was nearly impervious.

If Mira was in there, she would be safe. He had to believe that. Anything less was far too much of a distraction.

A shadow crossed over his living room floor, giving away his opponent's approach. Adam's mind filled with a list of ways to take the man out without killing him. There were too many questions to ask to let the man die. Besides, chances were he was acting under orders—possibly against his will—and since Adam was working with the good guys now, capturing over killing was going to win him some points in the TRUST ADAM column.

That, he desperately needed.

He waited where he was, putting his faith in the armored door he'd installed to keep him safe.

The doorknob rattled as the attacker tried to turn it. Locked.

The man reached in through the broken glass and worked the lock. Adam let him. It was better to have the confrontation go down behind closed doors, where his neighbors couldn't see it happen.

Not that any of them were still awake at this hour. He'd purposely picked a neighborhood filled with elderly inhabitants so that they were less likely to hear anything he did and less likely to stay awake during the hours in which he did his best work.

The door swung open slowly. Adam moved to allow it.

The man led with his gun. Before his head could clear the door, Adam grabbed the man's gun and broke his wrist with one hard twist.

The gunman let out a gurgled cry of pain and rage as he charged. He knew exactly where Adam was now, and wasted no time in attacking with his good hand.

Adam dodged the blow. He didn't even realize that there was a combat knife in the man's grip until it went sailing past his eyes with only an inch to spare.

Usually, a cold, calm logic took over Adam at this point. He would analyze options, assess his enemy's skills, and plan his attack, all in the blink of an eye.

This time, all he could think about was what would happen to Mira if he let this man win.

In the cold place where his logic usually lived, a hot kind of frantic concern blazed to life. It made him faster, stronger. He felt his body reacting more quickly, even as his mind was a distant, hazy thing.

Instincts took over. He closed into close-quarters combat with the man. Within seconds, the knife went flying across the room.

The intruder snarled and reached for a holdout weapon on his ankle. His left hand was slow, unused to the action of drawing the gun. That slight hesitation gave Adam the space he needed.

He drew his silenced weapon, aimed for the man's knee, and fired.

The gunman crumpled on a cry of pain, but fury was still riding his features. He wasn't giving up simply because he was shot.

The small revolver cleared the ankle holster. No suppressing that noise. One shot from that loud weapon, and the whole neighborhood was going to be awake, dialing 911.

Adam charged. He kicked the man's weapon hand, but the gun stayed in his grip. His aim was way off, pointing far too close to the pantry where Mira hid for Adam's comfort.

He dropped to his knees, pinning the unbroken arm to the floor. As soon as Adam shoved the suppressor on his weapon into the man's cheek, he went still.

"Who sent you?" asked Adam.

"Where is Dr. S.?" demanded the man.

The question surprised Adam, but he tried to hide it. "Dead. Who sent you?"

The man said nothing, so Adam punched him hard

enough to break his nose. A fine mist of blood hit his chest, and the man choked as he tried to keep the blood out of his throat.

"Who sent you?" asked Adam again, his voice calm.

"We know you have Dr. S. Where is he? With his daughter?"

For some reason, even that nameless reference to her pissed off Adam until all he could hear was a buzzing in his ears. This man had no business talking about her. Even thinking about her was too much.

Mira was in Adam's protection now. Bella had given him a precious chance to prove himself, and that was exactly what he was going to do.

He slammed the butt of his gun into the man's temple, knocking him unconscious.

Only then could Adam pull in a full breath once more. Whoever this man was, for whatever reason he was here, he could no longer hurt Mira.

If Adam didn't walk away from him now, his chance to prove himself was going to start with a dead body.

Chapter Eleven

After what felt like an hour but was probably more like three minutes, Mira heard a deep voice from the other side of the pantry door. Adam.

"You can come out now."

She kept her weapon in her hand, just in case it was some kind of trick, but kept it aimed at the floor. The last thing she wanted to do was shoot Adam if he didn't deserve it.

The dead bolt slid silently open, and the door swung out.

Adam stood there, shirtless. A few drops of blood were splattered across his chest. Her stomach did a low, queasy dive, and she grabbed the wall with her free hand to steady herself.

He wrapped his long arm around her waist and practically lifted her into a kitchen chair.

"Please tell me that's not your blood," she said.

"It's not." He went to the sink and wet a cloth. A few seconds later, the blood was gone.

"What happened?"

"I took care of the problem. You should probably stay in here until I have time to clean it up."

"Problem? An armed man shoots at you, and you call it a problem?"

"What would you call it?" he asked.

"A catastrophe. A freakin' nightmare. Reason to call the cops."

Her hands were shaking harder now as adrenaline leaked from her system. Adam gently took her gun and slid it back into her holster.

"Nothing so dramatic as all that," he reassured her. "It was more along the lines of a message."

"How's that?"

"Norma Stynger isn't happy that I left her employ. This was her way of showing her displeasure." Something about the look on his face made her question if he was hiding something.

"Are you sure she sent the shooter?"

"No, but I'll go through his cell phone records in a minute. He's not going anywhere."

"Did you kill him?"

"No. Would you have preferred that I did?" His tone was only slightly curious, almost conversational.

"No," she snapped, disgusted at the idea.

"That was what I assumed your preference would be, especially if he happened to be one of your father's subjects."

The idea chilled her to the bone. Was there ever going to be an end to the damage that man had done? Or would she be constantly running into the ruined remains of the lives he'd destroyed?

Adam left the kitchen, returning a moment later with a blanket and a cell phone. He set the phone on the table in front of her and draped the blanket over her and the chair she sat in.

Grateful for the warmth and comfort, she wrapped the thick fabric more closely around her body while she powered up the phone.

"It's password protected," she said.

"Is that a problem for you?"

"No, but I'll need to take it back to my office. I came

with dinner, but not the right connection cables for his phone."

"Are you hungry?"

Even the idea of putting something in her stomach made it lurch in rebellion. "Uh, no. I may never eat again."

A minute later, a cup of hot tea appeared in front of her. She had no idea how he'd made it wink into existence. She hadn't seen him heat the water or even so much as pull a mug from the cupboard.

She must have been a lot worse off than she thought.

Mira glanced up at him. Her gaze made the long journey from his ripped abdomen, up over his sleekly muscled chest, all the way along his angled jaw, until she was looking into his eyes.

"How did you do that?" she asked.

"Do what?"

"The tea. I didn't see you make it."

"We all deal with fear in our own way. You were busy processing."

"What about you? How do you deal with it?" she asked.

He lifted one broad shoulder, which caused a symphony of muscles to dance along his torso. By the time the distraction ended she was once again able to look him in the eye.

He was blushing. "Not well."

"What do you mean? You seem to be dealing well with it to me."

"That's because that little incident didn't frighten me. It was merely a nuisance."

"If that was a nuisance, then what does it take to scare you?"

He stared at her for a long minute. "The last time I was truly afraid, your best friend was pointing a gun at your head."

"Oh."

"Indeed. We both know how that ended."

"You shot him."

Adam shifted, and despite the grace of the movement, it was still awkward. "I'm going to call Victor to have our unconscious friend in the other room picked up. If you don't want to see blood, I suggest you stay here."

Mira stayed as Adam left.

She still hadn't digested the information that he'd felt afraid for her, nor was she really sure how to. It wasn't the kind of thing she could easily swallow. What if he was lying?

There was no way to know, and if things went well, she'd never have the chance to test the truth of his statement. No way was she letting someone put a gun to her head just to see if the man was lying, because truth or not, a gun to her head meant she was screwed.

Sophie floated around Riley's apartment like a ghost. She didn't make a sound or touch anything, but her fingers coasted just above his possessions, as if she could somehow pull from them a sense of the man who owned them.

There wasn't much here. A few photos of family and friends, a single shelf of books, a few roughly painted pictures made by children she assumed were the little ones in the family photos, and a small collection of music and movies. His towels were new but mismatched. His closet was filled with more tactical gear than office attire. There were weapons stashed in every room—several easy to spot and access. Probably more hidden. Her appearance here hadn't encouraged him to hide any of them away.

He trusted her not to shoot him in his sleep, which made him either really brave or really stupid. Even she wasn't sure which.

Sophie went to where he lay sleeping on the couch.

His arm was curled under his pillow, which made his biceps flex, even in his sleep. His head was shaved, with only a hint of growth showing beneath his skin. The sheet he'd tossed over his bare chest had worked its way down to his waist—just low enough for her to see that he'd undone the top button of his jeans for comfort.

Shadowed, intriguing masculine flesh covered him in a tempting display. She traced his muscular contours with her eyes, enjoying the view as she went.

There had been a time in her life when she would have simply climbed on board and took what she wanted. But that time was over now. She was a responsible adult, forcing herself to stay on a road that would lead her nowhere near the same neighborhood as where her useless father had subsisted.

Sophie was going to make something of herself. She wasn't entirely sure what yet, but—despite what she'd told Riley about never wanting to love again—the secret truth was that she wanted the whole package. A respectable job, a kind husband, and a couple of kids she would love as much as she had the baby she'd lost.

The whole white-picket-fence-in-the-suburbs thing might have been a nauseating cliché to some, but it was one she desperately wanted to live.

She placed one hand over Riley's heart, hovering but not touching, just as she'd done with the rest of his possessions. With less than an inch between them, she could feel his body's heat as she followed the even rise and fall of his chest.

The urge to close the distance between them was strong, but she reminded herself that touching strange men was not part of her journey now. Her straight-and-narrow path was laid out in front of her, gleaming and bright. Nothing would get in her way—not her father's past mistakes, and certainly not one perfectly built man.

She was just about to move her hand away when he grabbed her wrist. His eyes opened. They were a dark, rich brown the color of damp, fertile earth. There was no grogginess lurking there, only acute alertness.

She didn't try to tug her hand away or hide that she'd been almost touching him. She hadn't done anything wrong, and fighting him would only make him think she had.

"What are you doing?" he asked.

"Thinking about touching you. I didn't, though."

"I know. I would have woken if you had. It's a good way to get hurt, sneaking up on me like that."

"You and your catlike reflexes?"

He lifted his arm out from under his pillow, and in his hand was a gun. "No, me and my Glock."

He set the weapon on the end table as he sat up. He still didn't let her wrist go.

She still didn't try to pull away.

"Why would you touch me?"

She shrugged. "You're pretty."

"Pretty?" he nearly sputtered.

"Do you prefer handsome? Manly?"

"Yeah, I kinda do."

He uncurled her fingers like he was checking to see if she'd been holding something.

"What? You think I'm going to stab you?"

"I'm actually more worried about hypodermic needles. After all the crazy sh—stuff I've read lately about human experimentation, I'd rather not become some insane doctor's lab rat."

"You think I'd come here, give you a sob story about being abducted, then drug you in your sleep?"

"Stranger things have happened."

"Do you want to pat me down?" she asked. "Make sure I'm not hiding something?"

His gaze slid over her body. "I definitely want to pat you down, but not to search for weapons."

The idea that he was into her thrilled her all the way to her toes. That straight, narrow path suddenly sprouted a scenic route.

She lifted her arms. "Go ahead."

His jaw tightened. Muscles flexed all the way across his scalp. "Not going to happen."

"You don't like me?"

"I like you a hell of a lot more than I should."

"Then why not?"

"Because if I put my hands on you, I'm going to want to have sex with you."

"That's kind of where I was headed with this. I'm not naïve."

He stood, took a step back, and scrubbed his hands over his head. "Maybe not, but sex is out of the question."

"Because I'm a client?"

"Has nothing to do with it, though it should."

"Then why?"

He stared at her for a long second. "I'm abstinent."

Sophie stood there, waiting for the punch line. It didn't come. "Really?"

"Yes, really."

"You're a virgin?" she nearly shouted.

His face turned red. "Hell no."

"Are you going into the priesthood?"

"No."

"How, exactly, do you think you're going to manage abstinence looking like you do. I barely know you and already want to jump your bones."

He hastily buttoned the fly of his jeans, but not before she got a glimpse of his swiftly growing erection tightening the fabric. "Just let it drop, Sophie. It's really none of your business."

"I get that. I really do. I simply don't care. This is way too confusing for you not to explain."

"I don't owe you an explanation."

He was right. He didn't owe her anything. She was the one racking up all the debt here. "Okay. Fine. I give. Keep your impossible secrets."

"Can we just focus on you?"

"Me? I'm not the one with the big ol' . . . secret."

He turned and stalked into the kitchen and started a pot of coffee. "I'm going to go into the office first thing in the morning and try to access video footage of the men who abducted you. See if we get any leads."

"Nice change of topic."

"Thanks. Let's keep it changed."

She took pity on him. "I'll come with you and see if I recognize anyone."

"Good. You'll be safer at the Edge than you will be here."

"With all the weapons you have in this place, I'm not sure how that's possible."

"Weapons only get you so far. Hell, I didn't even wake up until you were close enough to kill me."

"I wasn't even touching. And if you keep bringing it up, I'm going to keep thinking about it. And if I keep thinking about it, I'm going to keep wanting you."

"Don't. I'm a dead end. Your best option is to get on with your new life in your new hometown and find some nice accountant or something to date."

An accountant? A nice husband was part of the white-picket plan, but that just seemed so . . . boring. Bet they didn't sleep with a gun.

It didn't matter. Boring was good. Safe. She needed to learn to love boring.

"Okay. Office it is," she said.

He set out two mugs on the counter and gave her a positively paternal frown. "No touching."

She lifted her hands. "Fine."

"Good. Now, sit down and start writing out everything you remember from the time you spotted the men tailing you. When you get to the part where they grabbed you, include towns, shops, street names—anything you can think of that might help us locate the right cameras."

Sophie sat and started writing. With her luck, it was going to take the rest of the night.

*   *   *

Sophie was going to kill Riley.

Since that whole pregnancy fiasco with his ex, Riley had been the model of responsibility and good behavior. He'd barely even glanced at a woman, and every time he had, he'd scolded himself for it.

His days of trying to be a bad boy were over. He hadn't been very good at it, anyway. He was going back to being the Boy Scout he'd been taught to be. Life was way less complicated that way.

At least it had been until Sophie showed up.

The first time he'd met her, she'd been weak, defenseless, and in pain. He hadn't allowed himself to think about her as more than someone who needed his help. But she was different now. Stronger. More aggressive. So damn beautiful it nearly stopped his heart every time he looked at her.

He couldn't do this to himself. He couldn't allow himself to get involved with a woman who was—very likely—going into hiding for the rest of her life. It was the only way to keep her safe, at least until Dr. Stynger was six feet under.

Riley carried his coffee into the living room where he could no longer see Sophie. Maybe if he kept his eyes off her, his brain would start to function again.

She needed his help, not his dick. And as disappointing as that might have been for him, he was raised well enough to know that sometimes disappointment now saved a whole hell of a lot of heartache later.

He was going to keep repeating that to himself until he believed it.

Chapter Twelve

Adam regretted admitting his weakness. He knew it was imperative that Mira learn to trust him, and revealing intimate information was a fast way to make that happen, but he never should have handed her such a powerful weapon by telling her how terrified he'd been when her life had been threatened.

She now knew how to make him afraid, and if that wasn't a strategic advantage, he didn't know what was. Had she handed him that kind of power, he wouldn't hesitate to use it if he thought it could bring them closer together the way partners were supposed to be.

Before his mind could lock itself into a constant loop that would serve only to distract him, Adam compartmentalized his worries, tucking them away for later, and focused on the task at hand.

The unconscious man lay motionless in the center of Adam's living room. His head was shaved. Beneath the layers of duct tape that restrained him, he had the kind of build that said he was used to some kind of intense physical exercise. There had been several weapons strapped to his body, but no kind of communications equipment.

Which indicated he was working alone.

Adam dialed Victor Temple.

The man answered his phone on the first ring. "Yes?"

"I have another pickup for you. My house."

"Busy night," said Victor, sounding impressed.

"This one came to me. Shots were fired, but our weapons were suppressed, so there wasn't a lot of noise. It's been long enough since the incident that if my neighbors were going to call the police, they would have already been here."

"Did you get hurt?"

"No, but he did. I stopped the bleeding, but he's going to need medical attention."

"How serious?"

Adam glanced at the bright red blood seeping through the towel he'd tied around the intruder's leg. "Not life threatening. He'll probably need surgery and a few bones set."

"Who is he?"

"I can guess, but I'd rather not. No ID. Mira's going to hack into his phone so we can get some answers."

"Was she still with you when it happened?"

"Unfortunately. There were no indications that the man had backup, but I'd like to get her away from here, just in case." Adam turned the man onto his stomach so he could do one more check for weapons and information.

He found nothing, but something was wrong. As hard as he tried, he couldn't put his finger on what it was.

"Understood," said Victor. "I'll send a detail to deal with the situation. Restrain him and get out now. Someone will be there within twenty minutes."

"Thank you."

"Sure," said Victor. "And when you do find out what's going on with this guy, you'll let me know so I can get him the help he needs, right?"

"Of course." That's when it hit Adam. The man lying on his living room floor had no surgical scar at the base of his skull. If he'd been one of Dr. Stynger's subjects, the telltale scar should have been there.

But if she hadn't been the one to send this man to find Adam, then who had?

"Adam?" said Victor, his tone one that made Adam think he'd missed a question.

"Yes?"

"Mira isn't combat ready. You know that, right?"

"I do."

"I mean, I know Bella has been working with her for a long time, and she's tough and determined, but some people just aren't cut out for what we do. I'm afraid she's one of them."

"Of that I am acutely aware."

"So you'll keep an eye on her?"

"Both of them," promised Adam. "If any harm comes to her, it will be only because I'm no longer around to stand in its way."

"Bella was wrong about you. You're a decent guy."

"No, I'm not. But I am the kind of guy you all need, whether or not you want to admit it."

"Yeah. Well, I'm going to pretend I didn't hear you say that."

"Why?"

"Because if I heard you say that, then I'd have to tell Bella. And there's no way in hell I'm going to be standing within range of that woman to deliver bad news."

"Afraid?" asked Adam.

"Hell yes. You would be, too, if you knew what was good for you. She thinks of Mira like a kid sister. Anything happens to her, it's your ass."

This conversation was veering far too close to home for Adam to continue. "We'll be gone in five minutes. I'll leave the doors unlocked."

"Copy. Stay safe."

Adam hung up and went back to the kitchen.

Mira sat cradling the hot mug. She didn't see him come in. Her head was down, and her focus was on the steamy surface of her tea. The blanket he'd given her dwarfed her frame and impeded her ability to move quickly if the need arose.

It struck him in that moment just how vulnerable she was, how little it would take for a bad man to put the barrel of his weapon against her skull and pull the trigger. She wouldn't even see it coming until it was too late.

He couldn't let that happen. He had to find some way to keep her safe, though he had no idea why the need was so compelling.

Guilt over what he'd done to her? Perhaps. But it felt like more than that.

He eased into her line of sight so as not to startle her. She looked up at him, and the vibrant green of her eyes gave away that she'd been fighting tears. Perhaps even crying.

Her pain taunted him, demanding that he fix it.

He had no idea how.

"We should go now," he said, keeping his voice quiet and nonthreatening.

He held out his hand and her fingers settled in the center of his palm. They were shaking and overwarm from holding the mug. He closed his grip, and something about holding her hand winged through him, settling in a content little ball in his gut.

Adam drew her up from the chair. He eased the blanket off her shoulders, letting it pool on the floor. The move put him squarely inside her personal space, but she didn't seem to mind.

Normally he didn't let anyone get this close. At this distance, someone could pull a knife and jab it into his heart faster than he could react. It was deadly to have someone this close, and yet with Mira, he sensed no danger.

At least not to his body. She did, however, send rippling quakes through his usual calm. She made him worry over things he would normally not notice, like the slight chill that lifted the fine hair on her arms, or the tiny quiver wrinkling her chin.

She was still suffering from her scare, and all he could think to do was get her as far away from the memory of it as possible.

The gunman's cell phone went into Adam's pocket. He tucked Mira under his arm and headed out the back door, around the house, toward the car.

"Where are we going?" she asked.

"I'm taking you home."

"What about the man?"

"Victor's on it." Adam opened the car door and settled her inside.

"Don't you need to stay?" she asked when he got in beside her and started the engine.

"Not as badly as you need to leave. Besides, we need to find out who this man was working for."

"I thought you said that Dr. Stynger was mad at you for leaving her."

"I'm certain she is, but this was not one of her men."

"How can you be sure?"

"No incision at the base of his skull." He took the fastest route through the neighborhood, making quick time through the short distance separating him from the highway—another of the benefits of the neighborhood he'd chosen.

"Are you sure his hair wasn't just covering the scar?" she asked.

"He's bald."

He pulled onto the highway. Even though he wasn't looking at her, he could feel her growing tense beside him. "He could be like Clay. Someone could be controlling him with a trigger phrase."

"No sense in jumping ahead to conclusions. We need to find out for sure what's going on."

She didn't seem to hear him. "My father is dead and his evil is still living on. In what world is that fair?"

"Fair has nothing to do with our world. Only facts matter."

"Take me to the office," she said, her voice solid and steady enough for it to sound like an order.

"Why?"

"I'm cracking into this phone tonight."

"You need to go home."

"I can do it from home, but the best equipment is at work. It'll be faster there."

"You need your rest. After last night, you really shouldn't be out of bed, much less being shot at."

"He wasn't shooting at me, Adam. You were his target. He was there when I arrived. That's why you were acting so weird."

"I was only trying to get you to leave so you wouldn't be in the middle of danger."

"What about us being partners? If you'd warned me about the danger, I could have given you backup."

"I didn't need backup. All I needed was a clear shot that wasn't going to hurt any of my neighbors."

"I'm surprised they didn't hear the noise, even with the silencers."

"It's a neighborhood filled with the elderly. Most of them don't hear so well—one of the reasons I chose it."

"Do you make any decisions that aren't based on you possibly needing to shoot someone?"

"Rarely." He glanced at her, watching the glow from streetlights caress her face as they passed. She was far too pretty for his peace of mind. With most women, he hardly noticed more than he needed to in order to do his job—namely, whether or not they were enemies or possible targets. With Mira, he couldn't help but notice the shape of her thighs as she warmed her fingers between them. Even the way her fitted shirt clung to the curve of her breasts was far more intriguing than was the bulge of the weapon she carried under her jacket.

There had been a time not so long ago when she would have let him kiss her. Now he wished that chance would come along again. Maybe then he would be able to clear his mind of all these pesky feelings and focus on his job.

"How long will it take for you to get information from the phone?" he asked.

"Not long. It will take longer to print it all out than it will to gain access to what's on it."

He turned toward the office to take her where she could best do her job.

At least it was a place where he could ensure her safety.

He pulled into the underground garage and escorted her inside to her office. The moment she entered the room, with its deep chill and low hum of machines, he could sense her relaxing.

Her shoulders lowered. Her breathing slowed, as did the flutter of her pulse in her throat. A sense of calm purpose radiated from her—one he swore he could feel lapping against his skin.

Adam simply watched her as she worked. Her fingers flew over the keyboard, without a single mistake. He could see her mind working as she split her attention between the man's phone and her computer screen.

A few minutes later, she sat back in her chair and finally glanced his way. "The phone was mostly clean."

"Mostly?"

"There was one number in memory. It had been deleted, but not well enough."

"And that number?"

"No record attached. Burner cell."

"Then why do you look so pleased with yourself?"

"Because he had location services enabled. I was able to figure out where the man lives, or at least where he spends his nights. I suppose he could drop his phone off somewhere while he slept, but that doesn't make a ton of sense."

"You have an address?" asked Adam.

"Even better. I have GPS coordinates."

She was good at her job. It was a shame that Bella was willing to risk such rare talent by putting Mira in the field.

She glanced at him, and he couldn't help but notice how much he enjoyed her like this—pleased, relaxed.

It made him wonder how lovely she would be if he could please and relax her even more.

He stood, being cautious about his size so as not to intimidate her. What he wanted from her now could not be had with force. She had to give it to him.

Adam propped his hips on the edge of her desk, widening his thighs enough that there was plenty of space for her in front of him.

She sat perched on her rolling chair, well within his reach. Still, he made no move toward her once he was settled.

"What shall we do next?" he asked, keeping all signs of intent from his voice.

She looked up at him. He saw the second she realized just how close he was now. Her eyes widened, her lips parted slightly, her breathing sped.

"Go to his apartment? Look for clues?" Her voice broke slightly.

"Aren't you tired?" No judgment, just curiosity.

"I should be after everything that happened tonight."

"But you're not," he guessed.

"Don't you want to know why this man came after you?"

"I already know. He was looking for someone and thought I knew where to find him."

"Who?"

Not yet. He wasn't ready to tell her that part. Any discussion about her father could wait until she was rested and fed and able to handle the emotional strain it would put on her.

Adam shrugged. "It doesn't matter."

She rose to her feet, which served only to put her closer to him. With the chair behind her, keeping her from backing away, she was standing squarely between his knees.

It took every bit of discipline Adam had not to fit his hands into the curve of her waist and bring her closer.

What was it about this woman that stirred his mind, sending it into a chaotic twirl of thoughts that had no place in this business?

She stared up at him and nervously wet her lips.

Need surged in his body, rising so swiftly, he was sure she would notice his growing erection if she so much as glanced down.

"You're not supposed to hide things from your partner," she said.

It took Adam a second to realize she was continuing their earlier conversation, rather than making comments about his state of arousal.

"My old life is in the past," he said. "I'd like to keep it there."

"*I* was in your past."

"There are some things worth clinging to."

She shook her head slightly. "I don't get you. I'm not sure I ever will."

But he wanted her to. For the first time in his life, he wanted someone to see him all the way through. She already knew that he was capable of violence. What was it going to take for her to see that there were still parts of him that were unblemished? Parts that bordered on good.

"I'm a product of my creation. Just like you. I did what I thought I must to survive—to protect those for whom I was responsible."

"A woman?"

The idea that he would have jumped through hoops and done shady things for a woman would have been ridiculous had Mira not been standing right in front of him. For her, he could see himself bending the rules. Crossing lines he wouldn't otherwise cross. Just as he'd done for Eli.

"No," he admitted. "A brother."

Her gaze softened, causing those golden threads to dance through her irises. "Did the scientists hurt him, too?"

Adam didn't want to talk about it, but she was open. Receptive. He didn't want that to end, either. How else was she to see the man he really was if he didn't let her in, just a little. "No more than the rest of us."

"That is more than enough." Her hand settled on top of his. "Is he still alive?"

Her touch swallowed up all of his attention. The heat of her skin, the slight trembling that still vibrated through her limbs, the soft texture that only women and babies could attain—it all swirled together in a heady mass of sensation he couldn't ignore.

"Yes," said Adam without thinking. "Though I only recently discovered that was the case."

Mira went still. "That's what was in the envelope, wasn't it? The one you traded me for to my father? He told you where to find your brother, didn't he?"

Shame haunted his skin, leaving behind its heat. "If I'd known you then, I never would have made the trade. I would have found another way."

Her hand slipped away, leaving his cold. "It doesn't matter now. It's in the past, just like you said. We should try to leave it there."

Adam felt her close up. All that warm attention drifted away, and he found himself hunting for a way to get it back again.

He reached for her despite all his warnings to keep his hands to himself. He cupped her shoulders and rose to his full height.

She glanced at his left hand, then up at his face. "We

should go. It's late—the perfect time to slip into his place while everyone is asleep."

He couldn't let her go. Not yet. Even though there was no logical reason for him to keep touching her, his hands stayed right where they were.

His fingers tightened slightly. He could feel the intricate pattern of muscle and bone under his fingers. For once, there was no thought as to how he could disable or damage what he touched.

All he wanted for Mira was pleasure.

Her scent rose to greet him, both light and teasing. The artificial scent of plastic and heated circuit boards did nothing to disguise the woman beneath. If anything, the contrast served to highlight just how vital and sweet she was.

She looked up at him expectantly. She'd asked a question and for the life of him, he couldn't remember what it was.

Her tongue swept over her bottom lip, leaving behind a sheen of moisture.

Adam's hands flexed around her arms as he lifted her slightly. The need to get closer to this woman rang through him, blocking out all logical sense.

"How can you do this to me?" he asked, wondering if she wielded some kind of secret genetic weapon against him. Perhaps she'd been designed to distract and tempt him.

"I'm not doing anything," she said.

If that was true, then he really was doomed. "I replay that night we had together in my head, over and over. No matter how many times I order my mind to stop, it betrays me, just as I betrayed your trust that night."

Her hands settled on his chest. "Memory lane isn't a good place for us. We have to work together."

She was right. He knew that, but knowing and acting on that knowledge were two different things.

"I could quit," he offered.

"Well, I can't. I need this job. I need to find the people my father hurt and do what I can to right his wrongs."

"You'll never be able to undo all the damage he caused."

Her hands fell away. She took a long step back, prying her arms from his hands. "Maybe. Maybe not. But I'm sure as hell going to try. Are you coming with me?"

There was nothing else to say. "Yes. Of course."

Chapter Thirteen

Mira was glad Adam was driving, because there was no way in hell she would have been able to keep the car on the road.

That man got under her skin. She didn't know how or why, but from the first moment she'd seen him, some intelligent part of her brain had simply melted into a puddle and leaked out her ears.

Geez.

She was such a mess. She had actually been feeling him back in her office—feeling him in a way that made her forget all about what he'd done to her. How he'd betrayed her.

For his brother.

What would Mira have done to find her brother if she'd had one? More important, what *wouldn't* she have done?

She glanced at Adam as he drove to the attacker's place. Every move he made was fluid and smooth. There seemed to be no thought in his actions, only reaction and instinct. His gaze was watchful, on the road ahead as well as behind them. He constantly switched lanes and went around blocks to ensure that no one followed them.

He was cautious, capable, and as sexy as hell.

Admitting that was hard, but it was her only chance at denying the pull he had on her. And she had to deny it.

Didn't she?

Of course she did. Bella had a strict no-fraternizing policy. Plus, Adam had betrayed Mira's trust. She'd be a fool to trust him again.

But what about forgiveness? What about understanding his motives and knowing she would have done exactly the same thing if it had been Clay she had lost?

Her head thumped against the headrest. No way was she going to make sense of all the emotions rioting in her brain. Not when she was so recently concussed, sleep deprived, queasy, and confused.

Best just to focus on the job and pretend Adam was a eunuch.

Yeah, right.

He pulled to a stop in the parking lot of an industrial building that was well past its prime. Even the FOR SALE sign had been there long enough to rust. It was a three-story construction, complete with both office space and a warehouse on one side. Boards covered more of the windows than not, and the parking lot was filled with enough potholes that their drive across it could be considered off-roading.

"I don't suppose there's any point in asking if you would prefer to stay in the car, is there?" he asked.

"None," she agreed. "Based on the vertical component of the GPS reading, he spent a lot of time on the third floor."

"Then we shall as well."

He reached into the pocket behind her seat. That simple shift of his frame brought him close to her and gave her a girlish little thrill.

She tamped down on the inappropriate reaction and steeled herself against his scent. No matter how good he smelled, she was keeping her hands—and all her other parts—to herself.

Adam righted himself and handed her a flashlight.

"Are you okay?" His deep voice wove its way into her chest and hung out there for a second before passing through.

"Uh. Yeah. Fine."

"I should have fed you before coming here."

"Not interested. Let's just get this over with."

She reached for the door handle. His fingers settled on her thigh, right above her knee.

Instantly, her nervous system went haywire, shorting out all over the place. A whole cheering section in her brain lit up, chanting at him to slide that hand higher. While that was going on, her motor skills abandoned her, and she went completely still.

"There's something you should know before we go in there," he said.

She tried to say *What?* but all that came out was a pitiful squeak.

"The man I subdued—the one who attacked at my house—he said something."

"What?" she managed this time, though she strained her vocal cords to do it.

"He wanted to know where we were hiding Dr. S."

Mira went cold at the mention of her father. Just like that, all the heat drained from her body except for the wide patch of skin beneath Adam's hand.

"Did you tell him we killed him?"

"I did, but he seemed unconvinced."

"Maybe he wasn't looking for Dr. Sage. Maybe he was looking for Dr. Stynger."

"I don't think so."

"Why?"

"Just a hunch."

"I thought Payton made sure that the word got out that Dad was dead."

"He did, which is why I thought you should know what I heard before we go in there."

"Why? What are you expecting to find?"

"I don't know. I just thought that if there were any mentions of your father, you should be braced for them."

"My father definitely left behind a legacy. Too bad no one in his right mind would want a piece of it."

"Another reason to brace yourself. If someone is searching for him or his work, this person might not be in his right mind."

"Lovely. The fun never ends, does it?"

"If we make progress tonight, we'll pretend it was fun."

"Deal," she said.

It was time to get out of the car, but his hand was still on her thigh, ridding her of all ability to move away. Adam's hold on her was too strong in a way that went way beyond physical.

She didn't get it—didn't even want to—but that didn't change a thing.

"Shall we?" she asked, hoping he'd release her from his touch even as part of her wished for him to touch her a little more.

He stared for a long moment, and then lifted his hand. "Of course."

Getting inside the building was easy. The locks that had once been in place had long since been busted free of the doorframe. And even if they hadn't, all they had to do was climb in through one of the broken windows.

The air in here smelled damp and musty. Dead leaves and trash collected at the base of walls and in corners. At the end of the hall, Mira's flashlight reflected off the beady eyes of at least three rats.

She froze in place as a shiver of revulsion passed through her.

"Not a fan of rodents?" asked Adam.

"I only associate with wild creatures when forced." Her reference to him was clear in her tone.

"I'm hardly wild. My guess is that you have more of a social life than I do."

"Yeah, me, my couch, and my jammies are always having crazy parties."

"Were you cut off from other kids when you were young?"

"Sometimes. Usually Dad would bring kids home to play with me just long enough for me to get close to them. Then he'd take them away, just to see how I'd react. If I was lucky, he would forget I existed and neglect to feed me for a few days rather than make me watch him hurt them."

"If I'd known what he'd done to you, I probably would have killed him on sight."

"He had that effect on a lot of people. I'm glad he's dead." And that made her feel as guilty as hell. It didn't matter that he was a monster. She still felt like a traitor every time she remembered he was dead and felt a wave of relief.

He couldn't hurt anyone anymore.

Mira reached for the door handle on the stairwell leading up. Adam covered her hand and held her still.

"What?" she asked. "This is the right way."

"No foot traffic," he said, shining his flashlight at the floor. "The marks in the dirt indicate that he never used this door. I suggest we don't, either."

"Do you think it's booby-trapped?"

"Possibly. We're smarter not to risk it. There must be other stairwells in a building of this size."

He was right. And as soon as they found the second one, it was clear that this was the way the man in Adam's house traveled. There was no dust on the knob, and the floor was littered with footprints.

"Stand over there," said Adam, pointing down the hallway the way they'd come.

"Why?"

"To be safe."

"What about you?"

"If things go badly, I won't be missed nearly as much as you."

His words hit her in the gut, giving her a brief moment of sympathy. There was no question about whether or not he believed what he said. He was simply stating a fact—at least as he knew it.

"Is that why you stepped in front of that bullet for me?" she asked.

He lifted one shoulder in an elegant shrug. "I'd gotten you into that mess. It seemed fair that I would find a way to get you out."

The words welled up in her. All she did was open her mouth and "Thank you" popped out.

His pale gray gaze settled on her. "After what I did to you, you're going to thank me?"

"If you hadn't stayed, Clay would have killed Leigh. My father would have killed me. Your actions don't make up for the bad things you did, but that doesn't mean I shouldn't appreciate the good things."

He nodded slowly, and something shifted in him. She wasn't sure what it was, but she saw this change come over him. His spine straightened. He grew taller. The light in his eyes flared brighter. "I won't hurt you again, Mira. Not ever. No matter the personal cost to me."

She wanted to believe him. Maybe that was part of his dark magic—to lure her in and make her trust him again.

Now that Clay was with Leigh, Mira felt so alone. She never would have wished for her best friend to be anything but gloriously happy, but his relationship with Leigh was new. They spent all their time together. Just as it was supposed to be. But that didn't mean that Mira didn't feel left out. Lonely.

And here was Adam, eager to please and working to find some way back into her life. He was so . . . present— a potent force standing only a few feet from her.

Before she'd known anything about him, she'd been drawn to his charming graciousness and smooth strength. Before they'd even exchanged ten words, her body had responded to his.

That never happened to Mira. It seemed a cruel trick that her hormones would lure her to let down her guard when she'd had little use for the pesky chemicals before Adam arrived. She'd listened to her instincts once, and it had nearly gotten her killed. How could she possibly listen now, when her bullet wound was still new enough that it sometimes ached?

"You're upset," said Adam. "Are you sure you wouldn't prefer to wait in the car?"

She hated it that he could sense her moods so easily. Even when he didn't seem to be looking at her, he still had some way of knowing what she was feeling. "I'm your partner. I'll back you up."

He flashed her a warm smile that made her stomach do a slow dip and sway. The temptation to trust him was more than she could stand.

The stairwell door opened with no kaboom. On the third step, however, Adam shone his light on a tightly strung wire blocking the path. "Watch your step."

He held out his hand to help her make the long, uphill stride. She took it without thinking and remembered too late how intoxicating his skin could be on hers. It didn't matter if it was only a simple, helpful gesture—one he would have made to anyone weaker than himself—it still shook her down to her bones.

She released his hand as soon as possible, then wiped it on her thigh. She could still feel his heat lingering in her skin, still feel the casual strength of his grip around her fingers.

With a monumental force of will, Mira shoved out all feelings and emotions relating to Adam. She put her full focus on the task at hand and kept her eyes off his tight, muscular butt as he marched up the steps in front of her.

"Another trip line here," he said, showing her where to look with his flashlight beam.

She braced herself for his touch as she once again accepted his help over the obstacle. As klutzy as she was, refusing his help would likely end with them going boom. Her pride and peace of mind weren't worth dying for.

They made it all the way to the third floor. The door here was locked, but a few seconds with a set of picks, and Adam eased it open.

The area was cleared, with only support columns to break up the space. There were obvious signs on the floor that cubicle walls and desks had once resided here. A few rolling chairs with mouse-chewed cushions were clustered together in a corner. On the far wall, easily a hundred feet away, blue tarps dangled from the ceiling to section off an area.

Adam pulled his gun. Mira didn't know what prompted the move, but she followed his lead and took hers in hand, too.

His feet were silent on the concrete floor. He moved at a slow, steady pace that made it look more like he glided than walked.

Mira hung back, working through the sudden wave of apprehension that flooded her. She tried to tell herself that this was all part of the job—that being in the field meant her learning to cope with certain things. Like surges of adrenaline.

For a long moment, she pined for her frigid, noisy office and the safety those walls provided. If only she was an adrenaline junkie like Bella and the other women at the Edge, this would be a piece of cake. Instead, her eyes kept wandering, looking for the closest hiding place.

Adam disappeared behind one of the dangling tarps. Mira braced herself for gunfire, but none came. After a few seconds, she got brave enough to close in.

He must have heard her approach. He lifted the tarp to give her room to pass. "Stay close. I've already seen a couple more trip wires."

She planted her feet on the dirty concrete and stayed put.

The area inside the tarp walls had been turned into a sort of apartment. There was a bed, a minifridge with a microwave on top, a laptop on a rickety desk, and a worn office chair.

"Did he live here?" she asked.

Adam fired up the laptop. "Possibly. Or it could have been a place he came to work."

"Why here?"

"Why not? It's private, secluded enough that no one would track his comings and goings, and it has multiple exits if things go badly. Plus, there's a lot of ground to cover to get up here, and with all the security cameras along the way, there's little chance of someone sneaking in."

"Security cameras?"

He used the tip of a pen to lift the cover of a notebook. "I counted eight. There were probably more."

She hadn't seen any of them, which made her wonder just what else she hadn't seen. And whether or not she even belonged out here.

"Any idea what this is?" asked Adam.

She holstered her weapon and took a look at the scribbled marks in the notebook. "It's code."

"Can you break it?"

"Not that kind of code. It's a program. Software."

"What does it do?"

She read through the few lines she could make out. "Looks like some kind of random word/number-combination generator."

"What's it for?"

"It's not very sophisticated. Any college kid could have programmed it. My guess is he was using it to create passwords."

"Why not just make up something?"

Mira shrugged. "Maybe he was worried that anything he made up could be guessed. The better question is what was he protecting?"

The laptop screen blinked on, waiting for a password to log in to a user's account.

"Can you hack it?" asked Adam.

"Probably." She used one of the USB cords sitting nearby to attach her phone. After making a secure connection to the network back at the Edge, she accessed her decryption software and let it do its magic. Less than three minutes later, the current account opened up, giving her access. "What do you want to know?"

"Check mail first."

She did. "Looks like he's been getting orders from someone—someone who told him to go to your house and kill you."

"Can you tell who sent the e-mail?"

She pulled up the proper program and tried to trace the IP address. "They hid their tracks pretty well. I might be able to figure it out given enough time, but it wouldn't be fast."

"What else can you find?"

There wasn't much on the hard drive, but she did notice one folder filled with large files. "There are some videos here. They're all password protected, too. Hold on."

She started downloading the files to a server at the Edge, just in case she and Adam had to flee. While she did that, she focused on the most recent file and ran it through her electronic lockpick.

A recorded image of a video chat from two days ago popped up on the screen. In the small window was the man who'd attacked Adam's house. In the main window was a beautiful blond woman in a designer suit. She had an elegant look about her, with her hair in a fancy updo that showed off dainty diamond studs.

Mira hit "play."

The woman spoke. "Did you find him?"

"No," said the man. "There's no sign that he was taken anywhere. But I went to the cemetery. His grave was empty."

"I told you he was alive. They're holding him, likely torturing him for information. Find him. Now."

"I've looked. Wherever they've got him hidden, it's not nearby."

"Adam will know where to look. Find him. Question him."

"Yes, ma'am."

"And, Kyle?"

"Yes?"

"If you don't find where they've taken Dr. Sage by Friday, the next call I make is going to be with the man I use to clean up loose ends."

"I'm not a loose end."

"You will be if you don't find Dr. Sage. Understood?"

Mira didn't hear the rest. Her mind was reeling too hard and fast for her to concentrate on anything other than what she'd already heard.

They were talking about finding her father. Who was dead.

Wasn't he?

His grave was empty.

Mira hadn't made any of the final arrangements for her father. Payton had taken care of everything for her. He'd told her he didn't want her to worry herself or go to any trouble for the man who'd ruined her life and killed her mother.

His grave was empty.

She looked up at Adam. "Is my father still alive?"

The look on Adam's face was ferocious. Dark shadows lurked under his eyes and along his sharp cheekbones. "That woman is Ruby Rypan."

He'd said it like she should know the name, but she didn't. "Who's that?"

"Your father's assistant. She ran the show whenever he was busy working in the labs. I've only met her once, but it was clear to me that she was as dangerous as she was devoted."

"To Dad?"

"Absolutely."

"And she thinks he's alive."

"So it appears," said Adam.

His grave was empty.

"Why would Dad's grave be empty if he were dead?"

"Did he ever experiment on himself? Could someone have stolen his body for research?"

"I can't imagine him ever risking damage to himself. That was what his family was for."

Adam swallowed hard enough that she could see his throat move, choking down his anger. "We need answers."

Wheels in Mira's head started to turn. Vague, cloudy memories of the night her father was killed came back to her. "Everyone was airlifted out of that barn last year. Were you on the helicopter with my dad's body?"

"I don't know. I'd lost too much blood by that point and was unconscious."

She rubbed the scar where the bullet that had nearly killed her had left its mark. "I was taken away in the first flight. Payton was directing people—ordering them around."

"Then we should talk to him."

"He made all the funeral arrangements. I never saw Dad's body. Not even at the funeral. Closed casket. Payton said he didn't want me seeing him like that." She looked up at Adam, horrified at the thought that passed through her mind. "He ordered the airlift. He could have taken Dad anywhere. Even someplace private where they could patch him up and force him to talk."

"He would be an invaluable informational asset."

That was it. The truth. It made too much sense for it to be anything else. Dad was alive, and Payton had known it all along. He'd let her grieve, let her think it was over and that she was finally safe.

Adam must have seen something in her expression. He reached for her, but she couldn't stand the idea of being touched right now. She took a long step back, hitting the blue tarp wall.

Something tugged at the back of her calf. A trip line.

A small pop sounded nearby. Smoke began pouring from the computer. A strobe light flashed overhead, silent but bright enough to wake anyone nearby.

Adam grabbed her arm. "We've set off an alarm. Run."

Chapter Fourteen

Adam hauled Mira out past the tarps. She went where he led, but she was too pliant for his peace of mind.

Her father was still alive. The news had shaken her badly. As much as he wished he could sit her down and discuss it until she felt more calm and steady, there simply wasn't time.

Thick, black smoke billowed from under the stairwell door. A quick check of the one at the south end of the building revealed the same. There was no electricity to power the elevators, but whoever had set the trip lines would have had some way to safety. They wouldn't have wanted to be trapped here on the third floor with no means of escape.

Adam peered out the windows, hoping for some kind of fire escape. There was none.

If he was living here, how would he have slipped out?

There was a large plastic tub sitting by the elevator doors. He raced to it and dumped it out.

A crowbar. A length of two-by-four. Rappelling gear. But enough for only one.

Smoke lined the ceiling now, and the toxic smell of it burned his lungs. They didn't have much time.

"What are you doing?" asked Mira. "We have to get out of here."

"The stairwells will kill us. So will the fall from one of the windows. This is our exit." He pried the door open, seeing an open shaft below. "Shove that board between the doors to hold them open."

She did. "How are we getting down that way?"

Adam slipped the harness on and fastened it as fast as he could. The smoke was just over his eyes now and growing thicker by the second.

He slipped the crowbar into his belt and dangled the flashlight from its wrist strap. "You're going to hold on to me while I lower us down."

"I'm not strong enough."

He clipped the harness onto the line suspended in the elevator shaft. "You'll be fine. It'll be just like sitting on my lap."

Before she could argue with him more, he grabbed her around the waist and pulled her close. "Arms around my neck. Legs around my waist."

"I don't really—"

"Do it, Mira!" He hated shouting at her, but they were out of time. There were no other options.

She did as he asked. A second later, he pushed away from the ledge with Mira clinging to him like a monkey.

The trip down was fast, but not so fast that he didn't feel every frightened quiver that raced through her body. Each rapid breath that swept across his neck was one more reminder to be careful.

Before he touched bottom, he used the flashlight to check and make sure there were no more nasty surprises waiting for them. All he saw was dusty concrete with a few scuff marks to prove someone had come this way before.

Mira held him so tightly he could feel every inch of her curvy body plastered against him. She hid her face in the crook of his neck.

Adam put his feet on the floor and unclipped the harness from the line. She still hadn't realized it was safe to let go, and his mouth seemed glued shut.

He wrapped his arms around her, using one to prop up her curvy backside. He knew she would let go in a second and that this contact with her would end. But until then, he would relish every second of it.

Light from his tethered flashlight bobbed around, brightening the dark space. The stench of that smoke still hovered on their clothes, but the stale air here was a welcome relief.

For a minute, he just held her, reveling in her trust. Yes, he'd tricked her, betrayed her, but in this moment, she'd forgotten all about that, and every dark little corner of his soul warmed at her show of faith in him.

Why what this one woman thought of him was so important, he had no idea, but it was. He ached for her trust. Yearned for a second chance to prove to her that he wasn't a wholly evil man.

"It's okay now," he finally managed. "We're on the ground."

She lifted her head just enough to see that what he was saying was true. Then she looked at him, relief glowing in her canted green eyes.

Adam had never before seen anything half as beautiful as this woman's eyes. There was something mysterious lurking there—some feminine secret he could only imagine.

Before he could sense her intent, she pressed her lips to his and kissed him.

His heart stopped. His lungs ceased to function. The rest of the world dissipated, meaningless and unimportant.

She lifted her mouth too soon; her kiss of thanks and relief was over before it had really begun. And now the look on her face shifted to an expression of shock and dismay.

"I'm sorry," she said. "I shouldn't have done that."

He couldn't imagine her having *not* done it. Not now.

Her legs unwound from his waist, dangling just above the ground. "You can put me down."

He couldn't. If he let her go, she'd never kiss him again. He could already see her resolve hardening her mouth.

It had been so very soft only a second ago.

"Adam? I can't reach the ground."

He knew that. He could feel her weight in his arms, right where he wanted her to be. The sensation was strange and exciting, reminding him of the way other boys used to talk about girls when he was young. He'd never felt those things then.

But he did now.

Slowly, he forced his muscles to unclench and release her. She slid along his front until her toes reached the ground. His arms still shackled her to him, but there was nothing he could do to convince them to let her go. Not yet.

Her hands pressed against his chest in a subtle sign to move away. When he refused, she stopped pushing and relaxed inside his hold.

"What are you doing?" she asked.

"I honestly don't know. Why did you kiss me?"

"I lost my head for a second. It didn't mean anything."

A small part of him shriveled up and died. It had meant something to him. He didn't know what, but that she would toss the act aside so easily hurt.

That pain was the thing that saved him, allowing him to release her. Pain he knew. Understood. It was how the world worked, and the jab she'd given him reminded him of that.

He stepped away, turned his back, and pulled the crowbar from his belt. He shed the harness and went to work on the doors. As soon as he had the elevator doors open, Mira slipped out. He was right behind her.

The doors closed with a rattle, shutting him off from that secret little place where she'd kissed him.

In his mind, he tried to close the act behind another door, compartmentalizing it. Later he would take it out and study it. For now, his attention had to be focused elsewhere.

They were in a basement. He found a service entrance where deliveries had once been received. Within a couple of minutes, they were back outside, on their way to the car.

The night air was cold, clean, and so very welcome to his burning lungs. He hadn't breathed in much of that smoke, but it had been more than enough.

"Are you having any trouble breathing?" he asked her as they neared the car.

"No. You? You were a lot closer to it."

"I'm fine."

They got in, and she was once again close enough to him to touch.

He didn't.

The doors closing off the memory of her kiss shuddered and bulged.

"I'll take you home so you can get some rest," he said.

"Not a chance. I'm going to see Payton."

"It's the middle of the night."

"You say that like I care if I wake him up. The man has some questions to answer, and if that means he loses a little beauty rest, then so be it."

"You could call."

She shook her head, the movement stiff. "No. I'm going to look him in the eye. It's the only chance I have at finding out if he's lying."

"A man with his background and training will be able to lie to you no matter what."

"What do you know about his training?"

"Nothing for certain, but I recognize certain traits—the same ones that allowed me to lie to you without you knowing it."

"So I'm screwed either way," she said on a frustrated sigh. "Doesn't matter what he says; I'll never be able to trust it."

"Not necessarily."

"How's that?"

"If he tells you what you don't want to hear, you'll know he's not lying."

"Fine. Then let's go see Payton. I'm not getting any sleep tonight, anyway."

Neither was Adam, but for reasons much different and more pleasant than hers.

As he drove away, the only thought in his mind was, if he got Payton to tell her the truth, would she kiss him again? With even the slightest hope of that happening again, Adam began going through his training on interrogation techniques.

He would find the truth Mira sought. One way or another.

Chapter Fifteen

Mira had always considered Payton a friend. Almost like a father. The idea that he'd lie to her sat in her stomach like a hot coal.

Was she really so gullible that everyone could lie to her and get away with it?

She used Payton's dog tags to track his location. He was still at work despite the late hour. By the time she marched into his office, a little part of her had died. She knew the truth. Payton had lied to her about her father's death.

"Where is my father?" she asked as she went through his office door without knocking.

Payton looked up. Even at this hour, his hair was still perfect, his tie in place, and his suit unwrinkled. In spite of his perfect grooming, she could see his fatigue hanging on him. It shadowed his eyes and dragged at his skin, making him look older than he was.

He sat his pen down, lining it up precisely along the notepad in front of him. His gaze slid past her, moving over her head to where Adam stood at her back.

She could feel his bulk there, creating a sort of gravitational pull on her. He'd always had that kind of magnetic energy about him, but she felt it much more now.

She never should have kissed him.

It didn't matter that it was chaste, or that it had lasted for only a couple of seconds. It had been real. A genuine reaction to the way he made her feel. Denying that he had such power over her would only make it more likely she'd screw up and kiss him again.

Every cell in her body apart from one tiny little square inch of logic left in her brain wanted her to do just that. Only this time with tongue.

Payton stood and buttoned his suit coat. "Mira, what are you doing here so late?"

"You heard my question. Where is Dad?"

Once again, Payton's gaze moved to Adam.

His deep voice came out quiet but filled with warning. "We know Sage is alive."

Technically, that wasn't true, but Adam's lie had the desired result.

Payton let out a deep breath as if he'd been holding it for weeks. "I'm sorry you had to find out," he said to Mira. "My hope was that you'd find some peace, some closure."

She thought she'd been prepared for the truth, but the pain of betrayal lanced through her with surprising force. She swayed against it. Her palms tingled with shock, and her ribs seemed to constrict around her lungs, making it hard to breathe.

Adam's long fingers wrapped around her arms to steady her. His body moved closer until there was no space left between them and she was leaning on him for support.

How strange it was that Adam was holding her up under the pain of Payton's betrayal instead of the other way around.

The whole situation left her reeling and struggling to find level emotional ground. She didn't know what to do next. Didn't know what to say. Her world was upside down, and everyone she usually turned to in times of crisis was out of reach.

She was on her own. Except for Adam.

"Where is Sage?" he asked, his voice hard.

"In a secure location."

"Where you held Clay?" she asked.

Payton nodded. "We still don't know where all of Sage's lab facilities are. We still don't have all the research—all the names of those he experimented on."

"You're interrogating him," stated Adam, as if commenting that the sky was blue.

"Daily."

"He hasn't said a word, has he?" asked Mira.

"Your father is a stubborn man."

Adam's thumb stroked across her arm in a comforting sweep. "He has people on the outside. They're searching for him. He knows they'll come and he'll bide his time until they do."

"They'll never find him," said Payton.

"You don't know that," said Mira. "They could be at your secret facility right now, breaking him free. How would you even know?"

His hand jerked toward his phone. The move was tiny, but enough for her to tell that he was definitely connected to the people who held her father.

Maybe she should hack into his phone and find out what she could for herself. She sure as hell couldn't trust him to tell her the truth. Not anymore.

"The holding facility is secure," said Payton. "You have my word."

"Which is worth less than a bucket of spit." What would her father do to her if he was free? As a kid, she used to resist his attempts to test her. She'd fake ignorance or fail on purpose, just to piss him off. That's when he'd bring in the other kids from the lab and hurt them in front of her until she did as he wanted.

What would he do now that she'd lied to him, stolen precious data, and ruined his plans? Who would he hurt now to gain her compliance?

Her voice shook. "You should have killed him. You have no idea what he's capable of."

Payton eased down into his chair, moving with an uncharacteristic frailty. "Sadly, I do. That's why I had to let him live. He's hurt so many people. It's my duty to find as many of them as I can and try to help them. What I need to know is locked in his head. All that's left is finding a way to extract it."

"He'll never talk," said Adam. "Not so long as he knows his people are alive and working on a rescue."

"Then I'll tell him they're dead. Give me enough details to make it believable."

"He won't ever believe you," said Mira. "He's convinced that his control over his subordinates is absolute. Even if you tell him that some of them are dead, you have no way of knowing how many people he controls." She pulled in a deep breath and prayed she wasn't making a huge mistake. She doubted her ability to sway her father to do the right thing, but she was smart. She might be able to gain some bit of information that someone who didn't know him as well couldn't. "But he knows he has no control over me. Let me meet with him. Talk to him."

"No," said both Payton and Adam at the same time.

She could feel Adam's growl at her back. "You're not getting anywhere near that monster. I've seen what he's willing to do to you."

The bullet scar along her ribs burned.

Payton glanced up at Adam. "Maybe she's right. Maybe she can get information out of him that none of us have been able to pry free."

"It's worth a shot," said Mira.

Adam stepped around to face her. "I won't let you put yourself within his grasp again."

"It's the only way. We need to find his labs. The trigger phrases he used to control his subjects are still out there. If someone were to get his hands on them . . ."

Payton's fatigue seemed to vanish in a flash. Cunning brilliance brightened his eyes, and Mira swore she could see the pieces of some puzzle click into place inside his mind. She had no idea what it was he seemed to have figured out, but he was pleased.

His voice came through, calm and cool. "Adam, if you're so worried about Mira's safety, you can go with her."

"If I see that man again, I'm going to want to kill him," said Adam.

"You won't be allowed to go anywhere near him armed."

"I don't need a gun to kill. You know that." Adam tilted his head, staring at Payton. "Maybe that's what you want."

"If I wanted Sage dead, he'd be that way."

As much as she hated her father, she didn't like to picture him dead. All this talk of killing was making her stomach turn. She needed to move forward and figure out what to do with the information she now had.

"Why did you lie to me?" asked Mira. "Why not just tell me he was still alive?"

"Because I wanted your nightmare to be over. I've spent years trying to set things right, trying to undo some of the damage I've caused. I thought that it would be easiest for you if you thought he was dead."

"Did you ever stop to think how it would feel to know you lied to me?" she asked. "I trusted you. You were the closest thing to a real father I've ever had. Your betrayal of my trust hurts far more than the bullet my own father put in me."

As she said the words, the truth in them broke free. Payton had hurt her. Badly. She'd always seen him as an ally, and now he was just one more man willing to use her to get what he wanted.

The only solace she could find was that they both wanted the same thing: the location of the labs where her father hid his research and any information they could find to help those he'd damaged.

"I'm going to see him," she told Payton. "You have twenty-four hours to make it happen, or I find my own way."

He nodded slowly. "I understand. You'll have your meeting."

"I will be there as well," said Adam. "She's not going anywhere alone with either you or Sage."

Payton's face was stoic, but his posture seemed to relax. Mira couldn't help but think that she'd somehow just given him exactly what he wanted.

Adam trailed behind Mira, unsure what to do. It was clear to him that she was upset, emotional, and shaken, but those weren't the kinds of problems he knew how to solve.

He followed her to her office, slipping in behind her through the door without an invitation.

She stopped, turned, and looked up at him. "What?"

"I didn't say anything."

"No, I mean what do you want?"

To comfort her, but he didn't dare say that. "You just found out your father is alive. I thought you might want to talk about it."

She closed her eyes, and for a brief second, he thought she might actually accept his offer to help. Instead, she straightened her spine and squared her shoulders. "Talking isn't going to change anything. All I need to concentrate on now is being strong enough to get through seeing him again."

"Payton wanted the meeting," he said, feeling obligated to share his conclusion.

"I thought so, too. But why?"

Adam took her question as enough of an invitation to invade her private office space. It wasn't the warm welcome he would have liked, but it was as close as a man like him was going to get.

He slipped past her and took a seat in the guest chair at her desk. "My guess is that Payton thinks your father might tell you something he wouldn't tell anyone else."

"I haven't taken any interrogation training yet. I have no idea where to even begin prying information out of him."

"You don't need to know a thing. If Payton is right and Sage will give you information, then he'll do it because you're his daughter, not because you're skilled with a set of thumbscrews."

She eased into her chair as if she were made of glass and afraid she'd shatter.

Adam's fingers ached to reach out for her, but he kept them curled tightly around the arms of the chair.

"I just don't know anymore, Adam. I keep thinking I finally have a grip on my life, and then everything spins upside down and I'm left reeling." Her gaze met his, and he swore he could sense how hard she fought back her tears. "My father is alive. How could I not have known that? How could I not have suspected?"

"Payton is a skilled liar. There's no shame in being fooled."

"The way you fooled me? Am I really just that gullible?"

"You know how to trust. It's a rare and beautiful thing. You shouldn't let me, Payton, your father, or anyone else steal that from you."

She rubbed her eyes as if a headache was forming. All Adam could think about was where and how he could touch her to ease her suffering.

"Does your head hurt?" he asked.

"A little."

"You haven't had much sleep, and you've had too much stress."

Her rubbing motion stopped and she peeked at him through her fingers. "Same goes for you. Doesn't seem to be getting you down."

"I could make up one of the beds in the on-call room."

"Thanks, but I couldn't sleep, anyway."

"Do you want me to drive you home?" he asked.

She looked at him for an extended moment, and he couldn't figure out what was going on inside her head. It both puzzled and intrigued him.

When she finally spoke, the last thing he expected to hear was, "Maybe I don't belong in the field if I can't even tell when someone is lying to me."

"That's why you have a partner."

She stared again, and this time he stopped trying to guess what she'd say and simply enjoyed her undivided attention.

"Have you lied to me since Bella assigned us as partners?" she asked.

"No. I tried to shoo you away from my house, but I wouldn't consider that a lie."

"Would you tell me if you had lied?"

"No."

"Well, at least that's the truth."

He needed to find a way to prove to her that he was being honest. The only thing he could think of was to tell her something he didn't want her to know—something private.

He pondered the idea for less than three seconds before he decided that the risk was worth the reward.

"I want to touch you," he admitted. "All the time."

She lifted her head, her eyes wide with shock.

"I want to be close to you, to know you're safe. I want to make your pain go away."

"What?"

He couldn't tell if his attempt to reach out was working, but he'd gone too far to turn back now. "You make me want things I've never cared about before."

Her response was slow, giving him plenty of time to squirm. "Like what?"

"The ability to travel back in time, for starters."

She straightened, giving him her absolute attention. "To do what?"

"Kill your father. Before I met you. Before he used me to hurt you."

She swallowed, but she was still with him. She hadn't cringed or shied away from the violence of his words. "But then you would have never found out about your brother."

"I would have found another way."

"Why are you telling me this?" she asked.

"So you'll know I'm capable of honesty. I understand it won't change what I did to you, but it might change how you see me in the future."

"Why do you care?"

He opened his mouth, but there were too many thoughts for any one of them to come out. They all clumped together in a confusing mass that silenced him.

"Adam?" she asked again, her voice quieter now. "Do you care how Bella sees you?"

"No, so long as she knows I'm capable of doing my job."

"Payton?"

"No, so long as he knows I will kill him if he hurts you."

"Uh. Okay. Not exactly what I expected, but I can run with that." She covered the back of his hand with hers. "If you don't care much about how they see you, then why do you care what I think about you?"

The answer was so obvious, he didn't understand why she even had to ask. "Because you're important."

"So are the others."

He couldn't keep his hands to himself any longer, so he pulled her rolling chair closer, until she was perched between his widely spread knees. His fingers settled lightly on her cheek. So warm and soft. "Not like you."

Mira's breathing sped, as did her pulse. As close as he was, he could even see the minute changes in the size of her pupils as they expanded to swallow up the golden starbursts. "I'm not going to let you suck me in again. I'm not going to let you seduce me, only to learn later that it was all just a game."

Seduce her? That he even had a chance to do so was enough to make him want it. Need it. If he could make her feel toward him half of what he felt for her, it would at least level the playing field.

She *had* kissed him. It had been done in the heat of the moment, and hardly lasted at all, but it had been a kiss—something a woman would never do with a man she didn't trust, at least for one split second.

The notion gave him hope and thrilled him all at the same time.

He leaned forward and threaded his fingers through her hair. Her eyes fluttered closed before he once again had her full attention.

"No more games," he said. "If I manage to seduce you again, this time it will be for real."

She glanced at his mouth. He knew she was thinking about kissing him again. It took every bit of strength he possessed to resist giving her what she wanted. What he wanted.

But he did resist. He had no idea if there was something real between them or not—he'd never had anything real before, so there was no way for him to tell—but if it was, he wasn't going to ruin whatever fledgling trust she might have for him by moving too fast.

No matter how much he wanted her, he would control himself. She deserved at least that much from him after all the mistakes he'd made with her.

Adam let her go and stood. Her gaze went straight to the bulge in his pants, but there was nothing he could do about that. At least she'd know his desire for her wasn't a lie.

"I'll be in my office if you need me," he said as he went to her door.

She cleared her throat. "You're just going to leave?"

He paused by the door. "Do you want me to stay?"

She blinked a couple of times, then shook her head. "No, of course not. I'll check in with you later, after I do some research on our mystery lady."

"Ruby Rypan?"

"Yes."

"I plan to do the same. But I urge you to be careful. I don't know much about her, but I do know that she's dangerous."

"That's okay," said Mira as she stretched her fingers and rolled up to her keyboard. "So am I."

As Adam walked away and felt the immediate loss of her presence, he knew that what she said was true.

Mira was dangerous, and there was no body armor in the world that could save him.

Chapter Sixteen

Mira's research revealed that Ruby Rypan had no life. She rented an upscale apartment, owned a nice car, had suits sent to her from fancy boutiques, and got her hair done on a regular basis. Besides that, the woman did . . . nothing.

There were no meals out with the girls, no movie nights, no gym membership. She didn't even get cable TV.

"She doesn't scream *evil mastermind*," Mira told Adam, who hovered just behind her, reading over her shoulder.

"She calls no attention to herself. Can you find even a single parking ticket?"

"No, nothing like that."

"She wants to remain invisible to the authorities. I did exactly the same thing—made sure I looked respectable, kept my head down and my nose clean. People rarely noticed me."

"I have a hard time believing that. You probably had women all over you, even when you were trying to be in stealth mode."

He pointed to a video file she had in the background. "Watch it. I bet you see that she has her shields up—completely unapproachable, making no eye contact unless it's to warn someone away."

Mira played the video of Ruby inside a local grocery store. She was in a perfectly fitted suit and heels. Her hair was coiled up in a sleek roll. Her appearance was put together and polished, all the way down to the glossy color on her fingernails. Several men looked her way, but not one of them approached her. The two men who drew her attention enough that she glanced their way actually backed up a step and gave her a wide berth.

"See. Shields up. A man would be risking his life making a move on a woman like that."

"So how do we find out what she's up to?"

"I'd say we follow her, but I don't think we'd get far before she saw us. Our best shot is probably going to be to break into her apartment and see if she's sloppy enough to leave information lying around."

"That seems like a waste of time, doesn't it? I mean, a woman as meticulously groomed as she is, as careful as she is with her spending, giving away nothing about herself, with no friends or family popping up—she's not going to be the type to leave secret files to break my dad out of prison sitting on her kitchen counter."

"No, but she might have a hiding place. If I get into her apartment, I might be able to find it."

"You also might get blown up."

Adam pointed to the copy of Ruby's financial statements. "She has maid service. A woman who lets a maid come in and clean isn't leaving explosives lying about."

"Don't you think that would make it even more likely for her not to keep files at her apartment?"

"Possibly. But if she thinks her hiding spot is good enough, she might risk it."

"Why? Why wouldn't she just live in a dirty apartment?"

"When your life depends on your skills, you constantly test yourself. A maid going through your house every few days is an excellent test."

"I can't say it's how I'd want to live, but I guess it gives us a bit of an edge."

"How's that?"

"Because all I have to do is print up some T-shirts with that maid service logo on them, and we have our way in."

He nodded. "Do you have any surveillance devices handy?"

"Always. I'm not sure how long it will take her to detect them, but I'll break out the best stuff for this job."

"She should be at work for a few more hours. That will give us plenty of time to get there and do what we need to do before she gets home."

"Give me thirty minutes and I'll meet you in the garage."

Adam left and Mira went to work.

Adam was almost to the armory when he saw Gage Dallas turn the corner.

He was nearly as tall as Adam, with short black hair and an angular face. His eyes were a blue so faded, they were almost gray. His clothes were covered in dust and wrinkled enough that he had probably slept in them. The weapons strapped to his body, however, were perfectly clean.

Even after several weeks of working with the man, Adam still had trouble controlling his emotions every time he saw him. Relief, anxiety, joy. Heartache.

After decades of being separated from his little brother, wondering how he was and whether or not he was safe and happy, here Eli was, safe and walking around with another man's name.

Gage nodded in greeting at Adam as he neared. "How's the new partner?"

Adam used every bit of skill he'd ever learned about lying to pretend that Gage was just another colleague, rather than his baby brother. "Fine. A bit rocky at first, but I think she stopped plotting my death."

Gage grunted. "Softie."

"I wouldn't let her hear you say that. She's gotten pretty good in the sparring ring."

Gage grinned with pride, but he said nothing.

"I won't bother to ask you about how your assignment is coming. I know it's all hush-hush."

"Almost done."

"Will you be assigned to help Mira and me when your job is finished?"

Gage shrugged. "Bella's call."

Adam hesitated, but knew he'd regret it if he didn't say something. "I know you don't trust me, and I don't blame you—any of you. But you're one of the few people here who is at least willing to speak to me. I just want you to know how much I appreciate you giving me a chance to earn your trust."

Gage's skin tone darkened just enough to tell Adam he'd crossed a line and made his brother uncomfortable.

"When this job is done, drinks are on me," said Adam.

Gage nodded once in agreement. "Good luck." He walked away.

Adam slipped into the armory and leaned against the door. His heart was beating too hard. Something close to frantic desperation danced just under his skin.

He wanted to tell Gage who he was so badly, he could barely keep the words locked behind his teeth.

Part of him resented the fact that Gage didn't recognize him. He knew they'd just been kids when they'd been separated and that Eli had been two years younger—practically a baby. Still, every time he looked at Gage, he *knew* he was looking at his brother. He saw the genetic connection in the other man's eyes, height, build, and features. He heard it in his voice.

How could Gage not recognize him?

Maybe because Gage was a good and decent man—the kind of man who saw what was inside the hearts of others. And when he looked inside Adam, there was nothing familiar looking back at him.

*   *   *

Mira was shaking by the time she'd bypassed the security system and they'd made it into Ruby's apartment.

Adam shut the door behind them with a soft click. "Plant your surveillance devices while I look around."

"How much time do I have?"

"As little as humanly possible."

She made quick work of identifying the prime areas to target and moved as fast as she dared. She'd gotten three of the bugs planted when she heard keys jangling on the other side of the door.

She raced to the bedroom where Adam was and whispered, "She's here."

He didn't waste time asking her any questions. Instead, he grabbed her arm and shoved her into a small walk-in closet. He pushed her behind the open door and crowded her with his body.

"Close the door," she whispered.

"No. It was open when we came in. Just be quiet. It's probably the maid."

She squeezed back into the dark space as far as she could go. Adam shifted toward her and drew his weapon. With slow, practiced movements, he threaded a silencer onto the barrel.

Mira desperately hoped he wasn't going to need it.

He put his mouth next to her ear. "We'll wait until she starts to vacuum, then slip out."

But as the click of heels sounded on the kitchen floor, Mira realized the truth. That wasn't a maid. It was Ruby Rypan.

A second later, the woman crossed through the bedroom toward the bathroom. Mira could barely see her through the crack in the door, but what she did see made her skin go cold.

Ruby moved with precise, almost robotic motions. Her hair was so perfect it could have been molded plastic, and her skin flawless enough that it must have been airbrushed. None of that was what bothered Mira, though. There was something else—something that tickled the back of her mind, something she hadn't noticed on camera.

But what?

Mira studied her as she tried to let go of the frantic fear quivering in her chest.

Ruby tossed her suit jacket on the bed and slipped off her heels as she walked. She was much shorter now, but still easily as tall as Bella. There was a birthmark on her left calf that looked almost like a child's handprint.

That's when it hit Mira. She knew Ruby. They'd been kids together. She'd been one of the kids her father had taken down to his lab for hours, doing God knew what to her.

She disappeared into the bathroom. Water ran into a tub.

Mira didn't realize she was gripping Adam's shirt in her fist until he turned, gently tugging it free. One look at her face and he frowned in concern.

"What?" he mouthed.

She shook her head. She couldn't talk about this now. Not here.

They waited in silence while the tub filled. Ruby appeared again, this time in a silky black robe. Her hair was down and flowing about her shoulders. Gone were the stockings obscuring the birthmark on her calf—the same one Mira had seen on a scrawny child's leg years ago.

There was no mistaking it. Ruby was one of her father's subjects. And she wanted to free him.

The urge to flee pounded against the soles of her feet. Adam must have sensed her anxiety, because he reached back and stroked her arm in a slow, soothing sweep.

Her pulse slowed. She was able to pull in a full, deep breath. She laced her fingers with his, not even caring that it made her seem weak and afraid.

She needed to reach out to Ruby. To offer the poor woman help. She was a victim of her father's evil, and it was Mira's responsibility to do everything she could to clean up his mess.

Ruby went back into the bathroom. The water stopped running. Splashing sounded as she got into the tub.

Adam tugged on her hand. She followed in his wake, moving as silently as possible. They were out the door and on the elevator in seconds. It was only after the doors shut that Mira let go of the breath she'd been holding.

He cupped her face and tipped it up. "You're okay now. She didn't see us."

All Mira could do was nod. Her whole body was quivering with adrenaline, and it made her wonder what the hell junkies of the stuff saw in it. All it did for her was make her feel like she was going to puke.

His thumbs stroked across her shoulders as they rode down to the first floor. She let her forehead fall against his chest. His heart was beating slow and steady, as if nothing had happened.

She envied him his cool.

He turned as the car reached the ground. His hand casually circled her upper arm, forcing her to walk at a calm pace. When they were finally outside with the cold winter sunshine hitting her skin, she let go of her control and gave in to the single sob that absolutely needed to come out.

"You're okay," said Adam again. "Just keep walking."

She did. His firm hold on her arm made sure of that. He opened her door, settled her in the seat, then went around the car. As soon as he was inside with the door shut, she blurted out, "I know her."

His frown told her he didn't understand her meaning. "Of course you do. We studied her all morning."

"No. I mean I've seen her before. I knew her. When she was a kid."

That, he understood perfectly. "One of your father's subjects?"

She nodded. "I remembered the birthmark. She was about my age, wearing a bright yellow checked skirt. There was dirt on the hem, and it was too short for her, like she'd grown out of it. I remember her going down into the lab with some man. He came back out, but she stayed down there for a long time. When she came up, she was crying."

"What else?"

"This was back when Dad was working out of the basement. There weren't many kids then—just a few. Like Clay."

"Do you know what he did to her?"

"No idea. We can look at the records. They're not complete, but we might be able to figure out which subject she was."

"Ruby Rypan isn't her real name. Her background was too clean for it not to have been a false identity."

"Do you think she knows?" asked Mira.

"Knows what?"

"That the man she's working for now is the one who hurt her when she was a kid."

"The real question is whether or not she's choosing to do any of this. We've seen others acting against their will. She could be doing the same."

Mira hugged herself. "This is all my fault."

"Impossible," said Adam. "Your father's actions are his own."

"Yeah, but if it hadn't been for the success he had experimenting on me, he might not have hurt all those other kids. I'm the reason the Threshold Project went as far as it did."

"That's not true. You can't think like that."

He didn't understand. No one really did. How could they? It wasn't as though everyone grew up with a mad scientist father. "If only I'd known enough then to fudge the results of his tests, all the damage he'd done would have ended with me. I could have saved all those kids if I'd been smart enough."

"How old were you?" he asked.

Mira shrugged. "I don't know. Four? He might have done stuff to me earlier, but four was when I started remembering it."

"You were a baby. You didn't know any better." He pried one of her hands away from her tight hug and warmed it between his palms. "No four-year-old is responsible for the actions of her parents, no matter how smart she might be."

"Logically, I know that. But I wasn't your average four-year-old."

"Because of what he did to you."

"I should have used it against him then."

He gave her hand a squeeze. "There is no possible way your involvement could have made or broken the Threshold Project."

"What makes you so sure?"

"I was born before you. The research had been going on for years by the time you were four. You couldn't have stopped it if you'd tried."

"But I didn't try. Maybe I could have at least slowed it down."

"Stop it. All this second-guessing is doing is making you doubt yourself now. Do you really want him to continue to have such power over you?"

"Hell no."

"Then let it go. Do what you know is right now and destroy everything he's ever worked to create."

He was right. Her father might have made her what she was now, but she was determined to use every bit of brainpower and stamina she had to see that his betrayal ended with her.

She squared her shoulders and looked at him. "Take me back to the office. I want to look at the research and see if I can find out who Ruby really is. And how we can help her."

"She's not the kind of woman we help," said Adam, his voice ringing with the hard edge of steel on steel.

"No?" asked Mira, confused.

"No. Sadly, Ruby Rypan is beyond our help. She's the kind of woman we destroy so that others can survive."

Ruby lounged in her tub long enough to give her visitors time to escape.

It had taken them long enough to find her. She'd been waiting for this for weeks, and the second her silent alarm had been triggered, she knew her patience had paid off.

Adam Brink and Mira Sage were exactly what she'd been hoping for. They no doubt would have bugged her apartment, giving her the perfect way of conveying information to them that she so desperately wanted them to have.

Now all she had to do was set her plan in motion.

Dr. Sage would be free soon, and when he was, he would reward her for her faithful service.

Chapter Seventeen

Sophie spent hours going through videos of the area surrounding the location of her abduction. When she found nothing, she moved on to the area where she'd finally managed her escape.

Lila Mallory, a secretary who worked at the Edge, slipped into the room with a steaming cup of coffee.

The woman was about as interesting as a used brown paper sack. Her drab clothes and plain face were made appealing only by close proximity to her mousy hair and gnawed fingernails. There was a nervous quality to her, as if she were expecting someone to jump out and scare her at any second. Her nose was pink, as if she'd recently been crying, though Sophie doubted that was the case since she'd looked like that for the past several hours.

Every few minutes, Lila very sweetly popped her head into the conference room where Sophie was working, just to see if she needed anything. So far, she'd refused the kind offer, which, apparently, had led Lila to take matters into her own hands.

She set the coffee next to the laptop. "I don't know how you take it, so I brought cream and sugar."

"Thanks."

Lila slipped into the chair next to Sophie's and waited. For what, Sophie wasn't sure, but she wasn't about to ignore the other woman.

She sipped the coffee, covering the grimace over how awful it tasted.

Lila beamed. "Are you having any luck?"

Because it seemed to make her happy, Sophie kept drinking the coffee. "Not really. How did Riley get this footage, anyway?"

"Payton pulled some strings. He's got friends everywhere." She leaned forward and whispered, "He's rich, you know."

"I didn't, but good for him."

Lila just sat there, letting the uncomfortable silence roll on.

"I should probably get back to work here," said Sophie.

"Oh, sorry. I didn't mean to intrude. It's just that everyone around here is gone all the time, and I get a little lonely."

"Not enough work to do?"

"Not really. I usually finish before noon and just hang out the rest of the day."

"Boring."

"Very. But I'll let you go."

Sophie took pity on the woman. "No, it's okay. You can hang out here."

Lila smiled and relaxed in her chair.

Sophie drank more of the vile brew as she queued up the next video. "So what do you know about Riley?"

"He's a great guy. Works really hard. Takes care of his mom. Bella couldn't run this place without him."

Was that a hint of a crush Sophie heard in her voice?

"Is he seeing anyone?"

"Oh," said Lila. "No. He doesn't date anymore."

"Any idea why?"

"Something to do with his ex-girlfriend. Lots of

drama. I didn't hear much, but Bella was ready to shoot someone over the whole thing."

"I met Bella. She seems like the type who's always ready to shoot someone."

"She's not that bad. She took me in when I needed a job."

"And you're very loyal." Sophie stifled a yawn.

"It's easy to be. Everyone here is so glamorous. Did you know they have a whole room here just for evening gowns and tuxedos?"

"Why?"

"They've all got built-in armor and stuff. Pretty cool, huh?"

Sophie didn't know what it was about this woman, but she was practically falling asleep just listening to her. "Yeah. Cool."

"I put one on once. Bella made me do it. She said I needed to dress up once in a while."

"Is that so? Bet that was fun."

"Not really. It was stiff and itchy. And I didn't really have enough boobs to pull it off."

Sophie's head did this slow, lazy spin thing. Clearly, her exhaustion and dehydration were catching up with her.

"You look tired. I'll go now so you can concentrate." Lila picked up the empty coffee cup and slipped out.

Sophie pushed the laptop aside and laid her head down on her hands. She went lights-out in seconds.

Lila cracked the door open and made sure the drugs had taken hold. As soon as she saw Sophie's limp posture, she knew it was time.

She used the cell phone that had been given to her to dial the man who'd been waiting for her signal all morning.

"It's time," she said.

"Location?"

"First-floor conference room. Did she tell you when I can see my baby?"

"She'll be in touch."

"But that wasn't our deal. She said if I did this, I'd get to see him."

"Take it up with the doctor. I've told you all I know."

"But—"

"Listen, lady. If you don't do the job, neither one of us is going to like what the good doctor does to us. Pull the trigger, already."

He was right. She had no choice. "Cameras down on your mark."

"I'm in position. Go."

Lila temporarily deactivated the cameras inside the first floor of the office. "You have two minutes to get her out of the building."

"I'll only need one."

Chapter Eighteen

Riley couldn't concentrate. His mind kept wandering back to Sophie.

The way she looked wearing only his sweatshirt. The way she smiled at him. The way her eyes warmed when talking about sex.

With him.

He read the same paragraph for the tenth time, comprehending none of it.

What he really needed was a couple of hours in the gym to blow off some steam. Too bad there wasn't time for such things. The best he could do was take ten minutes in the john with his fist and his thoughts of a woman he knew better than to touch.

If the idea hadn't felt so wrong, he might have actually given in to the urge.

He pushed away from his desk and went to seek her out. If he couldn't get her off his mind, maybe he could help her with the task of working through hours of video footage that might or might not have caught a glimpse of a face or license plate of the bad guys on tape.

Without a solid lead to follow, there was no way to find and stop the men who were after her.

A repairman passed Riley's office, pushing the sagging remains of one of the gym's battered heavy bags on a cart.

The man smiled, but it was purely social, not quite reaching his eyes. "This thing's seen better days, huh?"

"We had a lot of good hours together. I left more than a bit of skin on that thing over the years."

The repairman pushed the elevator button to take him down to the garage. "Well, the new one's up and ready for a beating whenever you are."

Something wasn't quite right here. "Did Lila sign you out?"

"She was going to walk me out, but she's on the phone. I didn't want to bother her."

Riley's instincts were humming, telling him something about this guy was off. Bella normally didn't allow people to traipse around without an escort—especially not since they'd taken on the new government contract. There was way too much sensitive information floating around to let strangers wander the halls.

"I'll walk you out."

"Thanks," said the repairman, "but you don't need to."

The elevator doors opened.

"I was on my way out anyway," lied Riley.

The man nodded and pushed the cart inside. As it bumped over the threshold, the heavy bag shifted. Riley reached down to steady it.

It was warm and didn't feel at all like it had the thousands of times he'd thrown a punch at it. In fact, it felt . . . bony.

A female moan rose from the bag. He knew that voice, muffled or not.

Sophie.

There was a flash of motion from the left. Riley saw a glimpse of the man's weapon a second before it was too late.

He lunged for the man's arm, slamming it back into the mirrored wall. The glass cracked. The gun went off, blowing a hole in the ceiling of the elevator car.

Riley reacted as he'd been trained to do—with lethal force. He slammed the blade of his hand against the man's throat, hard enough to crush his larynx. The man pounded his fist into the side of Riley's head, ringing his bell. Still the gun stayed pinned up high, where it couldn't hurt Sophie.

There were a couple of wobbly images of the guy in front of him, and both of them were as pissed as hell.

The repairman hadn't yet realized he was dead.

Another hard punch to Riley's temple made his head snap sideways, but he didn't let go of the gun. The guy could beat on him all day long, and that gun was staying right where it was. If he let go, he was as good as dead.

Riley saw the moment the man realized there was no more air for him. His eyes widened and started to water. He clawed at his throat with the hand that had just been busy knocking the hell out of Riley.

He waited, defending himself the best he could from the man's thrashing. As soon as he started kicking—way too close to Sophie's head—Riley gathered enough strength to sweep the other man's legs and ripped the gun free from his grip.

The man toppled. Riley pushed the cart away with his foot. The elevator doors tried to close but kept hitting the cart before bouncing open again.

After a few more seconds, the man quit fighting. He stared up at Riley as he passed out from lack of oxygen. In a few minutes, he'd be dead.

Riley staggered back and wiped the blood from his mouth.

Pounding footsteps drew closer. He drew his weapon.

Payton appeared with Adam only a couple of steps behind him. Both men were armed and ready to fire. As soon as they saw the situation, they reholstered their weapons.

Riley didn't. "Move out of the way, Payton."

"Put the gun away," said Payton.

"Sophie's in the punching bag. Get her out."

"What happened here?" asked Adam, apparently san-
guine about Riley's gun being aimed at his head.

"You sold her out, didn't you?" asked Riley. "You let
that fucker in here to take her."

Adam lifted his hands. "I have no idea what you're
talking about. Put your weapon away and we'll clear up
everything."

Payton ripped the duct tape off the opening in the
heavy bag and pulled Sophie's limp body from where it
had been hidden. Sand spilled out.

"Is she okay?" asked Riley.

"She will be. Come see for yourself," said Payton.

"I'm a little busy."

"Is he dead?" asked Adam, nodding toward the fallen
man.

"Not yet. Give it a minute. Crushed throat."

"I'm going to help him," said Adam, his voice calm
but hard.

"If you think I'm going to let you save your buddy,
you're out of your ever-loving mind."

"He's not my buddy, but he may have useful information. Shoot me or don't, but I'm doing this."

As he spoke, he pulled a penknife from his pocket
and leaned down next to the unconscious man. Less than
ten seconds later, Adam had performed an emergency
tracheotomy, shoving the shaft of a pen in the hole to
give the man room to breathe.

"Hand me the tape?" he asked Payton.

He shifted Sophie's limp weight to one arm, then
ripped the duct tape free the rest of the way.

Adam finished the job by taping the pen in place and
stood.

Riley still hadn't shot him, though he wasn't sure why.
Probably because Bella would have given him hell over it.

"Search him for drugs," ordered Payton. "We need to
find out what he used to dose her."

"Drugs?" Riley's blood temperature lowered a degree or two.

Lila appeared in the crowded elevator doorway and immediately burst into tears. "What happened?"

"I don't know," said Riley as he steadied his aim on Adam, "but I'm sure as hell going to find out."

Adam kept his movements slow and nonthreatening. He didn't for one moment believe that Riley wouldn't shoot him where he stood if he felt the need to do so.

"Lila, go get some cuffs."

She scurried off to obey Riley's command.

Air hissed through the pen in the man's throat.

"I'm not going anywhere," said Adam.

Mira's pretty face appeared in the elevator doorway, and until this very second, he hadn't realized just how worried he'd been about her. Her office was one floor up, not far from the elevator shaft. It would have been nothing for the bullet to have ripped through the walls and hit her.

His whole body relaxed slightly against his will. Normally, he controlled such movements, but when it came to Mira, he had so very little control.

All he wanted to do now was wrap her up in his arms and carry her away from this place. Of course, had he done that, Riley would likely shoot him, thinking he was saving Mira.

Her voice was high with disbelief. "What the hell, Riley? Take that gun off his head."

"He did this. He drugged Sophie just like he did you, only this time he let this bastard do his dirty work and cart her off like so much dirty laundry."

Adam looked right into Mira's eyes. "I did not."

She pulled out her phone, tapped on it a couple of times. "He's not lying."

"How do you know?" asked Riley.

"I track him everywhere he goes. He's been in his office for the past hour."

"You mean his dog tags have been."

"No. All his trackers were in the same place."

"*All* of them?" asked Adam. He knew she kept tabs on him, but until now he hadn't realized just how far her mistrust of him had gone.

"Yes. All of them."

Riley lowered his weapon and went to Sophie's side.

Lila came back, her face wet with tears. In her fist was a pair of zip ties.

Adam used them to bind the unconscious man before searching his clothing. "He doesn't have any drugs on him. Just weapons, keys, and cash."

Sophie groaned.

"It's okay, honey. You're safe," said Riley.

It was a lie, but one Adam understood. What sense was there in distressing a woman who was so drugged she couldn't even keep her eyes open?

"Let's move this show elsewhere," said Payton. "I'm going downstairs to see if our friend has anyone waiting on him."

"I'll come with you," said Adam.

Riley shot him a violent glare. "No. You're staying in this building until I figure out how this went down. Mira, go check the video logs."

She didn't move. Instead, she accessed something on her phone again.

"I'll be fine," said Payton. "I may be old, but I have done this a time or two before."

Adam lifted the unconscious man, making sure his airway was still open. He set him on the cart and pushed him toward the nearest conference room.

Riley was right behind him with Sophie in his arms. Mira and Lila brought up the rear.

The conference room filled up fast. Adam tracked Mira's movements as she entered the space. He wished for a few minutes alone with her to make sure she truly believed that it wasn't he who'd tried to hurt Sophie. He wasn't sure why it should matter so much to him, but it did.

Riley settled in the far corner of the room with Sophie on his lap. She was awake enough now that she was clinging weakly to his neck, which was a good sign.

Lila moved the chairs to make room for the cart along the back wall.

Adam tried to catch Mira's gaze, but she was too busy with her phone to look up at him.

"We need to call an ambulance," said Lila.

"Not until we question him," said Adam.

"But he can't talk—not with that pen in his throat." She started to remove the tape, but Adam stopped her.

"If you take that pen out, he's dead. Leave it alone. When he wakes up—if he does—we'll make him write down what we want to know."

"He needs medical attention," said Lila.

"And he'll get it. As soon as he tells us who sent him." She paled and sagged into a chair.

Mira finally looked up from what she was doing. "Someone definitely let him in. Records show that the garage entrance opened about twenty minutes ago and never closed. Someone must have propped the door open."

"Whose key card was used to open it?" asked Riley.

"It was opened from the inside. No key card needed."

"There are cameras on that door. What did they show?" asked Adam.

"Nothing. They were disabled. Whoever did it knew enough to trick the security systems into thinking that nothing was wrong."

"Adam knows enough to do that," said Riley.

"But I didn't."

"Just about everyone here is smart enough to learn how, and they all have access to the building," said Mira.

"Do you want me to get you a log of who was inside at the time?" asked Lila.

"No, I've got that right here. Looks like there are about a dozen of us."

"We should gather the others," said Lila. "I'll go get them."

"No," said Adam. "Let them think their plan is still in place. Only we know the truth."

Riley stood with Sophie in his arms. "I'm taking Sophie to see Dr. Vaughn."

"I'll tell her you're on the way," said Mira as she sent the text.

Riley glared at Adam. "If I find out this was your doing, I will take you down."

Adam nodded. "I'd expect no less."

Riley left.

Lila leaned over the man's breathing tube. "He's sounding worse. You really need to let me call an ambulance. You can question him after they patch him up."

Adam doubted the man would survive his injuries, no matter what doctors did for him. But as the minutes ticked by, it was getting less and less likely that he would wake at all. "Go ahead, Lila, but have them come in the front doors. We don't want them destroying any evidence by coming in through the garage."

She got up and scurried away, sniffing and wiping her nose as she went.

As soon as the door closed, Mira looked up. "Tell me you didn't drug Sophie."

"I didn't," he said without hesitation.

She got up and crossed the room until she was right in front of him. She grabbed his shirt and pulled. He let her do as she pleased, following her lead.

As soon as he was on eye level with her, she asked again, "Did you drug Sophie?"

"No. I did not."

She stared right into his eyes for a few seconds before nodding. "Okay."

"You believe me?" he asked, keeping all signs of frustration from his voice. He hated it that she still didn't trust him, but he refused to hold it against her.

Mira would have had to be an idiot to trust him under these circumstances, and Mira was no idiot.

"I do. Which means we need to find out who did it."

"Are you sure that the only people inside the building are ours?"

She shook her head. "No. I wish I could say otherwise, but anyone with enough skills to do what was done to trick our security system could easily have found a way in from the outside. They could have been in here for hours—days, even—just waiting until it was time to strike."

"We should consider focusing less on who did it and more on why."

"Sophie is on the List. Riley had me research her."

"Looks like Stynger is still collecting subjects."

"Yes, but this was a risky hit. What makes Sophie so important that Stynger would be willing to take these kinds of risks?"

"Stynger wouldn't have seen it as a risk."

"Why not?" asked Mira. "Surely she's smart enough to know that sending people into the enemy camp is dangerous."

"It would be if she cared about the well-being of those she sent to do her work. But she doesn't. The men she employs are simply tools. If one gets broken, she'll find or make another."

"Are you sure?"

He went to the man and gently turned him onto his side enough to show Mira the surgical scar at the base of his skull—the same kind they'd seen before on Stynger's subjects. "If she cared about what happened to this man, she wouldn't have put a ticking time bomb filled with poison in his head."

Mira sighed. "Once he's stabilized, we'll need to have him transferred to our surgeons so they can remove the implant. Maybe then he'll talk."

"It's too late," said Adam, as he felt for a pulse that wasn't there. "He's already dead."

Lila hated improvising. There was no way to know if that little ball of paper she'd dropped in the man's breathing tube would be big enough to block it, but she hoped so. If not, she'd have to find another way to kill him without raising suspicion.

He knew who she was. If he lived, he'd talk, and Lila couldn't let that happen.

She went through a list of options in her mind as she revved up a new set of tears just in time for the paramedics. She held the door open and showed them to the conference room.

As soon as she heard them say he had no pulse, she scurried off, sobbing. She had too much to do to stand around and pretend to care what happened to a man too stupid to finish his job.

Dr. Stynger's new right-hand man was going to be making contact at any minute, asking for a report. When he did, Lila was going to need to be ready with some options for making this right.

Otherwise, she was as good as the corpse in the conference room. And so was her baby boy.

Chapter Nineteen

Sophie woke up with both arms attached to foreign objects. Her left arm had an IV tube sprouting from it, and her right hand was pinned in place by Riley's strong grip.

He looked like he was praying.

The room had no windows. There was a counter, a sink, and a few plain, laminated cabinets along one wall. Overhead was the kind of drop ceiling often used in offices, but the fluorescent lights were off. A soft glow filtered out from an open door, where she could see a bathroom sink.

He must have realized she was awake. His bowed head lifted. "How are you feeling?"

Her mouth was dry and her head spun a bit, but she managed to push out a few words. He so looked like he needed reassurance. "Okay. What happened?"

Something shifted in his posture. He sat straighter, became more alert. "You don't remember?" His voice was gentle, but his attitude told her that was bad.

"No. Did I hit my head?" No one spot hurt more than any other. She lifted the arm with the IV to feel for lumps, but Riley grabbed that hand, too.

"You were drugged. Dr. Vaughn found no injection sites, so she thought you might have ingested it."

Ingested? *Drugged?*

Sophie's hand tightened around Riley's as a spike of fear sped through her. She searched her memory for something that would explain her current state but came up empty. "The last thing I remember was driving to the office with you."

He stroked her forehead. His voice went low and soothing. "It's okay, honey. Don't worry about it. Doc said you're fine, and that's all that matters."

She felt okay. Groggy, but not sick. A little weak, maybe, but still herself. "Tell me what happened."

He nodded slowly and pulled in a long breath. "I found the man trying to abduct you. I stopped him, but you were unconscious, so I brought you to see Dr. Vaughn."

"Why abduct me?"

"There was no time to ask him." Riley's gaze slid past her to something on the far wall. "He didn't survive."

It was then she knew the truth. "You killed him."

He looked at her once again, and she saw a strange combination of fury and regret in his eyes. "I did."

It wasn't the first time he'd killed to save her, but she was going to make sure that it was the last.

She swung her legs over the side of the bed and sat up, ignoring the flash of dizziness that assaulted her. "Where are my clothes?"

"You're not going anywhere—not until all of that crap is flushed out of your system."

"I'm not staying here."

He surged to his feet, blocking her path to jump down from the bed. "The doc is in charge of how long you stay. And this time, I'm not leaving so you can sneak away."

"Do I look like I'm trying to sneak? If you get out of my way, I'll happily walk out while you watch."

"No. We don't yet know who did this to you. Or why."

"It doesn't take a genius to figure out that he's one of the guys Stynger was paying to get her hands on me. They know where I am now. I have no choice but to leave."

"I can protect you."

"Like you did at the office?" she asked, instantly regretting it as soon as she saw his face fall.

Her words had hurt him.

"Damn it, Riley. I didn't mean that. I'm sorry."

"No. It's fair. I thought the office was safe. I was wrong. I won't make the same mistake again."

"There's no way to stop them. The only chance I have is to run."

He seemed to grow taller. His shoulders squared and his jaw set. He looked right into her eyes and said, "If you run, I'm going with you."

"You can't. You have family to take care of. A job."

"My family will understand my need to see you safe. My job can go fuck itself."

"You wouldn't say that if Bella was standing here."

"If you believe that, then you don't know me at all."

He was completely serious, standing there, ready and willing to leave everything behind just to make sure she was safe.

In that moment, she fell in love with him. All the way.

Sophie swallowed down the swell of emotion, hoping it didn't touch her eyes. "I can't let you give up your life for me."

"Then stay. Let us work on getting you the life you deserve. Your new identity will be ready soon, along with a new job and a safe place you can call home."

It was too good to be true, and Sophie knew from experience that anything that sounded that way was. Still, she couldn't bring herself to leave him just yet. What harm would there be in sticking around for a few more days?

Whether she stayed here and took the new identity or ran off on her own, it was just a matter of time before Stynger's men found her. And if she was going to die, she'd rather her last few days be spent with a man who proved that there were still decent human beings left on the planet.

"Okay," she said. "I'll stay. But not here."

A little smile of victory twitched at the corners of his mouth. "That's fair. I'll help you get dressed and take you home, but only if you promise to stay. Deal?" He held out his hand, waiting for her to shake.

She didn't. Instead, she wrapped her arms around him, reveling in the solid strength of his body. "Deal."

Mira didn't think this day could get any worse until she pulled up the video feed from Ruby Rypan's apartment. It took her some time to figure out that all of her efforts to find out how Sophie's attacker had gotten in were in vain. Whoever had orchestrated the event was either smarter or better equipped than she was. Maybe both.

By the time she'd finished her report on the incident for Bella and fought off the need to hide from her boss's incoming wrath, it was well after quitting time. She fired up the video and settled in to watch.

Nothing happened in fast motion for a while, then Ruby got on the phone. Mira played the recording at normal speed, and what she heard made her want to puke.

Bella's fury was no longer such a big deal.

Mira had no idea what to do with the information, but she knew better than to keep it to herself. Strangely, as she wandered the halls, trying to figure out how to proceed, she found herself standing outside Adam's office door.

Since when did she trust him enough to tell him her secrets? Since when did she feel the need to turn to him in a time of crisis?

There was no time to figure it out before the door opened.

"I hadn't knocked yet. How did you know I was here?"

"I saw a shadow under the door."

"You notice things like that?"

"It's how I stay alive, so yes." He frowned as he looked down at her. "What's wrong?"

"Who says anything is?"

"Your pulse, the reaction of your pupils, the flush in your cheeks, and the slight sheen of tears in your eyes."

She'd never had anyone look at her that closely, and she wasn't sure if she was supposed to be flattered or creeped out that he paid so much attention to detail when it came to her. "Guess you got me."

He stepped back to give her room to enter. "Come in. Tell me what's happened."

His office looked very close to the way it had when he'd moved in. The walls and carpet were gray. The metal desk was sturdy and designed to withstand at least a few rounds of small-caliber gunfire before it crumpled. On its surface was a short stack of folders, one of which was open. Next to it was a tablet computer.

There were no framed photos, no kids' drawings. He didn't even have a paperweight or coffee mug sitting around. Just like in his home, there was nothing here to give away anything about the man who spent his time here.

For some reason, Mira missed that glimpse inside— that little hint as to what made Adam Brink tick.

She sat at the small round table that filled one half of his office. The whiteboard above the table was completely bare, as if he needed no space for planning or reminders.

The office door closed with a small click, and suddenly, Mira became aware of just how alone they were in here.

Amazingly, she felt no fear—only a slight buzz of heightened awareness as Adam closed the distance between them and sat across from her.

He said nothing, just sat there, waiting for her to tell him in her own time. There was no anxiousness about him, no impatience. He appeared to be ready to sit there all night if that's what it took.

Mira folded her hands and gathered her resolve. "I really don't want anyone to know what I'm going to tell you, but the information is too dangerous for me to keep it to myself."

"And you came to me?" Curiosity, but no judgment.

"You're my partner. It seemed like the thing to do."

"I'm honored."

"Don't be. All I'm doing is giving you a burden."

"My shoulders are broad and my arms are strong. I can handle it."

He could, too. Maybe that's why she ended up here, instead of with Payton or one of the others. Adam seemed to be able to deal with anything that came his way, and if someone had to act on the information she was about to give him, better Adam than someone who cared about her.

Mira drew in a bracing breath. "Apparently, I'm a ticking time bomb."

He didn't react. His face was just as smooth and impassive as it had been a second ago. "You're going to need to explain a bit more."

"I was watching the video feed from Ruby's place. I know now why Stynger hasn't come after me the way she has the others on the List."

"I assumed it was because she knew you were too skilled and well armed to be an easy target."

"I wish. More like she doesn't have to bother. I have an expiration date."

"I don't understand."

"My dad, the kind and loving soul that he is, put a clock on me. Guess if I don't hear him utter a specific phrase every few months, I'm programmed to kill myself."

Adam fell silent, but the look of fury on his face was so intense, she swore she could feel the heat of it hit her across the table. "I will not allow that to happen."

"I'm on board with that, but how do you plan to stop it?"

"I'm taking you to see your father tonight. He'll give us this phrase and tell us how to fix you, or I will torture him until he does."

He was completely serious. In fact, so serious, he was already on his feet, moving like he was preparing to go right this minute.

"You can't *make* my father do anything. Believe me — many people have tried."

"Has anyone tried removing parts of his body an inch at a time?"

Mira's stomach heaved at the mental image that created. "No."

"Then we still have some avenues to investigate."

"You can't be serious," she said. "There's no way Payton's going to let you march in and cut my dad to bits."

"I'll be surprised if he doesn't offer to help."

Adam headed toward the door. Mira grabbed his arm. "I didn't tell you this so you'd kill him."

He turned and faced her, looking more than a bit intimidating from his impressive height. "Then why did you?"

"Because I needed someone to keep an eye on me. If I started acting strange, I needed to know that someone would take me out before I could hurt anyone else."

He looked stunned, blinking several times before he could speak. "You came to me because you thought I'd kill you?"

"There's no way to know if I might be programmed to hurt others before I take myself out. I thought you would get that."

"I understand the concept on an intellectual level, but what I don't understand is why you'd come to me."

"You're logical. You do what you think needs to be done, even if it's abhorrent."

"I promised I'd never hurt you again. It's clear to me now how little my word means to you."

"Are you saying I told the wrong person?" she asked,

unsure if she should be pissed or relieved that he refused to agree to kill her.

"I'm saying that the person I am and the person you believe I am are two different people. Now, are you coming with me to see your father, or should I have Payton arrange for you to have the cell next to his for your own protection?"

Chapter Twenty

A dam was furious.

Mira actually thought he would agree to kill her? Did she have no clue how protective he felt toward her? How far he'd go to ensure her safety?

Apparently, their relationship boundaries were a bit unclear to her. Which wasn't entirely her fault, as they weren't completely clear to him, either.

As they rode to meet their armed military escort—courtesy of Payton—Adam forced himself to calm down. Compartmentalize. Shove his feelings in a box where they would wait for him to sort out later.

Mira sat beside him in the backseat, completely silent. Payton drove, glancing back at them in the rearview mirror every few seconds.

"What's up with you two?" he asked.

"Nothing," snapped Mira. "We're doing what you want, so just leave it alone."

Adam refused to stay silent. "Mira is upset because she found out that her father made sure she wouldn't outlive him by long."

Mira punched his leg and shot him a poisoned stare.

"What the hell is that supposed to mean?" asked Payton.

Adam relayed the information to Payton, leaving nothing out.

By the time he was done, Mira was no longer looking at him. "Way to keep a secret, partner."

Payton glanced in the mirror. "That's not the kind of secret anyone should keep, Mira. And you know it."

"She thinks I'll kill her if she starts showing signs of cracking."

"Not if I kill you first," she said under her breath.

"Adam's right. You don't get to keep this kind of thing from us. Now that we know, we can deal with it."

"Oh, I'm going to deal with it, all right. Just put me in a room with Dad and lock the door."

Mira talked big, but Adam doubted she'd be able to follow through. Her heart was far too tender. It was one of the things he admired about her. "You know that won't work. There's no way of knowing if he can hurt you with just a few words—if he can activate some dormant program he imprinted in your mind when you were a kid."

She crossed her arms over her chest and turned away. Her position wasn't enough to hide the way her shoulders trembled or the slight change in her breathing as she fought off a sob.

Adam's heart—such as it was—broke for her. No one as brilliant and sweet as she was should have to suffer the way she did now.

"We're almost there," said Payton. "Take the drugs."

Adam and she had been forced to agree to a certain protocol meant to hide the location of the facility where Dr. Sage and several others were kept. One of the requirements was that they be drugged unconscious so there was no way for them to track where they were going. All electronics stayed behind. They were stripped, dressed in clothes provided for them, and searched for any kind of tracking or surveillance devices.

It didn't make Adam happy, but he knew that cooperation was his only option.

He opened the case and took out the syringe with the smaller dose. "Here," he said as he handed it toward Mira.

She shook her head. "I can't do it. Needles wig me out."

Probably because she'd been subjected to more than her fair share as a child.

"Will you let me?" he asked.

She nodded, pushed up her sleeve, and looked away. Adam carefully disinfected her skin and did the job as fast as he could. She slumped before he finished pushing the plunger.

Rather than shove the rest of the drug into her, he blocked Payton's view with his body enough to hide his hand for a second. He shoved the needle through the seat fabric and wasted the remains of the drug in the cushion.

"Your turn," said Payton.

Adam heard the sound of a helicopter in the distance. Up ahead, he could see the lights of a helo pad surrounded by armed guards. They were out in the middle of nowhere, and the only choice now was to do as he was ordered.

He injected himself.

When he woke, he was lying on a narrow bed. There were three more beds in the room, and one of them had rumpled covers about the same size as Mira.

Two armed men stood outside a steel door with a reinforced glass panel. Payton was with them and saw Adam was awake.

He pushed a button activating an intercom that piped his voice in through the wall. "You good?"

Adam ignored the question. "Where's Mira?"

"We woke her up a while ago."

"Why?"

"I wasn't sure how you'd react to what needed to be done. You've seemed a bit too close to her."

"What, exactly, did you do with her?"

"She's safe. She's on her way to see her father now."

Her father? The man who might be able to order her to kill herself with a single word?

All that rage Adam had boxed away came flying out. He hit the window in front of Payton with his fists, hard enough to shake the glass. "You let her near that bastard without backup?"

"See? This is why I didn't wake you first."

"Let me out of here right now. Someone needs to be with her to ensure her safety."

"I've got men on it. She's as safe as she can be."

"Why are you doing this? I thought you cared for her."

"I do. I also care about all the other people Sage has hurt. The only way to find them is to find his files, find out where all his labs are, and destroy every one of them so that nothing remains but rubble."

"What can Mira possibly do to help you with that?"

"Sage promised to talk to her and only her. He gets what he wants, and we get what we want."

Adam pounded on the door again, converting some of his helpless rage to blunt force. "You can't use her like that."

"It's already done."

"When I get out of here, you and I are going to discuss this further."

Payton shook his head. "When it's over, you'll see I was right. It's the only way."

"If Mira gets hurt—"

"No need for threats. If that girl gets hurt because of my decision, you won't have to lift your trigger finger. I'll do the job myself."

Mira walked down the corridor with one armed guard leading the way and one on her tail. Neither man looked at her as they escorted her to the room where her father was waiting. She wasn't sure if it was their training or if they didn't want to associate more than necessary with the spawn of an evil man.

The guard in front opened a solid metal door for her to enter. She walked into a large room that was equipped with a small table and two chairs. A pitcher of water and a pair of clean glasses sat waiting for use. The chairs faced each other. On the far side of the room was a large mirror that took up half of one wall.

She looked up at the guard. "Where's Dr. Sage?"

"Have a seat, ma'am," was all he said.

Mira did as she was told. The guard shut the door, and she heard the distinct sound of a lock being bolted into place.

Now that she was sitting, she saw two cameras mounted in plain sight. Her guess was there were more than those that she couldn't see.

No light shone in through the window. As she sat there, growing more nervous by the second, she realized what was going to happen next.

The door was going to open. Her father would walk in. Sit down on the far side of the table. She'd be able to see him. Touch him.

He wasn't dead.

Mira sloshed some water into the glass and clutched it in both hands. Trembling rings rippled the surface of the water, giving away just how much this meeting affected her.

She wished Adam were here. As crazy as it sounded, she would have felt better knowing he had her back. He was stronger than her father and just as cunning. He could think like Dad and had a better chance of seeing the blows coming than she did.

When it came to her father, she'd always had a wide blind spot.

She had almost talked herself into asking for Adam to be brought in when the lock moved. The door opened.

And there was her father.

Shock hit her hard enough to rattle the breath in her lungs. She'd known he was alive, but until this moment, she hadn't actually believed it. Even though the man standing there looked nothing like the man she remembered.

His beard had grown out, as had his hair. His usual clean-cut look was replaced by a shaggy, unkempt appearance. The bright orange jumpsuit he wore made him look pallid. It hung on his frame, showing just how much weight he'd lost. A few old bruises colored his face, but the look in his eyes was not one of an old, feeble, conquered man.

He was furious. Determined. Scheming.

Mira's chair screeched as she reeled back from the man who'd tried to ruin her life.

Sage smiled. "Good to see you, dear. You look well."

She tried to cover her dismay with spite. "You don't. You look old. Used up."

"Orange isn't my color."

The guard walked him to the chair across from hers and pushed him down into it. She recognized the soldier as one of the men who'd arrived to clean up on the night her father had shot her. He had a hard, cold edge to him that silently screamed *badass*.

He stayed right next to Sage—well within striking distance.

Slowly, some of Mira's anxiety trickled away. The brittle feeling in her muscles faded, allowing more room for her to pull in oxygen.

"Tell me the phrase," she ordered her father.

He frowned, doing a great job of pretending that he didn't understand. "What phrase?"

"The one that keeps me alive. The one that deactivates whatever fucked-up programming you shoved in my head."

He stared at her, his eyes so like hers it made her want

to claw them out. "You think that kind of information is something I'd give away for nothing?"

Another small part of her died in that instant. She'd thought he'd already hurt her as much as possible, but she'd been wrong. That he would treat her life as a bargaining chip hurt. Bad.

She tried to hide her flinch but wasn't sure she'd pulled it off. The spark of excitement in his eyes told her he'd seen something—smelled blood and wanted more.

"What do you want?" she asked.

"Release, of course, but I'm not stupid enough to think that's possible. I do, however, believe I at least deserve a more comfortable cell in exchange for my cooperation."

"Throw in the location of every one of your labs, and I'll see what I can do."

He eased back in his chair, the perfect image of a man in his element. "I did promise that if you came to see me, I'd tell you the truth. I'm a man of my word—"

Mira snorted. "Fucking liar."

He gave her a paternal frown of disappointment. "Language, Mira. Really. I taught you better."

She gave him a sweet smile. "You tried to teach me a lot of things, like how to inflict pain. How to treat people as disposable objects. How to suffer in silence. Guess you failed on all accounts, you motherfucking asshole. Now tell me, *where are the other labs*?"

He crossed his arms over his chest and looked away.

"Really?" she said. "You're going to try to punish me with the silent treatment? Do I look like I'm four?"

He said nothing.

Mira shrugged. "Fine. Keep your secrets. Whatever time I have left, I'll enjoy every second of it thinking about how you're rotting away in here. Just know that there will be no more visits from me—no more reason for them to stop beating on you to give the bruises time to heal."

Sage paled. She'd hit a mark. Despite his mental cunning and power, he was an old man and had the body of one. Whatever torture they subjected him to, it must have been enough to scare him.

"Don't go," he said. "I'll tell you what you want to know. Just get them to promise not to hurt me anymore."

"I have no authority to make them promise anything. Your only chance is to do the right thing and take away their reason for torturing you. Tell them what they want to know, and they won't have to hurt you anymore."

He looked at the floor. His voice was small. Weak. "There is no phrase."

"What?"

"Whoever told you that I programmed you is wrong. Even if I'd wanted to do it, you were never susceptible to that kind of conditioning. Your mind was always too strong for that. I made sure of it so you couldn't be used against me."

"But you tried."

He looked at her, and for the first time in her life, she saw regret in his eyes. "I did. I'm sorry."

He held out his gnarled hand to her.

How many times had she dreamt of this? How many times had she prayed for her father to turn himself around and do the right thing?

She couldn't count that high. And now, staring into the face of the thing she wanted most, she cracked. Weakened.

Mira put her hand in his.

Sage jerked her out of her chair and across the table. Her chair hit the far wall hard enough to shatter. Her legs flew out, slamming into the guard next to her father. The guard toppled over just as she slammed into her father's chest.

By the time she realized what had happened, she was being held against his body, serving as a human shield. He had some kind of sharp point digging into her throat.

The guard regained his feet and pulled his weapon.

"I will kill her," said Sage.

Whatever hope had sprouted in Mira's chest, it died a swift, painful death. Of course her father had no intention to repent. Of course he would use her to get what he wanted. He always had.

Whatever the guard saw in her father's face made him lower his gun. "There's no way out. This whole place is secure."

"If they want her alive, they'll clear a path."

"Don't listen to him," said Mira. "It's obvious he lacks the ability to tell the truth."

"The truth is I'll kill her if they make me."

She didn't doubt that for a second.

The door opened, revealing several more armed soldiers. Sage shifted her body to cover his own. He inched along the wall toward the door. "Let me pass."

None of the men so much as flinched.

"Shoot him," she said.

"They'll hit you," said the guard to her right.

"I've been shot before. I'll deal. Just pull the trigger."

Another voice boomed from down the hall. "Let him go."

Payton. He'd given that order.

"I will not risk Mira's safety. Let the man pass."

The soldiers cleared a path. They shuffled out into the hall.

"What the hell are you doing, Payton? Tell them to shoot."

Sage tightened his hold and dug the point of his weapon deeper into her skin. Blood trickled along her neck, making her stomach give a queasy flop.

Payton looked past her. "I have snipers on the roof. If you try to take her past the gate, they will fire."

"What's to stop you from shooting me after I let her go?"

"My word."

Sage laughed. "That never used to be worth much."

"It is now. I love Mira like a daughter—something you could never understand. Her life is worth more to me than yours."

"Tell your men to back off. Open the doors. If I see one soldier or one locked door on my way out, Mira will be the one to pay."

"Just like old times, huh, Dad?" she snapped.

"Shut up. The grown-ups are talking."

More blood flowed over her skin—enough to wet the collar of her shirt. She briefly thought about fighting back but couldn't think of a move she could make that wouldn't jab that weapon deeper into her neck. He was poised right above an artery, and she was likely miles away from the nearest hospital.

"Clear the way," ordered Payton. "Let him go."

Mira couldn't let this happen. She couldn't be the reason Sage went free. If he did, he'd hurt more people, and the list of his victims was already too long for her to ever make right. She couldn't allow him to add to the pile of bodies in his wake.

Somehow, somewhere between here and the front gate, she had to find a way to kill her father.

Chapter Twenty-one

As soon as Adam heard the alarm sound, he knew Mira was in trouble.

The guard posted outside his door disappeared. Adam wasted no time making his escape. He pried the plastic light-switch cover from the wall and ripped the switch free from its moorings. It took a few seconds to break off a couple of pieces of electrical wiring. Once the wires were free, he slammed the post of one bed down on them to flatten and harden them.

Lockpicks in hand, he made quick work of unlocking the door before his guard returned.

Finding the commotion was easy; figuring out what had gone wrong was irrelevant. As soon as he saw Sage dragging a bleeding Mira out into the night, all he cared about was getting her back.

Sage was halfway across the open space between the building and the gate. Mira had no coat. Blood oozed from her neck where Sage held what looked to be some kind of improvised weapon made from a spoon. The tip gleamed with her blood, less than an inch from a major artery.

If Sage shoved that sharpened spoon into her throat, she'd bleed out in seconds.

"Steady," Payton ordered the soldiers around him. "Hold your fire."

Adam started toward Mira. He wasn't going to let her father drag her away.

"Stop!" shouted Payton.

Adam ignored him.

There was some commotion behind him. He was vaguely aware of the guards asking if they should go after him. Whatever Payton told them held them at bay.

"I'm not letting you take her," said Adam.

Mira's face was pale, but she seemed solid. Coherent. "Shoot him, Adam."

He didn't have a weapon. He wasn't even wearing his own clothes. The cold air stroked his skin, bleeding away the heat of his fury. "I can't."

Her green gaze hit his with the force of a large-caliber round right in the chest. "I need you to stop him. Whatever it takes."

He understood her message: Don't worry about her. Take out the bad guy. But even though he understood it, he couldn't act on it. Not when she was in such clear danger.

Maybe she didn't realize how close to death she really was—how little her father cared about her safety. After all he'd done to her, she should have known, but children often had superhuman powers of denial when it came to their parents.

"Let them go," called Payton from behind him.

"You can't let him go," said Mira. "Neither can I."

She was going to act. He could see it in the slight change of her posture. She was coiling, preparing to strike.

If she did, she was dead. That weapon would go right through her and Sage would use her bleeding out as a distraction.

"Don't," was all he said, looking right into her eyes. "I've got this."

Mira relaxed. Adam closed the distance.

They were almost to the gate. He could feel the heat of crosshairs against his back from the men aiming at him.

"He'll let her go at the gate," said Payton. "If he doesn't, my men will shoot."

And hit Mira in the process.

The gate was only ten feet away. Adam calculated how long it would take him to do what needed to be done. He checked the ground for obstacles and sped his breathing to oxygenate his blood.

Sage must have seen what Adam was preparing to do, because he shoved Mira toward Adam, forcing him to catch her or let her fall.

He caught her.

By the time he had her flattened on the ground, out of the path of flying bullets, he shouted, "Fire!"

"No!" countered Payton, his voice booming into the night.

No one fired.

Adam shoved himself to his feet and took off at a dead run, hot on Sage's heels.

A motorcycle came out of nowhere. The rider swung past Sage and slowed just enough for him to hop on back.

Adam surged forward, but the bike headed for the trees. Within just a few seconds, it disappeared.

Sage was gone. Not a single shot had been fired.

Something about that was off, but he was too distracted to waste time figuring out what. Mira was on the ground, bleeding, and that was unacceptable.

Soldiers were rushing past Mira by the time Adam reached her. She tried to stand, but he held her down. "Not yet. Let's see to your bleeding first."

He ripped a strip from the bottom of his shirt and folded it into a pad. He pressed the fabric against her wound, being careful not to block the flow of blood to her brain.

"Follow him," ordered Payton. "Plan Delta."

Adam had no idea what Plan Delta was, but boots pounded the ground as men veered off in various directions. In the distance, he heard small engines roar to life. A helicopter's motor started to whine.

"He's gone, isn't he?" asked Mira.

"We'll find him."

"I tried to stop him, but I couldn't figure out how. Every move that Bella taught me would have shoved that knife into my throat."

"You were about to do it anyway, weren't you?" he asked.

"I didn't see any other way."

A medic appeared by her side and checked the wound. "It's not bad, ma'am. A little surgical glue and you'll be good to go."

Mira clutched Adam's hand as the medic worked. It didn't take long to do the job, and the soldier was off again, ready to join the others.

Adam helped her stand, angling her body so she wouldn't see the bloody mess left on the ground. Payton stepped in front of them.

"I'm sorry about that, Mira," he said.

She balled up her fist and slammed it into his face. His head snapped to the side. Blood leaked from his split lip. Mira sagged at the sight of it, forcing Adam to grab her around the waist.

"I deserved that," said Payton, rubbing his jaw.

"You let him go. You could have shot him, but you let him walk out. How could you? You know what he's capable of."

"We'll follow him. See where he goes. Maybe he'll lead us back to one of the labs."

"That was your plan all along, wasn't it?" asked Adam. "You wanted him to escape."

"No, I wanted him to tell Mira where his labs are hidden. This was the backup plan."

Her whole body was shaking now. She'd been through

too much, too fast. He needed to get her somewhere she felt safe.

"You're taking us back now," said Adam. "No drugs this time."

Payton shook his head. "No need. This wasn't our secure facility. We just wanted you to think it was so you would play along."

Mira pushed away from Adam and stepped back. "Can I just say how fucking sick to death I am of being played? I am not a tool that either one of you can use for your own purposes. If either one of you tries to use me again, I'm going to use every single one of my many and talented brain cells to ruin your lives. I might create false warrants for your arrest, or alter your medical records so that you can't get a Band-Aid without a psych hold. I'll bug your houses and cars and follow you everywhere until I have the most embarrassing video footage possible, which I will then post online. I'm not above a little creative editing. And as soon as you think the humiliation and pain is over, that's when I'll really put my mind to fucking up every facet of your existence."

Adam didn't doubt for a second that she would do just as she said.

"You're upset," said Payton. "Come back inside and lie down."

Mira got up in the older man's face and growled. "Where is my gun?"

Adam moved slowly, as he would when approaching a rabid animal. With care, he settled his hand at the small of her back and pitched his voice too low for Payton to hear. "Let me take you home."

She looked up at him, fury and fear evident behind the golden starbursts in her eyes. "Home? I can't go home. Dad is out there. We have to go find him."

"We will," said Payton. "My men are following him."

"Your men let him go once. What's to say they won't do it again?"

"They'll do as ordered, just as they did a few minutes ago. You don't have to like it, Mira, but it's not going to change the way things are."

"I can't believe he's alive. Out there. Free." Tears pooled behind her lashes. "I was supposed to finally be safe."

"You are safe. I'll make sure of it." Adam wrapped his arm around her waist in a show of support. She leaned into him just enough to make him hate the man who'd weakened her to the point that she needed Adam's help.

"No one can promise that. Not while he's still alive."

"Let me worry about Sage," said Payton. "Go home. Get some rest. I'll be in touch."

"Where are we?" asked Adam.

"About a hundred miles outside of Dallas. I'll have a driver take you back."

Adam shook his head. "No. Just give me the keys. I'll take her home myself. You've done enough damage for one night."

Payton stared at him for a long second. "Fine. We'll do it your way. I'll pick up the car tomorrow."

Mira stood up straighter, leaning less of her weight on Adam. He wasn't sure if he liked that she was strengthening or if he liked having her pressed against him more. "I want to stay until you find him."

"No, Adam's right. You need to get some rest. You've been through hell tonight."

"I've been through much worse than this and survived."

Some of which was Adam's doing. That fact was not lost on him.

Never again.

"Go. I'll call you when he's back in custody. There's nothing more you can do here but get in the way."

Before she could argue more, Adam said, "I'll have my cell on. Call the second you know something."

"I will," said Payton. "Cars are that way. I'll see to it you get what you need."

For some reason, Adam was certain that while Payton's words were true, there was still something he was hiding.

Had Adam been alone, he would have pushed for answers. But he wasn't alone, and Mira was in no shape to drive. Strangely, seeing her home safely held more interest for Adam than digging for answers.

But answers would come. Once Mira was safe, Payton's secrets would not be.

Chapter Twenty-two

It took nearly two hours to get home, and Mira fought the urge to cling to Adam's hand the whole time.

Her father was alive. Free. Walking around.

How in the world was she ever going to relax again? How would she ever sleep again?

"Do you want to talk about it?" asked Adam. He reached over and curled his fingers around hers. The heat of his skin surrounded her, giving her something to think about other than the fact that her father was a free man.

Mira shook her head and tightened her grip around his hand. She felt better when she touched him. Safer. It made zero sense that that would be the case, but she was too exhausted, both emotionally and physically, to fight whatever brought her comfort.

"He won't come for you," said Adam. "At least not tonight. He'll be too busy trying to get away to go someplace he thinks we'd look for him."

"I guess that's a blessing, at least. I don't know how I'm going to sleep knowing he's out there." She turned toward him in her seat, watching the play of lights across his angular jaw. "Did you know he put cameras in my home? In my office?"

His finger stroked across the inside of her wrist, magically slowing her rioting pulse. "We'll sweep for bugs when we get you home if you like."

"I do that every day as a matter of habit now. Even when I thought he was dead."

He pulled into her driveway and left the engine running. "You don't have to stay here tonight. We could go somewhere else."

"No. I won't let him run me away from my own home. If I give him that much control, it's like letting him win. I won't do that." She forced herself to get out of the car and go inside.

Between the car and the front door, she caught herself checking the bushes and shadows for signs of her father lurking nearby. Of course he wasn't there, but even knowing he could be was enough to make her feel uneasy and skittish.

The moment they walked through her front door, Adam locked it behind them. Her hand had already grown cold with the lack of his touch, and in that moment, she realized just how close to the edge of crumbling she really was. If she didn't pull herself together, she was going to end up sobbing in a ball in the middle of the floor.

She hadn't felt that way when Adam had held her hand. There was something about his silent support that gave her enough room to lean on him, just a little. Tomorrow she might hate herself for the weakness, but tomorrow was a whole, long, dark night away from now.

Mira gave in to the need for human contact and crushed herself against his body. He didn't hesitate to put his arms around her. In fact, if she hadn't known better, she would have thought he lurched at the chance to hold her.

She buried her face against his chest, breathing in his scent. His hand stroked down her back from her nape to the swell of her butt. Over and over, he petted her, and with each passing touch, more of her tension drained away.

His heartbeat was a steady, calming thrum under her ear. It urged her own chaotic pulse to follow his lead. Each deep, even breath he took rocked her slightly, instilling a sense of lazy peace way down in her core.

She hadn't been held like this in a long time. Maybe it never had been like this. It was both powerful and tranquil, weaving the two together in a way she hadn't known was possible until now.

Mira had no idea how long they stood there. Time was irrelevant. And he didn't seem to be in any kind of hurry to break the connection.

A few days ago, the only interaction she wanted with Adam was with him behind bars. Now she couldn't imagine him not being here, right where he was, solid and strong enough to keep her on her feet.

Finally, when she felt steady enough to move forward and calm enough to think, she lifted her head to thank him for being here.

Before she could open her mouth, the words dissolved and disappeared.

She and Adam were standing close, but she hadn't realized just how intimate it was until his head tilted down to look at her. Their mouths were only a few inches apart, and she couldn't seem to take her eyes off his.

She'd kissed him once before. She knew how warm and pliant his lips were. She even had a hint of how he'd taste.

It wasn't enough.

Her fingers curled over his shoulders. She lifted up onto her toes. He didn't so much as twitch, giving her no sign if she should keep going or back away.

She hesitated—and felt the slightest tightening of his hands at her waist. The motion pulled her forward just enough that she could feel the thick length of his erection against her stomach.

Right or wrong, this man wanted her, and the sheer power of that went to her head. Something inside her snapped. Years of pent-up hormones burst free, and she kissed him with all the enthusiasm of a teenage girl.

For a second, she thought he wasn't going to respond. His lips stayed still beneath hers, warm and soft but immobile. How he could be as aroused as he was and still maintain self-control was beyond her. Even without him kissing her back, she was swiftly getting excited.

She tilted her mouth, hoping to coax him to give her a taste. Her tongue flicked out along the seam of his lips.

In an instant, everything changed.

She felt herself lift from the ground. His big, hot hands cupped her butt, holding her against him so tight she could barely breathe. His mouth opened, and he took control of the kiss, his tongue sweeping inside and bringing with it his unique, intoxicating taste.

A moment later, he lowered her to the couch. She couldn't remember how she got across the room, but every bone in her body had melted just a little, and the horizontal surface at her back was more than welcome.

Adam cupped her face in his hands. His hold was gentle but firm enough that she could feel exactly how he wanted her to move as he kissed her.

Her body heated from the inside out. She floated in a state that was an odd mix of frenetic need and a languid kind of peace. It was just kissing, but it felt like so much more.

She wanted it to *be* more.

Her hands slipped up under the hem of his shirt. Sleek, smooth flesh met her fingers. Hot, hard, yet pliant. Each move he made shifted his muscles, giving her a tantalizing feast for her fingertips. There was so much strength there, yet each touch he gave her was gentle.

He lifted his head. His gray eyes had darkened, leaving behind a single, silvery ring around his pupils. His mouth had reddened, and there was a sheen of moisture along his bottom lip she desperately wanted to lick away.

She leaned toward him to do just that, but he splayed

one hand at the base of her throat and held her in place. For some reason, that simple act of restraint made a naughty surge of heat flare in her belly.

Mira melted beneath him. Her thighs widened, giving his body more space to settle close. The thick ridge of his erection grazed across the seam of her pants, causing it to inflict the most exquisite pressure against her clit.

Her nipples tightened. Her back arched, the move completely involuntary.

Adam gave off the sexiest sound she'd ever heard. It was somewhere between a purr and a growl, and so low she could barely hear it. But she felt it. The sound vibrated through her, quivering in her bones as it passed.

"Kiss me again," she said.

His jaw bulged as he gritted his teeth. She could see him struggling for control, and all she wanted was to strip it away so she could have the real man lurking under the surface.

She rolled her hips toward him—this time the move was anything but accidental. "Kiss me."

His long fingers curled against her skin. His hand was big enough to span both collarbones, and the casual strength he wielded was enough to make any red-blooded girl swoon.

"If I kiss you again, it won't end there."

"I'm okay with that." Was she? A few days ago she wanted to punch him and now she was going to let him sleep with her?

"Are you?" he asked, echoing her thoughts. "Do you really want me inside your body? Moving within you? Coming inside you?"

Just the words made a violent swell of heat sear her from the inside out. "Yes."

"That's not the Mira I know. You're not thinking clearly."

"I don't want to think. I just want to feel."

"And then what? When it's over, will you smile and curl against me while we sleep? Or will you hate me for violating you in a moment of weakness?" He rolled away and stood in a single, smooth motion. "I can't stand the idea of you hating me any more than you already do. I'm sorry."

Before she could gather a coherent thought to argue, he walked into the bathroom and closed the door. The lock clicked into place.

Mira's body ached with unsated need, but as the seconds rolled by, that shimmering heat began to fade. Her instincts receded, and her mind started working again.

She'd almost fucked Adam. Just the thought was too strange to grasp. She'd wanted him more than she could ever remember wanting another man. He'd wanted her, too. That was painfully obvious.

And yet he'd stopped.

She owed him for that. Big-time. And as soon as she could look at him again without wanting to jump his bones, she was going to thank him.

Adam clenched the sink and breathed. Anything more than that was beyond him. He'd used up everything else he had to walk away from Mira and her sweet offering.

He could have been inside her right now, stroking deep, feeling her body clench around him as he found what pleased her.

But at what cost?

The moments of pleasure would end and reality would set in. She'd realize what she'd done and hate him even more.

The fear of that was a far more powerful motivator than any biological need he possessed.

He tried to shove his feelings into a box. Compartmentalization was how he survived. He lived and breathed it, pushing things aside so that he could deal with what was too urgent to ignore. His skills had rarely failed him before, but they did now.

Mira and all of the feelings she aroused in him could not be contained.

There was nothing he could do but suffer through this odd kind of helplessness—no other option than to let his emotions run their course. So he stood in front of the mirror, holding on to the sink like it was the only thing anchoring him to this planet. And breathed.

He didn't know how long he stayed like that, but his body slowly relinquished control back to his mind, and he was once again himself.

His sigh of relief fogged the bathroom mirror. He wiped it away and stared at himself. The features looking back at him were the same as they'd always been, but he felt different. Altered.

Mira's pull on him had changed him somehow, and until he figured out exactly how, he needed to tread lightly.

He left the safety of the bathroom, feeling like he was walking into battle.

She was curled up on the couch, her legs tucked under her, gripping a mug. As soon as she saw him, she went still. Even the tendril of steam curling out from her mug seemed to freeze in place.

Maybe it was just him.

After a moment, she looked down at what she was drinking, depriving him of the power she held within her direct gaze. "Thank you."

"For what?" he asked.

"Getting me away from my father alive. Taking me home so I could breathe again. Not taking me once we got here and making me forever regret it."

Ah. There it was. The important bit saved for last.

Some small part of him had apparently hoped she'd still be ready, willing, and eager for him when he came out. He hadn't realized the fantasy of her acceptance was lurking in him until it died a swift and painful death.

"You're welcome."

"Your control astounds me. I have no idea how you

can stay so calm and cool with bullets flying, mad scientists spewing homicidal threats, and a woman throwing herself at you like some kind of hussy."

"The first one is easy. The second, difficult. The third . . . let's just say that I'm not sure how much more of that kind of control I have left in me."

A little grin kicked up one side of her mouth. "Message received loud and clear: Keep my lips to myself."

"Unless you change your mind about what you want," he said before he could think better of it.

Her grin vanished. Her throat moved as she swallowed. "We're not right for each other. It would be nothing more than a fling."

It could be.

The idea sprouted in his mind, fully grown and beautifully formed. If there was ever a woman he could love, it was Mira. Her spirit called to him. Her body haunted him. Her mind intrigued him. He wasn't sure he was capable of such an emotion as romantic love, but he knew what it was to care for someone so deeply that he would kill for them. It was how he felt about Eli, and why he'd been willing to hurt Mira to reach him.

Now the thought of doing exactly as he'd done before—of trading her for information about his brother—seemed impossible. Revolting.

How could his feelings toward an act so rational have changed in only a short time?

"Are you hungry?" she asked.

He checked in with his stomach. "Yes."

She uncurled her legs and stood. Her bloody clothes were gone. The baggy sweat suit she now wore was an obvious effort at self-defense. He couldn't see a single one of her curves, which was probably a blessing. He still wasn't sure how much control he had over his body, and sweet, sexy, brilliant Mira took up far too much of his attention to fit in one of his convenient mental boxes.

She went into the kitchen, and he trailed after her like a lost puppy. He swore he could smell her skin, even as far away as he forced himself to walk.

Her feet were covered by thin socks that clung to her high arches and dainty toes. His gaze kept straying to them, wondering how something as simple as a human foot could be so mesmerizing. Of course, her hands intrigued him, too, as did her eyes. And her mouth.

Her mouth.

He was getting aroused just thinking about the way it felt against his, so open and eager for his tongue. Her taste had gone to his head, addicting him in seconds. He wasn't sure how he was going to go the rest of his life without more of her mouth.

She laid out everything for turkey sandwiches. "It's not much. Sorry."

He didn't care about the food. None of it would taste like her, so it held no value other than fueling his body. "It's fine."

They sat down to eat, and once again he was struck by how close she was to him. The kitchen was small. The table matched. Her choice of seat had nothing to do with her desire to be within reach of him, and yet he was still acutely aware of just how easy it would have been to reach out and take her into his arms again.

Would she melt like she had before? Would she lose herself in the moment again? And if she did, would he be able to stop?

He knew he wouldn't. He was too weak to resist her again so soon.

Think of something else. Anything else.

"Something bothered me about tonight," he said.

She swallowed her bite. "Most of tonight bothered me."

But not all of it. Her blush spoke to just which part she'd enjoyed.

"Why didn't Payton have his men shoot?"

"He said he needed to know where Dad's labs were. It's hard to get a corpse to talk."

"There were two snipers on the roof. Either one of them could have wounded him nonfatally, but they didn't. It makes me wonder why."

She set down her sandwich. "You think Payton let him slip away?"

"So he could follow him, perhaps."

"Dad would assume he was being followed. He's smart enough to not go anywhere near where we'd want him to lead us."

That much was true. Sage was almost as brilliant as his daughter. "Then why not wound him?"

She shrugged. "Maybe they were worried he'd die. He's not exactly a young man. And he didn't look to be in the best shape, either. He seemed . . . frail. Old."

There was still something wrong about it all—something Adam could feel but not see. "Did he give you the phrase you needed?"

"He said there was no phrase. Said I wasn't programmable. Guess I'm like a VCR that way."

"Then why did Ruby say there was a phrase?"

"Maybe that's what he told her."

"Are you sure he wasn't lying when he told you there wasn't one?" he asked.

She paused for a second, picking at the crust of her wheat bread. "I don't think so. I could be wrong, but I know that he was always pissed that he couldn't force me to do stuff when I was a kid. At least not without threatening to hurt someone else."

"Like Clay."

Her gaze touched his, bounced off. "Yeah. He wasn't the first kid Dad had tortured to get me to cooperate, but he was the last. I hope it stays that way."

Adam's phone rang. "It's Payton."

She frowned. "Calling at two in the morning? Maybe they found Dad."

Adam answered.

Payton said, "Sage escaped. My men lost him. I need to see you and Mira first thing in the morning."

"Why?"

"Just meet me in my office at six."

"She hasn't slept yet."

"Neither have I. Deal." He paused; then his voice grew quiet. "You're with her now, right? She's not alone?"

"That's right."

"Keep it that way, Adam. There's no way to know if Sage will go after her."

"I'd already considered that. I'm on it."

"Good. One less thing for me to worry about, then."

"Anything else?"

"No. Just keep her safe. That's all I need." Payton hung up.

"Well?" Mira asked, her face wide with expectation.

"He got away. Payton wants to see us in four hours."

She slumped in her chair. "He knows something."

"Any idea what?"

"No. And every camera and tracker I plant on him, he finds. I know less about Payton than I do anyone else at the Edge. Except, perhaps, you."

He was not going to touch that comment. It was a toxic time bomb waiting to detonate, and he would not leave her side tonight, no matter how angry she was with him.

"Do you think Payton is on our side?" asked Adam.

"I used to."

"And now?"

"I think he's on the side that does the most to make up for his bad history. Even if that means letting a mad scientist roam free."

Adam filed Payton under suspicious. "What do you want to do?"

"First we meet with Payton to see what he has to say. Then I want to find my father," she said.

"And then?"

Her gaze met his, blazing with violent intent. "We kill him. This time for real. I'll never again believe he's dead unless I do the job myself."

Every minute felt like a year.

Mira lay in her bed, staring at the same pattern of acoustical texturing she'd stared at every night since she'd moved in. It had been only an hour since she'd lain down, but it had felt like a lifetime.

The house was silent. Adam had insisted on staying, and she hadn't fought him over it.

She didn't want to be alone. What if her father came for her?

He was out there somewhere, free to hurt people again. She hadn't realized until now just how much peace his death had given her. Now that she knew he was alive, she kept expecting him to jump out of the closet and come at her with a big honkin' needle.

Another few years passed in silence, and she finally gave up trying to sleep. It wasn't happening tonight. Her brain was running hot, her thoughts whirling at a million miles per hour. Sleep was an act of peace, and no matter how exhausted she was, there wasn't a speck of peace anywhere in her.

She padded across the floor on bare feet, headed for the kitchen and a cup of hot tea. As soon as she entered the living room, she saw Adam peering out the front window, watching the street.

"Did I wake you?" he asked without turning around. He was wearing a pair of running shorts and a white T-shirt that clung to every delicious inch of his torso. It took her a minute to realize that they were clothes her friend Clay had left here, because they'd never looked half as good on him as they did on Adam.

Mira tried not to give away how appealing she found him. "No. I thought you were asleep."

"I'll rest when Sage is dead or behind bars."

"You sound like you hate him."

Adam turned and looked at her. "He made you bleed. That's reason enough to hate anyone."

Okay. Not exactly what she thought he'd say, but it worked for her.

She found herself standing beside him. That hadn't been her aim, but he seemed to have some kind of gravitational pull on her she didn't even notice until it was too late. "Do you ever think about what you'll do when this is all over—when we've shut down all the research, found all the bad guys, and helped everyone we can?"

"No. I think about how to best get through tonight. What tomorrow will bring and how I'll live through that."

"No planning for the future?"

He hesitated, and there was a flicker of . . . something in his expression. It was important.

"What?" she asked. "You thought of something."

"Eli," he said. "I think about having a life with my brother in it again."

"Like cookouts and kids' swim parties?"

That pulled a smile from him, though she had no idea why. "No, more like weapons training and wilderness-survival exercises."

"Wow. You really know how to live, Adam."

"I didn't exactly have a conventional childhood. I've never been to a single cookout in my life."

"How is that even possible? You live in Texas, for heaven's sake."

"I never needed to go to one for a job or training, so I didn't go."

"That's so sad. We really need to get you some more friends."

His thumb swept over her cheek. She wasn't sure if he

brushed a hair away or if he was just touching her, but either way, she felt it streak like lightning all the way down to her toes.

"I don't need friends, Mira."

"Everyone needs friends."

His hand rested on her shoulder. It was an innocent touch, but one that made her think thoughts that were far from platonic.

"Are you offering to fill the vacancy?" he asked.

She wanted to. Maybe it was a side effect of that tight white T-shirt he wore, but she wanted to be his friend in a really bad way. And then some.

"Is that what you want?" Her voice cracked as she asked the question.

"What I want is irrelevant. Always has been."

Her heart broke for him in that moment. It broke for the boy who had been created through science instead of love. It broke for the boy who lost his brother and spent decades searching for him. It broke for the man who thought he meant so little to the world that having a friend was too much to ask.

She pressed her hands flat on his chest. His skin was hot, even through his shirt. It reminded her that she was playing with fire, but she simply didn't care. "It's not irrelevant to me."

He covered both of her hands with one of his, as if worried she'd pull away if he didn't hold her in place. "You only say that because you don't know what I'm thinking."

"Then tell me what you're thinking. Prove me wrong."

"I'm wondering how much of a disaster it would be to lay you down on your bed and kiss you until you come."

Her knees buckled at the potent image. His arm moved too fast for her to see but was around her waist, holding her up before she could crumple.

"Just kiss?" she squeaked.

"I'm almost certain that kissing would be enough to get you where I want you to go."

Just talking was doing a fine job of pushing her right along. Her blood had gone hot, and her insides liquefied. She had to lean against him just to stay upright. "And if it's not?"

"It'll have to be. No condoms. I realized that after I had time to . . . cool down from before." His hand moved to her wrists and pressed inward. The pressure made her inch closer. "But don't worry," he said. "We won't need them. I can be quite creative when I set my mind to a goal."

The noise that came out of her was an incoherent whimper of need.

His grip around her waist tightened. "But all of that still brings us back to the original question: How much of a disaster would it be?"

"Huge," she said.

"Gigantic," he agreed.

Her fingers clenched against his chest. "We're partners."

He nodded, and the move brought his mouth closer to hers. "We have to work together even when we're not partnered."

Her hands inched up over his shoulders and neck until her fingers were buried in his thick, dark hair. "Bella's rules say it's a no-no."

"So do yours, I imagine," he said.

"I'm not sure I care." She pulled on his head to try to get him close enough that she could kiss him.

He didn't budge. "I care. I won't ever betray you again, even if it means spending the rest of the night out in the cold where I can't hear you. Can't smell you. It's the only way I'll be able to keep my hands to myself."

She didn't want that. She liked his hands on her too much. It was a stupid, insane way to feel, but far too powerful for her to deny.

The time for thinking and analyzing was over. All she wanted now was his mouth and his tempting promises of creativity.

Mira pulled on his head again. "Kiss me," she told him.

Adam did.

Chapter Twenty-three

This kiss Adam gave Mira was not like the others. It was fierce, determined. It shimmered with purpose.

His lips moved over hers, hot and soft, with the slightest edge of demand. He kissed like he was on a mission, laying siege, conquering territory.

Mira was cheering for him to be victorious.

Everything he did made her hotter. Each minute change in pressure of his hands on her body made it sing. Every tiny little shift in the angle of his mouth against hers deepened their kiss until there was no more she could give. She reveled in every second, throwing herself into the string of sensations with abandon.

Her fingers curled around silky strands of his hair. She was on her tiptoes, straining to get closer to him. It didn't matter that she was already plastered against him; she wanted to climb him like a tree, wrap her legs around him, and slide back down.

Wide, hot hands eased beneath the hem of her shirt. She'd put on the bulky sweats in an effort to comfort herself. They were way too big and baggy for her to worry about needing a bra. And now that his hands were splayed across her naked back, she realized just how much of a barrier that little strap of fabric could be.

Adam groaned and lifted his mouth. "If I'd had any idea that you were naked under this shirt, I wouldn't have resisted as long as I did."

"I wish I'd told you."

His response was to lift her up and haul her into the bedroom faster than she would have been able to walk. He set her down near the edge of the bed, and a naughty little whim took her by surprise.

She stripped the baggy sweatshirt over her head, baring herself to him.

Adam went still as he stared. He didn't make a move to reach for her, and after a couple of seconds, she was starting to worry that she'd moved too fast.

Then his demeanor changed. A slow, dark look of possession spread across his eyes, and he swallowed visibly. His fingers clenched at his sides as if he were fighting the need to touch. Finally, his gaze lifted from her breasts to her face. "I'm going to put my mouth on every inch of you. By the time I'm done, there won't be a place left on your body that I haven't tasted."

His words sent a thrill streaking through her. She eased onto the edge of the bed, hoping it hid the fact that her knees had given out on her.

She patted the mattress next to her.

Instead of sitting beside her, he knelt on the floor at her feet. He picked up one foot and stripped away her sock, then did the same with the other one. His fingers curled just under the edge of her waistband. "You're not going to need these, either. Give them to me."

She lifted her hips, and he stripped the bulky fabric away, leaving her wearing only a skimpy pair of panties.

The sudden exposure made her cover herself with her hands as best she could.

"What are you doing?" he asked, sounding genuinely perplexed.

"I'm not a skinny, toned, kick-ass chick like the rest of the ladies who work at the Edge."

"Maybe that's why I'm not attracted to any of them," he said, the remark so casual it was almost offhand. "But that doesn't explain why you're trying to hide from me. I thought you wanted this. Did you change your mind?" That last question came out a strangled string of words she could tell were hard for him to utter.

"No," she said quickly. The mere idea of him stopping now was devastating. "I'm just more comfortable in the dark."

His eyes were fixed on hers. "If it's dark, I won't be able to see you. And I really want to see you, Mira."

She didn't know why he would, but if he could look at her with that scorching heat in his eyes, then she could be brave and let him look.

Her body relaxed. Her shoulders inched back down where they belonged. She let her hands fall to her sides. The reward for her bravery was his wicked smile and his deep growl of satisfaction.

A shiver streaked up her body, making her nipples tighten into hard little points. His gaze zeroed in on them, but he didn't make a move in that direction. Instead, he lifted her foot and planted a kiss on the sensitive arch.

Mira shivered again, sagging where she sat. His mouth moved up her ankle, then along her calf, leaving behind a string of hot kisses. By the time he got to her knee, she felt boneless and languid while still tense with anticipation.

His hand splayed across her chest, so close to the swell of her breasts that she ached for him to shift just an inch in either direction. His skin was slightly darker than hers, and just rough enough that she could feel the shape of his palm grazing against her skin.

He exerted the slightest pressure. "Lie back," he said. "This may take a while."

It did. He made a slow, thorough exploration of her body, working his way up as he went. When he'd finally reached the barrier of her panties, she was almost certain he'd strip them away, but instead, he grabbed her hips and deftly flipped her over onto her stomach.

She had no idea how long he spent kissing her, touching her. By the time he made his way back to her panties, she was floating in a hazy, relaxed fog that shimmered with a growing sexual burn.

His hands skimmed over her butt, then pressed harder as they rose over her bare back. He straddled her thighs and began a long, hot trek up her spine with his tongue.

Each fingertip worked magic across her skin. He seemed to know just where to press to make her muscles uncoil, and just where to skim to make her shiver with the need for more.

He seemed to be in no hurry, but with each passing minute, Mira's need grew hotter and hungrier, demanding to be fed.

She squirmed onto her back beneath the cage of his legs. He towered over her. The cords in his neck were taut, disappearing down under that sinfully tight T-shirt. His sharp cheekbones stood out, dark with the flush of his arousal. Sweat dotted his hairline. The proof of how turned on he was strained against the front of his pants, almost too good to be real.

She reached for his erection, needing to feel it — wanting to give back a small fraction of the pleasure he'd been giving her.

Her hand made it only halfway home before he grabbed her wrist and held on tight. "If you touch me, I'll come."

"And that's a bad thing?"

"No, but I'd rather you not have proof of just how much control over me you have."

"You're the one on top, holding me down. I'd say you have plenty of control."

"It's safer that way."

"Why? Afraid you're going to fall in love with me if I

get you off?" she asked, grinning at how ridiculous the idea was.

A trace of fear flickered behind his eyes for a split second, gone so fast she was sure she'd imagined it.

Before she could ask him what she'd seen, his mouth covered hers, in a kiss so blistering hot it burned away all the oxygen in her lungs. Her body struggled to keep up with his demands, igniting faster than she'd thought possible.

Her hips bucked beneath his. She hadn't told them to, but her body was not her own—it was an alien thing that drove her to give Adam all she had.

He broke the kiss only long enough to cover the tip of her breast with his mouth. He drew her in hard and fast, giving her no time to adjust to the intense sensation.

She felt herself grow wetter, dampening the panties she wished she'd shed. With him pinning her down, she couldn't spread her legs or rub herself against him like she craved. All she could do was gasp and buck beneath him while she clung to his head so he wouldn't quit suckling her.

A quivering tension inside her core began a slow, steady climb. He shifted his body lower, freeing one of her legs as she went. One of his hot fingers slipped inside the leg of her panties and glided through her natural lube.

Adam gave off a deep sound of approval as he pressed just the tip of his finger inside her.

That was all it took. Mira's climax took her by surprise, and there wasn't a thing she could do to stop it. She'd gone too long without release, and Adam had been too thorough in his efforts to arouse her.

Her body clenched as she let out a breathless cry. The pulsing pleasure hit her in bursts, each one more intense than the last. As the pressure subsided and hard contractions settled into small, quivering ripples, she went limp.

Adam lifted his head. Her nipple was distended and

bright red from his mouth. His breath fanned out across her, cooling the wetness he'd left behind.

His finger was fully inside her now, and she vaguely remembered him thrusting it deeper as she came. She half expected him to pull out, but he didn't. Instead, he just stared up at her, breathing hard.

"That was what I wanted," he said.

"Then why do you sound like you're disappointed?"

"I'm not ready to leave your body. It feels too good being inside you."

His words made a little aftershock quiver to life around his finger. As she tightened, he groaned. His eyes fluttered shut, and when he opened them again, she knew she was in trouble.

Determination brightened his gray gaze. "I want to make you come again."

Oh, yeah. She was on board for that ride. "What about you?"

"I don't have any condoms."

"I do," she said, suddenly remembering.

"Where?"

"Under the bathroom sink. Brown paper sack."

He withdrew from her body slowly, giving her time to experience every millimeter of his progress. By the time she was empty, she was desperate to have him fill her up again. Only this time with his cock.

Adam came back with the bag in one hand and the condoms and receipt in the other. "Have you had them long?"

"I don't know. There should be an expiration date."

He glanced at the receipt and stopped in his tracks.

"What? Are they expired?" she asked.

His gaze met hers. She couldn't tell what he was thinking, but whatever it was, it was intense. She could see it in his posture and the way he shifted from relaxed to vigilant, as if expecting someone to attack him at any second. "No. You bought them the day we met."

She looked down, embarrassed. "I remember."

"You liked me."

"I wouldn't have agreed to go out with you if I hadn't."

"A lot," he added.

She sighed. "Yeah. I did. It was a silly thing to do, rushing out to buy condoms as if a guy like you would ever want to sleep with a nerdy girl like me. I'm sorry if my enthusiasm offended you."

"It's just the opposite. I've heard the men at work talk about you. Not one of them has been able to gain your attention."

She snorted. "Not one of them is interested."

"That's not true at all. You have no idea how sexy you are."

She snorted again. Louder this time.

"I'm serious. You're an amazing woman. You deserve an amazing man in your bed."

"You were holding your own pretty well a minute ago."

"I had my chance. I made my decision. I hurt you."

"It's in the past. I'm done dwelling on it." Especially if she could dwell on something better, like how much she wanted him to get back in bed with her.

"How do I know? How do I know that you won't regret sleeping with me?"

"You don't. But I know one thing for sure."

"What's that?"

She gave him the sexiest smile her nerdy self had to offer. "You'll regret not sleeping with me more."

Adam was one hundred percent certain that Mira was right. He was already regretting every second he spent out of her bed.

With deliberate care, he shed his clothes. Each piece of fabric that was stripped away made her lips part a bit more, made her green eyes go dark and her lids lower.

The stain in her cheeks flared to life, and he could see her body quiver in anticipation.

He'd never felt so powerful—so wanted—in his entire life.

He rolled a condom in place and settled in the center of the bed with his hands stacked behind his head. His erection thrust out eagerly, but she didn't seem to mind. Once he was settled, he didn't move.

"What are you doing?" she asked.

"Letting you make the next move. That way there will be no question as to what happened between us—not even the slightest chance that I forced myself on you. I won't push you. I won't even try to seduce you. You're wet enough to take me. I made sure of that. Whether or not you do is your choice."

He could see her mind working. It wasn't at all what he wanted, but he held his ground and laced his fingers together a little tighter so he wouldn't reach for her. It would have been too easy for him to toss her down, spread her legs, and drive himself to heaven within her sweet body.

If he did that, he'd never forgive himself. He had to know that this was what she wanted. He couldn't be the guy who seduced her just to get what he wanted before walking away. Not anymore. She deserved better.

"So—what? You think I'm just going to climb on board and take a ride?" she asked.

His cock bobbed in hope. "If that's what you want."

"What if I want you to kiss me?"

"My mouth is yours."

She leaned over him and gave him an experimental kiss. He let her take the lead but gave back everything she offered. By the time she lifted her mouth, he was shaking with the need for more. His hands ached to feel her skin gliding under his palms.

Mira purred and smiled. "That was nice. But what if I want you to kiss me somewhere else?"

His mouth watered. "Whatever you want. I'm game."

She pressed the inside of her wrist against his lips. Adam inhaled her intoxicating scent and went to work kissing every inch of flesh he could reach. All too soon, he was deprived of her skin and arching up as she pulled away.

He clenched his muscles to keep his hands to himself. As the contours of his chest and abdomen tightened, Mira let out a feminine sound of approval and splayed her hands right over his heart.

The organ lurched toward her, pounding double time in an effort to keep enough blood flowing to his brain. His cock was a throbbing reminder of just how little blood he had to work with.

Her fingers trailed along his abs, touching with open curiosity, like she was learning a new path to her favorite vacation spot. Each inch lower she went, he got more excited. His breathing kicked up, and his thighs tightened as if the effort could pull her questing hands down to where he wanted them most at the moment.

She took her time learning his body but never once got as close to his groin as he needed.

Maybe she was teasing him. Getting a little payback for what he'd done to her. Surely, this kind of exquisite torture was evening the score between them in some minute way. He was certainly suffering enough for it to feel like it.

Mira slid those sexy panties from her legs and straddled his stomach. Trimmed dark hair covered her mound, but he could see the telltale proof of her arousal gleaming on her flushed, swollen skin. He could still remember exactly how she felt gliding along his finger—hot, slick, tight. He needed to feel that same tight heat covering his cock, welcoming him in, all soft and accepting.

"Take me," he whispered, stunned at the need grating through in his voice.

She wiggled against him as if settling more comfortably in place. The move made her hot core graze his abdomen. A dark smile made her mouth all the more beautiful. "I thought it was my decision."

"It is."

"Then you can't go ordering me around. I'm still not sure what I'm going to do yet."

Heaven help him, this was a mistake. He'd given the woman a deadly weapon, and now she was using it against him. With glee.

She leaned down, propping herself up on her elbows. Her breasts flattened against his chest, and he swore he could feel her nipples harden as they made contact.

Adam gritted his teeth and held his ground.

Mira traced his bottom lip with the tip of one finger. He flicked his tongue over it and pulled it into his mouth. He used his teeth to hold her captive while he sucked the salt from her skin.

Her eyes fluttered closed and she seemed to soften against him. "Nice, but I have a better use for your mouth."

She shifted her body, and like a glorious, unexpected offering, her nipple was right there, all puckered and ready for his tongue. He arched up just enough to capture the peak in his mouth. His tongue glided over the hardened tip, and she gave up a sexy sound of pleasure.

He was going to make her give him more.

The scraping sound of her fingernails against the pillowcase told him he was on the right track. Just like before, she heated up fast.

He knew if he slid inside her right now, she'd come around him again. Only this time it wouldn't be just his finger. He'd get to feel every one of those divine feminine contractions around his cock.

Just the thought was nearly enough to make him come. He clenched his muscles to stave off the orgasm for a little while longer. But he wasn't going to last long.

Mira's breathing became panting. She pulled her

breast from his mouth. He looked up at her to protest, but words died on his tongue.

She was beautiful. Glorious. Like some kind of ancient goddess, all golden and glowing. Her eyes were as dark as the forest at dusk, and her bottom lip was imprinted with indents from her teeth.

She'd been holding back on him, but one look at her now told him the time for restraint was over.

She reached behind her and gripped his penis in her hand, positioning herself to take him into her body.

Adam once again barely staved off the need to come. Once he slid home, he wasn't sure how long he'd make it.

She aligned their bodies and began taking him.

The heat of her scalded the tip of his cock in the sweetest way. She was tight, but so wet he slid in without hurting her. He knew, because the look on her face was one of intense, exquisite pleasure without the slightest hint of pain.

She rocked against him, completely lost in the act of joining their bodies. He was so enraptured by the sight that he managed to stave off his own need for just a bit longer.

Finally, she stopped and opened her eyes. The woman looking back at him was more sensation than intellect now. He was so used to seeing Mira's mind that he was shocked at the sheer level of sensuality she possessed.

"There," she said. "My choice. All mine."

She hadn't taken all of him yet, but she would. He couldn't imagine any possibility other than having every inch of him buried within her when he finally set himself free.

His voice was strained from his efforts at self-control. "Your decision is made, then. That's good."

"Why's that?"

"Because I'm going to take you now."

"I thought I was taking you."

"You did. Now it's my turn." He freed his hands from

their prison and sat up. The move forced another inch of his erection inside of her.

She moaned and gripped his shoulders. He wrapped his armed around her, cradling her close and pinning her in place. His mouth covered hers, and his tongue thrust inside as his hips surged upward.

One stroke, two. She cried out and tensed around him as her orgasm consumed her. He rode her through it, and by the time she reached the height of her pleasure, he'd worked every inch of his cock inside her soft body.

It was too much for him. The clenching heat of her release, the sweet smell of her body joined with his, the sexy sounds of completion she made into his mouth. He gave in to the needs of his flesh and let his orgasm have him.

The throbbing pressure exploded until he was blinded by it. Little sparkling dots danced in his vision, and his skin seemed electrified. There wasn't enough oxygen in the room to keep his body fed, but he didn't care.

Adam collapsed backward, carrying Mira with him. She covered him—a hot, soft, fragrant blanket. Her body rose with each of his labored breaths, and he felt the need to cling to her just so she didn't go away.

The world finally started spinning again and he found enough air to erase the stars from his eyes. He had no clue how much time had passed, but he was still deep within Mira's body, his cock twitching happily, all snug and cozy in its new home.

Sanity returned, and he realized the potential danger their comfortable position posed. He shifted her just enough to take care of the condom before he pulled her back where she belonged, right against him, and covered her up with the blankets.

His cock wanted to snuggle up again, too, but he ignored it. If he was good, careful, he would have her again. And if that wasn't motivation enough, he had no idea what would be.

After a few minutes, he realized that she was asleep. In his arms. Completely vulnerable and trusting.

That show of trust made something fierce and hot rip through his chest. He'd never felt anything like it before. Had no idea what it was. It hurt and felt good all at the same time.

Adam studied the feeling, wondering if it was something that belonged in its own special box. As he considered it, the idea of shutting it away became irritating. Then impossible. This feeling was his, and he was keeping it.

Just like he was keeping Mira.

The idea hit him out of the blue, but he didn't question it. Didn't need to. He had good instincts and knew when something was utterly and completely right.

Mira was his now. All that was left was convincing her that she wanted to be.

Chapter Twenty-four

It was the middle of the night, but Riley was wide-awake. Sophie had fallen asleep on his couch, her head in his lap. The TV was still on whatever channel it had been on, but the movie they'd been watching was long since over.

Not that he'd spent much time paying attention to whatever was on the screen. His entire focus was on Sophie—the pretty curve of her cheek, the way her strawberry blond hair clung to his shirt, the scattering of freckles he could just barely see beneath the loose collar of her shirt. He remembered just how enticing he'd found those freckles on her shoulders the first night he'd seen her. She'd been wearing a plain white cotton nightgown, and there had been few nights that had passed in which he didn't dream about her wearing it just for him. There should have been nothing sexy about it, but on Sophie, a brown paper bag probably could have turned him on.

An infomercial started up, spewing fake exuberance and excitement over some new gadget that was going to change the world. He didn't care about that, but the increase in volume worried him. Sophie hadn't been sleeping well after her attack, and the last thing he wanted was to wake her.

He muted the TV. She shifted in her sleep, giving off the cutest little sigh. The sound brushed across his nerves, setting every one of them ablaze. His imagination flared to life, tossing him in the midst of a full-on, Technicolor daydream that included a whole lot of sweat, moaning, and naked Sophie skin.

With a force of will, Riley pushed the unhelpful thoughts away. All they were going to do was make his jeans uncomfortable.

Abstinence sucked, but that was nothing new. It still beat the hell out of the guilt he'd suffered every day since his one-night stand with Lucille.

Riley's phone buzzed on the coffee table. Payton's name popped up, and at this hour, the man wouldn't be calling if it weren't important.

"Sage escaped," he said without preamble or social niceties.

Riley stifled his shock and did his best to keep his voice quiet. "Dr. Sage? As in Mira's dad? The guy who died last year?"

"He didn't die. It's a long story and none of your damn business. But this part is: Whoever helped get Sophie's attacker in the building knows who she is and that she was one of Sage's subjects."

"That news is already out. Why do you think she was attacked in the first place?"

"Yes, but with Sage free, there might be more people searching for her."

"How long until her new ID is ready?"

"A day or two. Good covers—the kind that stand up to close scrutiny—are hard to create. It takes time."

"She doesn't have a lot of that, Payton."

"I know. I'm pulling all the strings I can. But there's something else."

"What?"

"I need to know what Sophie remembers about her

time with Sage. Anything she can remember might be important."

"You want me to let you interrogate her? Hell no."

"No. Not me. You. She trusts you. Get her to talk, Riley."

"No way. She's been through enough. Just let it go. We'll find another way."

"We're running out of options. We have a tracker on Sage, but we need to give him bait — a reason to make his move and go to his labs. Once we have that, we're going to need every advantage we can get. What Sophie knows can give us an edge. Make it happen."

"Or what? You'll fire me? Bella would have your ass if you try."

"Bella doesn't scare me nearly as much as Sage does. With him free, there are a lot more people like Sophie in danger. We're giving her a new life. The least she owes us is whatever information is in her head."

"The least she owes you?" he nearly growled. Fury made his grip on the phone tighten. "You're the reason she's in danger at all. You did this. To Sophie, to Mira. Where the hell do you get off making demands?"

Payton's response was even toned, but it held no less power. "I'm doing everything humanly possible and then some to make up for what I did. But I can't undo the damage alone. I need help. It's bad luck and timing that Sophie's the one who can do the helping, but that's the way things work sometimes. It's your job to do what I say. So do it. Understood?"

"I understand that you're an asshole. I like to be a team player and all, but I'm not going to push her. I'll ask her. That's it. You don't get the answers you want? Tough shit."

"Okay, but if you don't get her to talk, I'm afraid I'll have to play hardball."

"Like you weren't doing that already."

"I've been a fluffy puppy up to now. There are more

lives at stake than you know. If I have to turn into the
Big Bad Wolf to save them, then so be it. I suggest you
get Sophie's cooperation so that I don't have to start getting ugly."

"Fine. Whatever," snapped Riley.

"Excellent. I'll wait for your call."

"And, Payton?"

"Yes?"

"Fuck you."

Sophie heard the whole conversation. She'd been drift-
ing in and out of sleep, enjoying the feel of Riley's fingers gliding through her hair and stroking her face. He
thought she was asleep, so she stayed that way, soaking
up his touch and feeling safe for the first time in weeks.

He set the phone down. She could feel tension quivering through his powerful body.

"I don't remember much," she told him. "But I'll tell
you what I can."

He stiffened. "You heard?"

"Yeah. Payton's voice carries."

He pulled in a deep breath. Let it out slowly. After he
was done, his anger seemed back in control, none of it
spilling over into his tone. "You don't have to talk about
it. I'll tell Payton to fuck off and leave you the hell alone."

"You kinda already did that. My guess is it's not going
to change anything." She rolled onto her back so she
could look at him. The feel of his hard thighs under her
head and shoulders comforted her, reminding her that
he could handle any thugs that came her way. For tonight, she was safe.

"I'll tell you what I can. If it can help someone
else . . ."

He touched her face. His big, rough hands landed so
gently, it reminded her of butterfly kisses. "I don't want
you to suffer."

"I'm tough."

He nodded slowly. "Okay. But if you change your mind at any point, that's fine. No pressure."

"It's a deal."

He picked up his phone. "I'm going to record what you say. That way, I won't forget anything, and any little details that I don't think are important won't get missed, even if they are."

"Okay. But do me a favor?" She almost hated herself for her weakness, but she was stretched too thin not to ask for his help. She wouldn't make it through this otherwise, and he needed her to make it through her story. Even the ugly parts.

"Sure."

"Keep touching me?" she asked. "It makes it easier to stay calm, be brave."

He leaned down and kissed her forehead. She wanted his mouth on hers more than she could ever remember wanting anything, but it wasn't to be. He'd already made his position clear: He didn't want her—not in that way. If she didn't accept that, it was only going to cause her pain in the long run.

His hand settled on her cheek. His thumb stroked the skin just beneath her eye. "Ready?"

Sophie nodded.

He started the recording, and she immediately wished it was anyone else hearing her story. She didn't want Riley to know about this part of her life. It was too sad. Too pathetic.

Still, if embarrassing herself was going to save even one other person, she owed it to them to suck it up and deal.

"I don't remember much about the first time I met Dr. Sage. I think I was four at the time, maybe five. Dad said I was going to see the doctor; then some guy came and picked me up. I rode in his car for a long time. I remember being bored, then afraid. I cried and the guy bought me ice cream. Then I went home."

"Do you remember what Sage did to you?"

"No. I don't remember anything that happened, except there was a stain on his white coat. A pen had leaked in his pocket, and it made the shape of a blue squirrel."

"Where were you living at the time?"

"I don't know. It was hot. Sticky. We moved around so much—Dad always trying to outrun some irate bookie."

"Great guy," said Riley, sarcasm heavy in his tone.

"Yeah. A real peach. I think he got a few hundred bucks every time he let the man take me."

"He didn't deserve to be a father."

"Believe me, letting some doctor poke at me wasn't the worst thing that man made me do to earn some quick cash."

As soon as she saw his face darken with anger, she realized her mistake. She never should have opened that door. There was no way she was going to talk about that part of her life—not to a man as good as Riley.

He would never understand.

"I'm sorry. Just forget I said that," she said.

"I wish I could. You can't imagine all the things that are going through my mind right now. It makes me wish he were still alive so I could kill him myself."

"He wasn't worth the time in prison killing him would have cost you. Just let it go. I have."

Riley slid his fingers into her hair and massaged her scalp. She wasn't sure if he did it because he could feel how tense she was or if he was simply trying to offer comfort. All she knew was that it felt good, and on the heels of so many crappy memories, she welcomed whatever good she could find.

"Do you remember any other details that might help us find Sage? Like buildings or roads?"

"No, the place I remember most was isolated. I remember pulling in the first time and wondering where the doctor's office was. All I saw were a couple of cars, and trees and a big, open area. The road was gravel."

"Are you sure?"

"Yeah. I bent down to pretend I was tying my shoe once and grabbed up a handful of rocks. I threw them at the head of the man who had picked me up. While he was cleaning grit out of his eyes, I ran."

"What happened?"

"He caught me. I didn't make it far. He shook me hard enough to rattle my teeth and dragged me right back where he wanted me to go. I was too little to fight."

Riley's fingers clenched against her scalp before he realized what he was doing and relaxed again. "Tell me more about this place. Was it a private airstrip, maybe?"

"No. No aircraft that I saw. We went down in an elevator. The guy with me tried to get me to stop crying by telling me about how we were going on an adventure. He said something about how far down we were going, but all it did was scare me more."

"Underground? That could be useful. Do you remember anything else? Where the elevator was, maybe? How far down you went?"

She'd worked hard to purge all those thoughts from her mind over the years. Even to this day, she couldn't see a person in a white coat coming at her with a needle and not freak out like a crazy woman. Just thinking about it made her start to sweat. Riley's hand kept stroking her head, and his touch was the only thing that kept her from shaking.

"I remember a big metal door."

"Like a garage door?"

"No. More like a cellar. It was flat in the ground, hidden inside a bunch of bushes. I never would have found it without help."

"Was it guarded?"

As soon as he asked the question, she remembered the men in sunglasses. They had big guns and never smiled. For a long time, she'd thought they were robots. "Yeah."

"Did you go anywhere else or just to the underground lab?"

"I went to a house when I was really young. There was a little girl living there. She cried every time I came over."

"Why?"

The memory of pain flooded Sophie. She couldn't scream. Something was in her mouth. There was a man standing over her, hurting her fingers somehow. Her head was strapped to a table, so she couldn't see what he was doing. But the little girl was there, in the room. She was crying and promising to be good.

Sophie bolted upright, nearly hitting Riley in the chin with her skull. She flung back the blanket he'd draped over her and paced to the far side of the room.

She couldn't stay still, not with the memory of the little girl haunting her.

Riley was beside her in a second, his hands moving over her arms as if he was afraid she'd been hurt. "You don't have to say another word. You've helped enough."

What about that little girl? Was she still out there, hoping someone would save her?

"I can do this. Just give me a sec."

She paced around, hugging herself. No matter how fast she went, that memory clung to her.

He watched her, and the sympathy in his eyes made her cringe. She had to find a way to toughen up. Stand tall and hide her fear. It was the only way he'd ever respect her.

And she really wanted Riley's respect. She'd had so little of that in her life, and what he thought about her was far more important than it had been with anyone else she'd ever met.

He was such a good man. If he liked her, then maybe there was something good in her, too. Maybe she wasn't just a street rat from bad blood who stole and conned people so her dad could gamble and piss away other people's money.

She glanced Riley's way. He had one broad shoulder propped against the doorway to his bedroom. He'd given her the space she needed, simply waiting until she got her shit together. He didn't push, didn't try to rush her. He was a monolith of patience and honor.

And she loved him so much it made her chest ache to know there wasn't a single spark of hope that she could ever have him. Not even just for sex.

It would have been nice to pretend that a guy like him could fall for her, if only for as long as it took him to get off. Even a few minutes with a man like him would be potent enough to fuel her fantasies for a long time to come.

A man like him, a nice little house, a couple of kids . . . what she wouldn't give to live a dream like that. She wouldn't be like her parents. She'd stick around, take care of her kids, never let anyone touch them.

She'd kill anyone who tried.

"I've seen that look before," said Riley. "Bella wears it all the time. That's the face of a woman planning violence."

"Nothing to worry about. The people I'm willing to do violence for aren't even born yet. Probably never will be."

"Not born?"

"Yeah. I was just thinking how I'd never be the kind of parent mine were. Mom just ran off. Dad . . . well, you know what a gem he was. I kinda thought I'd get a chance to set everything right with my own kid, but that didn't work out, either."

"You're going to be a great mom one day."

Sophie wasn't so sure. Just how deep did her dysfunction go? Was it in her blood? Would she pass on her damage to her children?

"In all of this research you've uncovered, was there ever any sign that what Sage did to us could be passed on to our kids?"

"None that I've seen. Besides, any kid that got your brains, looks, and strong will would be lucky."

She let out a hollow laugh. "Yeah, right. The daughter of a junkie and an alcoholic gambler. Real top-notch genetics."

"You're not like them."

"How do you know? You've known me for about forty-five seconds. I could be conning you right now—just like I did all those other men."

He pushed away from the door and stalked toward her. "What other men?"

She hadn't meant to tell him. She didn't want him looking at her like that—like he was right now, all skeptical and fierce.

Sophie backed up a step and tripped over the leg of the coffee table. She started to topple backward, but Riley grabbed her arms and held her up.

"What other men?" he asked again.

She lifted her chin and tried not to let him see just how terrified she was. "There were too many to remember."

"What did you do?"

"Whatever it took to get their money."

"Did you ever sleep with them?"

She'd never gone that far, but it had been close. Dad was pushing her to step up her game. He needed more money and told her it was no big deal. Women gave it up all the time for cash. She wasn't any better than any of those women.

But she wanted to be.

"It's none of your business," she said, raising the emotional shields that had kept her safe for years. She couldn't let this man hurt her. He had way too much power over her, and any blow he delivered would be devastating.

Slowly, he let go of her arms. He stepped back and shoved his hands into his pockets. "You're right. It's none of my business who you sleep with or what you had to do to survive. I'm just glad you stayed alive."

"That's it? You think I'm a whore and that's as mad as you're going to get?"

"What did you expect?"

"Screaming. Throwing things. At me."

"That's not the kind of man I am. Besides, I have no right to judge you. I'll admit that the idea of you being used as an ATM machine gets under my skin, but it's only because no one should have to be used like that. You deserve better."

"I got exactly what I deserved—getting abducted, knocked up, and nearly killed by a man I thought would sweep me away from my old life." She shook her head. "I was such an idiot."

"You didn't deserve that, Sophie. It happened and it sucked, but it was something that was done to you, not something you asked for. Not something you earned."

"You can't know that. You have no idea what I've done."

He pressed his hand over her heart, just above her breast. Her body lit up at his touch, and her soul ached for more. "Did you ever hurt anyone for fun?"

"No. But I did hurt people."

"By choice?"

"What do you mean?"

"Did you con anyone your dad didn't make you con?"

"Just you," she admitted.

"Me? I never gave you money."

"No, but I let you think I was good so you'd save my life."

"Honey, I would have saved your life if you'd had horns sprouting from your head. I saw you standing there in that white nightgown, terrified and vulnerable, and I was a goner. No way was I leaving that place without you in tow. It didn't matter who you were or what you'd done. All I knew was that I saw you and knew I had to make you safe."

If she hadn't already loved him, she would have now.

She reached up and kissed him before she could think better of what she was doing.

His response was immediate and powerful. He grabbed her and lifted her feet from the ground while he took her mouth, kissing her hard enough to steal her ability to think.

Her back hit the wall, freeing his hands to slide along the sides of her waist and down onto her hips. She wrapped her legs around his waist to help support her weight and gave in to the demands of his mouth.

So good. So right. He tasted like the sweetest dreams.

Sophie's body heated so fast she thought her skin might ignite. Her nipples tightened against the hard planes of his chest. She needed to feel his skin on hers— as much as she could get.

With a hard tug, she ripped his shirt over his head and bared him to the waist. Delicious.

The second his lips left hers, she felt him stiffen, felt the heat of his skin go cold.

"I can't." His words were a choked strand of sound.

He eased her feet to the floor and backed away like she was on fire. His lips were red, and the slashes of color across his cheeks and forehead matched. His chest expanded and contracted heavily with several deep breaths.

She had to bite her lip to keep from reaching for him, but she did. She didn't have much to claim as her own, but her dignity was still mostly intact. Pawing at a man who refused her would change that.

He ran his hand over his face. "I can't . . . you're too . . . I just can't."

"I'm too what?" she asked, sure she would regret her curiosity. "Whorey? Needy? Broken?"

His gaze met hers, so dark she was completely drawn in. "Too sexy. You make me forget the things I need to remember. Important things. Vital things."

She wasn't buying it. He was just letting her off easy. Man and woman alone together in a house with lots of tension and danger around? It was a potent hormonal stew. He might have been turned on by her, but he was smart enough to know she wasn't a keeper.

No matter how much she wanted to be.

"I understand," she said. "Won't happen again."

She went into his bedroom—the one he'd let her claim as her own—and closed the door. She was about thirty seconds from tears, and she didn't want a witness to her waterworks.

Tomorrow she'd leave. Either go to her new life, or get another bodyguard, or just take her chances alone. The longer she stayed with Riley, the harder she'd fall for him, and she was smart enough to know that if she fell any harder, she wouldn't survive the landing.

Chapter Twenty-five

Payton was waiting in his office when Adam and Mira arrived that morning. His hair and clothes were in perfect order, as usual, but Mira had never seen him looking so tired. Haggard.

He looked ancient.

"Have a seat," he said as they walked in.

"I'm not sure why I even showed up," said Mira. "You've been lying to me for weeks. Doubt that's stopping now."

"You showed up because you want your father back in custody as much as I do."

"Actually, I was happier with him dead."

"If it makes you feel any better, he detested every second of his stay."

"It's something," she said. "Not enough for me to forget you lied to me, but something."

Payton's face sagged a bit more. "I did what was necessary. I hope you'll come to see that one day."

"Whatever. Let's just get this over with. Bella sent a new assignment to me and Adam. I can't waste all day listening to you not apologize for being a flaming asshole."

"We know where your father is. Generally."

"What?" she asked, rising from her chair. "Why the hell aren't we out there getting him?"

"It's not that simple."

"Where is he?" asked Adam. His tone was casual, but his posture was anything but. Mira could feel some kind of intense vibe shivering out of him.

Payton shook his head. "Not yet. I tell you that, and you're out of here before I finish the sentence."

"Then say what you want us to hear. Fast."

"Sage was badly wounded when we captured him last year. We sewed him up, but not before surgically implanting him with a tracking device. I don't think he's aware it's there."

"You mean you've been able to find him all this time?" bellowed Mira.

Adam grabbed her hand and urged her back into her seat.

Payton's gaze zeroed in on the contact, and his eyes narrowed. "Nice the two of you are getting along so well."

"Fuck off, Payton," said Mira. "You've got sixty seconds before I start figuring out how to track him down myself."

"You can't. The tracker isn't activated. We didn't want his people to sweep for bugs and detect the signal, so it's deactivated until we send a signal."

"And then what?"

"We move in. Take him down."

"What the hell are you waiting on?" asked Mira.

Again, Adam calmed her down by stroking her palm. His touch had the desired effect, and she could actually feel her blood pressure drop.

"We need to find his labs. I'm almost certain that that's where he'll head, but not until he's sure he's lost us."

"How long are you calculating that will take?" asked Adam.

"I can guess. I was hoping Mira might do a better job at it."

"Guessing?" she asked. "What makes you think I can do any better?"

"He's your father. You know him better than anyone alive."

"Only because he's killed everyone else who ever loved him."

"Still, it puts you in the valuable position of helping us determine when to strike."

"Now is good," she said.

"You know better. Just think about it—think about what could be gained from having access to his current lab. All the data, all the lives we can save before he can ruin them."

"You're sure he's still doing research?" she asked.

"I am. A team of forensic accountants traced some off-shore money to him. We followed the trail and it led back to a group that's also been contributing to accounts we think are linked to Dr. Stynger. That's not a coincidence."

Mira slumped back in her chair. This was all supposed to be over. The experiments, the terror and pain—it was all supposed to have ended last year with her father's death.

"What do you want me to do?"

"He needs a reason to go back to his lab. I need you to find one."

The muscles in Adam's forearm shifted as he gripped the chair. She had no idea what had made him tense, but she had bigger worries.

"Like what?"

"You know him. You lived in a home with one of his labs. What made him scurry off, unable to stay away from his work?"

"A new subject—a new toy to destroy—but there's no way in hell we're giving him someone to play with."

"Agreed," said Payton. "What else?"

"He's fiercely competitive. If he thinks that someone else is about to surpass him, that might get him to act."

Payton nodded. "Someone like Stynger?"

"Yes. He hates her. His professional jealousy is definitely a big lever we could use. But how? We know less about her than we do my dad."

"We could make something up," suggested Payton.

"It won't work," said Adam. "He has spies at her facilities. He'll detect a lie and he's smart enough to figure out why we would."

"We can't raise his suspicion. One body scan or X-ray would reveal the tracker and give away our only advantage."

"There is one other thing he wants," said Mira, trying hard not to sound as terrified as she was.

"What?"

"Me."

"No," said Adam.

"It could work," said Payton. "We'd have to be careful, but—"

"No," said Adam again, and this time the word carried a sledgehammer's worth of force. "It's not an option. We've been looking for his location for months. If even the slightest thing goes wrong and Mira is taken, we may lose her, too."

"It's not my idea of a good time, either, but it could work," she said. "I can go in armed. Get my own tracking device installed."

Payton shook his head. "It's too dangerous. Even if things went perfectly, we already know that your father isn't beyond shedding your blood."

"Or taking her life," said Adam. "But there is another option. I could go in."

"No," said Payton. "He saw the way you reacted to Mira being taken hostage. There's no way he'd ever believe you would cooperate."

"So where does that leave us?" asked Mira. "We can't just wait for him to relax enough to go back to his work. That could take weeks. He can do way too much damage in that time and it gives him too much of an opportunity to find the tracking device."

"There is someone else," said Payton. "Someone skilled enough to be at minimal risk. Someone Sage would kill to get his hands on."

"Who?" asked Mira.

"Gage."

Adam exploded from his chair, sending it toppling backward. "No!"

Payton held up his hands. "Whoa. Easy. I know you two are partners, but it's a logical choice."

"It's not a choice at all."

"Think about it. Gage can handle himself in a bad situation. He was one of the few subjects from a lab we shut down early. Sage has been itching to get his hands on the research that came out of that facility for years. If he thinks he's got a shot at getting Gage in his lab, he might just take it."

Mira looked from Payton to Adam. There was something going on here—more than what it appeared. "Gage was one of the kids on the List?"

Payton nodded. "He was one of the first ones I found. I got him trained, set him up with a job, made sure he was on the straight and narrow. He doesn't remember anything that was done to him, but he knows it was. We've talked about it recently."

"I had no idea," said Mira. "I've worked with him for years and didn't even suspect."

"That's because he's quiet," said Adam. "Keeps to himself."

"That's true. I doubt I've heard him utter more than a dozen words in a day before."

"We're not using him as bait." Adam gave Payton a hard stare.

"He's right," said Mira. "I'm not going to volunteer people for my dad to torture. We'll find another way to drive him to his current lab."

Adam righted his chair. "You said you had a general idea of where Sage was."

"We're turning on his tracking device at random intervals for short bursts of time so he doesn't get too far away. The last two contacts we made indicated he was moving north."

"Where?" she asked.

"You don't need to know."

Mira stared at Payton across the desk. "You know I could find him if I put my mind to it."

"Please don't. This is bigger than your own personal vendetta."

How long could she sit back and wait? How long could she let that monster wander around, planning out his next move? He was smart. He had people to do his bidding and apparently an income stream to pay them. "If we don't move soon, he could go underground. Even the best trackers are going to have trouble with that. And once he's settled, he may not come out for years."

"We could use Ruby," said Adam. "If she's not with him, then she could lead us to him."

That was right. They still had bugs in Ruby's place. "Or she might say something that could tell us where he's headed." Mira used her phone to access the cameras in Ruby's apartment. "She's not home, but I'll set up an alarm to alert us if there's any movement or sound at her place."

"You do that," said Payton. "I'm going to work another angle. Let me know if you learn anything useful."

"Will you do the same?" asked Adam. "Or is this a one-way street?"

"I want him found as much as either of you. Possibly more. I won't do anything that will get in the way of that."

"That wasn't an answer," said Mira.

Payton crossed his arms over his chest. "It's the only one you're going to get."

*   *   *

"I'm not sitting around waiting for Dad to do something horrible," said Mira as they followed the hallways to her office.

"Of course you're not. Neither am I."

"So what are we going to do?"

She unlocked her office door. He held it open for her and followed her inside.

The cold hum of this room was something he would forever associate with Mira. Beneath the scent of plastic and electrical components, he swore he could smell her in the air here. Every time he came in, his senses perked up and his shoulders relaxed. It made him wonder what his chances were that she'd let him set up his desk in the corner, so he could be close to her.

"Do you really think you can find the signal they're using to track your father?" he asked.

"I know I can. It's just a matter of how long it takes and how many laws I have to break to make it happen."

"Okay. You do that. I'm going to begin working on another angle."

"What angle?"

"The less you know, the better."

"I don't like the way that sounds."

Adam leaned down and kissed her the way he'd been dying to do since they'd stepped foot into the office. Something about the forbidden called to him, making him want her even more than he had only an hour ago.

He hadn't thought that possible.

When he pulled away, her eyes were glazed, and the sweetest flush colored her cheeks. "What was I saying?"

"How anxious you were to start breaking some laws to find Sage."

"Oh, right. That."

"I'll be back to pick you up for lunch."

The smile she gave him was so pretty it weakened his knees. He realized in that moment that of all the people he'd encountered in his life, she was the most dangerous.

She had the power to tear his world apart if she chose, and she didn't even know it.

He hoped she never would.

Somewhere in the part of his mind he kept boxed away, the idea of never swirled. It was such a long time, and yet every second of it was filled with thoughts of Mira. He'd never had a romantic relationship before. He'd dated. Had sex. But it was almost always as part of a job or a plan to angle himself better in his search for his brother.

This desire to be with a woman? It was completely new to him. Completely strange and terrifying.

What if she changed her mind? What if she walked away and never came back? It happened all the time.

An odd, jangling panic built at the base of his skull. "You will be here when I come back, won't you?"

"Will you kiss me like that again?" she asked.

"Twice."

"Then, hell yeah. I'll be here."

Adam waited until she sat down and started working. Once her fingers started flying across the keyboard, he was finally able to inch away.

He'd never been needy before. Or clingy. He'd never felt the desire to be close to someone the way he felt with Mira. And this time, there was no obligation involved. He wanted to be near her simply because he wanted to know she was safe and happy. He wanted to be close enough to touch her.

He forced himself to leave and shut the door behind him. He'd made a few contacts in his work gathering test subjects for Stynger. With any luck at all, one of them would still take his call.

As soon as that happened, they'd have the bait they needed to take Sage down for good.

Chapter Twenty-six

Payton looked up as Sophie Devane walked through his open office door. He rose to greet her, wondering if she recognized him.

She'd seen him once in Sage's home. It had been after one of her treatments, and she'd been barely coherent, but he remembered exactly how she'd stared at him, silently begging for help.

That night had been the first time he'd had a twinge of conscience about what he was doing. He knew that Sage's treatments weren't fun for the kids, but he'd still believed that they'd thank him for it when they were older and realized how much stronger and smarter they were.

How wrong he'd been.

"Lila said you were on your way to see me. I thought you were supposed to be with Riley," he said.

"I was. Snuck out his bedroom window. He still thinks I'm at his place."

"Why are you here?"

"Riley said that I might be able to help—that something I'd seen or heard might lead you to Sage."

"He sent me the recording you made. I'm sure it will be helpful."

"It's not enough."

"I don't understand."

"I heard your conversation with Riley. I heard that you need to give Sage a reason to leave his hiding place and go to wherever it is he does his evil deeds." She pulled in a deep breath and squared her shoulders. "I'm that reason."

Payton slipped past her and shut his door so no one would overhear them. "I think you're mistaken."

"I'm not. I spent enough hours being tortured by that man to know how his mind works. I heard the fights that he and that lady doctor—Stynger—had. She already tried to get her hands on me twice. If Dr. Sage finds out about that, he'll want me. He won't let her get to me first."

He turned her words over in his mind, looking at them from various angles. As hard as he tried, he couldn't find a single hole in her logic. "What are you telling me?"

"If you want to draw someone out of hiding, you need juicy bait. Well, I'm standing right here."

"You're offering to let us use you? Do you have any idea how dangerous that is?"

"Actually, I do. It's probably just about as dangerous as trying to live a normal life when evil scientists are after me to use me as some kind of lab rat."

"Your new identity is almost ready. All that's left is finding you a secure place to live. Tomorrow, you can walk away a free woman."

"If you believe that, then you're an idiot. I've conned enough people to know that hiding is only a temporary solution. They'll find me. I've changed my name before. Moved. They always find me."

"A real identity—one that can stand up to scrutiny— is quite different from taking on an alias."

"Doesn't matter. They've got the time, manpower, and money to do whatever they want. Until every last one of them is dead or behind bars, I'll never be safe."

"If you do this, you could be killed."

"I'm tired of looking over my shoulder all the time. I'm tired of not having a life. I want to settle down and have a family. How in the world can I have a child if I have to spend my life on the run?"

"You'll never have a child if you die."

She shrugged. "I'm not an idiot. I realize this is a big risk, but if your team is there, I'll be okay."

"What does Riley say?"

"You don't have to ask to know that. Neither do I. That's why I crawled out of his window and stole his car to come here and talk to you in person."

Sophie was exactly what they needed to force Sage into action. One leaked rumor that Stynger was after her and his professional jealousy would flare to life. A few well-placed calls, a staged accident, and Sage would be on his way to his lab by dawn.

Payton looked at her, waiting until he was sure he had her undivided attention. "You have to be sure. If I set this plan in motion, there will be no stopping it—nowhere for you to hide. Once Sage learns of your whereabouts and that Stynger wants you, he won't rest until he's got you."

"I know."

He had to be graphic—had to be sure she understood what she was doing. "He'll put you through God knows what kind of tests. He'll drug you, hurt you. He may even kill you just to autopsy your brain. Are you really sure that you want to sign up for that kind of risk?"

"I don't, but it's the only way to take him out. Isn't it?"

"I could have killed him a hundred different times, but unless we take down his work and all of the people doing it, another one just like him will pop up and take his place. This is about destroying his life's work and making sure that every scrap of research is burned to ash."

"And this Stynger chick? What about her?"

"We're working to do the same thing to her. But right

now, Sage is the one on the ropes. We actually have a hope of digging up his work from the roots and annihilating it."

"Then sign me up. I'm all about annihilation when it comes to that man."

Payton nodded. "Do you want to tell Riley, or shall I?"

"Let me," she said. "He might hit you if he thinks you talked me into it."

"It's no less than I deserve."

"Yeah, well, we've all done shitty things. Seems to me it's time I started making up for some of mine."

Sophie left his office. Her steps were a little lighter, her head a little higher.

Payton knew in that instant that he was doing the right thing. That feeling of undoing past wrongs—it was more important to him than breathing. Maybe Sophie felt the same way.

She should have been afraid—and maybe she was—but she was facing her demons on her own terms.

He respected her for that. More important, she would respect herself. After all the pain he'd caused, it was the best gift he could give her.

Payton texted Riley to have him come in to the office. However this mission went, Payton knew that Riley would be on it. Period. There was no sense in trying to change that man's mind once it was made up. Besides, with Riley on the team, Sophie's chances of survival were much, much higher.

One of Mira's alarms went off, dragging her attention away from her efforts to access Payton's personal files.

She was expecting the alarm to be an indication of activity in Ruby's apartment, but instead found it was one of the triggers Mira had set up on Adam's phone weeks ago.

Confused, she squinted at the name and number displayed. She didn't recognize it, but her computer did. A few keystrokes later, the database pulled up the rest of the information attached to that phone number.

It was one flagged as being part of Stynger's network of goons.

Adam was calling Stynger? Why would he do that?

Unless he was a traitor.

Her heart chilled, and a wave of pain sloshed through her insides, freezing them over. For a long second, she couldn't think, couldn't breathe.

Adam had fooled her. He'd fooled her so completely that she'd slept with him.

The shock and pain melted in the face of her growing fury. How dare he? Seducing her once was bad enough, but this time . . . she was taking him down.

Mira used his trackers to locate him in his office. He had the nerve to make that call from inside the building, as if they were all so stupid they'd never even bother to keep tabs on him.

She slammed out of her office and down to the floor below, where he worked. Her weapon was in her hand, though she had no recollection of putting it there. Not that it mattered. The man deserved whatever he got for what he'd done.

She'd slept with a traitor. The mere thought made her sick.

She didn't bother to knock—just barged in through his office door and watched as he hung up the phone.

His smile of greeting faded as he saw how pissed she was.

"Why were you calling her? Getting ready to sell me out to the highest bidder again?"

He looked at the phone sitting on his desk, then back at her. Understanding dawned on his face. "You think I betrayed you?"

"Seems to be your habit."

"You're jumping to conclusions. If you give me a minute, I can explain."

It was a trick. He was an excellent liar, and she so desperately wanted there to be a logical explanation.

She didn't want him to be a bad guy—not when she felt about him the way she did.

"I'm listening. But you keep your hands where I can see them."

He pressed them flat against his desktop. "I was searching for bait."

She blinked, unable to make sense of his words. "What?"

"We needed someone to entice your father back to his lab. I still have the number of the people who used to send me out to find subjects for Dr. Stynger. I thought one of them would be able to help me find someone suitable to play bait."

"Suitable?"

"A murderer was my first choice. There are three convicted killers in prison right now who were victims of the Threshold Project—men so loathsome they make me look like an angel. I just found out where they are. I thought Payton might be able to pull some strings to get one of them released into his custody."

Now the pieces were clicking into place. As they did, her gun sagged in her grip. "You weren't turning on us?"

He stood and moved around his desk toward her. "I know you track all my calls. I know you probably listen to every word I say. Why in the world would I use a company phone inside of this office if I were planning to turn on you?"

"Because you think you could get away with it?"

He wrapped his hands around hers, angling the weapon toward the floor before easing it from her fingers. He set it on the desk behind him.

Mira probably should have fought him but didn't. She so desperately wanted him to be telling the truth. She wanted him to be worthy of the way she was starting to feel toward him—scary, deep feelings that would ruin her life if she let them bloom and he betrayed her again.

"I'm not trying to get away with anything." He wrapped his arm around her waist and pulled her against him. "I have exactly what I want. I'm not going to do anything to ruin that."

He smelled so damn good, she couldn't think straight. Every one of her brain cells were dancing around, celebrating his touch.

"What you want?" she asked, sounding breathless and vapid.

"You can check my phone logs. Listen to whatever recordings you make of me every day. You'll see I'm telling the truth."

"How do you know I record your calls?"

"Because you are a brilliant woman who has every reason not to trust me. I'd expect no less."

She was brilliant, but hearing him say it made a little warm spot in her chest flare to life. She tried to resist being sucked in by it—knowing that his praise had been designed to make her feel that way—but she couldn't seem to stop herself from reveling in his compliment.

His eyes were such a pretty shade of gray. They were normally pale, almost silvery, but when he touched her, they always shifted to a deep, richer slate. A man couldn't fake that response, not even one as skilled as Adam.

Could he?

"The next time you want to make alarming calls, you should at least warn me first."

A slow smile smoothed out the harsh angles of his cheekbones. "And miss you running down here to stop me and my nefarious ways, all armed and fierce? I don't think so. You're positively stunning like that."

"And that part where I was ready to shoot you in the foot didn't bother you?"

"Once you found out I didn't deserve it, you would have felt so guilty, you'd have nursed me back to health. Absolutely worth the pain."

"You underestimate my queasiness and overestimate my capacity for guilt."

"I don't think so. Everything you've done all year has been in an effort to erase your father's bad deeds. None of them were your fault, but you've still worked yourself into exhaustion trying to undo the damage he did."

"That's different."

"How?"

"If not for me, he never would have hurt those kids. I always resisted Dad's efforts to get me to cooperate, so he'd bring in some kid, let me play with them long enough to get attached, then hurt them until I did what he wanted. If not for me, none of those kids would have been tortured."

His big hand splayed across her back, stroking her in a slow, soothing sweep. "Those were the acts of a deranged mind, not of an innocent child victimized by her own father."

She looked away, unwilling to share her pain with him. "That's easy to say. Much, much harder to believe. I keep thinking that if I help enough of the people he hurt, it will tip the scales. Maybe then I can sleep at night."

He tipped her chin up, forcing her to look at him. "Then that's what we'll do. Once we find him and put a stop to any future pain he might cause, we'll gather every record in his lab and make it our life's work to restore balance."

Our life's work.

That he would tie them together in that way shocked her. It was almost as if he was saying that the two of them had some kind of life together.

But they didn't. Not really. Sure, they could work together and even sleep together, but in the end, he'd move on. Or she would. There was too much bad history between them for any other outcome.

"I can tell by your silence that I've overstepped my

bounds," he said. "But I don't care." He walked her backward until she was against the office door. "I don't want to make you uncomfortable, but you keep looking at me like I'm some kind of passing phase you'll outgrow in a day or two. But I'm not. I spent my entire adult life searching for my brother. I never slowed or faltered, and I never let anything get in my way, no matter how appealing or attractive a diversion it might have been."

Just the idea of that kind of potent force of will and undivided attention from him made Mira shiver. "And you found him."

"I did. And do you know what?" he asked.

She was almost afraid to say, "What?"

"I find I miss the quest. The challenge. Or I did until I met you."

"So the quest to find my dad has taken the place of the one to find your brother?"

He leaned into her just enough that she could feel his bulk, his power. The act sent a delicious thrill racing through her. It pooled in her knees, liquefying them until his weight was the only thing keeping her upright.

"No," he said. "Your father has nothing to do with what I want now."

"I don't understand."

Sexual hunger blazed in his eyes. His growing erection pressed against her, and she could feel every hard inch of it along her abdomen.

The idea that she could turn him on made her melt. No other man had ever responded to her the way Adam did. No other man had ever gone to her head the same way, either.

He lowered his head, his gaze on her mouth. "I know. But you will."

Chapter Twenty-seven

Adam craved this woman. The fact that Mira didn't even realize the power she held over him made her that much more intoxicating.

He kissed her because there was no other choice. He knew it was bad form to allow physical displays of affection in the workplace, but he simply didn't care. He wasn't letting a single chance to possess this woman pass him by.

She responded fast, softening against his body as his tongue swept in to claim her mouth. She offered up sweet noises of desire and clung to his head as if worried he might disappear.

Adam wasn't going anywhere.

He'd been thinking about this all morning—wishing he could find some reason to draw her away from work long enough to taste her again. And here they were, still at work, breaking who knew how many rules.

Still, he didn't care.

He reached past her and locked the door. There were no windows in his office—no way for anyone to see what he was about to do to her unless they had a key.

Adam lifted her up and inched toward his desk until her bottom was perched on the edge. He kept little clutter on his work surface and was glad of his tendency toward tidiness more now than he'd ever been before. Just a single sweep of his arm, and the desk was clear.

He laid her back, kissing her cheek and neck as he moved down. The buttons on her shirt were barely an obstacle. He was careful not to tear any of them free and ruin the shirt she had to wear all day, but that was as far as his restraint went.

Each inch of flesh he bared was more alluring than the last. He kissed his way along her collarbones, then down over the swell of her breasts. The lace of her bra's cups tickled his tongue as he slid it just beneath the edge.

Her nipples clenched hard enough that he could see them standing up beneath the fabric of her bra. The pink satin taunted him and turned him on all at the same time.

He layered hot, open-mouthed kisses across her ribs as he worked the clasp of her bra open. As soon as the cool office air hit her nipples, she gasped and arched up off the desk.

"We shouldn't be doing this," she said.

"Don't care." His words were mere grunts of sound, but she must have understood. She settled back down and gripped his hair in her fists as he worked his way back up to one of her breasts.

Once his mouth closed over her nipple, her grip tightened against his scalp. She sucked in a breath and it came out as a slow, sexy moan of pleasure.

His hands skimmed along her ribs, reveling in her curves. She was so soft and rounded in all the right spots—just perfect for the long span of his fingers. He could have spent all day touching her and still wouldn't have been satisfied that he'd memorized every swell and hollow her body had to offer.

Her hands left his hair and went to work on the button of his slacks. She had them open, his cock in her grip, before he had time to decide just how far he was going to let this go. Once her fingers were around him, he knew that the choice was no longer in his hands. It was definitely in hers.

He was going to take her, right here on his desk.

"Tell me you were smart enough to grab one of those condoms from my place," she said.

"I grabbed two."

"You are possibly the most brilliant man on the planet." She worked her fist over him, using a touch so light it made him grit his teeth against the need to beg for more. "Gimme one."

Adam did, and she had him covered in the space of a few seconds.

He should have slowed down but couldn't seem to find the brakes. His body was flying high and fast—the way he always did when he was with Mira. He couldn't seem to think about anything but getting inside of her. Right now.

She was one step ahead of him.

She stopped stroking him just long enough to unfasten her slacks and push them down. Pinned beneath him on the desk, she couldn't push them far. There was no room for her to spread her legs the way they were trapped by the fabric, so he flipped her onto her stomach.

The urge to shove into her loomed large behind him, chanting at him to rush. Take her. Claim her.

Not yet. He wanted this to be good for her. He knew that once it was done, he'd want more, and if he screwed this up and hurt her because she wasn't ready, he'd never forgive himself.

His usual patience had disappeared, but it reemerged just long enough to drive him to his knees. The scent of her arousal pulled him in. The first taste of her went to his head. Sweet, womanly need on his tongue.

She was already silky and wet, but he didn't pull away. He kissed her, thrusting his tongue deep to gather more of her addictive taste.

Her hips undulated. He pinned her in place, forcing

her to hold still while he feasted on her. The sounds she gave him were nothing short of beautiful, telling him wordlessly just what she liked and what she loved. The volume of her cries grew until she was loud enough that someone might be able to hear her on the other side of the door.

He didn't care. No man in his right mind would interrupt that kind of noise. There was no mistaking it for anything other than pure, consuming pleasure.

The office went silent. She sucked in a big breath and held it. Her body began to shudder with her climax, and he knew he needed to feel it around his cock.

With one smooth motion, he rose to his feet and drove his erection into her trembling body. As soon as he did, she exploded around him, gripping the edge of the desk until her knuckles turned white.

Adam couldn't hold still. He followed her body's demands, moving in time with the pulses of her orgasm. The act seemed to draw it out in an endless string of breathless cries and trembling contractions around his cock.

She was panting now, sweating, her body gleaming from the grip of her orgasm. A gentleman would have given her a minute to recover, but Adam was feeling like anything but a gentle man. He needed to leave an impression on her—make it impossible for her to forget that her body was his.

He covered her and pinned her wrists against the desk. He could feel her pulse pounding beneath her skin, feel her lungs working to refuel her blood.

He'd done that to her. He'd made her explode. She had no choice but to let him do it again.

Adam moved heavily against her, driving himself deep on every stroke. He could feel the force of it shake her body, but she didn't complain. If anything, he felt her pulse start to speed again, saw her skin flush with a new batch of heat.

He felt primal, fierce. The cool intellect that had been his constant companion disappeared, leaving behind the animal lurking beneath.

He bared his teeth and set them against the curve of her shoulder. Her pussy clenched in response and grew hotter and slicker around him. The gentle flutterings that served as the prequel to her release rippled across his cock, and he knew she was once again going to give him what he needed.

"Adam." His name fell from her lips, somewhere between a plea and an order. He didn't know what she wanted him to do, but it hardly mattered. His body was moving on instinct now, driving him fast and hard toward a powerful climax.

Her hips arched back toward him. He changed the angle of his penetration to pin her down again, holding her where he needed her to be.

That was what sent her over the edge. He heard it in her voice and the sharply cut off cry that stalled as she held her breath.

Adam let go of his control and came. He poured himself into her, letting his pleasure consume his world. Mira was at the center of it, a bright, burning star that singed him all the way to his bones.

By the time the last spurts of his release were squeezed from his cock by her body, he was breathless and weak. His grip on her wrists failed, and it was all he could do to hold himself up so he didn't crush her.

His lungs bellowed as he gathered his strength. The sweat from his forehead mingled with that glistening along her spine. When he was finally able to lift his head, he saw the teeth marks he'd left on her glowing in bright red detail.

He opened his mouth over the mark and used his tongue to rub away the sting. Mira groaned in approval and went limp beneath him.

Once again, he wanted to stay inside the warm, snug

confines of her body, but the risk of the condom leaking was an ever-present worry nagging him. "One of these days, I want to get my naked cock inside you and stay there for about a week."

He saw her cheek lift with a smile. "That would make going to work interesting. Besides, that's not exactly the kind of thing casual sex partners do—not if they're smart."

Casual sex partners? Was that how she saw him?

Of course it was. Why would she think of him as anything else?

And why the hell would that label made him angry?

He had no idea, but he was certainly feeling something like anger. He did his best to hide it as he moved away from her and went to work righting his clothing.

She hadn't gathered the strength to move yet, and the sight of her naked body draped over his desk was going to be with him for a long, long time. Every time he sat down to work, he knew that this was the image he'd see in his mind—Mira's sweetly rounded ass, the teeth marks he'd left on her shoulder, and her dark pink pussy lips all flushed and shiny from his mouth and cock.

He'd just had her, and still his erection wouldn't fade.

He zipped his slacks closed over it, then moved to help Mira cover herself. It was the only way he wasn't going to need that last condom, which was burning a hole in his pocket.

The waistband of her pants was in his grip. He tugged it up but stalled out before the pink curve of her bottom was covered.

Just one more taste. He needed it like his next dose of oxygen.

He lowered his head to kiss her pussy one more time, but before he could, she grabbed her pants from him and slid them all the way on.

Another hot flash of anger ignited beneath his skin. He didn't like being deprived of her taste and of the sexy sounds she gave him when he kissed and licked her just the way she liked it.

She stood as she fastened her pants. Her breasts were bare. Full, flushed with arousal, and stained with pink where he'd suckled her a little too hard. As tall as he was, he had no trouble seeing the teeth marks he'd left on the delicate skin between neck and shoulder.

Those weren't fading anytime soon, and all he could think about was the fact that any man who saw them would know she was taken.

He liked that thought—the idea of claiming Mira as his own.

Casual sex partners.

Like hell. That wasn't enough for him. When it came to Mira, he wasn't sure that anything would be enough. Even everything.

That thought scared the hell out of him.

Commitment, marriage, children . . . those were things that other people had. Not Adam.

It was better to accept the casual nature of their relationship—let her see him as nothing more than a distraction. When their time together came to an end, he would find a box where he could lock his memories of her away for safekeeping.

So far, none of his compartmentalization tricks had worked with her—there wasn't a box strong enough to contain the power she had over him. But that would change. Someday. It had to. He couldn't imagine spending the rest of his life feeling as unsettled and out of control as he did now.

"What in the world is going on in your head?" she asked.

He stroked her face and fought the urge to let his hand stray lower. "Nothing important."

She leaned up and locked her arms around his neck. The move pressed her naked breasts against his chest, which in turn made his heart try to beat through his ribs in an effort to reach her.

"You're a complex man," she said.

"Hardly. Like all men, there are only a few things I truly want." And she was most of them.

She grinned and kissed his mouth, moving away far too soon. "Well, after that, what I truly want is another hour with you naked, but it's not going to happen. We both have to work."

She started to pull away, but he held her against him so she couldn't. He lowered his head and kissed her the way he needed, with plenty of leisurely exploration. When he lifted his head, her eyes had a soft, dreamy look that told him he could take her again and she wouldn't resist, despite the work that awaited them.

Instead of taking advantage, he decided to be satisfied with the knowledge that he could do that to her anytime he wanted.

Mira didn't know it yet, but she was his. And despite his efforts to hold himself apart and stay detached, he was hers, too.

Adam's phone vibrated on the floor where it had landed earlier. He picked it up. "Yes?"

Payton answered. "Sage is on the move. Find Mira and get up here. Now."

Riley paced like a caged animal, waiting for Sophie to return.

She'd stolen his car. Snuck out. Gone to see Payton for some mysterious reason the man wouldn't admit.

She'd left him.

She was a free woman, a grown adult, perfectly capable of making her own decisions and going wherever the hell she wanted. He had no claim to her at all.

And that pissed him off.

She slipped through the back door and locked it behind her. One look at his face and she stopped in her tracks. "You know."

"Yeah. Kinda hard not to notice my car missing."

"I thought you were working and wouldn't see."

He hadn't for a while, much to his everlasting shame. He'd been so worried about people trying to break in that he'd never once thought she might try to break out. "How did you get past the security system?"

"Magnet from your shaving case closure."

"You shouldn't even know how to do that."

"A girl's gotta do what a girl's gotta do." She held out her hand with his keys in it. "I'm sorry if I scared you."

"If? *If* you scared me? Good Lord, woman, you took ten years off my life. If not for Payton's call telling me you were fine, it would have been twenty. What were you thinking? You could have been seen. Followed." His voice had gotten louder through his tirade, and with each increase in decibels, her shoulders rose a notch.

"You talked to Payton? He said he was going to let me tell you."

"Tell me what?"

She shifted her position so that there was a solid length of kitchen countertop between them. "I volunteered to help."

The words all made sense, but he still could find no meaning in them. "Help who?"

"You guys."

"I don't understand."

"Stynger wants me."

"Which is why you can't go running off alone whenever you feel like it."

She ignored his scolding. "Sage wants what Stynger wants."

"So? That just means that there are two bad guys out there who are after you. All the more reason to *stay the hell home*."

Her voice was calm, but small. "This isn't my home."

He wanted it to be. That thought hit him upside the head, rocking him down to his boots. It took him a second before he gathered himself enough to form a coherent sentence. "It's your home for as long as you need it."

She glanced down at his crappy vinyl flooring. He could afford better, but it had just never mattered to him. Taking care of his mom had always been his top priority.

Her floor was nice. That had to count for something.

The urge to take Sophie to see his mom flared to life. Maybe if she saw how he took care of his family, she wouldn't be so quick to take off whenever she felt like it. Maybe if she knew that his priorities were straight, she could trust him.

He really wanted her to trust him and see him as a good provider. Why, he wasn't sure, but the desire was there, so big it distracted him from moving on with any other thought but how he could get Sophie out to his mom's place.

Sophie and his mom would love each other. He was sure of it. Just thinking about it made some of his anger start to dissolve.

"Thank you," said Sophie. "That's really sweet. But I need to do this."

"Do what?"

"You and Payton talked about needing bait to drive Sage to his lab."

He stared at her, unable to fathom what she could possibly mean.

She lifted her gaze to his, and her green eyes were bright with determination. "I'm that bait."

It took him a second for the words to sink in. He simply couldn't put them in any kind of context that made sense. She wasn't talking about fishing. She was talking about Sage. And his labs. There was no possible world in which her life would intersect any of that.

Unless she actually thought she was going to put her life in danger.

He rounded the counter and took her by the arms.

Understanding was setting in now, and while he could not even imagine a scenario where he would let her risk herself, she apparently thought it was an option.

"You think you're going to put yourself in harm's way so that Sage will abduct you and take you to his labs?"

"I don't think I am," she said. "I am."

"No fucking way." He normally would have never used that kind of language in front of a lady, but she had to understand how serious this was.

"You don't make decisions for me, Riley."

"But Payton does?"

"This wasn't his decision. It was mine. I went to him of my own free will and offered to help."

"Tell me he turned you down."

"He realized that it was the best way. The only way."

"No. There've got to be other options."

"Name one."

"Easy. We wait until someone more suitable comes along to be our bait."

"Who? And how long will that take?"

"Doesn't matter."

"It does to me. I need this to be over, and the only way that can happen is if Sage is dead and his work dies with him."

"Stynger was the one who sent goons after you."

"Yes. And she'll be next."

"So—what? You're just going to dangle yourself out there until someone takes a big ol' bite out of you?"

"It wasn't *my* plan to use bait. And I didn't hear you arguing about whether or not it would work when you were on the phone with Payton."

"Your hearing is way too good for my peace of mind."

She pulled in a long breath. He did his best not to notice how it thrust her breasts out at him, like a soft, curvy invitation to touch. "This isn't about you, Riley. I need to feel safe."

He needed that, too, but even more, he needed to be the one who made her feel that way. "Then stay with me. Move in. I'll make sure no one hurts you."

"You know that won't work. Eventually, the bad guys will find me here, and then you won't be safe, either. We have to take them out."

"You're not trained for this kind of job."

"I survived having a miscarriage in the Colombian jungle while dodging bullets and running from madmen. I'm not exactly fragile."

"But I was there to keep you safe. If Sage takes you, I can't come along."

"But you won't be far behind. Will you?" Her shoulders curved inward, making her look vulnerable and fragile.

He couldn't stand this. He had to make her see reason. "I'd never leave you when you needed me. But please. Don't terrify me like this."

"There's nothing for you to worry about. I'll be fine. And if I'm not, it's okay. No hard feelings."

He nearly sputtered in outrage. "*No hard feelings?* What the hell does that mean?"

"You don't have to understand it. All you have to do is accept it."

Time to pull out the big guns. "I forbid you from doing this."

She smiled and patted his cheek. "You're sweet. But you're not my husband, and even if you were, you still wouldn't get to forbid me from doing anything."

"I could tie you to my bed and convince you to stay."

Her eyes darkened at that. "Nice try, but you already told me you're abstinent."

"What if I change my mind?"

"Thanks, but no thanks. I want you, but not like that." Her hand covered his heart. "I'm doing this, Riley. You can come along and help, or stay back and worry. Your choice."

"Oh, I'm going to help, but I'm still going to worry like hell."

"Like I said, you're sweet." She covered his mouth, giving him a slow, leisurely kiss. By the time she lifted her head, he was panting against the need to pin her to the wall and fuck her.

Abstinence sucked.

It seemed to take her just as long as him to gather her wits. She clung to him, her body shaking. Or maybe it was his. He had no idea anymore. All he knew was that this woman went to his head and did crazy things to it.

"Let's forget all of this," he said. "Leave the danger behind. Fly to Aruba or something."

"What about all the people here you love? Your co-workers, your mom?"

He hadn't thought that far ahead. "I'll figure it out."

"And what will we do with ourselves? Lounge around all day, not having sex?"

"No, we'd get married. And have lots of sex."

"We have to get married to have sex?"

He gave a stiff nod. "Yeah. We do."

"Why?"

"I was always the responsible one. Followed the rules. Tried to do the right thing. Always respected women. Then I met Lucille. She didn't want anything serious, just a one-night stand. I'd never done that before, and I thought, *Why the hell not?* Everyone does it." He took a deep breath. Then another. "I accidentally got her pregnant. We were careful. Used condoms. But one broke. I had to take off for an overseas assignment before I knew about the baby. She'd thought I'd abandoned her, because I didn't call back for weeks. She didn't see herself being a single mom."

"She got an abortion," Sophie guessed.

"Yeah. I didn't even have a chance to talk to her about it, and even if I had, it wouldn't have mattered. She wouldn't have changed her mind. She did what she thought was right. I don't hold it against her—I know she was scared and freaked-out—but I won't let it happen again. As a man, the only control I have is to keep my dick in my pants, so that's what I'll do. Until I marry."

"So you think you can control a woman if she's your wife?"

He snorted. "Hell no. I could never marry a woman who was that spineless. But any woman I'd want to marry would be ready for kids, just in case one came along by accident."

Her expression softened. "You think I'm that kind of woman? You don't even know me."

"Bullshit. I saw the love you had for the baby you lost. I've seen you in the worst possible situations. That's the kind of thing that strips away all the masks and glitter, leaving behind only what's real. I've seen you like that— the real you—and let me tell you, Sophie Devane, I loved what I saw."

Did he just use the L-word? The look on her face said he had.

Funny thing was, he actually meant it.

Suspicion crept in around the edges, hardening the sweet curve of her mouth. "You don't mean that."

"I do. Marry me. Run away with me. We'll leave right now and hit Vegas on our way out of the country."

She started shaking again, and this time he was certain it wasn't just him. "You're a responsible man. If you drop everything and run away, you're going to end up resenting me."

She hadn't said no. That was the only part of her response that really registered in his mind. He'd asked her to marry him and she hadn't said no.

Then again, she hadn't said yes, either.

"Let's go," he urged. "My bag is already packed. We'll buy you whatever you need along the way."

Her lip trembled. The longer she didn't say no, the more he wanted her to say yes.

After what felt like forever, she finally said, "You need time to think about what this means. If you really feel that way, then you'll still feel that way after Sage goes down."

Something in the general vicinity of his heart crumpled. "So that's a no, then."

She swallowed several times. "I won't leave with you now. I won't . . . marry you now. But once we finish this job, you should ask me again. If you still think you should."

He wasn't sure he'd have the guts. Her rejection had hurt too much for him to volunteer to get stomped on again.

"You're right," he said, pretending that his heart was still intact. "This was all too soon. I was just trying to save you from making a terrible mistake."

She swallowed again and nodded slowly. "So was I."

Chapter Twenty-eight

Mira's hands were shaking when she entered Payton's office. She didn't know if it was because of the mind-blowing orgasms Adam had given her or because she dreaded what Payton might have to say.

"We found what we needed," said Payton the second Adam closed the door behind them.

"What's that?" she asked.

"Sophie has volunteered to force Sage to his lab."

"She has no training," said Adam. "We can't send a lamb to the slaughter like that."

"He's right," said Mira. "I want my dad taken down more than anyone, but not at the risk of Sophie's life. What if we don't track him down in time? What if he vanishes right along with her?"

"The decision is made. I've already put plans in motion. Gage is on his way to pick her up now."

"Gage?" asked Adam. "I thought he was on assignment."

"He was. Now he's on this assignment."

Adam shifted in an uncharacteristic show of anxiety. He almost seemed more upset about Gage's involvement than he did Sophie's.

Mira studied him as she asked Payton, "What's the plan?"

"Gage will pick Sophie up at Riley's to take her to start her new life. They're stopping at a safe house not far out of town, where she will wait for her transport to arrive."

"You let all the details leak," guessed Adam.

"It's already done. Sage's men should be on their way."

"What about Stynger's men?"

"Gage will be nearby. He'll deal with them if they show up first."

"I need to go help him," said Adam. "I'm his partner."

For some reason, that comment stung a little. She'd begun to think of herself as Adam's partner, and she didn't like it that someone else was taking her place. Though there were certain things Adam would do with Mira that he wouldn't do with Gage.

"You're not his partner on this assignment. He can handle himself. I've made sure he's wearing plenty of body armor and is stocked with enough weapons to hold off a small army."

Mira tensed, picturing poor Sophie caught in the middle of a firefight. "What about Sophie?"

"She'll be locked away in an underground safe room. Sage's men will have to work to find her. Just so it looks authentic."

"What can we do to help?" asked Adam.

"Sage won't be with the team who goes after Sophie. He may or may not be headed to his lab, but I need eyes on him."

Adam nodded. "You want me to close in?"

"Us," said Mira.

Payton looked from her to Adam and back again. "We're going to need her. Whatever security he may have at his lab, Mira will be able to counter it. We may not get another chance, so we can't screw this up." He

fixed her with a hard stare. "You're going only to disable
the security measures. If you take one step past what you
absolutely must do to accomplish that, it will be the last
time you ever go in the field. Understood?"

"What I understand is that Bella is the one who
makes that decision. And she's not too happy with you
right now."

"Mira," he said in a warning tone.

She held up her hand. "No, I get it. Nerdy girl does the
nerdy job and leaves the rest to the big, bad fighters. I'm
fine with that, but only because I hate adrenaline rushes.
It has nothing to do with you ordering me around."

Payton looked to Adam. "Keep her out of trouble."

Mira turned to Adam and stared at him, silently warning him to tread lightly.

He shifted his stance so that he was facing Mira, completely ignoring Payton. "I'm going to do everything in
my power to keep you safe. Not because you're weak
and not because of any order. I'm doing it because you
and I aren't done. Not even close. Once this is over, I
want you whole and safe so that we can continue where
we left off."

Just like that, she was thinking about the sex they'd
just had. Hot, against-the-rules, on-the-desk sex. "We're
not done?" she asked, her voice a mere squeak of sound.

"Far from it. So when I tell you to duck or run or hide,
know that I'm telling you that so we can keep breaking
the rules."

Payton cleared his throat. "I don't know what you're
talking about, nor do I care. But I think you should go
now." He slid a piece of paper across the desk. "This is
the access ID for Sage's tracker. Don't activate it unless
you must. As long as the tracker is hidden, we have a
chance at finding him."

Mira glanced at the paper and memorized the code.
"Where was he last spotted?"

"I'll send you the coordinates while you gear up. Just don't be long. Sophie's life is on the clock now."

Riley had asked Sophie to marry him. She still couldn't get her head around it.

Who did that? What man in his right mind asked a woman he hardly knew to run off to Aruba with him?

And what woman in her right mind said no to an offer that good?

Sophie still couldn't believe she'd had the strength to say no. Only the certain knowledge that he'd wake up one morning soon, resenting her for ruining his life, had kept her from saying yes.

She'd so desperately wanted to say yes.

Riley sat in the backseat, glowering. Gage drove the car, his eyes covered with shades so that she couldn't see where he was looking or what he was thinking.

"This is idiotic," said Riley.

"You promised," said Gage. "No complaints."

"You can't tell me you think this is a good idea— taking Sophie out in the middle of nowhere and dropping her off so that she can be abducted."

"Not my call," said Gage.

"It's brilliant," said Sophie. "Out in the country there's little risk of anyone getting hurt or calling the cops. As long as I don't fight back, they won't hurt me." Much. "They want me alive, remember?"

"How will we even know which men are Stynger's and which are Sage's?"

The reflective lenses of Gage's glasses lifted toward the rearview mirror. "I'll know."

"There's still time to rethink this," said Riley. "We can turn around and take you back to my place. That sounds a whole hell of a lot better, doesn't it?"

She shifted in her seat to face him as best she could.

"I want this over as much as you do, but it's a done deal. You said you wouldn't make a fuss."

"No, you said I wouldn't make a fuss. I said I was coming with you. I never stipulated that I wouldn't try to stop you."

"Deal or get out," said Gage.

Riley leaned back and crossed his arms over his powerful chest. "I'm dealing," he told Gage. "Not well, but I'm dealing."

They drove awhile. Riley watched her the whole time, and she couldn't figure out why. He seemed to be studying her, or possibly looking for something he couldn't quite find.

"What?" she finally asked him.

"Why aren't you afraid?"

"It's not time to be afraid yet. Once it is, I promise I'll be all over it. But right now, in this moment, I'm safe and comfortable. Might as well enjoy it while it lasts."

Gage's glasses flicked back to the mirror. "She's a keeper."

"Hands off," said Riley. "I saw her first."

Gage grinned and kept driving.

"You know what to do when we get there?" asked Riley.

"Yes. I go in and hide in the basement until the bad guys huff and puff and blow my door in."

"Use your weapon to thin their numbers, but try not to kill them all."

The idea of taking a life repelled her, but she'd do whatever it took to take Sage down. Besides, she could aim for arms and legs as well as anyone.

"Gage and I will be nearby, but not so close that you'll be able to see us."

But they would be there. About that, she had no doubt.

She couldn't remember the last time she'd trusted a man as much as she did Riley. Maybe she never had. She sure as hell hadn't trusted her father. And the string of boyfriends she'd had over the years . . . she trusted them to steal her cash while she slept, but that was about it. She'd trusted Lorenzo Soma enough to let him coax her into bed, and all that had earned her was a miscarriage that had nearly broken her heart.

"I'll try not to look for you," she said.

"You're tagged with multiple tracking devices. We'll be able to find you no matter where you go, okay?"

"Yeah. Okay."

Gage turned onto a dirt road.

Now she was starting to get nervous.

Riley cupped her shoulder and leaned forward. His voice was quiet, and even though Gage could hear him, the words seemed to be for her ears alone. "I won't leave you. You won't see me, but I will be there, Sophie."

Just like he'd been there for her before, in Colombia. She wouldn't have lived through that night without him. He'd stayed behind with her when they'd been trapped inside the villa. He'd stayed with her when she couldn't keep walking. Even when the bullets were flying at them and they were being hunted through the jungle—her leaving a trail of blood behind that was way too easy to follow—he hadn't left her.

She covered his hand, soaking in the hot power of his skin against hers. "I believe you."

Gage slowed as he pulled into a long, gravel driveway. A little house sat at the end of the drive, aged and unassuming.

"This is it," said Riley. "From here on out, it's just like we planned. They may be close, so watch what you say."

"I'll go in with her." Riley pulled his hand away and donned a cool mask of indifference. Gone was the warmth in his eyes. She knew it was for show, but it still made her insides curl up to see it.

Gage shook his head slightly but said nothing.

"I should be the one to get her settled."

"You're too close."

Sophie desperately wanted Riley to stay with her for

just a little longer, but it was more important that they did this right. "We stick with the plan."

The car stopped. She reached for her door handle.

"No," said Riley. "Wait for Gage to come around and get you out."

"And then it's just like we planned," she repeated.

"That's right."

She nodded. "I go inside and wait to be taken."

Chapter Twenty-nine

"In position." Gage's voice came over the comms.

Beside Mira, Adam went tense.

"You're really worried about him, aren't you?" she asked.

He shifted in his seat and said nothing. The armored car they waited in near her father's current location seemed to grow smaller.

The sky was heavy with clouds the same shade as Adam's gray eyes. The bare branches of the trees in the park where they waited swayed on a cold wind. Even with the windows closed, Mira could smell snow in the air. Weather reports indicated that they were in for some flurries, but she hoped that it was no more than that. Anything that obscured visibility was going to make it easier to lose sight of her dad.

"He's a good man," said Adam. "Not much of a talker, but you can see it in him—that inner core of goodness running all the way through him."

Mira had never really thought about it, but now that she did, she realized Adam was right. "He's always been there whenever anyone has needed him. That's probably why Bella partnered you with him. He's not the kind to throw your past deeds in your face every day. Like I did."

He flashed her a smile. "You haven't tried to use that against me in at least twelve hours."

She stared in the direction her father was hiding. She couldn't see him from here, but she knew he was close. That was enough to make her skin crawl. "The last two times I saw my dad, he tried to kill me. If I see him again, he might succeed. There doesn't seem to be much point in carrying a grudge against you—especially since you were the one who kept me alive both times."

They sat in silence for a while, watching the sky darken as the day ended and the storm moved in.

"There's something I want you to know," said Adam. "Just in case things go . . . badly."

He had her complete attention now. She stifled a spurt of worry and turned in her seat to face him. "Nothing is going to go badly. I forbid it."

He gave an amused grunt. "I like your plan, but there's still something you should know."

"Save it for after the job."

"No. It can't wait. I need at least one other person to know the truth."

And he was trusting her? That made a little warm spot light up right in the middle of her chest. "Okay. If it's that important."

He looked past her, taking several deep breaths as if to gather his nerve. "Gage is Eli."

Eli, his lost little brother.

Shock streaked through her, leaving a numb path in its wake. "Gage is your brother?"

Adam nodded.

"Does he know?"

"No. No one does. Except me and your father."

"How is that even possible?"

"He was adopted when he was young. I don't think he even remembers that he has a brother."

"Why haven't you told him?"

"Everyone sees me as suspicious at best and the enemy at worst. I wanted a chance to prove to him the kind of man I really was before I let him know we shared blood."

"You should have told him."

"Not yet. I mean, how would you have felt to know that your only biological sibling was working for the people you dedicated your life to destroying?"

"But you were only working for them so you could find him. That has to count for something."

"Does it? Does it change the way you feel about the things I've done?"

Mira thought about it. Really thought about it.

If Clay went missing, what would she do? How far would she go to find him? She loved him like a brother, and she couldn't think of very many things she wouldn't do if his life was at stake.

Did that make her a bad person? She didn't think so. And the more time she spent with Adam, seeing how he ticked, the more she came to realize that they were more alike than she'd ever suspected.

She took Adam's hand in hers. "You should tell Gage who you are. He deserves to know that he has a brother who would do anything for him, the way you did."

"If he rejects me, I don't think I could handle it. I've searched for him for so long . . ."

"He won't reject you. And if he does, you'll simply win him over, the way you did me."

His fingers tightened around hers. "Have I won you over, Mira?"

"I don't want to kill you in your sleep anymore. That's got to count for something, right?"

"I know I have a long way to go to truly earn your trust, but I will. Even if it takes me the rest of my life."

Mira was reeling from that proclamation and all the attached implications when the comms squawked to life. There was a loud boom, like a tree crashing into a roof. Then a woman let out a terrified, blood-curdling scream.

Sophie. Gunfire erupted, filling the car with its explosive noise.

Silence filled the line for a second, giving Mira time to count every one of her frenetic heartbeats.

"They have her," said Riley, his voice coming through gritted teeth.

Mira had to breathe deeply to stem the urge to vomit. That poor woman. She'd done nothing to deserve the fear she suffered. She was innocent—another victim of a man Mira could have killed a dozen times over.

If only she'd had the nerve.

A little poison in his morning coffee. A bullet in his head as he slept. Or she could have made it look like an accident, just like he'd done to Mom.

If Mira had taken her father out when she first realized just how twisted he really was, she could have saved so much suffering.

But she hadn't. He was her dad, and she'd let that cloud her better judgment.

Mira's phone buzzed, alerting her that her father's tracking device had begun to move.

She turned on her mic as she held the screen up for Adam to see. "Movement on this end. We're in pursuit."

Adam started the car. His expression changed as he went into work mode. Gone was the sweet warmth she'd glimpsed a moment ago. In its place was the stony-faced badass she recognized all too well.

She turned off her mic again. "Are you going to tell me what you meant by that 'rest of my life' remark?"

He didn't even look at her as he pulled out into traffic. "Only if we survive."

Riley had to be physically restrained from going after Sophie. If not for Gage's unbreakable hold on his arm, Riley would have been hot on the heels of that van that carried her away, screaming and sobbing.

He prayed to God her terror was more for show than real.

"We need to go," said Riley.

"Patience," said Gage.

"Fuck patience. We can't let them take her far. What if we lose her signal?"

"We won't."

This was part of the plan. Riley kept telling himself that as he counted off the seconds.

Payton's voice came over the comms. "I see the van on satellite. We're tracking them now."

They stayed in place, hidden from sight, just in case there was a backup team covering the van's getaway. He had no idea how much time passed, but it felt like way too much.

"Now?" he asked.

Gage laid a hand on Riley's arm. "Patience."

Riley growled. "If that was your woman being dragged away, you wouldn't be so damn calm."

Gage looked at him then, blinking twice as if surprised. "Your woman?"

"Yeah. She is. I even asked her to marry me."

Gage let out a low whistle.

"Don't worry. She said no. Well. Actually, she told me to ask her again if we survived."

"Smart woman."

"Why? Because she didn't say yes or because she waited to tell me no?"

Gage grinned. "Idiot."

"What the hell is that supposed to mean?"

His grin widened. "She'll say yes."

"How do you know?"

He shrugged.

"You don't even know the woman. How can you possibly know she'll say yes after this is all over?"

Gage grinned. "You're cute."

"I'm cute? That's why she's going to marry me? I've been *cute* for a long time and I'm still single."

"Right woman this time."

So Gage thought Sophie was going to say yes.

That meant a lot to Riley. Gage didn't talk much, but he was always listening. And he was as astute as hell. If he thought Sophie was the right woman and that she was going to say yes, then odds were she was.

That thought bolstered Riley's spirits and made him straighten his spine. The woman he was going to marry had just given herself up to be used as bait. She was taken, and he was going to do everything in his power to see to it that she came back to him alive and well. Even if he had to pry her away from the bad guys with his bare hands.

And as soon as he got her back in his arms, he was never letting her go again.

Chapter Thirty

Sophie did her best not to pee her pants in fear.

The guys who had abducted her were silent, practically ignoring her where she crouched in the back of the van.

They'd cuffed her to the wall, forcing her to brace herself every time the van turned so she wouldn't slide across the slick metal floor and dangle by her wrists.

Her ribs ached where one of the men had hit her. She'd shot him in the leg for his effort. Three times. He was laid out on the floor of the van, leaking blood.

He glared at her over his crooked nose, his gaze promising payback.

Sophie was smart enough to not spit in his face, but she was definitely entertaining some vivid fantasies of doing just that.

The van lurched and rocked as they sped to wherever it was they were going. After what she thought was about an hour, they stopped.

One of the men stepped in front of her. He was in his late thirties, with a receding hairline and a fresh scar bisecting his chin. "Strip."

"Not only no, but hell no."

"Don't flatter yourself. This is about making sure we're not followed. Now, do it, or I will help."

She held out her arms. "Unlock me. I can't do anything without my arms free."

He hesitated for a second, then did as she asked.

The second he unlocked her and stepped back, she bolted for the door. She knew she wasn't going to get away. That wasn't even her intention. But if she didn't make her desire to get away look real, they'd start to suspect that she was exactly where she wanted to be.

Kind of.

Chin Scar grabbed her around the waist before she hit the door. He hauled her back, while she kicked and clawed the whole way. The second he dumped her on her ass, she cowered, pretending to be suitably fearful.

She curled up and covered her head with her hands. "I'm sorry. Don't hurt me."

He let out a noise of disgust. "Just change. We don't have all night."

She turned her back and took off her jeans.

"Panties, too. Everything goes."

Lovely.

She gritted her teeth and did the job as fast as she could. He bundled up her old clothes and tossed them out the back door. Then he picked up some kind of electronic gadget and started sweeping it over her in a slow grid.

She tried to cover her nudity, but he kept pushing her hands aside as he waved the gadget over her. "What are you doing?"

"Checking for bugs."

She still had one on her, but Riley had told her that they wouldn't activate it until they had to. It was hidden beneath a patch of fake skin under her arm—barely visible even to her.

As the gadget got close to the bug, she had to consciously try not to hold her breath and give her nerves away. There was nothing she could do about the shaking of her limbs or the chill in her fingers and toes, but he didn't seem to attribute that to anything other than her crappy situation.

The gadget passed without beeping or flashing, and it was all she could do not to let out a long sigh of relief.

When the man was satisfied that she was clean of bugs, he handed her an ugly set of oversized sweats. They were stiff and itchy, but she would have willingly put on a dress made of live snakes if it meant not being naked with these men.

As soon as she was covered, he pounded on the front wall near the driver's head. The van started up again. The shackles went back on her wrists. "Where are you taking me?"

"Doctor wants to see you."

She played stupid. "What doctor? I'm not sick."

The man she'd shot grinned. "He's going to cut you up, honey. He's going to saw open your skull just to see what makes you tick. Hope you enjoyed your day, 'cause it's your last."

"Shut up," ordered Chin Scar.

The man shut up but didn't stop looking at her with glee in his eyes.

What if it was her last day? What if Riley and his friends didn't find her in time?

At least she'd gotten to spend some time with a man worthy of her love, unlike all those asshole bastards who had marched in and out of her life.

She'd never get to see him again. Never kiss him again. But she'd had the chance to see what a real man was like up close before the end. That was more than most women ever got.

As those bleak thoughts crept in, she had to forcibly shove them away.

Today was not her last day. She would see Riley again. He would kiss her again, and a hell of a lot more, too. Even if she had to seduce him every day until he gave in.

Riley was going to be hers in every possible way.

The image of a baby with her mouth and his eyes popped into her head. Need unlike anything she'd ever felt came close on its heels.

That was what she wanted. A real life. A real home and family. A man who made her heart jump with joy whenever he walked in the room, and a child who would fill her with more love than she could stand.

Sophie stared at the man on the floor of the van and smiled. "At least I got to spend my last day putting three bullets in your leg. How in the world are you going to live down getting shot by a woman? I bet your buddies help you remember me for a long, long time. *Honey.*"

He started to sit up, moving like he was going to come after her, but Chin Scar stepped between them. "Stop it. Both of you. It's a long drive, so just settle down and be quiet."

Sophie relented rather than risking her secret tracking device being found. She went quiet and closed her eyes, fantasizing about her, Riley, a private beach, and all the things they were going to do once she got him naked.

Mira checked her phone again, activating Sophie's tracking device just long enough to get a single read on her location. Then she did the same for her father.

They'd both stopped. In the same place, in eastern Texas, almost at the Louisiana border.

"I think this is it," she told Adam.

He stopped the car about a mile away from where she wanted to be and opened his mic. "What does the satellite show?" he asked Payton.

"The van just now pulled into the same barn where Sage's car pulled in about two minutes ago."

"Do you see the lab?"

"Negative. Only trees and a small farm."

Adam shifted in his seat. His hands curled around the

steering wheel until his knuckles paled. "Something isn't right. Why aren't they moving?"

Mira pinged the trackers again, and both the one on Sophie and the one inside her father's leg were still active and stationary. "They're still in there."

"I'm going in for a closer look," said Riley.

"No," said Payton. "Stay back. There's nowhere for them to go."

"Too late," said Gage, who was stationed with Riley. "He's gone."

"This is definitely wrong," said Adam again. "They've been still for too long with no good reason. I wish we had audio."

"I've got a parabolic mic in back. We could try that." She leaned over the backseat and opened the black case. The compact mic took only a second to set up, but all she heard was the wind whistling through bare branches and pines.

"Anything?" he asked.

"Nothing. Maybe we're just out of range."

Payton's voice came over comms. "I just switched to thermals, and there's definitely something wrong."

"What?" asked Adam.

"There are warm bodies inside the barn, but none of them are moving. In fact, they're cooling down. Fast."

"Cooling down?" asked Mira. And then it hit her. "They're dead."

"Moving in," whispered Riley.

Adam was out of the car before she could stop him. He sprinted across the dark ground, so fast he disappeared into the shadows coating the landscape.

"Looks like it's a party," said Mira as she slid over into the driver's seat and adjusted it so she could reach the pedals. "I'm on the move."

She reached the barn in time to see Adam and Riley disappear inside, weapons in hand. A thick layer of anxiety coated her skin, making it clammy. As soon as she got out of the car, the cold wind hit her hard, stealing her breath.

She turned on her flashlight, holding it in the hand not filled with her gun. So far, there had been no screams or sounds of combat from inside the barn. That gave her the courage she needed to slip in through the rotting door and do what she could to help her friends.

The first thing her flashlight beam touched was a grotesquely overinflated blowup doll—the kind men used when they couldn't get a real woman. Her arms and legs were stiff, and her plastic skin was heavily wrinkled in places.

"He filled them with hot water," said Adam. "Sage knew we were watching him."

"That's not all," said Riley from across the barn.

Mira went to where he stood, passing several more blowup dolls as she went. Inside the car her father had been in was an array of surgical instruments on a metal tray. They were all covered in blood, and in the middle of them was a tiny tracking device she knew was rated for surgical implantation.

"It's the tracker we put in my father. He found it and took it out."

Adam picked up a patch of fake latex skin with another tracker attached. "They found Sophie's, too."

Riley let out a strangled cry of frustration and anger that made the hair on the back of her neck lift in warning. She stepped away from him. Adam shifted his body so that he was between her and Riley. Apparently, Adam had felt the same scary vibe she had.

"How the hell did they get away?" Riley snarled.

"I don't know," said Mira. "There's no one here. We had satellite support the whole time. It saw the blow-up dolls, so the images must be real."

"They are," said Payton over comms. "I can see the heat signatures of the three of you moving around."

Mira looked around, searching for some way of escape. There were no separate rooms where they could hide. "Is there a false wall or something?"

Riley opened the back of the van.

Adam crouched and looked beneath the car. "There's something under here. Some kind of cellar door."

Riley bent to look. "Cellar door? Sophie said something about going through one of those when she was taken to the labs as a kid."

"Help me move the car."

The keys were missing, but Mira dragged the warm, person-shaped water balloon from behind the wheel and found the key slot, which allowed her to put the vehicle in neutral. The men shoved the car out of the way, revealing a pair of rusted doors set in the dirt floor.

Riley pulled on them while Adam readied his weapon.

"They're locked," said Riley. "Barred from the inside."

Adam nodded. "We're going to need a welding torch. Or some explosives."

Chapter Thirty-one

Sophie had been in enough bad situations to know one when she saw it.

Two burly men dragged her down the long, filthy corridor. The walls were a mix of rock and dirt, with supports bracing the tunnel every few feet. It smelled like mildew. Dim electric lights glowed over her head, giving the space just enough light to let her see how dangerous this place really was.

She didn't know what it was for, or where it led, but one good sneeze and the ceiling might come caving in on them.

She tried really hard not to sneeze in the midst of all the mold spores that were doubtlessly floating around.

Dr. Sage limped ahead of her, leaving a drop of blood every few steps. She only hoped that even though the bad guys had found her tracking device, Riley and the others would follow the tunnel and find her before it was too late.

The ground beneath her feet sloped up. Water dripped from the electrical conduit overhead. The temperature changed, growing colder as they went up.

She prayed it meant they were nearing the surface and some fresh air. If she had to die tonight, she really didn't want it to be down here.

One of the men escorting them opened a heavy steel door to her left. There had been a few others along the never-ending path, but they all looked too old and rusted to move on their hinges. This one was in a bit better repair, as if someone had made sure it still functioned.

Steps led up. Sage had a hard time using his injured leg, but she didn't feel a second of pity for him.

"If you want to fall and crack your skull open, that works for me," she said.

The fist around her left arm tightened painfully.

Sage glowered at her over his shoulder. "I'll let that pass since I owe you a debt of gratitude."

"I've never once willingly done anything for you."

"Your will is irrelevant. That tracking device they so cleverly tried to hide on you? If not for that, I never would have suspected that I might also have a similar object under my skin. I should have thought of that, but I've been a bit . . . distracted over the past few weeks. All the torture and whatnot."

"Whatever they did to you, it wasn't enough."

He stopped on the top step and turned. His head cocked to the side as he studied her. "I remember you now," he said. "You were the screamer."

She clamped her lips shut around the bubble of fear that tried to escape.

She had screamed at his hands. A lot. The memories of those times seemed to shove their way to the top of her brain, forcing her to remember.

Sage grinned. "Don't worry. I only need you alive for one little thing. You won't have to scream for long."

*   *   *

Mira's phone rang while Riley and Adam were working on opening the metal doors. Gage had brought in enough plastic explosives and det cord to take the building down, but they were worried about what it might do to anyone on the other side of the door.

Namely, Sophie.

She didn't recognize the number, so she stepped outside, away from the noise, to answer it.

A cold wind whipped around her head and froze her fingers. "Hello?"

"By now you know I'm not in the barn," said her father.

Suddenly, the temperature outside seemed balmy when compared to the ice freezing over her insides.

"Where are you?" she managed to ask through chattering teeth.

"You'll see soon enough. First, I want you to head south, back out toward the main road, and wait for your ride."

"You think I'm going to just hop in the car with one of your goons? You're fucking crazy."

"You won't find me any other way. And I know how much you want to find me."

"We're nearly through the door," she lied. "We'll be on your trail in less than thirty seconds."

"Let me save you the trouble. The tunnel beneath the barn leads to a little clearing where I had a helicopter waiting. Your friend and I are getting on it now. You can join us, or you can let her die."

"You won't hurt her. You want her for your experiments too much."

"Is that what you really believe?" he asked, using a paternal tone that made her stomach heave dangerously. "Are you saying you don't remember the lessons I taught you? You don't remember just how far I'll go to make sure my daughter obeys?"

Memories swirled in her head, choking her. He'd hurt so many kids to get her to cooperate. She knew that. But the tone in his voice, the sound of his words buzzing in her head, made old memories resurface—ones she thought long gone.

She'd tried so hard to forget them—the kids who hadn't lived through her father's attempts to teach her some lesson or other.

"You won't kill her," she said, but this time her voice was weak and trembling with uncertainty.

"I will. Just like I killed the others when you were too stubborn to do what you knew I wanted. Just like I killed your mother. The only thing that matters to me now is the work. You were my greatest creation. It's time you accept that and come home."

She could barely push out a whisper. "Home?"

"You belong with me. My work on you is almost done. Just a little more and you'll be perfect—just like I always dreamed."

Realization dawned, and with it came a blinding wave of emotion. Disgust, anger, fear. Betrayal.

"This is about me, isn't it? This was always about me."

"No. It's about me. My work. My dreams. You've always been too selfish to see that. From the moment you were born I knew you would be my greatest achievement."

Something inside of her—some small, hopeful part that had always wanted a real, loving father—died, screaming in pain. There was no more hope. No more possibility for redemption.

"I won't let you win," she said. "I won't give you what you want."

"You will." The wrenching sound of a scream of pain flooded the phone. It was Sophie's voice, pitched in agony. "Or your friend will suffer before I kill her."

Mira had been here before. Too many times to count.

Her father knew she would give in. She couldn't stand the sound of another person's pain, couldn't stand the sight of another person's blood.

He knew that. It was how he defeated her, how he gained her cooperation. It always had been.

"Please, don't hurt Sophie anymore." Mira started walking south. "I'm coming."

Chapter Thirty-two

Something wasn't right. Adam could feel it in his bones. He double-checked the explosive charge Gage was setting. That seemed perfect. There were no words of warning from Payton, who served as their eyes in the sky. Riley was helping Gage get the shaped charge set to blow. Mira had taken a call and slipped outside, safely away from the blast radius.

That had been ten minutes ago. She should have been back by now.

Heart thudding with dread, Adam raced outside to search for Mira.

She was gone.

He dialed her cell. A familiar ring and blinking light came from a pile of leaves a few yards away.

His stomach bottomed out, and his ribs took a beating as the queasy adrenaline of fear hit his system.

He activated his mic. "Anyone have eyes on Mira?"

"Negative," said Riley and Gage in unison.

Payton's voice held a hint of panic that mirrored Adam's own. "Nothing on the satellite, but we're at the extreme edge of its window now. I can only see half of the area."

"Redirect it. I think she's been taken."

Riley said, "Hold on. I'm checking the location of her dog tags right now." He came out of the barn, phone in hand, making a beeline for Adam. He brushed past him by a few feet, then bent over.

When he stood up, the silver, barcoded tags she always had on her were dangling from his fingers. So was her gun.

"It's not good news," said Payton in his ear. "I backed up the image and got a split-second glimpse of someone getting into a car at the road leading into the property."

Adam had to struggle to pull in his next breath. Panic—something he'd rarely allowed himself to feel— shoved its way in, shaking his voice. "Where did it go?"

"There's no way to be sure. The satellite's range didn't reach that far."

Adam closed his eyes and allowed himself one deep breath. He had to focus. Think. He couldn't let his emotions run rampant.

But this was Mira, not just any woman. This was the woman he loved.

Shocked by the realization, he turned it over in his mind, studying it for just a moment before he boxed it away for another time. Strangely, the feeling and all its associated thoughts wouldn't be hidden. Like so many other things about Mira, his love for her was too powerful to contain.

He had no choice but to let it dwell in his mind while he tried desperately to think around the consuming feeling.

How did anyone function like this? How could they possibly go about their lives with so much going on in the background?

However they did it, he needed to learn. Fast. If his head wasn't clear, Mira might be lost to him forever.

Rage bloomed at the thought, swelling to the point that he had trouble taking his next breath.

"Easy," said Riley, laying a steady hand on his arm. "We'll find her. She's got to be with Sage. That asshole's been trying to get her in his grasp for years. He was the only one who knew where we were. We'll find her, find Sophie, and bring them both home."

"Do you know where to even begin looking?" Adam asked. "Isn't that the whole point of this expedition—to find Sage and his lab and take them both out? We lost him. What do you propose we do now?"

Gage's voice came over the comms, low and quiet. "Take cover."

Adam and Riley both turned away and covered their heads just as the charge went off.

"Door's open," said Gage.

Adam and Riley ran back into the barn. The metal doors were twisted and smoking, but the path down was clear.

"It heads west," said Riley.

"One of us should follow in a vehicle," said Adam.

"Not me," said Riley. "Sophie went down there. So am I."

Adam looked at Gage. "Go with him. I'll follow in the vehicle with all the weapons and ammo."

Riley nodded. "We probably won't have working comms down there, so if you don't hear from us, don't worry. We'll resurface when we can."

Gage stared at Adam with eyes that were too much like his own. Those eyes narrowed. "I know that look."

"What look?" asked Adam.

"Gonna do something stupid."

"We haven't been partners long enough for you to know me that well."

"But I do."

"Just go," said Adam. "I'm not going to do anything stupid."

Gage continued to stare long enough that Adam grew uncomfortable under the scrutiny. Finally, he gave a single nod, then followed Riley down the steps.

Adam hurried out of the barn, making sure his microphone was off. The call he was about to make was not one he wanted anyone to overhear.

He'd worked for Dr. Norma Stynger just long enough to know that she was as brilliant as she was ruthless. If anyone knew where Sage's lab was, it would be her.

It took several minutes for a string of personnel to connect him to the woman. He was already behind the wheel and speeding away when her voice came over the line.

"Adam. How good of you to contact me. It's been too long."

Not nearly long enough, but he had no choice. "I need a favor."

"Really? And you called me? You must have me confused for someone else. I don't *do* favors."

He ignored her and said what he needed to say. "Sage has gone missing."

"So he's not dead after all. Seems that condition is contagious. Where was he hiding?"

"He was in custody."

"But he no longer is. Too bad. He's always been a thorn in my side."

"One I'd like to remove. Permanently."

"Now, here's a conversation I'm interested in having. It's been a long time since you wanted to work for me. Why the change of heart?"

"I don't have a heart. You know that. All I need to know is where to find Sage. Tell me that and he'll be out of your way for good."

She let out a quiet sigh. "That's too bad. I have no idea where he is."

"You know his patterns. You know where he'd go to continue his work."

"All the old labs were destroyed. Bainbridge, Norwood, and the rest of them made sure of that."

"All of them? If that's the case, then where are you working?"

"Me?" she said with fake sincerity. "I'm retired."

"Bullshit. I was collecting people for you only a few months ago. In fact, I met one of your employees recently while at work—the one who you sent to collect Sophie Devane."

"That name doesn't ring a bell."

"Enough with the games. You know where Sage is headed, and even if you don't, you have a better guess than anyone else will."

"Where was he when you last saw him?"

Adam gave her the location of the nearest town.

"Ah. Right. The underground tunnel network." She sighed as if reminiscing over the good ol' days. "I remember them."

"Where is the closest lab? He left on foot. He's got to be headed somewhere nearby."

"Let's say I do know the place where he might go—an old facility that has seen quite a bit of renovation activity over the last few weeks. What would that kind of information be worth?"

"You think we're going to help fund your research? You're insane."

She let out a laugh that sounded like nails on a chalkboard. "I have no desire for your money. I receive plenty of that from my eager investors. But there is something you have that I don't."

"What's that?"

"I'm developing a new protocol that has been designed to work on even the most . . . resistant subjects. I've read your files. So many times. Nothing else I've designed would work on you, but I think this will. I'd like to test my theory."

Adam went numb with shock. His hands felt like lead weights around the steering wheel. He nearly swerved off the road. The tires slid over the edge of the pavement, trying to drag the whole car into the ditch.

He righted the vehicle, but not before the noise he'd just made carried through the phone.

"What did you think I'd want, Adam?" she asked. "You have so little of value."

"You want to experiment on me? See if you can control me? Use me against my will?"

He swore he could hear her lips smacking in eager glee. "I do."

Even the suggestion made him queasy, but he couldn't think of any other options. Sage was in the wind. Mira was in danger. So was Sophie. If Adam didn't find them soon, he knew exactly what would happen—the same thing he'd barely prevented from happening last year. Sage would end up killing his daughter.

He sucked in a deep breath, hoping it would calm his churning gut. "If I agree to let you use me as a test subject, you'll tell me where to find Sage?"

"Yes. You will kill him. When you're done, there will be a man waiting for you. You'll come along quietly and not make a fuss. Agreed?"

"Are you going to kill me?" he asked.

"Not intentionally, but I can't make any promises. All those pesky side effects, you know."

"Promise you will leave the people I work with at the Edge alone." He didn't dare give her names for fear she'd use the knowledge of his love for his brother and Mira against him.

She chuckled. "You've made emotional attachments. That's interesting."

"Promise," he grated out, "or I take my chances finding Sage on my own."

"Fine. As long as you're a nice, docile test subject, I'll leave your friends alone. But you're going to have to sweeten the pot."

"How?"

"Sage has something of mine—some research notes that were stolen by one of my lab techs."

"You want me to get them back," he guessed.

"No. I want you to convince him you know the password protecting the file—one I'll give you."

"You're going to let him open the file?"

"No. It's a built-in safeguard to protect the data. You enter the right password and it will activate a program destroying all the information as well as any computer and network it can reach."

"What's the password?"

"Not yet. Tell me you'll do the job first—to save your emotional attachments."

The fewer people with her research the better, as far as he was concerned. "Fine. I'll find a way to destroy your research notes."

"Good boy." Her condescending tone ground against his nerves.

He gritted his teeth. "We have a deal. Now tell me where I can find Sage."

Chapter Thirty-three

Mira desperately wished for some bread crumbs to leave behind.

The black sedan sped over the landscape, taking her deeper into uninhabited countryside. She could see nothing but trees and more trees.

Every tracking device on her was gone, including the ones in her shoes. Those had been tossed out after a quick sweep of her escort's bug detector. She was without means of communication, with no way of letting her coworkers know where to find her.

For the first time since childhood, Mira was truly on her own.

The training Bella had forced on her sped through her mind. The first thing she needed to do was figure out where she was headed so that if she got the chance to alert anyone, she had something to tell them.

"Where are we going?" she asked the driver.

He barely glanced in her direction. His expression was a cold, blank wall. His eyes were empty, and his lips were so thin his mouth looked like a cut slashed across his face.

"The quiet type, huh?"

He ignored her and kept driving.

"At least tell me how long it's going to take. I have to pee."

He rolled down his window, tossed the dregs of a cup of coffee out and handed her the empty paper cup. "Go ahead."

"Yeah. Not that bad."

Clearly, she wasn't getting anywhere with Chatty Pants, so she started searching for landmarks that might tell her where they were. Anything more specific than *middle of nowhere* would have been helpful.

The moon rose in the sky, muted by a thin layer of clouds. The terrain grew steeper and more dense with trees. With each passing mile, her skin itched a little more, as if she was going through withdrawal from her friends.

Or maybe just Adam.

The man had definitely worked his way under her skin. No doubt about it. Sadly, she liked him there.

Caring about him was a huge mistake. Monumental proportions on an epic scale. And yet she couldn't bring herself to mind.

She liked Adam. Maybe even loved him.

Nice that she figured that out just in time to meet her demise.

The sedan made a hard turn onto an unmarked road she hadn't even seen coming. The path was nothing more than some compacted earth through the trees showing tire tracks. She held on tight, trying to steady herself against the deep, lurching ruts and bumps along the way.

They went over a hill and then nearly skidded down a steep bank into an area that was well hidden from the road.

High, razor-wire-topped fences surrounded a building in the center of a large clearing. As soon as the sedan neared, floodlights flicked on and followed their progress like a spotlight. The closer they got to the fence, the more she was able to make out the shape of armed men guarding the perimeter.

The driver came to a full stop and rolled down his window. The barrels of about three different weapons were trained on them.

Mira tried to shrink out of existence, hugging herself good-bye.

"Delivery for Dr. S.," said the driver to an armed guard.

"Open the trunk," ordered the guard.

The driver did, and after a thorough search of the vehicle, the guard seemed satisfied that there was no one hiding inside. He let out a shrill whistle.

The metal gates rolled open, allowing them to pass.

Mira briefly considered getting out of the car and taking her chances with the armed men. At least getting shot would be a fast way to go. Whatever her dad had in store for her was likely going to make an appearance in front of a firing squad feel like a day at the spa.

But if she bailed now, what would happen to Sophie?

Mira knew the answer to that one. It was why she'd come in the first place.

Sophie might not get out of this alive, but if Mira hadn't come, there was exactly zero chance of Sophie's survival.

The sedan came to a stop outside of a U-shaped building. It wasn't as huge as some of the facilities her father had used for his work, and it was definitely showing signs of age and wear, but no matter how old or small it was, there was still plenty of room for suffering inside.

And she was going in there.

Her heart started beating so hard and fast her head began to swim. She couldn't get enough air. Fireworks bloomed behind her eyes, and every muscle in her body grew weak.

Panic. Mira had felt it enough times to know it well. In fact, they'd been BFFs for a few months the summer her father had killed her mother. Mira hadn't known how she'd survive without her mom as a blanket of protection to keep her safe.

There was definitely no blanket this time. No one knew where she was. No one could come to save her. She'd checked her phone before dropping it as ordered, and the satellite feed was already out of range when she'd stepped into the sedan.

She squeezed her eyes shut and held her breath for a slow three-count. She could do this. She had no other choice. She would face her demons and take them down.

Or die trying.

The panic set in again, gripping her even harder. She didn't even have her gun. The driver had made her drop that, too. Her training wasn't strong enough to get her and Sophie out of this without a weapon. She wasn't like Bella or Riley or Adam. Her body was not a deadly weapon. It was more like a complicated transportation device for her brain. She wasn't calm under pressure. She freaked out. Hard.

The thought of Adam brought his image to mind. Like some kind of talisman, picturing him made her pulse slow enough that she could take a single, deep breath.

She gripped his image, letting it flare to life in perfect detail. His tall, lean body, which moved with the grace of a dancer. His starkly handsome face, complete with those inky brows and pale gray eyes she found so intriguing. His long-fingered hands, which knew just how to touch her and set her on fire.

Was she really going to give up and never have the chance to feel that again?

Fuck no. That was not the kind of thing a girl gave up easily once she got a taste. She was going to make her way out of this torture chamber, with Sophie. They were going to call for reinforcements and blow the whole facility to hell. And then, when that was done, she was going to find Adam and make him kiss her until she couldn't even remember what fear felt like.

With that plan in mind, she started to relax. Her shoulders dropped down from her ears. Her fists unclenched. Her lungs unlocked, giving her room to breathe.

She could do this. She didn't know how, but she was smart. Smarter than her father.

All she had to do now was find a way to be just as ruthless.

The moment Adam saw the lab in the valley below, he knew what it was.

His birthplace.

It had seemed so much bigger then. So much brighter. Now all he saw was a small, run-down building that had been the place of far too much pain and suffering.

That ended tonight.

"I'm moving in," said Adam for whoever was listening on the other end. He didn't know if Riley and Gage had made it out of the tunnel yet or not.

"You need to wait for reinforcements," said Payton. "General Norwood has men on the way."

"I can't wait." Mira's life was too precious. Every second he let her linger inside that place was one more too many.

Sage might simply kill her out of spite. Adam had seen it before.

"Stand down, Adam."

He ignored the order. He was no soldier. Orders were things for puppets and men of honor. Adam was neither.

He had the tools he needed in the trunk of his car. It was easy for one man to slip in unnoticed. He was good at blending in, sticking to the shadows, and using his instincts to tell him when to move and when to freeze. He'd done it before so many times. This would be just one more.

Perhaps his last if Stynger's protocol killed him.

He forcibly emptied his mind of that possibility, shoving it in a sturdy box where it belonged. The only thing he couldn't stop thinking about was Mira. There was no box strong enough to hold the power she had over him.

Interestingly enough, he no longer minded. He liked having her as his constant companion, warming his thoughts and strengthening him. She was the reason he was here. She was the reason he would be victorious.

Adam gathered what he needed and set out, hiking down through the darkness to where the fence was the most vulnerable.

The building was U-shaped, and the back side was protected by thickly wooded, steep, nearly impassible ground. Because of that, security was lighter there, and perfect for his approach.

He'd played on these grounds as a child. He knew where all the dips and valleys were. He used that to his advantage as he made his way through the fence and to the back of the building.

Two armed guards patrolled this area. There was a ten-second period in which they no longer had line of sight with each other—the time when they were both too close to a fenced-in area that held trash and maintenance equipment to see each other. If he didn't take the first guard down during that interval, the second one would alert the others before Adam had time to take him out.

He waited in the shadows, biding his time until the perfect moment. A short, silent sprint across the ground, and he was within reach of the first guard.

He took control of the man's body, covered his mouth and nose, and injected him with a heavy tranquilizer. The whole thing took all of five seconds, and the man slumped to the ground.

Adam drew another syringe from his bag and crouched, waiting for the second guard to come investigate what had happened to his buddy.

The nonlethal method was strange to him, but these men were only damaged, not entirely broken. His work finding others on the List had proven that much to him. And interestingly, saving lives made him feel proud. Like he was really one of the good guys instead of walking around in disguise, wearing one of their suits.

Life was what Mira would have wanted for her father's victims, and that was enough to motivate Adam to take the extra effort and risk.

A few seconds later, the second guard came around the corner and Adam pounced. The man let out only a grunt before the drugs kicked in and he joined his buddy on the ground.

They'd both be out for hours.

Adam didn't dare go for the door. He knew it would be equipped with an alarm. Instead, he went to where he remembered the kitchen being and searched for the window with the broken lock.

He'd escaped tests and lessons too many times to count using that window. And no matter how many times he was caught and punished for slipping away against the rules, he'd never divulged his means of escape.

The kitchen storeroom was dark. The door leading into the cooking area was closed. He shone his light through the dusty glass and saw that the latch was still the same old one—it hadn't been replaced in all these years.

He used his knife to slide it open and then crawled inside.

The storeroom was covered in dust. Old canned goods lined the shelves, along with a few mouse-chewed boxes of dried pasta and bags of beans that had been left behind.

He pressed his ear to the kitchen door, listening for signs that anyone was on the other side. He heard nothing, so he eased the door open.

The second he smelled fresh coffee brewing, he knew he wasn't alone.

A man stood at the industrial kitchen counter, sipping a cup of coffee. He saw Adam open the door.

The coffee dropped and splashed over the concrete floor. Steam rose from the hot liquid as the man reached for his weapon.

Adam's choices were few. He could draw his suppressed weapon and fire. He was faster than this man—just as he'd been designed to be. But even with the silencer, the sound of the weapon discharging would still be loud enough to alert anyone nearby.

He could also pull his knife and sink it into the man's chest. He was unarmored—clearly off duty. With the right placement, the man would bleed out in seconds, and the only noise coming out of him would be easily cut off with a hand over his mouth.

Adam could turn and run, but that was likely to get him shot in the back. Even with his body armor, he had no desire to take a hit from this short distance.

That left only one option—the one that was the most likely to keep both this man and Mira alive.

Adam lifted his hands and surrendered.

Chapter Thirty-four

Mira's reaction to seeing her father was potent and violent.

First there was the fear.

He was wearing his usual lab coat, his pockets bulging with the sinister outline of syringes and vials of who knew what. His hair was long and messy, adding to the mad-scientist vibe he always gave off. His cheeks sagged with the weight of his scraggly beard.

Mira had seen him looking unkempt and haggard before, always when he was in the throes of proving some new hypothesis. He'd disappear into his lab for weeks, and when he came out, that wild light in his eyes was always burning bright with excitement.

That's when the experiments—the suffering—would start.

As she breathed through the familiar bout of fear, anger began to burn it away.

She wanted to kill him with her bare hands. She wanted to watch the life flicker from his eyes and know with complete certainty that he was really dead this time.

This man had hurt so many people. Not just Mira, but countless others. Her office was stuffed with files of those he'd used and damaged—subjects who were cast aside as unfit because his latest protocol failed to do whatever it was he'd been working toward.

It was never his fault that things didn't go as he'd hoped. It was always the subject's fault.

Just like it hadn't been his fault that he'd killed her mother. It had been her ignorance that forced his hand, her lack of intelligence. If she'd been smarter, she would have understood why he'd been so driven to finish his work.

Because Mira's mom had tried to stop him from using Mira in his experiments, he'd killed her. Said she was small-minded.

Mira had never forgiven him. Never would.

But she could kill him. It was the only way he'd ever stop hurting people.

Dr. Sage offered her a smile of greeting as she entered the lab. The room was smaller than his usual setup, but it still contained all the necessary equipment—the scientific and medical gadgets that made her skin crawl and her stomach churn dangerously.

Sophie was lying on a gurney, strapped in place so she couldn't escape. An IV line pumped something into her arm, and whatever it was couldn't be good for her.

She lifted her head slowly, as if it was too heavy to hold up. Her eyes were glassy and unfocused, but there was a flash of recognition in her expression that told Mira she knew who she was.

Mira shoved her chin up and glared at her father. "I'm here. Let Sophie go."

Her father motioned to one of the two men in the room with him. She didn't know if they were guards or merely burly lab techs, but both were armed.

One of them pulled out a chair at a desk in front of a laptop, indicating she should sit.

"What's this?" she asked.

"I've come across some information from my competitor."

"You mean Dr. Stynger."

"Yes. Sadly, none of my staff is capable of breaking her encryption. That's why you're here."

"Really?" she asked, staring at him in disbelief. "The last time you asked me to do this for you, I destroyed every file I could. What makes you think I'll do any different this time?"

He shook his head in disappointment. "You always did need the proper motivation. It's sad, really. It makes me feel like I've failed as a father."

He went to Sophie's IV port and injected something. She started to scream in pain.

"Stop it!" Mira covered her ears and looked away. She'd always been queasy when it came to seeing others suffer, and she was incapable of watching poor Sophie without breaking down.

If Mira was to have any chance at staying strong, she had to pretend that none of this was happening. It was just a TV show. A bad dream. Not real. No pain.

The screaming stopped. Mira looked up, praying Sophie was still alive.

Sage pulled a different needle from Sophie's IV. "She's resting comfortably now. How long is up to you." He glanced pointedly at the laptop. "The next dose will probably kill her."

"Then you'll have no leverage," spat Mira.

He smiled like he knew a secret, then nodded toward a curtained-off area. One of the guards opened the curtain and behind it was Adam, struggling against the heavy leather straps holding him down. His mouth was covered with tape, and his eyes promised payback as he glared at Sage.

Ruby Rypan stood beside him, carrying what she needed to start his IV—just like the one Sophie had that pumped those pain-inducing chemicals into her.

Mira's stomach clenched, and a raging swell of nausea

churned in the back of her throat. She swallowed hard to keep from throwing up, but she wasn't going to last long if she couldn't find some kind of calm.

"I have all the leverage I need, Mira," he said. "And when these two are used up, if you still need motivation, I'll find more. Clay. Bella. Riley. Leigh. Gage. And so many others you call friends. I know them all. I have men watching them, just waiting for me to give the order to bring them in. So ask yourself this: How much motivation do you need?"

Her head fell forward in defeat. She was beaten. Her father knew just where her weakness was. He knew just how hard to push and how often. And there was not a single doubt in her mind that he would kill Sophie and Adam and everyone else if he felt he needed to in order to get what he wanted.

"No more," she whispered. She was too weak to even find her voice. "I'll do it."

"That's my girl."

"When I'm done, you'll let them go?"

"Is that what you want?"

"Of course it is."

"Then be a good girl and open those files. If you do it fast enough, I may be in a charitable mood."

He was lying. Her father wouldn't know what charity looked like if he sat on it.

"And in case you're thinking of trying something cute, know that if anything goes wrong with this process—if even one file is corrupted by your antics—you won't like what happens to your friends."

That was the truth. At least he still knew how to tell it sometimes.

"I won't mess anything up," she told him. "It doesn't matter if you have access to this information or not. The only way to stop you is to kill you."

"Patricide?" he asked, grinning. "You, who can't stand

the sight of blood, are thinking about killing me? That's adorable." He patted her on the head. "Get to work. Your friends don't have all night."

Mira started working. It didn't take long before she realized that this encryption was something she'd never seen before and was way beyond her skills—at least in the short time she had. With each passing minute, her father's pacing sped, and she knew she was running out of time.

She stared at the screen, trying to clear her mind enough to think. Nothing she did helped. She couldn't hack into these files. She wasn't that good.

Stynger's files were safe, but Sophie and Adam were going to die. There wasn't a thing Mira could do to stop it.

Adam could tell by watching Mira that it wasn't going well.

Her lip was clenched between her teeth so hard she'd drawn blood. Her hands shook as they sped over the keyboard. Her face was pale, and a trickle of sweat eased along her hairline, despite the chill in the room.

He'd spent the last few minutes working to loosen his bonds whenever Sage's men looked the other way. He'd made no progress before Ruby had come in and halted his efforts. Despite his best efforts, the cuffs around his wrists and ankles were holding fast.

Mira wiped her sweaty brow. Sage stopped pacing and glanced at Sophie. It was easy to see the man was about to hurt her again. Possibly kill her.

Adam started grunting and thrashing to get Sage's attention.

Ruby came over and checked Adam's bonds, tightening them down. "He's good."

Only then did Sage come within reach of Adam.

Smart man.

Sage loomed over him. "What?"

Adam grunted behind the tape, trying to give the noise a sense of urgency.

Sage ripped the tape free, leaving an angry sting behind. "This had better be important."

"It is. I know the passcode."

"Impossible."

He glanced nervously at Mira. There was no way for him to communicate to her that he was conning her father. Once she heard what he had to say, she was going to think he'd betrayed her. Again.

"Spit it out," said Sage.

"Can't we talk somewhere private?"

"This is as private as it gets for a man with your skills. I'm not about to put myself alone in a room with a killer like you."

Mira's fingers stilled on the keyboard.

Adam lowered his voice, hoping it wouldn't carry across the lab. "I . . . work for Stynger. She knew the files were missing. I was sent to find them and steal them back. That's why I was working with Mira. Stynger thought she had them."

Mira turned in her chair to face him. She'd heard every word. He could see the painful gleam of betrayal wavering in her eyes. "You were lying to me the whole time?"

"I didn't mean to hurt you, Mira. It's not what it seems."

"Did you sleep with me to get me to trust you? Was that part of the plan, too?"

Sage's shrewd gaze flashed between them. "Stynger wanted your child, didn't she? That's what this research she's hiding is about. Second-generation enhancements. With your altered genetics, Adam, it makes perfect sense. Of course."

Whoa. Sage was veering way off track, into territory that Adam knew would be dangerous for him, Mira, and any children they might have.

Strangely, he had no trouble picturing what their child would look like, how it would feel to hold his son or daughter. Profound, joyful. Right.

But what scared him was that he could also imagine the lengths to which he would go to see their child safe.

Based on the speculative look Sage was giving his daughter, it was clear where his mind was headed: forcing Mira to have a child Sage could study.

There was only one response Adam could muster to such a threat.

Sage had to die. Here. Tonight.

Adam cleared his throat. "She came to the conclusion first. The research idea is hers and hers alone."

Sage's face went red and mottled with rage. "That bitch stole my idea. Any work she's done on the subject rightfully belongs to me." He turned to Mira. "Open those files. Now."

She shook her head, horror clear in her expression. "I can't. And even if I could, I wouldn't. I won't have a hand in you or Stynger or anyone else hurting more children."

Sage took the weapon from a guard near him and leveled the barrel at Adam's head. "Do it now, or I kill him."

"You don't want to do that," said Adam, trying to sound as calm as possible. "Not only do I have the correct passcode; I'm also the only one with genetic alterations. What you did to Mira and the others probably won't pass on to their children. Me, on the other hand . . ." He let his thought hang in the air, giving Sage plenty of room to come to the proper conclusion.

He lifted the weapon. "You're not the only one," he said. "Don't forget, I was the one who told you where to find your brother."

Another burst of rage hit Adam hard, but he shoved it in a box and kept his cool. "Let me go. I'll type in the passcode and you can see how far Stynger has come with her research."

"You mean *my* research."

"I don't give a fuck whose research it is," said Mira. "You can't do this, Adam. You can't give him access to those files."

He kept his face cold and hard, as if he weren't aching to hold her and chase her pain and fear away. "It's the only way to survive."

"A heightened instinct for survival was part of your enhancements," said Sage. "I can hardly fault you for doing as you were designed to do."

"Don't," said Mira. Tears quivered in her eyes, breaking his heart.

"I have no choice. If I do this, we survive. It's that simple."

"What about the people he's going to hurt?" she asked.

He wanted to tell her that he'd changed. He wasn't the same man he'd been when she met him. He knew what it felt like now to put the safety of others above his own. He wasn't just some cold, calculating creation who did what he was told to do.

There was no way to tell her any of that now. His plan worked only if everyone believed he was the same Adam Brink he'd been before he met her.

He shrugged as well as his bonds would allow. "I can't let that be my problem."

Sage smiled and patted Adam's shoulder. "This is the right choice, son. You won't regret it."

"Don't," said Mira. A tear fell down her cheek.

Adam lurched against his restraints. "Please, Mira. Forgive me."

She shook her head. "I can't. Not for this. You have no idea what he's capable of doing. I do."

"Tell me the code," ordered Sage. "My patience is already worn thin."

Adam wanted to look away from Mira as he gave the passcode, but that was the cowardly way out. He couldn't touch her to comfort her that way, so the only thing he had left to give her was eye contact.

He only hoped that she'd see past his lies. Somehow.

"Second chances," he said. "That's the passcode. All lower case, no spaces."

Mira flinched, but she didn't look away. "You have no idea what you've just done."

"I saved your life," he said. "And Sophie's."

"You're wrong. You just delayed our deaths." She turned to her father. "Isn't that right, Dad?"

He was too busy typing in the code to respond.

Adam waited for the fallout to start. He almost expected sparks to start shooting out of the laptops and tablets nearby. But none of that happened.

From this angle, he could see the screen fill with data. Text, charts, graphs, data logs. Nothing exploded. Sage didn't curse as the screen went blank.

He practically cackled with giddiness.

"This is it," he said. "Everything I need."

Pieces in Adam's mind began to shift. He wasn't sure exactly what was happening, but he knew it wasn't good.

Stynger had set him up. She'd wanted Sage to get his hands on those files.

But why?

"Ruby, take one of the guards and put our guests in one of the holding cells," said Sage, his tone distracted.

"Together?" asked Ruby, giving no indication of her preference.

"Absolutely. I'm looking forward to grandchildren."

"Yes, Dr. Sage," said Ruby.

Mira bowed her head in defeat.

Adam realized in that moment that, despite his good intentions, he'd been outmaneuvered. Stynger had whatever crazy thing she wanted out of this. Sage had the data he wanted to leapfrog Stynger's work. And Adam had lost Mira forever. She'd never believe he was only trying to help—not with the history they shared.

"I'm sorry," he said as Ruby began wheeling him out, still strapped to the gurney.

"Don't," Mira said. "Just don't."

The second guard pushed her ahead of him. "Move."

Mira marched ahead without a single glance back at Adam.

Chapter Thirty-five

Adam's message led Riley and Gage right to Sage's lab. They'd had to steal a car to get here, and Riley prayed it wasn't too late.

He wanted to rush in and find Sophie, but Gage's hand on his arm held him back and reminded him that they had to be smart about this.

Smart and fast.

Every second she was in there was one too many.

"Four out," said Gage as he peered through his binoculars. "Ten inside."

"Sophie? Mira?"

He shook his head. "Can't tell."

"How do you want to play this? Stealth or force?"

"You're all force."

"I know. I can't calm the fuck down—not with Sophie and Mira in there."

Gage nodded and pulled a sniper-rifle case from Adam's trunk. "Stealth part's mine."

"How long do you need?"

He started assembling the rifle. "Not long."

"We could wait for reinforcements."

"Can't. Other plans."

Riley blinked. "We're going on a rescue mission and you're thinking about other plans?"

"Bella's orders."

"If she were here, she'd change her orders. She'd want our friends safe."

Gage stared at him over the rifle. "They will be. Go."

Riley moved away from Gage's position so he wouldn't give it away if he was detected. As soon as Riley was through the opening in the fence that someone else had made, Gage opened fire.

Riley broke into a sprint, counting shots as he went. Each distant boom of Gage's rifle was another enemy down. No question. He was just that good.

As the fourth shot rang out, Riley fired a breaching round through the lock on the back door and barreled inside.

The only thought on his mind was finding Sophie before she got hurt.

As soon as the first shot went off, Mira knew her friends had arrived.

A nearly overwhelming sense of relief swept through her, making her knees go wobbly.

"You stay with them," said the guard to Ruby as he handed her a gun. "I'm going to see what's happening."

Ruby took it, looking completely capable and at ease with the weapon. Not a good sign.

As soon as the guard was out of sight and only Ruby remained, Mira channeled Bella and struck.

All those hours in the sparring ring came back to her. Endless drills had created enough muscle memory that her body flew through the moves with no thought. Before she even realized what had happened, the woman was on the floor, unconscious.

Mira picked up Ruby's gun and used a strip torn from the bedsheet to restrain her.

"Free me," said Adam. "I know a way out."

They were in the middle of a long hallway. Anyone could come around a corner at any second and shoot them. She believed her friends were outside, but it could have just as easily been Stynger's men invading the facility.

Mira didn't care.

She stared down at Adam, trying to find some control over the emotions raging through her.

"Why should I trust you?" she asked. She could think of no reason to trust him other than that she so desperately wanted to.

"The thing with the passcode looked bad, but I swear it was all an act. I didn't betray you."

"No? You just pretended to?"

"Yes. I needed to know where to find you. Stynger knew. I called her."

"And she just told you out of the kindness of her heart?"

"No. There was a price."

"What was it?"

He hesitated.

"What? Trying to think up something on the fly?"

"No. She told me that Sage had some files of hers and that if I agreed to give him the passcode, she'd tell me where to find him—where to find *you*. She said the code would destroy the information as well as his internal network."

"That's not what happened."

"I know. The only thing I can think of is that she wanted him to have the information."

"Why would she want that? Those two hate each other. They've been having the same pissing contest since I was a child. She's not just suddenly going to change her mind and share research."

"I don't know why it went down the way it did. All I know is what I was told."

Mira nodded as another volley of gunfire erupted somewhere inside the building. "Me, too. Only I'm not stupid enough to believe your lies this time."

"So—what? You're just going to leave me here, strapped to this bed, unable to defend myself?"

She couldn't do that. She so desperately wanted him to be telling the truth. Just wishing for it made her weak enough to consider the tiny chance that he was. If anything happened to him because she walked away, she'd never forgive herself.

Chances were he was counting on that.

The radio Ruby carried clipped to her waistband was still active. Mira pulled the earphone from Ruby's ear to listen in.

Dad's voice filled Mira's ear. "Execute the escape plan. Ready the helicopter."

He was going to escape. Likely with all of his new-found research that Adam had unlocked for him.

If her dad got away again, she'd never be able to sleep at night. She'd always worry that he was coming for her. Coming for her children, if she ever had them.

She wasn't going to let him do that to her. He'd terrorized her all her life. It ended here. Now.

Mira shoved Ruby's gun in her waistband. She unfastened one of Adam's wrist cuffs, found the nearest exit, and then ran off toward the sound of a helicopter's engines revving to life.

Her father wasn't going to make it onto that helicopter alive.

She kept to the shadows as much as possible. Floodlights lit up the area but left deep pools of darkness here and there where obstructions blocked the light. She heard gunfire in the distance, heard men shouting nearby. She passed two bodies on her way to the helipad and made a point not to look at them too closely. The last thing she needed now was to start puking.

The helicopter was bigger than she expected. One

man was in the pilot's seat, getting ready to lift off. Two more men were carrying several boxes out to the aircraft. One of them took a shot to the leg and went down screaming. The boxes toppled to the ground, spewing papers and electronics.

Her father was trying to escape with his research intact, presumably so he could continue torturing people indefinitely.

Mira clung to the shadows behind a fenced-in area that held the facility's garbage. She pulled the gun and held it while she waited for her father to appear.

The air was freezing, but despite that, sweat pooled in her palms. Hatred for the man burned deep in her gut, doing little to quiet the queasy churning there.

She didn't want to shoot anyone. Just imagining the blood spraying out and bones crunching under the impact was enough to make her sick. But if she let her father get away, she knew he'd never stop working. He'd never stop hurting people.

Unless she pulled the trigger.

Mira sucked in a series of heavy breaths, trying to gather her nerves enough to steady her hands. Dad would walk outside any second, and when he did, her aim had to be true.

She might not get a second shot before one of the guards took her down.

The shouting grew louder. She couldn't hear what they said, but it didn't matter. Her path was set. Her finger was on the frigid trigger. All she needed was her target.

Her father scurried toward the helicopter carrying a cardboard box. A leather laptop case was slung over his shoulder, bobbing against his hip with every hurried step.

She had a clean shot. No one was in the way. She'd reliably hit the center mass on targets farther away than he was now. They hadn't been moving, but she was good with patterns, understood physics, and could predict exactly where her aim should be.

A slight adjustment for the slope of the ground, the wind, and his clumsy gait, and her sights were lined up just right.

Her finger tightened on the trigger, but before she could finish the pull, something hard shoved against the base of her skull.

"Don't," came a quiet command. A voice she didn't recognize. "Drop the weapon. Your finger so much as twitches and I'll shove a bullet through your brain stem."

Mira froze. The owner of that voice was not fucking around.

She let her weapon dangle from her index finger, then slowly set it on the ground. The whole time, she watched as her father climbed onto the helicopter with his precious boxes.

"Stand up and walk."

Mira did. The barrel of the gun against her head shoved her toward the helicopter. Her hair flew around her face in a wild storm. She could barely see but didn't dare move her hands to hold it away from her eyes.

Her father saw her approach. Disappointment covered his face in a familiar mask.

Funny how it no longer bothered her. She'd spent most of her childhood trying to please him, and she'd finally reached a point where she truly didn't care what he thought anymore.

"Bring her," her father yelled over the heavy pounding of the helicopter's blades. "She's finally going to be of some use."

The gun barrel scraped across the back of her neck as it ripped away. The man holding it screamed in pain. She heard the shot, instinctively looking toward the noise.

Adam held the weapon that had just fired at her captor. He fired again, hitting the man on the ground. The guard didn't move again.

Nearby, another man fired, and this time it was Adam

who went down. Blood erupted from his leg, splashing the wall behind him.

Adam rolled and shot his attacker. A small hole bloomed in the middle of the other man's forehead, and he crumpled.

Another man nearby flew back onto his ass, following the pink spray that bloomed from his head. A second later, Mira heard the distant boom of a rifle.

Adam tried to regain his footing. Before he could, the last remaining guard kicked the gun from Adam's hands and hauled him up to serve as a shield.

"Bring him," shouted her father.

The shock of being in the middle of a gunfight started to fade, but not soon enough for her to realize just how precarious her position was. She was within reach of her father. He grabbed her arm and hauled her onto the helicopter before the thought of fighting back even tickled her mind.

By the time she had her wits gathered enough to think straight, her father had his own weapon out and pointed right at her.

Adam was shoved inside, bleeding everywhere. He slumped in his seat, clutching his wound to slow the bleeding.

Her father looked at the guard who was covered in Adam's blood. "Stay here and destroy what's left."

The guard loped away and the helicopter began to lift.

In that moment, Mira realized just how screwed they were. Adam was seriously injured and bleeding badly. He was in no shape to fight, assuming he was even on her side anymore. She was weaponless and trying not to throw up, both of which left her at a serious disadvantage. She had no idea where they were going. And her father had that look in his eye that promised the kind of punishment she wouldn't soon forget.

As the ground became out of reach, it became clear to Mira that they were well and truly fucked.

Chapter Thirty-six

Riley had to force himself to move slowly through the halls, checking every doorway and corner for another possible threat.

So far, his path had been clear. He'd seen a couple of men scurry by with their arms loaded with boxes, but none of them had seen him. Yet.

Gage's voice sounded in his ear, calm and low. "All but two men down."

"Can you see where Sophie is?"

"Smaller heat signature north of you."

"That could be her. Or Mira. Is she okay?"

"Not moving."

Cold dread poured down his back. He picked up the pace and switched his weapon to the nonlethal tranq gun. "Where are my targets?"

"Twenty yards."

Riley went silent and swept down the hallway. After a few paces, he heard voices.

"Doc said to torch the place. Start the timer."

"How long?"

"Set it for ten minutes. That'll be enough time for us to get clear."

"What about the girl?"

"She's research. Goes up with the rest."

That was all Riley needed to hear. He used the last bit of his remaining willpower not to switch back to his Glock and kill the assholes for discarding a life so easily. It almost didn't matter that they were victims, too.

In the end, Bella's orders to save as many lives as they safely could took over, and he moved in on his targets.

He hit the closest one. The man swayed on his feet but managed to get a couple of shots off before he toppled. The second man swung around just as Riley ducked into a doorway and readied his next shot.

A bullet tore through the wall, grazing his calf. Pain streaked up his leg and landed at the base of his brain in a searing pile. By the time he was able to breathe again, the second target was on top of his position.

Riley turned the knob at his back and fell through the doorway just as another volley of gunfire came screaming in his direction.

The shots flew over his head. He jackknifed up, took aim and fired. The tranq stuck in the man's throat, but Riley didn't wait to see how long it would take to work. Instead he rolled away, scampering to get out of the way of whatever finger twitches the man still had left in him.

Three more shots went off, ripping holes in the wall next to Riley. The heavy thud in the hall told him the job was done. The man was down.

"Anyone else moving around?" he asked Gage.

"Negative. You hit?"

"It's not bad. Just keep looking for Sophie and warn me if anyone comes my way."

Riley pulled a small roll of duct tape from his pack and wrapped a strip tightly around his wound. He used his sleeve to wipe away the blood on his boot so he wouldn't leave visible tracks on the floor and pushed to his feet.

He continued down the hall, each step burning. The damage was minimal, but it still hurt like hell. When he reached the spot where the first man had fallen, all thoughts of physical pain disappeared.

There, recessed in the concrete floor, was a timer counting down toward zero. Dread hit him hard.

"Looks like they've rigged the place to blow. You need to get clear," said Riley.

"How long?"

"Nine minutes. Is the building clear?"

"No one's moving."

Riley started running. "I don't know if it's Sophie or Mira at the end of the hall, but I'm grabbing them and getting out. If there's time, I'll come back for the men."

"I got them."

"No," said Riley. "Do not come in here. Stay clear."

No response.

There wasn't time for him to deal with that now. He had a job to do.

Riley hit the door at the end of the hall at a dead run. It swung open against his weight, and his eyes immediately fixed on Sophie lying on a hospital bed. She had a tube dripping drugs into her body, but he couldn't see any sign of blood or damage.

Without pausing, he rushed to her side and peeled off the tape holding the IV in. The tube came with it, as well as a trickle of blood.

He took the fact that she was bleeding as a good sign and scooped her up in his arms.

She groaned as he carried her out of the room. It was the sweetest sound he'd ever heard.

Sophie was alive.

In his mind he traced his steps back to the nearest exit. He'd passed several on the way but needed the one that would get her to safety fastest. The sooner he could get her on the other side of some solid earth, the better.

He sped past the timer, glancing at it as he went.

"Seven minutes," he said into his mic.

Gage didn't respond.

Fuck.

As gently as he could, he repositioned Sophie over his shoulder so he could use his hands to open the door.

The cold night air hit him in the face. He kept searching for signs of danger, but every man he passed was dead or tranqed.

Gage had done a thorough job of taking care of the men outside. Just like always.

Riley hit the button that opened the rolling gate. Out of the corner of his eye, he saw a dark shape streaking toward the building.

He drew his weapon before he realized that it was Gage.

"What the hell are you doing?" he demanded.

"Working."

"Get out of there. There's no time."

Gage said nothing.

"If you're not out of there in two minutes, I'm coming in after you." That was how long it was going to take to get Sophie to safety, and he couldn't bring himself to set her down just anywhere.

As much as he cared about his buddy, he loved Sophie more. It made no rational sense that he would love her, but that didn't seem to stop his heart from stretching out to nearly painful proportions every time he thought about her.

He couldn't leave her in danger. It was simply impossible to even contemplate.

Riley hurried up the sloping ground, doing his best to ignore the burn of his protesting leg.

"Riley?" Sophie's voice was weak, but it was still music to his ears.

"It's me, honey. Stay still. We're almost there." He patted her in a lame effort to offer her comfort, and the feel of her full bottom against his palm was more than enough motivation for him to hurry the hell up.

An ass like that was definitely worth risking his life to save.

He skidded down the far side of the hill, going as fast as he dared. Her head was unprotected, and one wrong move on his part would bash it into the tree branches.

Their vehicle sat in the distance, gleaming under the moonlight. Riley opened the back door and eased her inside.

Her eyes tried to open, but he could tell it took a lot of effort to keep them that way.

"Just rest," he told her. "I'll be back in just a second."

"Don't leave me." The fear in her tone nearly tore him to pieces.

He crawled in enough that she could see his face. "I won't be gone long. I promise. When I get back, you're going to say yes."

"Yes?"

"That's right. You told me to ask you again, and that's exactly what I'm going to do. So you get your mouth all set while I'm gone."

She didn't seem to understand him, but it didn't matter. As long as she stayed here, she'd be safe.

He checked to make sure the car was running so she could drive off if he and Gage didn't make it back. Of course, with a childhood like hers, hot-wiring a car probably wasn't beyond her skills.

He closed the door and watched her eyes drift shut.

His internal clock said there was less than five minutes left on that timer, and far too many men in there for Gage to save them all by himself.

Riley gritted his teeth against the pain in his leg and sprinted back up the hill.

Chapter Thirty-seven

Adam had been shot before, but never like this. He was losing blood fast enough that he could feel his strength fading.

Mira unlaced her shoe and handed him the string.

At least she didn't actively want him dead. It wasn't much, but it was something.

Then again, maybe she just didn't want his bleeding making her sick.

Adam counted the seconds. Each one put them farther away from help and closer to whatever it was Sage had in store for them. His back was to the pilot, facing the rear of the aircraft, so he couldn't see where they were headed. His internal compass told him they were going south, but there was no way to know how far.

Adam was not going to let Mira's father hurt her the way he had planned. Sadly, there were only two ways to stop it from happening: kill Sage or kill Mira.

He knew which one he was capable of doing and which he wasn't.

The helicopter cleared the ridge hiding the clearing, then headed over the building, hugging the ground. They flew over a sea of trees with no landmarks to guide them.

"Staying off radar?" Adam shouted at Sage so he

could be heard over the rotors. As he spoke, he tied the makeshift tourniquet and tried to pretend he wasn't growing weaker by the second.

"Norwood is always sticking his nose into my business. No sense in making it easy on him."

Blood pooled on the metal floor at Adam's feet. "But you know he'll come for you."

"He hasn't found me yet."

"Where are we going?" asked Mira.

"To your new home."

She shuddered visibly at that. "You and your new home can go fuck themselves."

Sage scowled at her use of language. "Unless you've decided to be more trouble than you're worth. Like your mother."

She swallowed and looked away, but not before Adam saw furious tears shimmer in her eyes.

Mira was planning something. He could see the wheels in her head turning. And if he knew her well enough to see it, then so did her father.

"It won't work," said Sage. "Whatever you're planning, there's nowhere to run. Nowhere to hide."

She peered out the open side of the helicopter. That's when Adam saw what she was going to do.

She was going to jump.

"Don't," he said, reaching for her.

She saw the blood on his fingers and recoiled. "Don't what?"

"He's not worth it."

Sage moved the gun to Adam. "Stop talking to her."

Adam stared at Mira, silently begging her to stop planning whatever it was she had in mind. As soon as they landed, they'd join forces and fight Sage together. Until then, she just needed to stay alive.

She glared at him. "Like you care."

"I do. Deeply. More than you know."

"I doubt you're even capable of such depth."

"I hope to live long enough to prove it to you."

She glanced at his wound and blanched. The bleeding had slowed significantly, but he'd already lost enough that he was well below peak performance.

"You will," she said. "Men like you always survive. However they can."

"Stop talking!" shouted Sage.

Behind them, the sky lit up in an orange glow. A moment later, a deafening blast shook the helicopter.

The lab and everyone in it went up in flames.

Chapter Thirty-eight

Riley shook the dirt from his body. The unconscious man beneath him was alive, as were three others he and Gage had pulled out of the building. Nearby, a blond woman's body lay still and charred. She hadn't been there a second ago, leaving Riley to assume she'd been thrown from the building. There was a piece of metal embedded in her chest. It had torn cleanly through her prim suit, leaving no chance for survival. Her empty eyes stared up at the night sky as her blood soaked the frozen ground.

Gage stood and started jogging toward the car Adam had left behind. It was closer than the one where Riley had put Sophie, well out of the blast radius. The car's paint job was destroyed, but it seemed drivable.

"Where are you going?"

"Chopper took off."

"And you're going to follow it?"

He nodded as he kept running. "They have our friends."

No arguing with that. "I'll be right behind you."

Gage didn't respond. He was already behind the wheel, sliding over the dirt road in the same general direction the helicopter had gone.

Riley pulled the unconscious men a bit farther away

from the flames before he cuffed them and left them to wait for reinforcements. These men would get the help they needed or, at the very least, be put where they would never hurt anyone again.

It was the best he could offer.

As soon as it was safe, he jogged back to Sophie. The blast had apparently woken her enough that she was sitting up when he arrived. Whatever drugs they'd pumped into her seemed to be wearing off fast.

He was so relieved to see her moving under her own steam that the last few steps he made toward her were on wobbly knees.

"You're hurt," she said, her voice still a little weak.

"Just a little."

"What was that noise?"

"The lab went boom. Good riddance."

She frowned and a distant look haunted her eyes as her memory came back. "Sage had me. I saw Mira and Adam. Sage was hurting me. Mira was crying." She sucked in a terrified breath. "Oh no. They were in there, too. Please tell me they got out okay."

His hands were dirty, but he didn't let that stop him from stroking her hair in an effort to soothe her. "They got out. Gage is going after them now."

"Going after them?"

"Shh. It's okay. Nothing for you to worry about."

"Are they safe?"

"They will be. Everything is going to be fine."

She flung her arms around his neck and held on tight. "I didn't think I was going to make it out of there alive. Thank you for coming for me. Again."

He leaned back just enough that she could see his eyes. It was important to him that she saw he was telling the truth. "I'll always come for you, Sophie. Every single time. But do me a favor, okay?"

"Anything."

"Try to stay safe this time? Knowing that the woman I love is in danger is taking years off my life."

She offered him a watery smile. "You love me?"

"I do."

Her smile widened, brightened, until he could barely stare into the face of so much beauty all at once. "I love you, too."

And that was it. Riley knew in that moment that the woman looking at him was his future. His whole life. And he was going to do whatever it took to keep her. "Marry me," he urged, his tone almost bordering on desperation.

"What about the goons that are after me?"

"If we see them, I'll take care of it. They won't bother you again."

She smiled. "You are kind of a badass, aren't you?"

"I am. Especially when it comes to protecting you. That's why you should marry me."

"You're not worried I'm going to crack from what was done to me as a kid and try to kill you in your sleep?"

"Never."

"Why?"

"One, I've seen what cracking looks like, and you're nowhere close to the breaking point. I'd never let you get that far before getting you help. Two, I sleep with a gun. And three, I don't think either of us is going to be getting much sleep anytime soon."

"How can I contradict such a well-thought-out argument?"

"You can't. Marry me, Sophie."

She blinked back a few happy tears. "Yes. The answer has always been yes."

"I don't want to wait. Vegas?" he asked, grinning, so eager to start their new lives he could hardly wait for her response, much less some lengthy set of wedding plans.

She nodded, her smile radiant. "Hell yeah, Vegas. Babies?"

"Hell yeah, babies." The sense of rightness that fell over him was so powerful it almost choked off his air. He saw his entire life stretching out before him, all in this woman's pretty eyes. He had to struggle to say, "Let's go save our friends. We have a plane to catch."

Chapter Thirty-nine

The laboratory explosion was the final straw. Mira's friends had come to rescue her and Sophie. For all she knew, they'd been inside that lab when it blew.

Sophie had been, drugged and bound to a bed. Completely helpless.

If Mira let herself think about it too long, she would break down in a soggy puddle of tears, right next to that pool of Adam's blood.

She had to stay calm and cool—at least until her father was dead. Once that happened, she'd let go and crumble. But not yet. Not while Richard Sage still drew breath.

Mira's father's killing spree ended here.

"How many people did you just kill?" she asked.

He shrugged. "None that count. I have what I need from that facility."

"And where will you go now?"

He glanced at the man piloting the helicopter. "He is always making contingency plans. It's how I designed his mind to work. If only you'd been so useful."

The cold air whipping in through the opening chilled Mira to the bone. She had no coat. Her fingers were almost numb. Only her fury kept her core temperature up above dangerous levels.

Adam shivered visibly. He also had no coat, was wet with blood, and was running a couple of pints low.

The second her gaze strayed to his, his eyes seemed to focus. Intensity burned there, and while she had no idea what he was thinking, she had no doubt that he, too, was making contingency plans.

They were still flying low to the ground—so low she thought about jumping until she actually peered over the side. Her head made a dizzying spin, and her already twisty stomach rebelled at the thought.

"Don't," said Adam, the single word cutting through the roar of the rotors easily.

"I have to do something."

"Not here. Not now."

Her father shifted in his seat and re-aimed the gun at whoever was talking. "Shut up! Both of you."

This was her chance. The farther away from her friends she got, the more likely she was never to be found again. If her father had a hiding place, it could be years before Bella and the others uncovered it.

Mira wouldn't survive that long.

"I'll say whatever the fuck I want," she snapped.

"Mira," said Adam. "Don't."

She scowled at him. "You can't tell me what to do."

"You're going to get yourself killed."

"I'm dead anyway."

"But not like—"

When the barrel was pointed halfway between the two of them, Mira pounced. She lunged at her father, grabbing the weapon in both hands.

The steel was so cold her clammy hands stuck to the metal. Instantly, her father tried to pull it away, but he was old and she was pumped full of adrenaline and hate.

She managed to control the gun enough to keep it away from both her and Adam. It barked in her hands as her father's finger squeezed the trigger. She didn't know if he'd meant to or not, but the effect was all the same.

The bullet ripped through the back of the pilot's head. Blood and brains splattered across the inside of the windshield.

The helicopter lurched and started to go down.

Chapter Forty

As low as they were flying, Adam had only a few seconds to keep them from crashing into the trees.

He shoved his way into the cockpit, opened the door, unlatched the pilot's seat belt, and pushed his body out. Adam regained control of the helicopter, but not before it clipped the top of some trees.

The aircraft canted sideways, and Mira let out a scream of fear.

A quick glance behind him showed her dangling from the open doorway with only her death grip on her father's sleeve holding her inside.

If Adam didn't land now, the woman he loved was dead.

His view was obscured by the interior of the pilot's skull, so he swiped it away with frozen fingers.

The ground here was too hilly and covered in trees to find a safe landing spot. The best he could think to do was turn around and land near the small lake they'd flown over a couple of minutes ago.

He deployed the emergency floats, just in case, and made a beeline for the tiny ring of flat, clear ground near the water's edge. "Hold on, Mira. We're landing."

*   *   *

Mira wasn't going to be able to hang on that long. Her frigid grip was already failing. She couldn't feel her fingers, but she could see them slipping on the slick nylon of her father's winter coat.

"Don't let me fall," she begged.

His eyes were empty as he looked at her. No fatherly love. No humanity. He was a vacant shell held together only by his work. She was nothing more to him than the growth at the bottom of a petri dish.

She'd known that for a long time, but she *felt* it now. Saw it in his eyes. She really meant nothing to him.

No fucking way was she going to let him take her down.

Mira gathered her strength and tightened her grip. Her feet were dangling over the edge, but she felt them bump against something hard. She found that surface and pushed herself up, climbing up her father's arm as she went.

He fired the gun. She felt the heat of the explosion against her cheek, but he had no control of his aim with her clinging to him like she was.

He fired again and again. Her eyes stung and watered from the gunshot residue that hit her face. Her tears were swept away by the frigid wind before they could fall.

The helicopter was moving fast. The trees under her seemed to be only inches away. Up ahead she saw moonlight gleaming on water and the headlights of a car speeding toward them.

Friends? Enemies? There was no way to know, and they were so far out of reach it hardly mattered.

Her father stopped trying to pry her away and used his free hand to unzip his coat.

Mira knew what was coming next. Once that coat was loose, she would have nothing left to cling to. She'd fall to her death and he would still be alive to hurt more people.

She couldn't let that happen. She needed this to be over, even if it meant going with him.

With no other options coming to mind, Mira reached up and grabbed the latch on her father's seat belt. He saw what she was doing too late.

The metal clicked open. She let her feet fall from their perch. Her weight dragged him out of his seat. He tried to grab something, but it was no use. They both fell from the helicopter.

Mira's last thought was one of relief. There was no way she was going to survive the fall, but neither would her father.

His days of hurting people were finally over.

Chapter Forty-one

Adam felt the weight of the helicopter shift as he began his landing. He glanced back. Saw Sage and Mira were both gone.

His world went dark. Mira was gone. He was still too far up for anyone to survive the fall.

A crushing weight of agony fell on him. Grief. He knew how it felt, how debilitating it could be. He'd mastered his skills of emotional containment because of that pain, and yet now, as he tried to gather it all up and shove it in a box, his ability failed him.

Mira and the power she had over him could never be contained.

A low moan of mourning rattled in his chest. He was powerless to stop it, just as he'd been powerless to both fly the craft and keep her from falling.

Either failure would have killed her just the same.

This was all Sage's fault. If the man wasn't dead, Adam was going to make him beg for death before he gave it to him.

He spun the aircraft around to see where Sage landed. All he saw was a pair of ripples spreading out over the lake.

They'd landed in the lake. Both of them.

A tiny beam of hope lit him up inside. The water might have cushioned their fall enough to make it survivable. But as cold as it was, Mira wouldn't last long.

His need to see her safe strengthened his weak body. He'd lost a lot of blood, but there was still some fight left in him. He was going to use every ounce of it to save the woman he loved.

Without a second thought, Adam maneuvered the helicopter where he needed it to be, abandoned the pilot's seat, and dove into the water.

How could Mira be so numb and in so much pain at the same time? The mystery consumed her, swamping her sluggish mind.

She couldn't breathe. It took her a second to realize that it was because she was underwater.

It was too dark for her to figure out which way she could find air. She couldn't even see bubbles in front of her face.

Then, to her left, she saw a brilliant yellow flash.

The sun? That didn't seem right, but she swam toward it all the same.

The water's surface shimmered above her like fire. She didn't know why, but her lungs were driving her now, urging her to ignore everything else.

She was almost to air when something grabbed her leg and tugged her back down.

Frantic, clawing hands ripped at her body, desperate to use her to reach the surface. She kicked and fought against her captor, but nothing helped. She was too weak from lack of oxygen to do more than try to shove him away.

He was stronger.

As his head passed hers, she saw her father's face in the fiery light from above. He saw her, too, and yet he didn't let go. He held her down as he resurfaced.

Maybe he knew she'd kill him if she survived.

Mira fought harder, punching him as hard as she could. His fist was tight in her hair, holding her under while the last of her oxygen ran out.

Then something happened.

She felt a heavy current push against her. Saw a glimpse of powerful arms above her. The next thing she knew, her father had let go of her hair and she was free.

Mira exploded out of the water, gasping for air. She heard a violent splashing behind her, along with heavy, pained male grunts.

Her head was so dizzy, her body so numb, she couldn't quite figure out how to turn around. Finally, after a few breaths had restored function to her brain, she spun around and saw Adam holding her father's head underwater.

Just as her father had done to her.

His eyes met hers. There was cold hatred there. The need to kill.

It froze her insides over so they matched her skin.

Beneath the water, there was a small flash, then a muffled boom.

Something hit her shoulder. Blood stained the water soaking her shirt.

She'd been shot.

Adam snarled and his whole body jerked as he gave a savage twist to her father's neck. She heard the bones breaking. Saw his body go limp and float off over the water.

Her father was dead.

All the strength left her body. The cold stole over her. She couldn't keep her eyes open anymore. She knew this was a bad thing but couldn't remember why.

It didn't matter anymore. She didn't have to keep fighting. Her father was dead. He couldn't hurt anyone else. She could just let go now.

Chapter Forty-two

Adam saw Mira go under and lunged for her. The makeshift tourniquet on his leg came loose, and he saw his blood billow under the surface of the water.

The burning helicopter nearby gave him just enough light to see the edge of the lake.

He grabbed her and kept her head above water as he swam toward the shore.

Each kick weakened him more. He was losing blood too fast. He could tell by the way his heart was racing just to keep pumping what was left through his veins.

Only a few more yards.

Headlights bounced over the ground. His breath fogged in the air, catching and holding some of the firelight.

He felt himself going down—felt unconsciousness drag at him. He had only a few seconds left before both he and Mira went under.

With the last of his strength, he lifted and threw her the last few yards to where the water became shallow. The move shoved him under, and he didn't have enough strength left in him to resurface.

Mira was safe now. That was all that mattered.

*   *   *

Mira woke being ripped apart by fire and ice. One half of her body was nearly blistered from heat, and the other was frozen stiff.

She opened her eyes and realized why.

Someone had pulled her from the water and set her near the burning remains of the helicopter for warmth.

It took a few seconds for her brain to start spinning again, and as soon as it did, she wished it hadn't. Those hazy moments had been a gift, and so much better than the stark reality that hit her now.

Her father was dead. She could see his body still floating facedown on the lake. Adam had saved her, but he was nowhere to be found.

That's when it hit her.

He was still in the water.

Mira shoved to her feet and limped toward the shoreline. The cold night air took her breath away, but she couldn't leave him down there to die.

She loved him too much to let him die.

As that realization struck, two dark heads broke the surface of the water. Adam was one of them, but his body was limp. The other man was Gage, who swam toward her with powerful strokes.

Within seconds, he had Adam lying on the ground and was administering CPR.

"Is he alive?" she asked, her voice a terrified thread of sound.

"Barely." He took off his belt and looped it around Adam's leg. Adam groaned as Gage increased the pressure to stop the bleeding.

"He lost a lot of blood," she said.

Gage looked at her then, his face a mix of fury and fear. "Get the med kit."

Mira ran toward the car as fast as her numb legs would allow. The bullet wound in her shoulder was still cold enough that she couldn't feel much, but that was changing as her blood pressure skyrocketed.

She grabbed the med kit from the trunk and hauled ass back to Gage and Adam.

With movements faster than she could track, Gage started an IV and handed the bag to Mira. "Squeeze."

She did, pushing fluids into Adam's body, praying they would keep him alive until help came.

While she did that, Gage filled an empty bag with his blood and pushed that into Adam's IV as well.

"Are you sure that's safe?" she asked.

Gage nodded as he began filling another bag with his blood. "I'm a universal donor. He's my brother."

"You know?"

His eyes met hers, so like Adam's it was a wonder everyone hadn't guessed. "I do now."

The sound of a helicopter in the distance grew closer.

Mira held out her hand. "Give me your spare weapon, just in case they're not friendly."

She was in no shape to fight, but Gage did as she asked.

As the helicopter landed, Mira raised her weapon. Payton leaned out and took off his helmet. "Don't shoot."

The last of her adrenaline faded. She slumped to the ground.

She must have passed out, because the next thing she knew, she was in a hospital room with Gage at her side.

Her first thought was, "Where's Adam?"

"Surgery."

"Will he be okay?"

Gage nodded.

She leaned back in relief. "What are they going to do with him?"

"Do?"

He didn't know his brother was a traitor.

Mira's heart ached. It hurt like hell that she loved a man who'd betrayed her and everyone she cared about. She could only imagine how much it was going to hurt Adam's brother.

"He's working for Stynger. He has been all along, I guess."

"You're wrong."

"No, I'm not. I was there when he told my father the passcode to those files. Only someone working for her would know that."

"You're wrong," Gage repeated.

"I was there, Gage. I witnessed his betrayal. He's working for Stynger."

Gage leaned down. His voice was quiet but no less powerful. "He traded his life for you. Made a deal with her to find you."

"You can't know that."

"His phone was in his car. I got her call. He promised to let her experiment on him if she told him where you were."

"Experiment on him?" The horror of that image rolled through her, lighting every nerve ending on fire.

"You were lost. He thought it was the only way to find you."

"But . . . the passcode."

"Gave her access to Sage's network. She stole his research."

"And he didn't even know it." Of course. She could see exactly how that would work—she'd done the same thing herself. The classic Trojan horse.

As all the bits shifted into place, one critical point hit her. "Adam didn't betray me?"

"No. He didn't. And if I hadn't been there to pull him from the water, he would have died saving you."

Mira had thought she loved him before, but she'd been wrong. Those feelings were a dim shadow compared to the blazing bonfire she felt now. It was too much to contain—too much for someone her size to hold. She had to tell him and let it out.

He'd risked his life to save her. More than once. Never again was she going to question his loyalty. He deserved better than that.

He deserved her trust and her love—as much as she was capable of giving.

"I need to see him," she said, trying to sit up.

"Later," said Gage as he pushed her gently back down. "Sleep."

"But I have to tell him how much I love him. He needs to know."

Gage smiled, and there was so much relief in the expression, it confused her. "He will. Soon."

Chapter Forty-three

Lila scrambled to answer the phone she kept hidden in the bottom of her purse. She'd been dreading this conversation for so long, her fingers were numb by the time she managed to answer the call.

"Hello?" She slipped down the hall into the empty conference room where she'd killed a man. She'd never thought of herself as the kind of person who would be capable of murder, but that had been before her baby boy had been taken from her.

"You've been a bad girl." A woman's voice was on the other end of the line—one that made Lila's blood curdle in her chest. She thought she'd hear from one of the men, but instead, it was the devil herself calling, Dr. Norma Stynger.

Lila's fervent whisper wavered with fear. "No. I swear I haven't. I've done everything you asked."

Dr. Stynger's disappointment was clear in her tone. "You killed one of my men."

"He was going to talk. What if he told them about you?"

"None of my men talk about me. I make sure of it. But what about you? You've been free to talk all along."

Lila shivered at the memory of those pictures she'd

seen of men with surgical scars at the base of their skulls. She didn't know how Dr. Stynger managed it, but whatever electronic gadget she shoved in those men's heads worked. They'd die before revealing her secrets. Literally.

The autopsy photos Lila had seen of the men who'd died from poison were gruesome proof that the doctor knew what she was doing.

"I haven't said a word," Lila assured her. "Sophie doesn't know I was the one who drugged her."

"Does anyone there suspect you?"

"No. I've been so careful. Just like you said." Lila pulled in a deep breath for courage, and then asked, "When do I get to see my baby?"

"That depends on you, of course."

"I've done everything you've asked. Please let me see him."

"Soon. If you're a good girl."

Hot, silent tears slid down Lila's cheeks. "I killed a man for you. What more could you possibly want?"

"Stay where you are. I'm going to need your help soon."

Lila wanted to say no. She wanted to defy the woman who'd taken her boy and used him as leverage to gain her cooperation. He was only three. He had to miss his mommy. There was no way he could understand what was happening or why he was all alone.

"You're hesitating," said Dr. Stynger. "Is it because someone is there, or because you no longer care what happens to your son?"

Even the thought sent fear winging through Lila's body, making her shake. "Please don't hurt him."

"Ah, so you do care. That's good. He's such a sweet thing. I'd hate to see him orphaned."

Lila had no living family. Her ex had dumped her as soon as he'd found out about the baby. She'd raised her son on her own. If anything happened to her, no one would even know he existed. She hadn't dared tell a single soul at the Edge about him for fear of the questions his absence would raise. After all, she'd gotten the job because her son's life had depended on it.

Stynger's voice dripped with eagerness. "I need one last little favor from you, and then your boy can come home."

Lila wasn't stupid enough to believe something too good to be true, but at the same time, her heart betrayed her, jumping in hope. She wiped her tears away and said the only thing she could. "What do you want me to do?"

Gage left Mira's room as soon as he was sure she was asleep.

He wanted to see his brother and talk to him, but there was no time for that. He had an appointment to keep.

Stynger had been clear about what would happen if he was tardy. As it was, he was grateful that she'd allowed him to pay his brother's debt.

As weak as Adam was now, he likely wouldn't survive whatever it was Stynger had in store for him.

Gage dialed Bella on his way to the meeting.

"How did it go?" she asked.

"Mira and Adam are alive. Sage is dead."

"Are we sure this time? I don't want him coming back to life again."

"I checked."

"Good. And your assignment?"

"I found what we needed."

Excitement lit her tone. "Already?"

"Opportunity knocked."

"What happened?"

"I let it in."

"You'll be careful?" she asked. "Just like we planned?"

"Always," he said.

"I won't hear from you again, will I?"

"No."

"You're one of mine. I will come for you," she promised.

Gage only hoped he'd survive that long. But if he did, the outcome would be more than worth any suffering he might endure. "I know."

"Find her as fast as you can. Once you do, send the signal."

"Yes, ma'am," he said, then hung up and tossed his phone in the trash.

Where he was going, he wouldn't be needing it. All it could do was serve as a list of contacts that could be used against him.

Chapter Forty-four

Adam worked to shed the effects of the drugs from his system, unsure where he'd find himself. Had Stynger come for him already? Was this lethargy something she'd done to him? If so, the warm, soft cocoon she'd put him in was far from the torture he'd expected.

As soon as he was strong enough to strike, he allowed himself to open his eyes.

Mira was curled up next to him, her arm around his waist. She was wearing a hospital gown, and beneath the edge he could see a thick bandage on her shoulder. Their matching IV stands were next to each other, creating a tangle of tubes across his body.

He breathed in her scent, letting it drive away the antiseptic sting of the hospital air. Even in his sleep he had known to hold her tight against him—so tight she couldn't get away without him knowing.

His body was a matrix of pain, but he tucked all that away in tidy little boxes where it couldn't reach him.

Mira, however, took his full attention.

She lifted her head. "You're awake. How do you feel?"

"Fine," he said. He was weak, but that was fading by the moment.

"No pain?"

"Not with you here to distract me."

She smiled and rose over him, being careful of his wounds. "I got in trouble when the nurse found me, but I scared her away."

"You are a terrifying force of nature."

"I am when someone tries to tear me away from my man."

"Your man? I thought you hated me for betraying you again."

His smiled faded. "You didn't betray me. I know that now."

"How?"

"Gage told me."

"Gage?"

She nodded. "He pulled you out of that freezing lake. Gave you his blood when you'd lost too much." She stroked his forehead. "He knows he's your brother."

"How long has he known?"

"Not long. He left you a note, though. I was nosy and read it."

"What did it say?"

"He said they've got Stynger on the run and she won't be looking for you to visit anytime soon. What does that mean? You weren't actually going to let her touch you, were you?"

Adam didn't have to uphold his end of the bargain with Stynger? He could hardly believe his good fortune. He'd get to stay with Mira. That news was a priceless gift for which he'd never be able to thank his brother enough. As soon as he saw Gage again, he was going to make sure the man knew he had Adam's undying gratitude.

He touched Mira's face, marveling at how lucky he was. "It's unimportant. I'm just glad it's a debt I don't have to repay. Did Gage say anything else?"

Her mouth softened on a smile, and her green eyes glittered with joy. "He said he's proud to call you his brother, and that when he gets back from his assignment, you two are going to have a lot to catch up on."

"He doesn't hate me?"

"Not even a little. He defends you, just like a brother should." She shifted until she was right on level with his mouth. "If he'd stayed longer, I would have told him that I get first dibs on your time. You and I are going to go somewhere warm to recover. I'm going to make sure you stay in bed."

"Just how are you going to do that?"

She gave him a sexy smile that lit him up all the way to his toes. "With enthusiasm."

Adam wasn't sure what was happening inside him, but it felt . . . good. Part of him expanded in this warm ripple of relief and pleasure. No more cowering in a cold, dank ball inside one of his boxes. Whatever it was, he'd never felt anything like it before. If he hadn't known better, he would have said it felt like being forgiven.

He swallowed past his emotion but couldn't stop it from trembling in his voice. "I love you, Mira."

"That's good," she said, inching closer to his mouth. "Because I love you, too."

She kissed him as he smiled, and he knew in that moment that he would never need anything more than what he had right now. Mira forgave him for his sins, and he would die before hurting her again.

Their future was a clean, warm place filled with enough hope and happiness to sustain them for a lifetime. And it was all thanks to Mira. She'd taught him that love for a man like him was possible, and he was going to spend the rest of his life showing her what an excellent student he was.

Stay tuned for a sneak peak at
Shannon Butcher's next Edge novel,
coming in fall 2015 from Signet Eclipse.

Dallas, Texas, April 28

After two weeks of sleepless nights, little food, and endless hours spent working beside a man who lit her libido up like the surface of the sun, Bella Bayne wanted nothing more than a little quality time with her vibrator and a solid eight hours of shut-eye. In that order. Instead, what she got was the man of her fantasies—highly inappropriate ones at that—standing on her front porch, making her mouth water far more than the fragrant bags of Indian food he was toting.

"Thought you might be too tired to cook," said Victor Temple, the most perfectly formed male of any species ever created.

He stood a few inches over her five-foot-ten-inch frame, blocking out the streetlight behind him. He had aristocratic features that were made more interesting by the three scars decorating his face. They were small but broke up the sea of masculine beauty enough that she could look at him without sunglasses to mask the glare of perfection. His dark blond hair was cut with military precision, falling in line exactly as he pleased. After several missions with this man, she'd learned he defied the

laws of helmet hair in a way she still couldn't understand.
Blood pact with dark forces, no doubt.

His clothes were casual but neat and extremely high-
end. Victor came from money. Old, refined, nose-in-the-
air money, yet she'd never once seen him flaunt it. No
diamond cuff links, flashy cars, or pricey watches for this
man. No, Victor Temple had way more substance than
that, which was another reason she wished he was anywhere else than standing on her front porch. It was his
substance combined with those stunning good looks that
made him dangerous to her professional ethics.

"Hungry?" he asked.

Bella was hungry, but not for what was in those sacks.
If not for the fact that she was Victor's boss, she would
have feasted on him weeks ago. But her strict no-frater-
nization policy meant she had to keep her hands and
mouth off. Way off.

"You should be at home asleep," she said, forcing cen-
sure into her tone. "If you think I'm giving you the day
off tomorrow so a pretty boy like you can get his beauty
rest, you're wrong."

"I slept more than you did while we were away. And
when one comes bearing gifts, Bella, it's customary for
the receiver to at least pretend to be gracious."

"Sweetheart, I don't like pretending. And I'm not gracious."

He smiled as if he found her amusing. "Only because
you're hungry, which I have learned over the past few
weeks makes you cranky. Now, step aside, Bella. I'm
coming in to feed you. Then we have to talk."

Talk? At this hour? That couldn't mean good news.

He didn't give her time to move. Instead, he stepped
forward, and she had no choice but to step back or feel his
body collide with hers. As nice as his body was, as off-limits
as it was, she wasn't sure she'd survive the crash without
tossing him to the carpet and riding him until she got off. At
least twice. Maybe then she wouldn't be so cranky.

"Talk about what?" she asked as he strode past her like he owned her home, heading unerringly to a kitchen he'd never before even seen, much less navigated.

"It can wait until after food."

His clean scent lingered in the air around him, crossing her path and making her drag in a deep breath to capture it. For a moment, the urge to bury her nose against his chest took over and she forgot all about why she didn't want him here. She had to shake herself to get her brain working again. "You're *my* employee in *my* home, honey. If I tell you to talk now, then that's what you'll do."

He glanced over his shoulder at her, daring to give her a grin. "I'm off the clock. You can't order me around. Deal with it."

Fury struck her for a second before turning to lust. She had no idea what it was about this man. She was the owner of a private security firm. She worked with badass men all day long, every day. None of them had ever held her interest for longer than it took her to flatten them in the sparring ring.

But Victor Temple was different. He got under her skin and made it burn. It didn't matter that he was her subordinate or that he was on loan from the U.S. government to help her deal with a situation of nightmarish proportions. She couldn't seem to be near him without wishing they were both naked, panting, and sweating.

Maybe it had something to do with the one and only time she'd taken him on in hand-to-hand combat practice. They'd both been panting and sweating then, and while they hadn't been naked, she was acutely aware of just how skilled he was. How perfectly built he was. Not overblown or bulging with showy bulk, but his big frame was wrapped with sleek, functional muscles that rippled with power. She'd fought bigger men than him and won, but only Victor had been able to pin her to the mat.

She was a strong, independent, kick-ass woman, but even she had to admit she liked that in a man.

"I was half hoping you wouldn't answer the door—that you'd be asleep," he said.

"I needed to unwind a bit first."

He lifted a wayward lock of damp hair that had escaped her haphazard ponytail. Only then did she realize just how close he was standing. Too close.

"Shower didn't do the trick?" he asked.

No, but her vibrator would have if he hadn't shown up. After all the time she'd spent with him recently, she wondered if she'd still be able to keep his face out of her fantasies. "There's a heavy bag in the garage. A little time with that would have worn me out."

He stepped away, leaving her feeling adrift for a second before she caught up with reality. She could not be drawn to Victor. She had to lead by example, and fucking her employee on the kitchen floor whether or not he wanted it was not the kind of tone she wanted to set for her workplace.

"You're worried about Gage, aren't you?" He glanced over his shoulder as he washed his hands. Muscles shifted beneath his tight T-shirt, adding fuel to the naughty fantasies she already suffered for this man.

Her gaze slid past him to the window over the sink. She didn't want him to see how appealing he was to her. Even more than that, she didn't want him to see her fear for Gage. He had willingly walked into the hands of a monster in the hopes of taking her down for good. No one had heard from him since. Bella had to stay tough, appear confident, and provide leadership to her men. That included Victor.

She straightened her spine. "Gage has been gone for weeks. He was ordered to make contact with me as soon as he could. The fact that he hasn't is more than a little concerning. Sweetheart, any sane person would be worried."

Victor turned back around to her as he dried his hands. A flicker of sympathy crossed his features, making him even harder to resist. "He's smart. And tough. I'm sure his silence is a sign that he's working an angle with Stynger, not that he's in trouble."

"Easy for you to say. You weren't the one who sent him into that crazy bitch's hands."

"He volunteered for the job. He knew exactly what he was doing when he let her men take him into custody."

"He did it to save Adam by taking his place. I know Gage. The second he learned that Adam was his brother, his decision was made."

"Are you saying that he wouldn't have volunteered if it wasn't to save Adam?" asked Victor.

"No, he was on board the whole time, but now that he knows he has a brother, there's no telling what kind of sacrifice he's making to keep Adam safe."

Victor stepped closer, easing into her personal space like he belonged there. "There's more at stake here than one man. Gage knows that. He's smart enough to realize that the only true way to keep Adam safe is to take Stynger down for good."

"That's part of what worries me. It's personal for Gage. If he gets the chance to kill Stynger, he'll do it. Even if it means sacrificing himself." Maybe he already had, and that was why no one had heard from him.

Victor must have read her mind. "He's still alive, Bella. You have to believe that." He came toward her, compassion shining in his bright eyes. One lean, hard hand was extended. She knew he meant to offer comfort, but she was too fragile for that right now. She had to stay strong, stay tough. As tired as she was, as worried as she was, it would be too easy for her to crack under the strain and let her emotions run free. One touch from him might be all it took to shatter her self-control.

She hadn't cried in years—not since the night she killed her husband in a blind rage. She wasn't about to start now.

Bella moved away before he could reach her. "I'm

sure he's alive," she lied. "I'm also sure we'll find him soon. I just have to keep looking and stay vigilant for even the smallest signs of his whereabouts. We've been on enough missions together that I know how he thinks."

Victor's hand fell to his side. "You'll be a lot more vigilant after you get some food and sleep. You know him better than any of us. If we're going to see some obscure sign he left behind, you're the most likely one to spot it. But only if you're not exhausted."

She gave him a pointed stare. "I'd sleep better without one of my men in my kitchen, honey."

"When was the last time you ate?"

She couldn't remember, but that didn't make him right. "If it's that important to you, then feed me already so we can get to whatever it is you need to talk about. I'm wrung out."

"Maybe the talk should wait until tomorrow."

"I'm busy tomorrow. Talk now."

"I don't think so. Your blood sugar is too low for my peace of mind. It'll only take a minute to warm up the food."

She watched him move around her kitchen, opening cabinets and finding what he was looking for. The smell of curry filled her kitchen, making her stomach rumble.

He set a plate of food in the microwave, pushed some buttons. Nothing happened. He frowned as he checked to make sure it was plugged in. "It's not working."

Bella went to his side and tried to make the appliance go with no luck. "Sorry. It's one of the few kitchen tools I know how to use. I must have worn it out."

"No worries. We have other options." He opened her oven door and pulled out her box of business receipts, staring at them as if they might bite. "You keep paperwork in your oven?"

"It's a handy spot. Nothing blows away when I open the windows."

"What about when you cook?"

She laughed. "Honey, I work eighty-hour weeks, minimum. I spend more than half of my time out of the country, run a reputable business where lives are on the line every day, and you think I have time to cook? You're adorable."

A blush brightened his cheeks and made his glacier blue eyes stand out. She knew he was a poster boy for the military, all upright and honorable, but there was something about the clarity of his eyes that really sold the whole look. She swore she could see right through him, like he had nothing to hide.

No one was that honorable. Especially not her.

"Does your oven even work?" he asked.

Bella shrugged. "Who knows? Never tried it."

He turned a knob to get the gas-fueled contraption working. She probably should have been paying attention to how he operated it, but all she could concentrate on was the way his fingers gently gripped the knob, giving it the slightest twist.

Her nipples puckered in response.

After a few seconds, his brow scrunched up as he turned the knob again. "Your pilot light's out."

"I didn't want to set my receipts on fire. The IRS frowns on excuses like that during an audit."

"Got any matches?"

She pulled a lighter from her junk drawer and handed it to him. He knelt down, making his jeans go tight over a manly ass carved by God himself. She was so busy admiring him, she barely heard his question.

"Did you move the oven out recently?"

Bella shook her head to get it set on straight again. "Why on earth would I do that?"

"To clean under it."

She grinned. "So adorable. I just want to pinch your cheeks." His ass cheeks, if she had her choice.

"Right. Got it. You don't clean, either."

"I have a housekeeper who comes in once a month to keep the place livable."

"When was she here last?"

"I don't know. While we were gone sometime. Why?"

He pointed to some crumbs on her floor next to a rusty brown smudge line, his face taut with concern. "Scuff marks. Someone's moved your oven."

Before she had time to follow why he was upset by her oven's position, he turned on a flashlight app on his phone and shone it back behind the oven.

"Bella," he said, his voice that same eerie calm he got during a firefight. "Turn around and walk out the way I came in. Don't touch anything."

Serious worry settled in between the cracks in her arousal and fatigue. "What's going on?"

He took her arm and forced her to start walking. "Someone tied what looks like an explosive device into your gas line. Time to go and call the bomb squad—from outside."